PENGUIN CLASSICS

SILAS MAR...

MARY ANN (MARIAN) EVANS was born i̶... ...̶shire. She attended schools in Nuneaton and Coventry, ...ng under the influence of evangelical teachers and clergymen. In 1836 her mother died and Marian became her father's housekeeper, educating herself in her spare time. In 1841 she moved to Coventry, and met Charles and Caroline Bray, local progressive intellectuals. Through them she was commissioned to translate Strauss's *Life of Jesus* and met the radical publisher John Chapman, who, when he purchased the *Westminster Review* in 1851, made her his managing editor. Having lost her Christian faith and thereby alienated her family, she moved to London where she met Herbert Spencer and the versatile man-of-letters George Henry Lewes. Lewes was separated from his wife, but with no possibility of divorce. In 1854 he and Marian decided to live together, and did so until Lewes's death in 1878. It was he who encouraged her to turn from philosophy and journalism to fiction, and she subsequently wrote, under the name of George Eliot, *Scenes of Clerical Life, Adam Bede, The Mill on the Floss, Silas Marner, Romola, Felix Holt, Middlemarch* and *Daniel Deronda*, as well as numerous essays, articles and reviews. George Eliot died in 1880, only a few months after marrying J.W. Cross, an old friend and admirer, who became her first biographer. She was buried beside Lewes at Highgate. George Eliot combined a formidable intelligence with imaginative sympathy and acute powers of observation, and became one of the greatest and most influential of English novelists. Her choice of material widened the horizons of the novel and her psychological insights radically changed the nature of fictional characterization.

DAVID CARROLL is Professor of English at Lancaster University, and has taught in universities in Africa, Canada, the Middle East and Britain. Among his publications are *George Eliot: The Critical Heritage, Chinua Achebe* and the Clarendon edition of *Middlemarch*. He is joint General Editor of the *Longman Literature in English Series* and his most recent critical study was *George Eliot and the Conflict of Interpretations*.

Q. D. (Queenie Dorothy) Leavis (1900–1982) spent her academic career teaching at Cambridge University and was married to the distinguished literary critic F. R. Leavis. She was a regular contributor to the Cambridge-based quarterly periodical, *Scrutiny*, and published several volumes of criticism, including *Fiction and the Reading Public* (1932) about the relationship between literature and literacy, *Lectures in America*, and *Dickens the Novelist*.

GEORGE ELIOT

Silas Marner

THE WEAVER OF RAVELOE

Edited with an Introduction and Notes by
DAVID CARROLL

With the original Penguin Classics Introduction by
Q. D. Leavis

PENGUIN BOOKS

PENGUIN BOOKS

Published by the Penguin Group
Penguin Books Ltd, 80 Strand, London WC2R ORL, England
Penguin Putnam Inc., 375 Hudson Street, New York, New York 10014, USA
Penguin Books Australia Ltd, 250 Camberwell Road, Camberwell, Victoria 3124, Australia
Penguin Books Canada Ltd, 10 Alcorn Avenue, Toronto, Ontario, Canada M4V 3B2
Penguin Books India (P) Ltd, 11 Community Centre, Panchsheel Park, New Delhi – 110 017, India
Penguin Books (NZ) Ltd, Cnr Rosedale and Airborne Roads, Albany, Auckland, New Zealand
Penguin Books (South Africa) (Pty) Ltd, 24 Sturdee Avenue, Rosebank 2196, South Africa

Penguin Books Ltd, Registered Offices: 80 Strand, London WC2R ORL, England

www.penguin.com

First published 1861
This edition first published in Penguin Books 1996
Reissued with new Chronology and 1967 Penguin Classics Introduction by Q. D. Leavis 2003

042

Introduction and Notes copyright © David Carroll, 1996
Appendix: Original Penguin Classics Introduction copyright © Q. D. Leavis, 1967
All rights reserved

The moral right of the editor has been asserted

Set in 10/12 pt Monotype Janson
Typeset by Datix International Limited, Bungay, Suffolk
Printed and bound in Great Britain by Clays Ltd, Elcograf S.p.A.

ISBN-13: 978-0-14-143975-4

www.greenpenguin.co.uk

CONTENTS

INTRODUCTION

I

In Florence on 21 May 1860 George Henry Lewes had an idea. Having left London on 21 March, three days after the publication of *The Mill on the Floss*, he and George Eliot were well into a three-month tour of the Continent which had taken them from Paris over the Alps to Turin, Genoa, Pisa and Rome (for Holy Week); and then south to Naples before returning to Florence. Now, in the Hôtel de la Pension Suisse, he records in his journal: 'This morning while reading about Savonarola it occurred to me that his life and times afford fine material for an historical romance.' George Eliot, he writes, 'at once caught at the idea with enthusiasm'; and they quickly got to work – visiting San Marco, the Accademia, buying books and examining manuscripts in the Magliabecchian Library. Before they left Florence, Lewes even commissioned a painter to copy a Fra Angelico fresco so that the novelist could have it in view as she wrote.

This was a definite turning-point in the novelist's career and her plans were nothing if not ambitious. She was going to rewrite the history of the Italian Renaissance in the form of a historical novel, *Romola*, set in Florence in the final decade of the fifteenth century. The gods, Christian and Classical pagan, were to be reborn into the complex politics of the city through which the heroine has to pick her way in order to achieve a new kind of mythic understanding of the world. Romola will relive in the crucible of Florence the shaping myths of European civilization before she herself becomes the future madonna of the new religion of humanity. 'Many legends were afterwards told in that valley about the blessed Lady who came over the sea.' The novelist called it 'a rather ambitious project', acknowledging that it would 'require a great deal of study and labour'. This was the European idea George Eliot carried with her over the Apennines in June to Venice, and then back home through the Italian Lakes to Switzerland and London. It was to tax even her capacious mind.

'But I want first to write another English story,' she told her publisher, John Blackwood, in the August letter in which she revealed the closely guarded secret of her Italian novel. In November 1860, when she was already writing *Silas Marner*, she records in her journal that the idea for this new story 'thrust itself between me and the other book I was meditating'. And to Blackwood again a few weeks later: 'I am writing a story which came *across* my other plans by a sudden inspiration.' What, we might ask, was so urgent about this 'story of old-fashioned village life' as to delay her epic of European civilization? At this turning-point in her career – with the success of *Adam Bede* (1859) and *The Mill on the Floss* (1860) behind her, and the larger horizons of *Romola* (1862–3), *Middlemarch* (1871–2) and *Daniel Deronda* (1876) ahead – was she experiencing a loss of nerve? If there is a break in George Eliot's career it certainly occurs here. But *Silas Marner* – that afterthought which had to be written – appears on both sides of the fissure: it seems to belong to the earlier rural fiction and yet it cuts across the plans for *Romola* on which work had already begun. It is the key work that enables us to link the early and the late novels.

A clue to its significance is to be found in her remark to John Blackwood on 24 February 1861, after she had sent him the first thirteen chapters of the novel:

It came to me first of all, quite suddenly, as a sort of legendary tale, suggested by my recollection of having once, in early childhood, seen a linen-weaver with a bag on his back; but, as my mind dwelt on the subject, I became inclined to a more realistic treatment.

Silas Marner embodies both the legendary tale and its realistic treatment, and this accounts for its ambivalent reception, then and now. Like *Romola*, it dramatizes the emergence of a legend from a variety of conflicting myths and explanations, which the community as a whole finally agrees to accept. The 'realistic treatment' to which the legendary core – the golden guineas and the golden-haired child – is subjected, however, makes *Silas Marner* not only an example of George Eliot's myth-making but also an expression of her mythography – the study of the origin, development and meaning of myths. So the European drama of ideas has to wait while the novelist, in what is both a retrospect and an anticipation, offers a final virtuoso performance in her chosen medium of rustic realism. But the central question posed by both novels is the same: what is the process through which successive psychological and historical phases conduct us to a new vision of the world, whether in the form of a local legend or a new religion of humanity?

It was, however, the rustic realism that impressed the reviewers when *Silas Marner* was published in April 1861. After the evidence of *Adam Bede* and *The Mill on the Floss* they now accepted that George Eliot uniquely had the skill and insight to depict the life of the poor in a strikingly new way. For the critic of the *Saturday Review* this still had the force of 'a new revelation' when compared to 'the ordinary tales of country life that are written in such abundance by ladies':

There the poor are always looked at from the point of view of the rich. They are so many subjects for experimenting on, for reclaiming, improving, being anxious about, and relieving. They have no existence apart from the presence of a curate and a district visitor. They live in order to take tracts and broth.

As a result, the poor remain 'a distinct race': 'What they think of and do when they are not being improved and helped, remains a blank.' George Eliot fills the blank, cultivating this 'virgin soil' with her picture of a whole village from the squire down to the poacher. 'We know that these poor are like real poor people' (*George Eliot: The Critical Heritage*, pp. 171–2).

The novelist becomes a sympathetic anthropologist describing the way of life of a remote people, re-creating their rituals, hierarchies and dialects. Like her admired predecessor Wordsworth, George Eliot at all times endeavoured to look closely at her subject, and the subject, in her early novels, was, like Wordsworth's, the life of the farmers and peasantry. And it is as a result of their radical reappraisals of the pastoral conventions that we tend to take for granted what George Eliot's mid-Victorian readers still found revelatory. In fact, she had begun to define her own kind of realism five years earlier in the form of a critique of the pastoral in the pages of the *Westminster Review*. 'Idyllic ploughmen are jocund when they drive their team afield; idyllic shepherds make bashful love under the hawthorn bushes; idyllic villagers dance in the chequered shade and refresh themselves, not immoderately, with spicy nut-brown ale.' From a distance it is possible to maintain the illusion. 'Observe a company of haymakers,' she writes. The fresh hay, the golden light, the wagon, the meadow, the activity – the scene is 'smiling' and the labourers must be bright and cheerful.

Approach nearer, and you will certainly find that haymaking is a time for joking, especially if there are women among the labourers; but the coarse laugh that bursts out every now and then, and expresses the triumphant taunt, is as far as possible from your conception of idyllic merriment ... the only realm of fancy and imagination for the English clown exists at the bottom of the third quart pot.

This describes one of the primary motives in George Eliot's early fiction. 'We want to be taught to feel not for the heroic artisan or the sentimental peasant, but for the peasant in all his coarse apathy, and the artisan in all his suspicious selfishness.' Idyllic pastoral writes such characters out of literature; only by writing them in will 'the vulgarity of exclusiveness' be abolished (*Essays of George Eliot*, pp. 269–71).

That there was still work to be done is startlingly revealed by the language the reviewers use – whether they like the novel or not – to describe the subject matter of *Silas Marner*. E.S. Dallas in *The Times*, for example, commends the novelist for her unflinching truthfulness: 'We see the people amid all their grovelling cares, with all their coarseness, ignorance, and prejudice – poor, paltry, stupid, wretched, well-nigh despicable' (*George Eliot: The Critical Heritage*, p. 179). The reviewer of the *Dublin University Magazine* wears all his prejudices on his sleeve in his belief that there must be better people living in the countryside than '[t]hese dull clowns ... whose ideas and imagery seldom rise above the level of their native dunghills, whose highest faith in the powers above falls far below that of a good Mahommedan or an educated Hindoo' (*George Eliot: The Critical Heritage*, p. 191). Even Blackwood on 19 February 1861, mediating tactfully between the novelist and the demands of his readers, finds the first five chapters sad and almost oppressive: 'I wish the picture had been a more cheery one and embraced higher specimens of humanity, but you paint so naturally that in your hands the veriest earthworms become most interesting perfect studies in fact.' The challenge had been to make the lives of these earthworms meaningful in the folk culture to which they belong, and so earn the praise of the *Westminster Review*: 'It is impossible to dissociate any of the characters from the village in which they were born and bred – they form an organic whole with Raveloe' (*George Eliot: The Critical Heritage*, p. 187).

There were, however, at least two Victorian reviewers who saw beyond the rustic realism of *Silas Marner* to the larger and more pressing issues that point forward to *Romola*. In the *Economist* that versatile man of letters, Richard Holt Hutton, quickly realized that the novel was not simply a study of English rural life at the turn of the century. Like George Eliot's Italian novel, *Silas Marner* engages in its own way with the controversies of mid-Victorian England. 'One of the most striking features in this striking tale is the strong intellectual impress which the author contrives to give to a story of which the main elements are altogether unintellectual, without the smallest injury to the verisimilitude of the tale.' Behind the conversation in Chapter 6 in the Rainbow, for example, Hutton discerns the 'faint shadow of the intellectual phases of "modern thought"', with its distinctions between 'subjective' and 'objective', and 'form' and 'substance' (*George Eliot: The Critical Heritage*, pp. 176–7). And, one might add, the lengthy discussion there about the existence of ghosts runs, in its own idiomatic way, through the whole gamut of arguments, from historical evidence, experience, experiment, to analogy and belief. Similarly, the debate over Silas's lost gold is a parody of the continuing contemporaneous disputes in theology and history over the nature of evidence and its interpretation. But here in Raveloe the village consensus is always achieved through the ritual of debate, argument, disagreement and reconciliation; and it is by this means that the approved version of the legend of Silas Marner is eventually established in the community.

A second reviewer who discerned George Eliot's larger purposes was much more critical and suspicious. In 1863 Richard Simpson, the Liberal Catholic friend of Lord Acton, wrote an incisive survey of the first half of the novelist's career for the *Home and Foreign Review*. He explores with impressive authority the foundations of George Eliot's ethical beliefs in Strauss, Feuerbach, Comte and Goethe, in order to demonstrate that her positivist belief in 'the pure emanation of feeling' is incompatible with any system of religious doctrine. She is shrewdly aware, however, that doctrines are still necessary to enable people to convert their feelings into energies – 'for energy results from the union of belief and feeling'. Consequently, Simpson maintains, she appears to sympathize in her fiction with a variety of religious beliefs that she, in fact, rejects. But this is for her only a temporary expedient: in time the shell of Christianity will fall away and reveal the true inner substance, the feeling that it has been safe-guarding. Simpson's mistrust of Eliot's heterodoxy informs his remark-able essay. And as far as *Silas Marner* is concerned, he views the double plot of the novel as a means of explaining away rather condes-cendingly the workings of Providence so that 'Marner's conversion depend[s] altogether on human sympathies and love, while he, simple fellow, fails to see the action of the general law of humanity, and attributes everything to the "dealings" which regulate the accidents' (*George Eliot: The Critical Heritage*, p. 229). Indeed, George Eliot acknowl-edged to her publisher on 24 February 1861 that the aim of her story was to set 'in a strong light the remedial influences of pure, natural human relations'. It is just that Simpson objects to the way in which the religious beliefs of Raveloe are devalued to serve that humanistic end.

In their different ways, Hutton and Simpson recognized that *Silas Marner* was a contribution to a current Victorian debate about the nature of belief and, at the heart of this, the status of myth or sacred story in the modern world. It is clear from her early essays and reviews that George Eliot shared with other freethinkers the need for a new mythology in a world conscious of its own belatedness. The past and its traditions, creeds and doctrines had become remote and alien in a new and disturbing way. For Matthew Arnold, in his essay on Heine (1863), 'the awakening of the modern spirit' was a recogni-tion of 'the sense of want of correspondence between the forms of modern Europe and its spirit'. Carlyle in *Sartor Resartus* (1833–4) had responded to this belatedness with his Clothes Philosophy, which asserted the need for a continual discarding of old, unfashionable beliefs and systems, and the creation of new myths. And as early as 1851 George Eliot was calling for the social sciences to separate the old clothes from the new: 'Our civilization, and, yet more, our reli-gion, are an anomalous blending of lifeless barbarisms, which have descended to us like so many petrifications from distant ages, with living ideas, the offspring of a true process of development' (*Essays of George Eliot*, p. 18). The key term is 'development'. Religious beliefs, world-views, myths and legends, all represent stages in the progress of the intellect, a means of understanding the past and speculating about the future.

George Eliot, as a formidable intellectual, was at the centre of this debate in England during the first part of her writing career. She translated David Friedrich Strauss's three-volume *Life of Jesus* (1835) from the German in 1846 where he developed what he called his mythical method of interpreting the gospels. His aim was to reconcile modern culture and the ancient records, the rational and the supernatural interpretations of the gospel texts; and Strauss's lengthy introductory chapter provides a sophisticated discussion of the narrative criteria by which myth may be defined. In 1854 her translation of Feuerbach's *Essence of Christianity* (1841) transmitted further radical German ideas to England. The antithesis of the divine and the human was, Feuerbach maintained, altogether illusory and only arose because humanity projected its own ideals into an imaginary absolute, God. The gospels needed stripping of their theological accretions and returning to their human frame of reference: then, God is Love will become Love is God. As these ideas were being assimilated into English intellectual life, George Eliot remained at the cutting edge of radical debate in her role as assistant editor of the freethinking *Westminster Review* where she reviewed the latest works on philosophy, biblical studies, sociology and mythology.

One review that demonstrates clearly her confident grasp of the current debate was her lengthy discussion in 1851 of Robert William Mackay's *The Progress of the Intellect* (1850). Referring extensively to German writing on mythology, George Eliot shows that Mackay was developing and extending Strauss's ideas by defining myth as a form of hypothesis which arises naturally in all kinds of mental activity as a means of connecting the known with the unknown. '[E]very past phase of human development,' she writes, 'is part of that education of the race in which we are sharing; every mistake, every absurdity into which poor human nature has fallen, may be looked on as an experiment of which we may reap the benefit.' This is the premise, she maintains, that introduces 'a truly philosophic spirit into the study of mythology' (*Essays of George Eliot*, p. 36). Myth becomes a kind of experimental hypothesis through which the individual or the community formulates an explanation of life, so replacing the fixed systems and creeds of earlier generations. Inevitably, each hypothesis or world-view proves inadequate when subjected to harsh reality, and collapses. 'None of our theories,' comments the narrator in *Felix Holt* laconically, 'are quite large enough for all the disclosures of time.' But this is the education of the human race out of which new myths or patterns of meaning emerge. This is the disruptive yet evolutionary rhythm of life that is central to George Eliot's thinking, both at the level of individual consciousnesss and the larger movements of European history. Certainly, it is not difficult to discern the progress of the intellect in the rise and fall of competing myths in *Romola*, but how does it find expression in that humble tale of rural life, *Silas Marner*, the writing of which cut across the preparations for her European epic?

2

Far from the cultural hothouse of Renaissance Florence, *Silas Marner* explores the origins of folk myth in a rural community at the beginning of the nineteenth century. As a natural historian of religion, George Eliot is seeking to refine her ideas in a world she is most familiar with and where myth-making can be seen at its most primitive. There are several features of life in Raveloe that bring out this anthropological side of the novel. First, the community is remote in time and space, providing the narrator – and the Victorian amateur folklorist – with vestiges and remnants of a distant past to be deciphered: 'Such strange lingering echoes of the old demon-worship might perhaps even now be caught by the diligent listener among the grey-haired peasantry' (p. 6). And beyond these echoes, there are vestiges of an even more remote, mythical past to which the novel reaches out: 'In the early ages of the world, we know, it was believed that each territory was inhabited and ruled by its own divinities' (p. 16). Though superseded, such myths are an integral part of the genetic, evolutionary history through which we come to understand ourselves. 'The gods of the hearth exist for us still; and let all new faith be tolerant of that fetishism, lest it bruise its own roots' (p. 142).

Secondly, the novel creates a world full of mysterious gaps and uncertainties. Beyond Raveloe is an inexplicable region from which strangers manifest themselves like apparitions, or into which people disappear without explanation. Some things come (a child), others go (the gold). A dominant image is that of a lighted candle or lantern surrounded by encroaching darkness. Within the community, too, there are social gaps between the landed parishioners and their tenants that are accepted as unbridgeable and eternal, 'the Raveloe imagination having never ventured back to that fearful blank when there were no Osgoods' (p. 23). And this particular mystery is sharpened by a new development in George Eliot's fiction, the double plot of Silas and Godfrey Cass, which reflects these social divisions and in which the interconnections are minimal and mysterious. A further gap is the narrative hiatus of sixteen years between the two parts of the novel, whose significance becomes fully apparent only in the climactic debate.

To underline the indeterminacies of this fictional world even further, George Eliot endows the central character with catalepsy, 'the chasm in his consciousness' (p. 110), which baffles both the brethren of Lantern Yard and the rustics. This is an essential feature of the novelist's experiment in the basic logic of myth-making. In a hostile comment in *The Times*, E.S. Dallas wondered what was the point of writing a story about such 'a singularly unaccountable being' as Silas, since 'the pleasure of fiction depends mainly on our being able to count upon the elements of human character and to calculate results' (*George Eliot: The Critical Heritage*, p. 182). One can see his point, but the challenge of the novel is to depict a world unaccountable at many levels so that the crucial strategies by which people make sense of their lives may be explored in the most fundamental way. This is what separates the major characters, Silas and Godfrey, from the community. Whereas Raveloe relies on its shared beliefs, that mixture of superstition and religion which finds expression in its public rituals – the Sunday church service, the New Year's dance, the discussions in the Rainbow – the protagonists experience a series of sudden dislocations that make them revise repeatedly their ways of looking at life. To both of them can be applied the phrase that describes Silas's career: his 'inward life had been a history and a metamorphosis' (p. 9). The history belongs to the developing cause and effect of fictional narrative; the metamorphosis to legendary story. *Silas Marner* combines them so that they illuminate each other.

These are some of the features which enable the novelist to carry out her most fundamental experiment into what constitutes a minimally coherent myth or world-view. And the narrative commentary repeatedly refers the reader to even more extreme situations. Silas's desperate weaving, for example, is explained in these terms:

Have not men, shut up in solitary imprisonment, found an interest in marking the moments by straight strokes of a certain length on the wall, until the growth of the sum of straight strokes, arranged in triangles, has become a mastering purpose? Do we not wile away moments of inanity or fatigued waiting by repeating some trivial movement or sound, until the repetition has bred a want, which is incipient habit? (p. 19)

The prisoner in solitary imprisonment, Silas Marner, the author and the reader, are all brought together in the inescapable need to create meaning and purpose in a vacuum. And one of the best places to examine the relationship between the need and its expression is in those primitive communities untouched – unlike the Victorian reader – by critical self-consciousness. 'To people accustomed to reason about the forms in which their religious feeling has incorporated itself, it is difficult to enter into that simple, untaught state of mind in which the form and the feeling have never been severed by an act of reflection' (p. 14). The novelist enters this untaught state of mind, and then, through the disrupted careers of the protagonists, separates form and feeling, before finally reuniting them in order to examine and redefine their relationship.

The parallel careers of Silas and Godfrey, out of which the novel is constructed, dramatize the creation of mythical systems in response to the unpredictable. The retrospect of the first chapter shows how the religious sect of Lantern Yard has developed its own system of belief, a form of Calvinistic Dissent, in response to 'the currents of industrial energy and Puritan earnestness' (p. 23) of a northern city. Its vulnerability is revealed by the disputes over the meaning of Silas's cataleptic fits, and then by the theft of the church money. The trusting community which believes that immediate divine intervention, rather than an examination of the evidence, will answer their questions, has produced its darker progeny in William Dane, Silas's rival, who cunningly exploits the situation for his own purposes.

When the drawing of the lots declares Silas guilty, he blasphemes against 'a God of lies, that bears witness against the innocent' (p. 14), and leaves Lantern Yard as Dane's plotting becomes clear to him. In the search for absolute assurance, things have become their opposites: the certainty of divine intervention finds expression in the randomness of the lots, and innocent trust has generated devilish cunning.

The exile into which Silas moves is a limbo 'in which the past becomes dreamy because its symbols have all vanished, and the present too is dreamy because it is linked with no memories' (p. 15). This blank must – and it is one of George Eliot's imperatives – be filled with some minimal coherence if Silas is to remain a recognizable character. He has to be reconstructed virtually *ex nihilo*, from nothing. All he carries with him into exile is his skill in weaving, but around this a miniature creation myth is enacted as he weaves himself back into existence.[1] The stages are carefully defined. First, with both past and future cancelled, the threads of his weaving criss-cross the emptiness of his life. 'He seemed to weave, like the spider, from pure impulse, without reflection.' And the commentary provides the gloss for the educated reader: 'Every man's work, pursued steadily, tends in this way to become an end in itself, and so to bridge over the loveless chasms of his life' (p. 16). Then, Silas begins to find in the gold he earns a purpose in life: 'that habit of looking towards the money and grasping it with a sense of fulfilled effort made a loam that was deep enough for the seeds of desire' (p. 17). A new world is emerging in which time now acquires a structure and meaning: 'the money had come to mark off his weaving into periods, and the money not only grew, but it remained with him' (p. 19). Silas's 'life [is] narrowing and hardening itself more and more into a mere pulsation of desire and satisfaction that had no relation to any other being', and yet, past, present and future are being linked meaningfully together. Then, as the gold pieces begin to provide continuity in his life, Silas comes to love them as 'his familiars' and enjoy their companionship. And, finally, he celebrates his new life by creating a ritual, his Midas-like 'revelry', which expresses this vivid fetishism. At night he locks the door and closes his shutters, bringing out the golden guineas – the sacraments of his belief – for his love and worship. 'He spread them out in heaps and bathed his hands in them … and thought fondly of the guineas that were only half earned by the work in his loom, as if they had been unborn children' (p. 21). It is a wonderfully vivid account of a world of meaning conjured into existence by the mechanical and minimal rhythm of Silas's weaving.

Through this account of Silas's early life and his fifteen-year exile, Eliot is establishing the basic pattern of the novel, the metamorphosis of one world-view into its opposite. In this case, absolute trust in the divine has been replaced by materialism, the miraculous by the mechanistic, simple trust by self-dependence, and the believing community by a life of solitary utility. In neither case, George Eliot implies, is Silas fully human. His original naïve defencelessness, with his 'deer-like gaze', disengaged him from the world, while his embittered reaction has simply turned him into the engine that drives his loom. Having lost his god, Silas has turned himself into a machine for making gold. Though the phases of his life are not completely exclusive – the narrator is at pains to remind us that his 'sap of affection was not all gone' (p. 20) – these are the extreme polarities that have to be reconciled. And it is at this point that the Cass family, from the other mysterious half of the novel, intervenes in his life through the theft of his gold. Again, a 'sudden chasm' has opened up in his life but now he can only '[fill] up the blank with grief' (p. 77). How can he begin to make sense once more out of his dereliction? Was it a thief or a supernatural power 'which had delighted in making him a second time desolate?' (p. 44). This is the question that Silas, in his helplessness, is now forced to carry into the community.

He finds no clear answers. Instead, we have George Eliot's parody of the contemporary Victorian debates in theology and history as to the nature of evidence and its interpretation. But he has, crucially, been brought into the community, where he is initiated by his Job's 'comforters' into a new way of looking at his affliction. It is a mystery that Dolly Winthrop benignly explains through 'her simple Raveloe theology', which combines 'trust i' Them as knows better nor we do' (pp. 83–4) with good works, those two dimensions of life fatally separated in the first two stages of Silas's career. He has learnt that help must come from outside, and this is why on New Year's Eve he is waiting expectantly with his door open when he is again arrested 'by the invisible wand of catalepsy' (p. 110). The second impingement of the Cass family upon Silas's life then occurs with the arrival of the child and, with it, the most sudden metamorphosis in the novel. As his gold is transubstantiated into Eppie's curls before his eyes, Silas begins to evolve his third mythical explanation.

The event itself is neither good nor evil. It is how he responds to it; and, as with Job, the question is, what has survived his afflictions? The sudden discovery recalls to Silas the key events of his previous life, but these are now transformed by his response to Eppie, his act of intuitive love, a revelation to himself. It is upon this act of faith and natural affection that he begins to articulate the new myth of his life: 'My money's gone, I don't know where – and this is come from I don't know where. I know nothing – I'm partly mazed' (p. 118). Encouraged by Dolly to trust in this mysterious rhythm of life, Silas tentatively expresses the hidden logic of events: 'Thought and feeling were so confused within him, that if he had tried to give them utterance, he could only have said that the child was come instead of the gold – that the gold had turned into the child' (p. 122). This is the minimal confession of faith out of which the legend is finally constructed. And just as the mechanical repetition of the weaving generated one creation myth, so this mysterious sequence generates another, a contrary one, which links him organically to the community from which he has been isolated. Eppie 'created fresh and fresh links' between Silas and Raveloe: 'As the child's mind was growing into knowledge, his mind was growing into memory: as her life unfolded, his soul, long stupefied in a cold narrow prison, was unfolding too, and trembling gradually into full consciousness' (p. 126). Through Eppie, 'he had himself come to appropriate the forms of custom and belief which were the mould of Raveloe life' (p. 142). It is through love's mediation that Silas begins to gain possession of his life along with that of the community.

In the other half of the novel, the career of Godfrey Cass undergoes its own metamorphoses which chart the origins, self-contradictions and establishment of his coherent vision of the world. The context here, in contrast, is the aimless, indulgent and bored life of the rural landowners whose repetitive rituals are, in a compelling phrase, their only means of 'annulling vacancy' (p. 31). With the deft economy she employed in Lantern Yard, George Eliot again delineates in the Cass family a genealogy of world-views. The power in this semi-feudal society is Squire Cass, a widower, who is, unpredictably, both harsh and indulgent. His two sons have responded in contrasting ways, becoming, like Silas and Dane, polar opposites dangerously separated. Godfrey's passive creed is a belief in 'some unforeseen turn of fortune, some favourable chance which would save him from unpleasant consequences' (p. 73), while the decisive Dunstan believes actively in his own good luck, which he pursues with 'diabolical cunning' (p. 31). This is why Godfrey has to use him as his agent and intermediary. And through this agency, Dunstan expresses his brother's shadowy and illicit desires – his wish to marry the desirable Nancy, his 'good angel', with its accompanying dark corollary, his wish for the death of the 'demonic' Molly. Their interdependence is expressed vividly in their mutual recriminations, their reciprocal threats to tell all to the squire, and their shifting of responsibility on to each other. In this way, by means of a legend-like genealogy, George Eliot dismantles the indulgent tyranny of the father into the mutually hostile world-views of the sons, a passive reliance on chance and a cunning self-interest. Separated from each other, faith and works are again shown to be corrupting and self-defeating.

From this perspective, those mysterious interventions in Silas's life become successive expressions of the Casse's' world-view – the loss of gold becomes theft, the arrival of Eppie becomes her abandonment by her parents. For Godfrey, initially, it is as if his belief in the god of 'favourable Chance' (p. 73) has paid off: Dunstan, the blackmailer, has disappeared; the clandestine wife, Molly, is dead; and their unacknowledged child will now be looked after by Silas. But, in George Eliot's fiction, 'the orderly sequence by which the seed brings forth a crop after its kind' (p. 74) never falters; and it is always initiated by the response characters make to events. In this crisis, Godfrey first hopes that his wife is dead, and then fails to claim his own child:

The wide-open blue eyes looked up at Godfrey's without any uneasiness or sign of recognition: the child could make no visible [or] audible claim on its father; and the father felt a strange mixture of feelings, a conflict of regret and joy ... when the blue eyes turned away from him slowly, and fixed themselves on the weaver's queer face. (p. 118)

It is a momentous pause in which nothing apparently happens, but it is the turning-point of the novel. What Godfrey mistakenly thinks is the 'deliverance from his long bondage' is, in reality, Silas's – and Godfrey's own – punishment.

Godfrey's marriage to Nancy is both his salvation and his nemesis. The Lammeter family, as the other main landowners in Raveloe, represent contrasting values to the Casses, as their surnames suggest.[2] The head of the family is a sober, strong-minded widower, with two contrasting daughters. After the sixteen-year gap in the novel, we see that Nancy's sense of propriety, conventionalism and exactitude have transformed Godfrey's view of the world. Chance has given way to routine, order and accountability. But amid this order there is one omission, variously described as a 'blank' or a 'void', which corresponds to the gap in the text for the reader. This is their childlessness, which both unites and separates them. Godfrey seeks to repair the omission through the adoption of Eppie, but Nancy denies him this compensation for within the rigidly ordered Lammeter world there is a strong belief in providence, the acceptance of the *status quo*, the opposite of the chance from which she has rescued Godfrey.

Their married years run parallel to Silas's fostering of Eppie in the time-gap (sanctioned by legend)[3] between the two parts of the novel. This hiatus represents both steady growth and sudden metamorphosis in the two main characters when we rejoin the narrative. This occurs with the discovery of Dunstan's body. Godfrey's growing sense of order and retribution now turns into a full confession and acceptance of an omniscient divine power: 'Everything comes to light, Nancy, sooner or later. When God Almighty wills it, our secrets are found out.' Her shock is followed by Godfrey's when she replies: 'Do you think I'd have refused to take [Eppie] in, if I'd known she was yours?' (pp. 162–3). This finely prepared mutual misjudgement is an essential part of what the novelist called the mild nemesis of the story. But now, having reversed his earlier belief in chance, Godfrey is ready to accept his full responsibility in a divinely ordered universe, as he and Nancy set off to claim their daughter.

To whom does Eppie belong? In the weaver's cottage, the 'contest', as it is called, takes place between the two fathers with the recovered gold on the table. Who will get which? What principle will settle this semi-legal contest of a paternity suit? The reader has been well prepared for the difficulties attending the assessment of evidence upon which truth-claims can be based. The divided structure of the novel has guaranteed that all the major events are ambivalent – someone's loss is another's gain – while, in addition, the precise interpretation of these events is determined by particular world-views. Silas has passed from the other-worldliness of Lantern Yard through the machine-like world of his weaving to their synthesis of his life with Eppie. Now that the gold has been found, he is at his moment of 'transfiguration' (p. 165), in possession of his whole life and its meaning. Godfrey, on the other hand, is now intent on claiming Eppie as the 'blessing' denied his marriage and so putting to rights his sixteen years of secrecy and irresponsibility, impatient of any obstacles to 'his virtuous resolves' (p. 169).

Against Godfrey's claims of legality, duty and blood, Silas invokes what George Eliot calls in *The Mill on the Floss* 'the special circumstances that mark the individual lot', the claims of lived experience: '[T]hen, sir, why didn't you say so sixteen year ago, and claim her before I'd come to love her ...?' And later, 'Your coming now and saying "I'm her father" doesn't alter the feelings inside us. It's me she's been calling her father ever since she could say the word' (pp. 169–70). Godfrey wants, in the terms of the novel, the 'form' without the 'feeling'. But the proof is in the naming and the feelings that justify it, just as Silas's naming of Eppie had established their covenant in the first place.[4] This is the basis of Silas's claim. And he is now in a position to justify it by an interpretation of events which finally exorcizes his earlier blasphemy. He combines the language of Lantern Yard with that of Raveloe: 'God gave her to me because you turned your back upon her, and He looks upon her as mine: you've no right to her! When a man turns a blessing from his door, it falls to them as take it in' (p. 169). What was before a simple sequence – gold, child – now becomes a more complex statement of cause, effect and purpose, a kind of theology. Silas's 'transfiguration' at this moment is the final metamorphosis that encapsulates his whole career, his becoming fully human.

The final decision, the verdict in the trial, however, is left to Eppie, the living evidence of that sixteen-year time-gap in the novel, and the confirmation of one man's blessing and the other's nemesis. The princess in exile chooses to stay with her foster-father by reaffirming, in suitably biblical rhythms, the covenant Silas had made in adopting her. 'And he's took care of me and loved me from the first, and I'll cleave to him as long as he lives, and nobody shall ever come between him and me' (p. 172). The domestic reality out of which this statement comes is vividly dramatized, as Silas and Eppie, always conscious of each other, touch and hold hands in their cottage. It is a complex and moving scene, which recuperates the whole of the double narrative: two views of the world, painfully evolved, confronting each other. And, as so often in George Eliot's novels, there is no key of interpretation, no general principle, but only an appeal and confession. The appeal is to the sixteen-year gap in the novel during which Eppie has become the incarnate history of Silas's love. With great simplicity she confesses this as the evidence which ensures the keeping of their covenant.

Though the life and values of 'the poor who are born poor' (p. 171) are unintelligible to Godfrey and Nancy, they accept Eppie's decision and Silas's judgement, and through this rejection Godfrey is forced, in turn, to move on. He now begins to reconcile the passive reliance on chance of his earlier life with its opposite, his belief in a strictly providential order, neither of which has brought him his daughter. He, too, comes to acknowledge the evidence of the sixteen-year gap in the narrative, the final chasm to be bridged. This sad acceptance is expressed in terms of organic growth: 'While I've been putting off and putting off, the trees have been growing – it's too late now' (p. 174). This is the darker side of the community's belief in earned good luck. Neither he nor Silas is allowed to go back into the past, pay off their debts, clear up the mystery, and start afresh – for even Lantern Yard has disappeared when the weaver returns there at the end of the novel. It is left to the community, gathering in front of the Rainbow for Eppie's wedding, to authorize the interpretation of events that will pass into legend, that 'strange history' of Silas Marner by which 'he had brought a blessing on himself by acting like a father to a lone motherless child': 'and all differences among the company were merged in a general agreement with Mr Snell's sentiment, that when a man had deserved his good luck, it was the part of his neighbours to wish him joy' (p. 182).

If *Silas Marner* is a novel about a legend and its creation, what truth does the legend embody? A clue is to be found in a letter George Eliot wrote to her evangelical friend Sara Hennell on 9 October 1843, shortly after losing her Christian faith, where she recapitulates the stages of her own developing beliefs. First comes the liberation 'from the wretched giant's bed of dogmas', then the enjoyment of 'the full use of our limbs and the bracing air of independence', but soon the sense of 'our own miserable weakness' introduces a new awareness: 'Speculative truth begins to appear but a shadow of individual minds, agreement between intellects seems unattainable, and we turn to the *truth of feeling* as the only universal bond of union.' For George Eliot, the individual life develops, as we have seen, by a series of disruptive discoveries and disconfirmations. But finally – and here Richard Simpson's analysis is confirmed – all the partial truths fall away to reveal the genuine kernel of belief, the truth of feeling.

This truth of feeling has, however, to find expression in a recognizable form. To express his new-found sense of community and love, Silas Marner appropriates 'the forms of custom and belief which were the mould of Raveloe life'. But he could do this only after the forms and feeling of his previous beliefs had been dismantled; and the same applies to Godfrey Cass. In a similar way, the novelist appropriates and refashions traditional beliefs of various kinds in her narrative and commentary; the extent of her biblical quotations and allusions, for example, will be evident from the Notes to this edition of *Silas Marner*. All are assimilated finally to express, in her words, 'the remedial influences of pure, natural human relations'. This, in brief, is George Eliot's mythical method. Out of a conflict of personal myths emerges one generally accepted by the community, a myth that develops from these and genetically contains them. Silas's 'strange history' confirms the Raveloe belief in earned good luck,[5] a belief that encapsulates, without resolving, the agency of chance and that of cause-and-effect, out of which this novel – like all novels – is so strikingly constituted. In the future lie those other myths for the modern world – the future madonna in *Romola*, the modern St Theresa in *Middlemarch* and the putative messiah in *Daniel Deronda*. But it is here in this rustic tale that the dynamics of George Eliot's mythical method is fully presented for the first time.

Notes

1. Titus Burckhardt shows, in *Sacred Art* (London: Perennial Books, 1967), how the creation of the universe was frequently represented through the activity of weaving. Carlyle plays many variations on this theme in his account of the Philosophy of Clothes in *Sartor Resartus* (I. 8) where he quotes the Earth-Spirit from Goethe's *Faust*: ''Tis thus at the roaring Loom of Time I ply,/And weave for God the Garment thou seest Him by.'

2. Measure (meter) and chance (*casus*), respectively.

3. There are interesting parallels between the gold, the child and the sixteen-year gap in *Silas Marner* and the same elements in *The Winter's Tale*.

4. Isaiah 62: 4: 'Thou shalt no more be termed Forsaken; neither shall thy land any more be termed Desolate: but thou shalt be called Hephzibah, and thy land Beulah: for the Lord delighteth in thee, and thy land shall be married.'

5. See Q.D. Leavis's discussion of Luck, Chance and Providence in her edition of *Silas Marner* (Harmondsworth: Penguin, 1967), pp. 42, 259–60.

1. Further Writings by George Eliot

Essays of George Eliot, ed. Thomas Pinney (London: Routledge & Kegan Paul, 1963).

The George Eliot Letters, ed. Gordon S. Haight, 9 vols. (New Haven: Yale University Press, 1954–78).

Selections from George Eliot's Letters, ed. Gordon S. Haight (New Haven: Yale University Press, 1985).

George Eliot: Selected Essays, Poems and Other Writings, eds. A.S. Byatt and Nicholas Warren (Harmondsworth: Penguin, 1990).

2. Biography

Cross, J.W., *George Eliot's Life as Related in Her Letters and Journals*, 3 vols. (Edinburgh and London: Blackwood, 1885).

Haight, Gordon S., *George Eliot: A Biography* (Oxford: Oxford University Press, 1968; Harmondsworth: Penguin, 1986).

Uglow, Jennifer, *George Eliot* (London: Virago, 1987).

3. Collections of Critical Writings

Carroll, David, ed., *George Eliot: The Critical Heritage* (London: Routledge & Kegan Paul, 1971).

Draper, R.P., ed., *George Eliot: 'The Mill on the Floss' and 'Silas Marner': A Casebook* (London: Macmillan, 1977).

Haight, Gordon S., ed., *A Century of George Eliot Criticism* (Boston: Houghton Mifflin, 1965).

Levine, George, *An Annotated Critical Biography of George Eliot* (Brighton: Harvester, 1988).

4. General Studies

Auster, Henry, *Local Habitations: Regionalism in the Early Novels of George Eliot* (Cambridge, Mass.: Harvard University Press, 1970).

Beer, Gillian, *Darwin's Plots: Evolutionary Narrative in Darwin, George Eliot and Nineteenth-Century Fiction* (London: Routledge & Kegan Paul, 1983).

Burstein, Janet, 'Victorian Mythography and the Progress of the Intellect', *Victorian Studies*, 18 (1974–5), pp. 309–24.

Carroll, David, *George Eliot and the Conflict of Interpretations* (Cambridge: Cambridge University Press, 1992).

Hardy, Barbara, *The Novels of George Eliot: A Study in Form* (London: Athlone Press, 1959).

Knoepflmacher, U.C., *George Eliot's Early Novels: The Limits of Realism* (Berkeley and Los Angeles: University of California Press, 1968).

Shuttleworth, Sally, *George Eliot and Nineteenth-Century Science: The Make-Believe of a Beginning* (Cambridge: Cambridge University Press, 1984).

Wiesenfarth, Joseph, *George Eliot's Mythmaking* (Heidelberg: Carl Winter, 1977).

5. Some Articles

Carroll, David, '*Silas Marner*: Reversing the Oracles of Religion', *Literary Monographs* (Madison: University of Wisconsin Press, 1967), I, pp. 165–200.

Cohen, Susan, R., 'A History and a Metamorphosis: Continuity and Discontinuity in *Silas Marner*', *Texas Studies in Literature and Language*, 25 (1983), pp. 410–26.

Fisch, Harold, 'Biblical Realism in *Silas Marner*', in *Identity and Ethos: A Festschrift for Sol Liptzin*, ed. Mark H. Gelber (New York: Peter Lang, 1986), pp. 343–60.

Leavis, Q.D., Introduction to *Silas Marner* (Harmondsworth: Penguin, 1967).

McLaverty, James, 'Comtean Fetishism in *Silas Marner*', *Nineteenth-Century Fiction*, 36 (1981–2), pp. 318–36.

Shuttleworth, Sally, 'Fairy Tale or Science? Physiological Psychology in *Silas Marner*', in *Languages of Nature: Critical Essays on Science and Literature*, ed. L.J. Jordanova (London: Free Association Books, 1986), pp. 244–88.

Swann, Brian, '*Silas Marner* and the New Mythus', *Criticism*, 18 (1976), pp. 101–21.

1819   *22 November*, born at Arbury, Warwickshire.

1824–36 Attends boarding schools in Attleborough, Nuneaton and Coventry.

1836   *3 February*, mother dies.

1837   After sister Christiana marries, becomes father's housekeeper.

1841   Moves with her father to Coventry where she meets Charles
        and Caroline ('Cara') Bray. Reads Charles Hennell's *An Inquiry
        Concerning the Origin of Christianity* (1838) which leads her to
        question her religious faith.

1842   *January–May*, the 'Holy War' with her father when she refuses
        to attend church. Friendship with Charles and Sara Hennell.

1844   Begins a translation of Strauss's *Das Leben Jesu* (4th edn., 1840).

1846   *The Life of Jesus* published.

1846–7 'Poetry and Prose, from the Notebook of an Eccentric', pub-
        lished in the Coventry *Herald and Observer*.

1847–8 Nurses father.

1849   Begins to translate Spinoza's *Tractatus theologico-politicus*. *31 May*,
        death of father. *June*, sets off to France, Italy and Switzerland
        with the Brays; they return to England in July. Remains in
        Geneva, lodging from *October*, with the painter M. D'Albert-
        Durade and his wife. Begins journal.

1850   *March*, returns to England. Feels unwanted by her family and
        resides with the Brays. Decides to earn her living by writing.
        October, visits John Chapman in London.

1851   *January*, her first major article, 'The Progress of the Intellect',
        published in the *Westminster Review*. *September*, moves to London
        and becomes assistant editor of the *Westminster*.

1852   *January*, her first number of the *Westminster* published. Close
        friendship with Herbert Spencer.

1853   Working hard on the *Westminster*. *October*, intimacy with George
        Henry Lewes begins.

1854   translation of Feuerbach's *Essence of Christianity* published. Leaves for
        Germany with Lewes. Begins translation of Spinoza's *Ethics*.

1855   *March*, returns to England with Lewes; they set up house together.

1856   Trips to Ilfracombe and Tenby to collect materials for Lewes's

Sea-side Studies (1858). Begins to write fiction, 'The Sad Fortunes of Amos Barton'. 'The Natural History of German Life' and 'Silly Novels by Lady Novelists', published in the *Westminster.*

1857   'Amos Barton', 'Mr Gilfil's Love-Story' and 'Janet's Repentance', published in *Blackwood's Edinburgh Magazine*. Assumes pseudonym, George Eliot. Writes to her brother of her relationship with Lewes and he breaks off communication. *October*, begins *Adam Bede.*

1858   *January, Scenes of Clerical Life*. Travels with Lewes to Munich, then to Dresden via Salzburg, Vienna and Prague.

1859   *February, Adam Bede. April*, interrupts composition of *The Mill on the Floss* to write 'The Lifted Veil', published in *Blackwood's* in *July. June*, pressured into unveiling the identity of 'George Eliot'.

1860   *April, The Mill on the Floss*. Trip to Italy where she conceives the idea of *Romola. August*, writes 'Brother Jacob'. Begins *Silas Marner.*

1861   *April, Silas Marner*. Further trip to Italy for research on *Romola* which she starts to write in *October.*

1862   *July, Romola* begins serialization in *Cornhill Magazine.*

1863   *July, Romola*. She and Lewes buy the Priory, Regent's Park.

1864   Begins verse play *The Spanish Gypsy. July*, 'Brother Jacob', published in the *Cornhill.*

1865   *February*, temporarily abandons her verse play which is making her ill. *March*, starts writing *Felix Holt.*

1866   *June, Felix Holt*. Returns to work on *The Spanish Gypsy.*

1867   Trip to Spain to collect material. Subscribes £50 to the foundation of Girton College, Cambridge.

1868   *May, The Spanish Gypsy.*

1869   Writes 'Brother and Sister' sonnets, and begins *Middlemarch.*

1870   'The Legend of Jubal', published in *Macmillan's Magazine.*

1871   *'Armgart'*, published in *Macmillan's.*

1871–2   *Middlemarch* published in eight parts.

1874   *The Legend of Jubal and Other Poems.*

1876   *Daniel Deronda*, published in eight parts. Purchases the Heights in Witley, Surrey.

1878   *30 November*, Lewes dies.

1879   Preparing last volume of Lewes's *Problems of Life and Mind* for publication *The Impressions of Theophrastus Such.*

1880   *6 May*, marries John Walter Cross. *22 December*, dies in London.

Silas Marner was written in about six months between September 1860 and March 1861. Apart from the manuscript, which is in the British Library, three significant versions of the novel were published in George Eliot's lifetime. The first edition appeared in April 1861, in one volume at 12s., and was an immediate success. By September 8,000 copies had been sold, and a second edition (one volume at 6s.) was required later in the same year for which George Eliot made careful corrections. When a third edition was needed in 1863, the novelist informed her publisher, John Blackwood: 'I corrected Silas carefully for the last edition, so that the reprint may be made from that without any need for my revision' (*Letters*, IV. 76). The so-called Cheap edition of 1868 was printed from the plates of this third edition so that also has no textual significance. The next and last important version of *Silas Marner* was the Cabinet edition of 1878 when the novel was combined with the two short stories, 'The Lifted Veil' and 'Brother Jacob', to form one volume in George Eliot's collected works. It is usually assumed that the novelist paid relatively little attention to the state of her texts for this edition, which was prepared during George Henry Lewes's final illness; the author's corrected proof of *Silas Marner* shows, on the contrary, that she carried out a careful, final revision.

From the collation of these four versions of *Silas Marner* – manuscript, first edition (1861), second edition (1861), Cabinet edition (1878) – it becomes clear that George Eliot was concerned throughout with the accuracy of her text. Initially, the manuscript was made to conform, as with all her novels, to the Blackwood house style in matters of punctuation, spelling, hyphenation, capitalization and word-division, in all of which George Eliot's usage was frequently erratic; she accepted the heavier, syntactical Blackwood punctuation throughout her career without demur, changing it when she so wished. At the same time, she herself made over sixty substantive changes of meaning in the proof of the first edition. For the second edition in the same year, the author's corrected copy of the first edition shows a further thirty substantive changes, while the author's proof for the Cabinet edition reveals that the process of careful revision continued to the end: there are thirty-five substantive changes and at least ninety changes in accidentals, the majority of which are the removal of unnecessary commas. (I am indebted to Gillian Beer for the loan of a microfilm of the author's corrections for the second and Cabinet editions.)

It seems clear, therefore, that the Cabinet edition is the best choice of text as the basis of the present Penguin edition. The process of revision and correction that began with the manuscript continued up to 1878 when, it can be argued, the text of *Silas Marner* finally achieved stability under George Eliot's careful surveillance. A small number of emendations have been made to the copy-text to correct inconsistencies in spelling or capitalization, to provide a missing word and to return obviously misleading punctuation to its original form. These are recorded in the list of Emendations.

Two other kinds of information are provided in the textual apparatus to enable the reader to trace the genesis and development of the text of the novel. First, a list of Textual Variants records all substantive variants from the copy-text (Cabinet edition) in the manuscript (MS), first edition (1) and second edition (2). Secondly, a list of Manuscript Deletions shows the author at work in the early stages of her writing, clarifying, correcting and revising. Some of George Eliot's deletions are illegible, but where they are decipherable all complete substantive revisions are recorded. From these it should be clear how the copy-text readings achieved their final form.

Facsimile title-page of the first edition.[1]

SILAS MARNER:

THE WEAVER OF RAVELOE

BY

GEORGE ELIOT

AUTHOR OF "ADAM BEDE," ETC.

"A child, more than all other gifts
That earth can offer to declining man,
Brings hope with it, and forward-looking thoughts."
WORDSWORTH.

WILLIAM BLACKWOOD AND SONS
EDINBURGH AND LONDON
MDCCCLXI

PART I

In the days when the spinning-wheels hummed busily in the farm-houses – and even great ladies, clothed in silk and thread-lace, had their toy spinning-wheels of polished oak – there might be seen in districts far away among the lanes, or deep in the bosom of the hills, certain pallid undersized men, who, by the side of the brawny country-folk, looked like the remnants of a disinherited race. The shepherd's dog barked fiercely when one of these alien-looking men appeared on the upland, dark against the early winter sunset; for what dog likes a figure bent under a heavy bag? – and these pale men rarely stirred abroad without that mysterious burden. The shepherd himself, though he had good reason to believe that the bag held nothing but flaxen thread, or else the long rolls of strong linen spun from that thread, was not quite sure that this trade of weaving, indispensable though it was, could be carried on entirely without the help of the Evil One. In that far-off time superstition clung easily round every person or thing that was at all unwonted, or even intermittent and occasional merely, like the visits of the pedlar or the knife-grinder. No one knew where wandering men had their homes or their origin; and how was a man to be explained unless you at least knew somebody who knew his father and mother? To the peasants of old times, the world outside their own direct experience was a region of vagueness and mystery: to their untravelled thought a state of wandering was a conception as dim as the winter life of the swallows that came back with the spring; and even a settler, if he came from distant parts, hardly ever ceased to be viewed with a remnant of distrust, which would have prevented any surprise if a long course of inoffensive conduct on his part had ended in the commission of a crime; especially if he had any reputation for knowledge, or showed any skill in handicraft. All cleverness, whether in the rapid use of that difficult instrument the tongue, or in some other art unfamiliar to villagers, was in itself suspicious: honest folk, born and bred in a visible manner, were mostly not overwise or clever – at least, not beyond such a matter as knowing the signs of the weather; and the process by which rapidity and dexterity of any kind were acquired was so wholly hidden, that they partook of the nature of conjuring. In this way it came to pass that those scattered linen-weavers – emigrants from the town into the country – were to the last regarded as aliens by their rustic neighbours, and usually contracted the eccentric habits which belong to a state of loneliness.

In the early years of this century, such a linen-weaver, named Silas Marner, worked at his vocation in a stone cottage that stood among the nutty hedgerows near the village of Raveloe, and not far from the edge of a deserted stone-pit. The questionable sound of Silas's loom, so unlike the natural cheerful trotting of the winnowing-machine, or the simpler rhythm of the flail,[2] had a half-fearful fascination for the Raveloe boys, who would often leave off their nutting or birds'-nesting to peep in at the window of the stone cottage, counterbalancing a certain awe at the mysterious action of the loom, by a pleasant sense of scornful superiority, drawn from the mockery of its alternating noises, along with the bent, tread-mill attitude of the weaver. But sometimes it happened that Marner, pausing to adjust an irregularity in his thread, became aware of the small scoundrels, and, though chary of his time, he liked their intrusion so ill that he would descend from his loom, and, opening the door, would fix on them a gaze that was always enough to make them take to their legs in terror. For how was it possible to believe that those large brown protuberant eyes in Silas Marner's pale face really saw nothing very distinctly that was not close to them, and not rather that their dreadful stare could dart cramp, or rickets, or a wry mouth[3] at any boy who happened to be in the rear? They had, perhaps, heard their fathers and mothers hint that Silas Marner could cure folk's rheumatism if he had a mind, and add, still more darkly, that if you could only speak the devil fair enough, he might save you the cost of the doctor. Such strange lingering echoes of the old demon-worship might perhaps even now be caught by the diligent listener among the grey-haired peasantry; for the rude mind with difficulty associates the ideas of power and benignity. A shadowy conception of power that by much persuasion can be induced to refrain from inflicting harm, is the shape most easily taken by the sense of the Invisible in the minds of men who have always been pressed close by primitive wants, and to whom a life of hard toil has never been illuminated by any enthusiastic religious faith. To them pain and mishap present a far wider range of possibilities than gladness and enjoyment: their imagination is almost barren of the images that feed desire and hope, but is all overgrown by recollections that are a perpetual pasture to fear. 'Is there anything you can fancy that you would like to eat?' I once said to an old labouring man, who was in his last illness, and who had refused all the food his wife had offered him. 'No,' he answered, 'I've never been used to nothing but common victual, and I can't eat that.' Experience had bred no fancies in him that could raise the phantasm of appetite.

And Raveloe was a village where many of the old echoes lingered, undrowned by new voices. Not that it was one of those barren parishes lying on the outskirts of civilisation – inhabited by meagre sheep and thinly-scattered shepherds: on the contrary, it lay in the rich central plain of what we are pleased to call Merry England, and held farms which, speaking from a spiritual point of view, paid highly-desirable tithes.[4] But it was nestled in a snug well-wooded hollow, quite an hour's journey on horseback from any turnpike,[5] where it was never reached by the vibrations of the coach-horn, or of public opinion. It was an important-looking village, with a fine old church and large churchyard in the heart of it, and two or three large brick-and-stone homesteads, with well-walled orchards and ornamental weathercocks, standing close upon the road, and lifting more imposing fronts than the rectory, which peeped from among the trees on the other side of the churchyard: – a village which showed at once the summits of its social life, and told the practised eye that there was no great park and manor-house in the vicinity, but that there were several chiefs in Raveloe who could farm badly quite at their ease, drawing enough money from their bad farming, in those war times,[6] to live in a rollicking fashion, and keep a jolly Christmas, Whitsun, and Easter tide.

It was fifteen years since Silas Marner had first come to Raveloe; he was then simply a pallid young man, with prominent short-sighted brown eyes, whose appearance would have had nothing strange for people of average culture and experience, but for the villagers near whom he had come to settle it had mysterious peculiarities which corresponded with the exceptional nature of his occupation, and his advent from an unknown region called 'North'ard.' So had his way of life: – he invited no comer to step across his door-sill, and he never

strolled into the village to drink a pint at the Rainbow, or to gossip at
the wheelwright's: he sought no man or woman, save for the purposes
of his calling, or in order to supply himself with necessaries; and it
was soon clear to the Raveloe lasses that he would never urge one of
them to accept him against her will – quite as if he had heard them
declare that they would never marry a dead man come to life again.
This view of Marner's personality was not without another ground
than his pale face and unexampled[7] eyes; for Jem Rodney, the mole-
catcher, averred that one evening as he was returning homeward he
saw Silas Marner leaning against a stile with a heavy bag on his back,
instead of resting the bag on the stile as a man in his senses would
have done; and that, on coming up to him, he saw that Marner's eyes
were set like a dead man's, and he spoke to him, and shook him, and
his limbs were stiff, and his hands clutched the bag as if they'd been
made of iron; but just as he had made up his mind that the weaver
was dead, he came all right again, like, as you might say, in the
winking of an eye, and said 'Good night,' and walked off. All this Jem
swore he had seen, more by token that it was the very day he had
been mole-catching on Squire Cass's land, down by the old saw-pit.
Some said Marner must have been in a 'fit,' a word which seemed to
explain things otherwise incredible; but the argumentative Mr
Macey, clerk of the parish, shook his head, and asked if anybody was
ever known to go off in a fit and not fall down. A fit was a stroke,
wasn't it? and it was in the nature of a stroke to partly take away the
use of a man's limbs and throw him on the parish,[8] if he'd got no
children to look to. No, no; it was no stroke that would let a man
stand on his legs, like a horse between the shafts, and then walk off as
soon as you can say 'Gee!' But there might be such a thing as a man's
soul being loose from his body, and going out and in, like a bird out
of its nest and back; and that was how folks got over-wise, for they
went to school in this shell-less state[9] to those who could teach them
more than their neighbours could learn with their five senses and the
parson. And where did Master Marner get his knowledge of herbs
from – and charms too, if he liked to give them away? Jem Rodney's
story was no more than what might have been expected by anybody
who had seen how Marner had cured Sally Oates, and made her
sleep like a baby, when her heart had been beating enough to burst
her body, for two months and more, while she had been under the

doctor's care. He might cure more folks if he would; but he was worth speaking fair, if it was only to keep him from doing you a mischief.

It was partly to this vague fear that Marner was indebted for protecting him from the persecution that his singularities might have drawn upon him, but still more to the fact that, the old linen-weaver in the neighbouring parish of Tarley being dead, his handicraft made him a highly welcome settler to the richer housewives of the district, and even to the more provident cottagers, who had their little stock of yarn at the year's end. Their sense of his usefulness would have counteracted any repugnance or suspicion which was not confirmed by a deficiency in the quality or the tale[10] of the cloth he wove for them. And the years had rolled on without producing any change in the impressions of the neighbours concerning Marner, except the change from novelty to habit. At the end of fifteen years the Raveloe men said just the same things about Silas Marner as at the beginning: they did not say them quite so often, but they believed them much more strongly when they did say them. There was only one important addition which the years had brought: it was, that Master Marner had laid by a fine sight of money somewhere, and that he could buy up 'bigger men' than himself.

But while opinion concerning him had remained nearly stationary, and his daily habits had presented scarcely any visible change, Marner's inward life had been a history and a metamorphosis, as that of every fervid nature must be when it has fled, or been condemned to solitude. His life, before he came to Raveloe, had been filled with the movement, the mental activity, and the close fellowship, which, in that day as in this, marked the life of an artisan early incorporated in a narrow religious sect,[11] where the poorest layman has the chance of distinguishing himself by gifts of speech, and has, at the very least, the weight of a silent voter in the government of his community. Marner was highly thought of in that little hidden world, known to itself as the church assembling in Lantern Yard; he was believed to be a young man of exemplary life and ardent faith; and a peculiar interest had been centred in him ever since he had fallen, at a prayer-meeting, into a mysterious rigidity and suspension of consciousness, which, lasting for an hour or more, had been mistaken for death. To have sought a medical explanation for this phenomenon would have been held by Silas himself, as well as by his minister and fellow-members, a wilful self-exclusion from the spiritual significance that might lie therein. Silas was evidently a brother selected for a peculiar discipline;[12] and though the effort to interpret this discipline was discouraged by the absence, on his part, of any spiritual vision during his outward trance, yet it was believed by himself and others that its effect was seen in an accession of light and fervour. A less truthful man than he might have been tempted into the subsequent creation of a vision in the form of resurgent memory; a less sane man might have believed in such a creation; but Silas was both sane and honest, though, as with many honest and fervent men, culture had not defined any channels for his sense of mystery, and so it spread itself over the proper pathway of inquiry and knowledge. He had inherited from his mother some acquaintance with medicinal herbs and their preparation – a little store of wisdom which she had imparted to him as a solemn bequest – but of late years he had had doubts about the lawfulness of applying this knowledge, believing that herbs could have no efficacy without prayer, and that prayer might suffice without herbs; so that his inherited delight to wander through the fields in search of foxglove and dandelion and coltsfoot, began to wear to him the character of a temptation.

Among the members of his church there was one young man, a little older than himself, with whom he had long lived in such close friendship that it was the custom of their Lantern Yard brethren to call them David and Jonathan.[13] The real name of the friend was William Dane,[14] and he, too, was regarded as a shining instance of youthful piety, though somewhat given to over-severity towards weaker brethren, and to be so dazzled by his own light as to hold himself wiser than his teachers. But whatever blemishes others might discern in William, to his friend's mind he was faultless; for Marner had one of those impressible self-doubting natures which, at an inex- perienced age, admire imperativeness and lean on contradiction. The expression of trusting simplicity in Marner's face, heightened by that absence of special observation, that defenceless, deer-like gaze which belongs to large prominent eyes, was strongly contrasted by the self- complacent suppression of inward triumph that lurked in the narrow slanting eyes and compressed lips of William Dane. One of the most frequent topics of conversation between the two friends was Assur- ance of salvation:[15] Silas confessed that he could never arrive at anything higher than hope mingled with fear, and listened with longing wonder when William declared that he had possessed unshaken assurance ever since, in the period of his conversion, he had dreamed that he saw the words 'calling and election sure'[16] standing by themselves on a white page in the open Bible. Such colloquies have occupied many a pair of pale-faced weavers, whose unnurtured souls have been like young winged things, fluttering forsaken in the twilight.

It had seemed to the unsuspecting Silas that the friendship had suffered no chill even from his formation of another attachment of a closer kind. For some months he had been engaged to a young servant-woman, waiting only for a little increase to their mutual savings in order to [announce] their marriage; and it was a great delight to him that Sarah did not object to William's occasional presence in their Sunday interviews. It was at this point in their history that Silas's cataleptic fit[17] occurred during the prayer-meeting; and amidst the various queries and expressions of interest addressed to him by his fellow-members, William's suggestion alone jarred with the general sympathy towards a brother thus singled out for special dealings. He observed that, to him, this trance looked more like a visitation of Satan than a proof of divine favour, and exhorted his friend to see that he hid no accursed thing[18] within his soul. Silas, feeling bound to accept rebuke and admonition as a brotherly office, felt no resentment, but only pain, at his friend's doubts concerning him; and to this was soon added some anxiety at the perception that Sarah's manner towards him began to exhibit a strange fluctuation between an effort at an increased manifestation of regard and involuntary signs of shrinking and dislike. He asked her if she wished to break off their engagement; but she denied this: their engagement was known to the church, and had been recognised in the prayer-meetings; it could not be broken off without strict investigation, and Sarah could render no reason that would be sanctioned by the feeling of the community. At this time the senior deacon[19] was taken dangerously ill, and, being a childless widower, he was tended night and day by some of the younger brethren or sisters. Silas frequently took his turn in the night-watching with William, the one relieving the other at two in the morning. The old man, contrary to expectation, seemed to be on the way to recovery, when one night Silas, sitting up by his bedside, observed that his usual audible breathing had ceased. The candle was burning low, and he had to lift it to see the patient's face distinctly. Examination convinced him that the deacon was dead – had been dead some time, for the limbs were rigid. Silas asked himself if he had been asleep, and looked at the clock: it was already four in the morning. How was it that William had not come? In much anxiety he went to seek for help, and soon there were several friends assembled in the house, the minister among them, while Silas went away to his work, wishing he could have met William to know the reason of his non-appearance. But at six o'clock, as he was thinking of going to seek his friend, William came, and with him the minister. They came to summon him to Lantern Yard, to meet the church members there; and to his inquiry concerning the cause of the summons the only reply was, 'You will hear.' Nothing further was said until Silas was seated in the vestry, in front of the minister, with the eyes of those who to him represented God's people fixed solemnly upon him. Then the minister, taking out a pocket-knife, showed it to Silas, and asked him if he knew where he had left that knife? Silas said, he did not know that he had left it anywhere out of his own pocket – but he was trembling at this strange interrogation. He was then exhorted not to hide his sin, but to confess and repent. The knife had been found in the bureau by the departed deacon's bedside – found in the place where the little bag of church money had lain, which the minister himself had seen the day before. Some hand had removed that bag; and whose hand could it be, if not that of the man to whom the knife belonged? For some time Silas was mute with astonishment: then he said, 'God will clear me: I know nothing about the knife being there, or the money being gone. Search me and my dwelling; you will find nothing but three pound five[20] of my own savings, which William Dane knows I have had these six months.' At this William groaned, but the minister said, 'The proof is heavy against you, brother Marner. The money was taken in the night last past, and no man was with our departed brother but you, for William Dane declares to us that he was hindered by sudden sickness from going to take his place as usual, and you yourself said that he had not come; and, moreover, you neglected the dead body.'

'I must have slept,' said Silas. Then after a pause, he added, 'Or I must have had another visitation like that which you have all seen me under, so that the thief must have come and gone while I was not in the body, but out of the body.[21] But, I say again, search me and my dwelling, for I have been nowhere else.'

The search was made, and it ended – in William Dane's finding the well-known bag, empty, tucked behind the chest of drawers in Silas's chamber! On this William exhorted his friend to confess, and not to hide his sin any longer. Silas turned a look of keen reproach on him, and said, 'William, for nine years that we have gone in and out together, have you ever known me tell a lie? But God will clear me.'

'Brother,' said William, 'how do I know what you may have done in the secret chambers of your heart, to give Satan an advantage over you?'[22]

Silas was still looking at his friend. Suddenly a deep flush came over his face, and he was about to speak impetuously, when he seemed checked again by some inward shock, that sent the flush back and made him tremble. But at last he spoke feebly, looking at William.

'I remember now – the knife wasn't in my pocket.'

William said, 'I know nothing of what you mean.' The other persons present, however, began to inquire where Silas meant to say that the knife was, but he would give no further explanation: he only said, 'I am sore stricken; I can say nothing. God will clear me.'

On their return to the vestry there was further deliberation. Any resort to legal measures for ascertaining the culprit was contrary to the principles of the church in Lantern Yard, according to which prosecution was forbidden to Christians, even had the case held less scandal to the community. But the members were bound to take other measures for finding out the truth, and they resolved on praying and drawing lots.[23] This resolution can be a ground of surprise only to those who are unacquainted with that obscure religious life which has gone on in the alleys of our towns. Silas knelt with his brethren, relying on his own innocence being certified by immediate divine interference, but feeling that there was sorrow and mourning behind for him even then – that his trust in man had been cruelly bruised. *The lots declared that Silas Marner was guilty.* He was solemnly suspended from church-membership, and called upon to render up the stolen money: only on confession, as the sign of repentance, could he be received once more within the fold of the church. Marner listened in silence. At last, when every one rose to depart, he went towards William Dane and said, in a voice shaken by agitation –

'The last time I remember using my knife, was when I took it out to cut a strap for you. I don't remember putting it in my pocket again. *You* stole the money, and you have woven a plot to lay the sin at my door. But you may prosper, for all that: there is no just God[24] that governs the earth righteously, but a God of lies, that bears witness against the innocent.'

There was a general shudder at this blasphemy.

William said meekly, 'I leave our brethren to judge whether this is the voice of Satan or not. I can do nothing but pray for you, Silas.'

Poor Marner went out with that despair in his soul – that shaken trust in God and man, which is little short of madness to a loving nature. In the bitterness of his wounded spirit, he said to himself, '*She* will cast me off too.' And he reflected that, if she did not believe the testimony against him, her whole faith must be upset as his was. To people accustomed to reason about the forms in which their religious feeling has incorporated itself, it is difficult to enter into that simple, untaught state of mind in which the form and the feeling have never been severed by an act of reflection. We are apt to think it inevitable that a man in Marner's position should have begun to question the validity of an appeal to the divine judgment by drawing lots; but to him this would have been an effort of independent thought such as he had never known; and he must have made the effort at a moment when all his energies were turned into the anguish of disappointed faith. If there is an angel who records the sorrows of men as well as their sins,[25] he knows how many and deep are the sorrows that spring from false ideas for which no man is culpable.

Marner went home, and for a whole day sat alone, stunned by despair, without any impulse to go to Sarah and attempt to win her belief in his innocence. The second day he took refuge from benumbing unbelief, by getting into his loom and working away as usual; and before many hours were past, the minister and one of the deacons came to him with the message from Sarah, that she held her engagement to him at an end. Silas received the message mutely, and then turned away from the messengers to work at his loom again. In little more than a month from that time, Sarah was married to William Dane; and not long afterwards it was known to the brethren in Lantern Yard that Silas Marner had departed from the town.

Even people whose lives have been made various by learning, sometimes find it hard to keep a fast hold on their habitual views of life,
on their faith in the Invisible, nay, on the sense that their past joys
and sorrows are a real experience, when they are suddenly transported to a new land, where the beings around them know nothing of
their history, and share none of their ideas – where their mother
earth shows another lap, and human life has other forms than those
on which their souls have been nourished. Minds that have been
unhinged from their old faith and love, have perhaps sought this
Lethean[1] influence of exile, in which the past becomes dreamy because its symbols have all vanished, and the present too is dreamy
because it is linked with no memories. But even *their* experience may
hardly enable them thoroughly to imagine what was the effect on a
simple weaver like Silas Marner, when he left his own country and
people and came to settle in Raveloe. Nothing could be more unlike
his native town, set within sight of the widespread hillsides, than this
low, wooded region, where he felt hidden even from the heavens by
the screening trees and hedgerows. There was nothing here, when he
rose in the deep morning quiet and looked out on the dewy brambles
and rank tufted grass, that seemed to have any relation with that life
centring in Lantern Yard, which had once been to him the altar-place
of high dispensations. The whitewashed walls; the little pews where
well-known figures entered with a subdued rustling, and where first
one well-known voice and then another, pitched in a peculiar key of
petition,[2] uttered phrases at once occult and familiar, like the amulet[3]
worn on the heart; the pulpit where the minister delivered unques-
tioned doctrine, and swayed to and fro, and handled the book in a
long-accustomed manner; the very pauses between the couplets of
the hymn, as it was given out, and the recurrent swell of voices in
song: these things had been the channel of divine influences to
Marner – they were the fostering home of his religious emotions –
they were Christianity and God's kingdom upon earth. A weaver who
finds hard words in his hymn-book knows nothing of abstractions; as

the little child knows nothing of parental love, but only knows one face and one lap towards which it stretches its arms for refuge and nurture.

And what could be more unlike that Lantern Yard world than the world in Raveloe? – orchards looking lazy with neglected plenty; the large church in the wide churchyard, which men gazed at lounging at their own doors in service-time; the purple-faced farmers jogging along the lanes or turning in at the Rainbow; homesteads, where men supped heavily and slept in the light of the evening hearth, and where women seemed to be laying up a stock of linen for the life to come. There were no lips in Raveloe from which a word could fall that would stir Silas Marner's benumbed faith to a sense of pain. In the early ages of the world, we know, it was believed that each terri-tory was inhabited and ruled by its own divinities, so that a man could cross the bordering heights and be out of the reach of his native gods, whose presence was confined to the streams and the groves and the hills among which he had lived from his birth. And poor Silas was vaguely conscious of something not unlike the feeling of primitive men, when they fled thus, in fear or in sullenness, from the face of an unpropitious deity. It seemed to him that the Power he had vainly trusted in among the streets and at the prayer-meetings, was very far away from this land in which he had taken refuge, where men lived in careless abundance, knowing and needing nothing of that trust, which, for him, had been turned to bitterness. The little light he possessed spread its beams so narrowly, that frustrated belief was a curtain broad enough to create for him the blackness of night.

His first movement after the shock had been to work in his loom; and he went on with this unremittingly, never asking himself why, now he was come to Raveloe, he worked far on into the night to finish the tale of Mrs Osgood's table-linen sooner than she expected – without contemplating beforehand the money she would put into his hand for the work. He seemed to weave, like the spider, from pure impulse, without reflection. Every man's work, pursued steadily, tends in this way to become an end in itself, and so to bridge over the loveless chasms of his life. Silas's hand satisfied itself with throwing the shuttle, and his eye with seeing the little squares in the cloth complete themselves under his effort. Then there were the calls of hunger; and Silas, in his solitude, had to provide his own breakfast, dinner, and supper, to fetch his own water from the well, and put his own kettle on the fire; and all these immediate promptings helped, along with the weaving, to reduce his life to the unquestioning activity of a spinning insect. He hated the thought of the past; there was nothing that called out his love and fellowship toward the strangers he had come amongst; and the future was all dark, for there was no Unseen Love that cared for him. Thought was arrested by utter bewilderment, now its old narrow pathway was closed, and affection seemed to have died under the bruise that had fallen on its keenest nerves.

But at last Mrs Osgood's table-linen was finished, and Silas was paid in gold. His earnings in his native town, where he worked for a wholesale dealer, had been after a lower rate; he had been paid weekly, and of his weekly earnings a large proportion had gone to objects of piety and charity. Now, for the first time in his life, he had five bright guineas put into his hand; no man expected a share of them, and he loved no man that he should offer him a share. But what were the guineas to him who saw no vista beyond countless days of weaving? It was needless for him to ask that, for it was pleasant to him to feel them in his palm, and look at their bright faces, which were all his own: it was another element of life, like the weaving and the satisfaction of hunger, subsisting quite aloof from the life of belief and love from which he had been cut off. The weaver's hand had known the touch of hard-won money even before the palm had grown to its full breadth; for twenty years, mysterious money had stood to him as the symbol of earthly good, and the immediate object of toil. He had seemed to love it little in the years when every penny had its purpose for him; for he loved the *purpose* then. But now, when all purpose was gone, that habit of looking towards the money and grasping it with a sense of fulfilled effort made a loam that was deep enough for the seeds of desire; and as Silas walked homeward across the fields in the twilight, he drew out the money and thought it was brighter in the gathering gloom.

About this time an incident happened which seemed to open a possibility of some fellowship with his neighbours. One day, taking a pair of shoes to be mended, he saw the cobbler's wife seated by the fire, suffering from the terrible symptoms of heart-disease and dropsy,[4] which he had witnessed as the precursors of his mother's death. He felt a rush of pity at the mingled sight and remembrance, and, recalling the relief his mother had found from a simple preparation of foxglove, he promised Sally Oates to bring her something that would ease her, since the doctor did her no good. In this office of charity, Silas felt, for the first time since he had come to Raveloe, a sense of unity between his past and present life, which might have been the beginning of his rescue from the insect-like existence into which his nature had shrunk. But Sally Oates's disease had raised her into a personage of much interest and importance among the neighbours, and the fact of her having found relief from drinking Silas Marner's 'stuff' became a matter of general discourse. When Doctor Kimble gave physic, it was natural that it should have an effect; but when a weaver, who came from nobody knew where, worked wonders with a bottle of brown waters, the occult character of the process was evident. Such a sort of thing had not been known since the Wise Woman at Tarley died; and she had charms as well as 'stuff:' everybody went to her when their children had fits. Silas Marner must be a person of the same sort, for how did he know what would bring back Sally Oates's breath, if he didn't know a fine sight more than that? The Wise Woman had words that she muttered to herself, so that you couldn't hear what they were, and if she tied a bit of red thread round the child's toe the while, it would keep off the water in the head.[5] There were women in Raveloe, at that present time, who had worn one of the Wise Woman's little bags round their necks, and, in consequence, had never had an idiot child, as Ann Coulter had. Silas Marner could very likely do as much, and more; and now it was all clear how he should have come from unknown parts, and be so 'comical-looking.' But Sally Oates must mind and not tell the doctor, for he would be sure to set his face against Marner: he was always angry about the Wise Woman, and used to threaten those who went to her that they should have none of his help any more.

Silas now found himself and his cottage suddenly beset by mothers who wanted him to charm away the hooping-cough, or bring back the milk, and by men who wanted stuff against the rheumatics or the knots in the hands;[6] and, to secure themselves against a refusal, the applicants brought silver in their palms. Silas might have driven a profitable trade in charms as well as in his small list of drugs; but money on this condition was no temptation to him: he had never known an impulse towards falsity, and he drove one after another away with growing irritation, for the news of him as a wise man had spread even to Tarley, and it was long before people ceased to take long walks for the sake of asking his aid. But the hope in his wisdom was at length changed into dread, for no one believed him when he said he knew no charms and could work no cures, and every man and woman who had an accident or a new attack after applying to him, set the misfortune down to Master Marner's ill-will and irritated glances. Thus it came to pass that his movement of pity towards Sally Oates, which had given him a transient sense of brotherhood, heightened the repulsion between him and his neighbours, and made his isolation more complete.

Gradually the guineas, the crowns, and the half-crowns, grew to a heap, and Marner drew less and less for his own wants, trying to solve the problem of keeping himself strong enough to work sixteen hours a-day on as small an outlay as possible. Have not men, shut up in solitary imprisonment, found an interest in marking the moments by straight strokes of a certain length on the wall, until the growth of the sum of straight strokes, arranged in triangles, has become a mastering purpose? Do we not wile away moments of inanity or fatigued waiting by repeating some trivial movement or sound, until the repetition has bred a want, which is incipient habit? That will help us to understand how the love of accumulating money grows an absorbing passion in men whose imaginations, even in the very beginning of their hoard, showed them no purpose beyond it. Marner wanted the heaps of ten to grow into a square, and then into a larger square; and every added guinea, while it was itself a satisfaction, bred a new desire. In this strange world, made a hopeless riddle to him, he might, if he had had a less intense nature, have sat weaving, weaving – looking towards the end of his pattern, or towards the end of his web, till he forgot the riddle, and everything else but his immediate sensations; but the money had come to mark off his weaving into periods, and the money not only grew, but it remained with him. He began to think it was conscious of him, as his loom was, and he would on no account have exchanged those coins, which had become his familiars,[7] for other coins with unknown faces. He handled them, he counted them, till their form and colour were like the satisfaction of a thirst to him; but it was only in the night, when his work was done, that he drew them out to enjoy their companionship. He had taken up some bricks in his floor underneath his loom, and here he had made a hole in which he set the iron pot that contained his guineas and silver coins, covering the bricks with sand whenever he replaced them. Not that the idea of being robbed presented itself often or strongly to his mind: hoarding was common in country districts in those days; there were old labourers in the parish of Raveloe who were known to have their savings by them, probably inside their flock-beds; but their rustic neighbours, though not all of them as honest as their ancestors in the days of King Alfred,[8] had not imaginations bold enough to lay a plan of burglary. How could they have spent the money in their own village without betraying themselves? They would be obliged to 'run away' – a course as dark and dubious as a balloon journey.[9]

So, year after year, Silas Marner had lived in this solitude, his guineas rising in the iron pot, and his life narrowing and hardening itself more and more into a mere pulsation of desire and satisfaction that had no relation to any other being.[10] His life had reduced itself to the functions of weaving and hoarding, without any contemplation of an end towards which the functions tended. The same sort of process has perhaps been undergone by wiser men, when they have been cut off from faith and love – only, instead of a loom and a heap of guineas, they have had some erudite research, some ingenious project, or some well-knit theory. Strangely Marner's face and figure shrank and bent themselves into a constant mechanical relation to the objects of his life, so that he produced the same sort of impression as a handle or a crooked tube, which has no meaning standing apart. The prominent eyes that used to look trusting and dreamy, now looked as if they had been made to see only one kind of thing that was very small, like tiny grain, for which they hunted everywhere: and he was so withered and yellow, that, though he was not yet forty, the children always called him 'Old Master Marner.'

Yet even in this stage of withering a little incident happened, which showed that the sap of affection was not all gone. It was one of his daily tasks to fetch his water from a well a couple of fields off, and for this purpose, ever since he came to Raveloe, he had had a brown earthenware pot, which he held as his most precious utensil among the very few conveniences he had granted himself. It had been his companion for twelve years, always standing on the same spot, always lending its handle to him in the early morning, so that its form had an expression for him of willing helpfulness, and the impress of its handle on his palm gave a satisfaction mingled with that of having the fresh clear water. One day as he was returning from the well, he stumbled against the step of the stile, and his brown pot, falling with force against the stones that overarched the ditch below him, was broken in three pieces. Silas picked up the pieces and carried them home with grief in his heart. The brown pot could never be of use to him any more, but he stuck the bits together and propped the ruin in its old place for a memorial.

This is the history of Silas Marner, until the fifteenth year after he came to Raveloe. The livelong day he sat in his loom, his ear filled with its monotony, his eyes bent close down on the slow growth of sameness in the brownish web, his muscles moving with such even repetition that their pause seemed almost as much a constraint as the holding of his breath. But at night came his revelry: at night he closed his shutters, and made fast his doors, and drew forth his gold. Long ago the heap of coins had become too large for the iron pot to hold them, and he had made for them two thick leather bags, which wasted no room in their resting-place, but lent themselves flexibly to every corner. How the guineas shone as they came pouring out of the dark leather mouths! The silver bore no large proportion in amount to the gold, because the long pieces of linen which formed his chief work were always partly paid for in gold, and out of the silver he supplied his own bodily wants, choosing always the shillings and sixpences to spend in this way. He loved the guineas best, but he would not change the silver – the crowns and half-crowns that were his own earnings, begotten by his labour; he loved them all. He spread them out in heaps and bathed his hands in them; then he counted them and set them up in regular piles, and felt their rounded outline between his thumb and fingers, and thought fondly of the guineas that were only half earned by the work in his loom, as if they had been unborn children – thought of the guineas that were coming slowly through the coming years, through all his life, which spread far away before him, the end quite hidden by countless days of weaving. No wonder his thoughts were still with his loom and his money when he made his journeys through the fields and the lanes to fetch and carry home his work, so that his steps never wandered to the hedge-banks and the lane-side in search of the once familiar herbs: these too belonged to the past, from which his life had shrunk away, like a rivulet that has sunk far down from the grassy fringe of its old breadth into a little shivering thread, that cuts a groove for itself in the barren sand.

But about the Christmas of that fifteenth year, a second great change came over Marner's life, and his history became blent in a singular manner with the life of his neighbours.

The greatest man in Raveloe was Squire Cass, who lived in the large red house with the handsome flight of stone steps in front and the high stables behind it, nearly opposite the church. He was only one among several landed parishioners, but he alone was honoured with the title of Squire;[1] for though Mr Osgood's family was also understood to be of timeless origin – the Raveloe imagination having never ventured back to that fearful blank when there were no Osgoods – still, he merely owned the farm he occupied; whereas Squire Cass had a tenant or two, who complained of the game[2] to him quite as if he had been a lord.

It was still that glorious war-time which was felt to be a peculiar favour of Providence towards the landed interest, and the fall of prices had not yet come to carry the race of small squires and yeomen[3] down that road to ruin for which extravagant habits and bad husbandry were plentifully anointing their wheels. I am speaking now in relation to Raveloe and the parishes that resembled it; for our old-fashioned country life had many different aspects, as all life must have when it is spread over a various surface, and breathed on variously by multitudinous currents, from the winds of heaven to the thoughts of men, which are for ever moving and crossing each other with incalculable results. Raveloe lay low among the bushy trees and the rutted lanes, aloof from the currents of industrial energy and Puritan earnestness: the rich ate and drank freely, accepting gout and apoplexy as things that ran mysteriously in respectable families, and the poor thought that the rich were entirely in the right of it to lead a jolly life; besides, their feasting caused a multiplication of orts,[4] which were the heirlooms of the poor. Betty Jay scented the boiling of Squire Cass's hams, but her longing was arrested by the unctuous liquor in which they were boiled; and when the seasons brought round the great merry-makings, they were regarded on all hands as a fine thing for the poor. For the Raveloe feasts were like the rounds of beef and the barrels of ale – they were on a large scale, and lasted a good while, especially in the winter-time. After ladies had packed up their best gowns and top-knots[5] in bandboxes, and had incurred the risk of fording streams on pillions with the precious burden in rainy or snowy weather, when there was no knowing how high the water would rise, it was not to be supposed that they looked forward to a brief pleasure. On this ground it was always contrived in the dark seasons, when there was little work to be done, and the hours were long, that several neighbours should keep open house in succession. So soon as Squire Cass's standing dishes diminished in plenty and freshness, his guests had nothing to do but to walk a little higher up the village to Mr Osgood's, at the Orchards, and they found hams and chines[6] uncut, pork-pies with the scent of the fire in them, spun butter[7] in all its freshness – everything, in fact, that appetites at leisure could desire, in perhaps greater perfection, though not in greater abundance, than at Squire Cass's.

For the Squire's wife had died long ago, and the Red House was without that presence of the wife and mother which is the fountain of wholesome love and fear in parlour and kitchen; and this helped to account not only for there being more profusion than finished excellence in the holiday provisions, but also for the frequency with which the proud Squire condescended to preside in the parlour of the Rainbow rather than under the shadow of his own dark wainscot;[8] perhaps, also, for the fact that his sons had turned out rather ill. Raveloe was not a place where moral censure was severe, but it was thought a weakness in the Squire that he had kept all his sons at home in idleness; and though some licence was to be allowed to young men whose fathers could afford it, people shook their heads at the courses of the second son, Dunstan, commonly called Dunsey Cass, whose taste for swopping and betting might turn out to be a sowing of something worse than wild oats. To be sure, the neighbours said, it was no matter what became of Dunsey – a spiteful jeering fellow, who seemed to enjoy his drink the more when other people went dry – always provided that his doings did not bring trouble on a family like Squire Cass's, with a monument in the church, and tankards older than King George.[9] But it would be a thousand pities if Mr Godfrey, the eldest, a fine open-faced good-natured young man who was to come into the land some day, should take to going along the same road with his brother, as he had seemed to do of late. If he went on in that way, he would lose Miss Nancy Lammeter; for it was well known that she had looked very shyly on him ever since last Whitsuntide twelvemonth, when there was so much talk about his being away from home days and days together. There was something wrong, more than common – that was quite clear; for Mr Godfrey didn't look half so fresh-coloured and open as he used to do. At one time everybody was saying, What a handsome couple he and Miss Nancy Lammeter would make! and if she could come to be mistress at the Red House, there would be a fine change, for the Lammeters had been brought up in that way, that they never suffered a pinch of salt to be wasted, and yet everybody in their household had of the best, according to his place. Such a daughter-in-law would be a saving to the old Squire, if she never brought a penny to her fortune; for it was to be feared that, notwithstanding his incomings, there were more holes in his pocket than the one where he put his own hand in. But if Mr Godfrey didn't turn over a new leaf, he might say 'Good-bye' to Miss Nancy Lammeter.

It was the once hopeful Godfrey who was standing, with his hands in his side-pockets and his back to the fire, in the dark wainscoted parlour, one late November afternoon in that fifteenth year of Silas Marner's life at Raveloe. The fading grey light fell dimly on the walls decorated with guns, whips, and foxes' brushes,[10] on coats and hats flung on the chairs, on tankards sending forth a scent of flat ale, and on a half-choked fire, with pipes propped up in the chimney-corners: signs of a domestic life destitute of any hallowing charm, with which the look of gloomy vexation on Godfrey's blond face was in sad accordance. He seemed to be waiting and listening for some one's approach, and presently the sound of a heavy step, with an accompanying whistle, was heard across the large empty entrance-hall.

The door opened, and a thick-set, heavy-looking young man entered, with the flushed face and the gratuitously elated bearing which mark the first stage of intoxication. It was Dunsey, and at the sight of him Godfrey's face parted with some of its gloom to take on the more active expression of hatred. The handsome brown spaniel that lay on the hearth retreated under the chair in the chimney-corner.

'Well, Master Godfrey, what do you want with me?' said Dunsey, in a mocking tone. 'You're my elders and betters, you know; I was obliged to come when you sent for me.'

'Why, this is what I want – and just shake yourself sober and listen, will you?' said Godfrey, savagely. He had himself been drinking more than was good for him, trying to turn his gloom into uncalculating anger. 'I want to tell you, I must hand over that rent of Fowler's to the Squire, or else tell him I gave it you; for he's threatening to distrain[11] for it, and it'll all be out soon, whether I tell him or not. He said, just now, before he went out, he should send word to Cox to distrain, if Fowler didn't come and pay up his arrears this week. The Squire's short o' cash, and in no humour to stand any nonsense; and you know what he threatened, if ever he found you making away with his money again. So, see and get the money, and pretty quickly, will you?'

'Oh!' said Dunsey, sneeringly, coming nearer to his brother and looking in his face. 'Suppose, now, you get the money yourself, and save me the trouble, eh? Since you was so kind as to hand it over to me, you'll not refuse me the kindness to pay it back for me: it was your brotherly love made you do it, you know.'

Godfrey bit his lips and clenched his fist. 'Don't come near me with that look, else I'll knock you down.'

'Oh no, you won't,' said Dunsey, turning away on his heel, however. 'Because I'm such a good-natured brother, you know. I might get you turned out of house and home, and cut off with a shilling any day. I might tell the Squire how his handsome son was married to that nice young woman, Molly Farren, and was very unhappy because he couldn't live with his drunken wife, and I should slip into your place as comfortable as could be. But you see, I don't do it – I'm so easy and good-natured. You'll take any trouble for me. You'll get the hundred pounds for me – I know you will.'

'How can I get the money?' said Godfrey, quivering. 'I haven't a shilling to bless myself with.[12] And it's a lie that you'd slip into my place: you'd get yourself turned out too, that's all. For if you begin telling tales, I'll follow. Bob's my father's favourite – you know that very well. He'd only think himself well rid of you.'

'Never mind,' said Dunsey, nodding his head sideways as he looked out of the window. 'It 'ud be very pleasant to me to go in your company – you're such a handsome brother, and we've always been so fond of quarrelling with one another, I shouldn't know what to do without you. But you'd like better for us both to stay at home together; I know you would. So you'll manage to get that little sum o' money, and I'll bid you good-bye, though I'm sorry to part.'

Dunstan was moving off, but Godfrey rushed after him and seized him by the arm, saying, with an oath –

'I tell you, I have no money: I can get no money.'

'Borrow of old Kimble.'

'I tell you, he won't lend me any more, and I shan't ask him.'

'Well, then, sell Wildfire.'

'Yes, that's easy talking. I must have the money directly.'

'Well, you've only got to ride him to the hunt to-morrow. There'll be Bryce and Keating there, for sure. You'll get more bids than one.'

'I daresay, and get back home at eight o'clock, splashed up to the chin. I'm going to Mrs Osgood's birthday dance.'

'Oho!' said Dunsey, turning his head on one side, and trying to speak in a small mincing treble. 'And there's sweet Miss Nancy coming; and we shall dance with her, and promise never to be naughty again, and be taken into favour, and—'

'Hold your tongue about Miss Nancy, you fool,' said Godfrey, turning red, 'else I'll throttle you.'

'What for?' said Dunsey, still in an artificial tone, but taking a whip from the table and beating the butt-end of it on his palm. 'You've a very good chance. I'd advise you to creep up her sleeve again: it 'ud be saving time, if Molly should happen to take a drop too much laudanum[13] some day, and make a widower of you. Miss Nancy wouldn't mind being a second, if she didn't know it. And you've got a good-natured brother, who'll keep your secret well, because you'll be so very obliging to him.'

'I'll tell you what it is,' said Godfrey, quivering, and pale again, 'my patience is pretty near at an end. If you'd a little more sharpness in you, you might know that you may urge a man a bit too far, and make one leap as easy as another. I don't know but what it is so now: I may as well tell the Squire everything myself – I should get you off my back, if I got nothing else. And, after all, he'll know some time. She's been threatening to come herself and tell him. So, don't flatter yourself that your secrecy's worth any price you choose to ask. You drain me of money till I have got nothing to pacify *her* with, and she'll do as she threatens some day. It's all one. I'll tell my father everything myself, and you may go to the devil.'

Dunsey perceived that he had overshot his mark, and that there was a point at which even the hesitating Godfrey might be driven into decision. But he said, with an air of unconcern –

'As you please; but I'll have a draught of ale first.' And ringing the bell, he threw himself across two chairs, and began to rap the window-seat with the handle of his whip.

Godfrey stood, still with his back to the fire, uneasily moving his fingers among the contents of his side-pockets, and looking at the floor. That big muscular frame of his held plenty of animal courage, but helped him to no decision when the dangers to be braved were such as could neither be knocked down nor throttled. His natural irresolution and moral cowardice were exaggerated by a position in which dreaded consequences seemed to press equally on all sides, and his irritation had no sooner provoked him to defy Dunstan and anticipate all possible betrayals, than the miseries he must bring on himself by such a step seemed more unendurable to him than the present evil. The results of confession were not contingent, they were certain; whereas betrayal was not certain. From the near vision of that certainty he fell back on suspense and vacillation with a sense of repose. The disinherited son of a small squire, equally disinclined to dig and to beg,[14] was almost as helpless as an uprooted tree, which, by the favour of earth and sky, has grown to a handsome bulk on the spot where it first shot upward. Perhaps it would have been possible to think of digging with some cheerfulness if Nancy Lammeter were to be won on those terms; but, since he must irrevocably lose *her* as well as the inheritance, and must break every tie but the one that degraded him and left him without motive for trying to recover his better self, he could imagine no future for himself on the other side of confession but that of "'listing for a soldier"[15] – the most desperate step, short of suicide, in the eyes of respectable families. No! he would rather trust to casualties than to his own resolve – rather go on sitting at the feast, and sipping the wine he loved, though with the sword hanging over him[16] and terror in his heart, than rush away into the cold darkness where there was no pleasure left. The utmost concession to Dunstan about the horse began to seem easy, compared with the fulfilment of his own threat. But his pride would not let him recommence the conversation otherwise than by continuing the quarrel. Dunstan was waiting for this, and took his ale in shorter draughts than usual.

'It's just like you,' Godfrey burst out, in a bitter tone, 'to talk about my selling Wildfire in that cool way – the last thing I've got to call my own, and the best bit of horse-flesh I ever had in my life. And if you'd got a spark of pride in you, you'd be ashamed to see the stables emptied, and everybody sneering about it. But it's my belief you'd sell yourself, if it was only for the pleasure of making somebody feel he'd got a bad bargain.'

'Ay, ay,' said Dunstan, very placably, 'you do me justice, I see. You know I'm a jewel for 'ticing people into bargains. For which reason I advise you to let *me* sell Wildfire. I'd ride him to the hunt to-morrow for you, with pleasure. I shouldn't look so handsome as you in the saddle, but it's the horse they'll bid for, and not the rider.'

'Yes, I daresay – trust my horse to you!'

'As you please,' said Dunstan, rapping the window-seat again with an air of great unconcern. 'It's *you* have got to pay Fowler's money; it's none of my business. You received the money from him when you went to Bramcote, and *you* told the Squire it wasn't paid. I'd nothing to do with that; you chose to be so obliging as to give it me, that was all. If you don't want to pay the money, let it alone; it's all one to me. But I was willing to accommodate you by undertaking to sell the horse, seeing it's not convenient to you to go so far to-morrow.'

Godfrey was silent for some moments. He would have liked to spring on Dunstan, wrench the whip from his hand, and flog him to within an inch of his life; and no bodily fear could have deterred him; but he was mastered by another sort of fear, which was fed by feelings stronger even than his resentment. When he spoke again it was in a half-conciliatory tone.

'Well, you mean no nonsense about the horse, eh? You'll sell him all fair, and hand over the money? If you don't, you know, everything 'ull go to smash, for I've got nothing else to trust to. And you'll have less pleasure in pulling the house over my head,[7] when your own skull's to be broken too.'

'Ay, ay,' said Dunstan, rising; 'all right. I thought you'd come round. I'm the fellow to bring old Bryce up to the scratch. I'll get you a hundred and twenty for him, if I get you a penny.'

'But it'll perhaps rain cats and dogs to-morrow, as it did yesterday, and then you can't go,' said Godfrey, hardly knowing whether he wished for that obstacle or not.

'Not *it*,' said Dunstan. 'I'm always lucky in my weather. It might rain if you wanted to go yourself. You never hold trumps,[18] you know – I always do. You've got the beauty, you see, and I've got the luck, so you must keep me by you for your crooked sixpence;[19] you'll *ne*-ver get along without me.'

'Confound you, hold your tongue!' said Godfrey, impetuously. 'And take care to keep sober to-morrow, else you'll get pitched on your head coming home, and Wildfire might be the worse for it.'

'Make your tender heart easy,' said Dunstan, opening the door. 'You never knew me see double when I'd got a bargain to make; it 'ud spoil the fun. Besides, whenever I fall, I'm warranted to fall on my legs.'

With that, Dunstan slammed the door behind him, and left Godfrey to that bitter rumination on his personal circumstances which was now unbroken from day to day save by the excitement of sporting, drinking, card-playing, or the rarer and less oblivious pleasure of seeing Miss Nancy Lammeter. The subtle and varied pains springing from the higher sensibility that accompanies higher culture, are perhaps less pitiable than that dreary absence of impersonal enjoyment and consolation which leaves ruder minds to the perpetual urgent companionship of their own griefs and discontents. The lives of those rural forefathers, whom we are apt to think very prosaic figures – men whose only work was to ride round their land, getting heavier and heavier in their saddles, and who passed the rest of their days in the half-listless gratification of senses dulled by monotony – had a certain pathos in them nevertheless. Calamities came to *them* too, and their early errors carried hard consequences: perhaps the love of some sweet maiden, the image of purity, order, and calm, had opened their eyes to the vision of a life in which the days would not seem too long, even without rioting;[20] but the maiden was lost, and the vision passed away, and then what was left to them, especially when they had become too heavy for the hunt, or for carrying a gun over the furrows, but to drink and get merry, or to drink and get angry, so that they might be independent of variety, and say over again with eager emphasis the things they had said already any time that twelve-month? Assuredly, among these flushed and dull-eyed men there were some whom – thanks to their native human-kindness – even riot could never drive into brutality; men who, when their cheeks were fresh, had felt the keen point of sorrow or remorse, had been pierced by the reeds[21] they leaned on, or had lightly put their limbs in fetters from which no struggle could loose them; and under these sad circumstances, common to us all, their thoughts could find no resting-place outside the ever-trodden round of their own petty history.

That, at least, was the condition of Godfrey Cass in this six-and-twentieth year of his life. A movement of compunction, helped by those small indefinable influences which every personal relation exerts on a pliant nature, had urged him into a secret marriage, which was a blight on his life. It was an ugly story of low passion, delusion, and waking from delusion, which needs not to be dragged from the privacy of Godfrey's bitter memory. He had long known that the delusion was partly due to a trap laid for him by Dunstan, who saw in his brother's degrading marriage the means of gratifying at once his jealous hate and his cupidity. And if Godfrey could have felt himself simply a victim, the iron bit that destiny had put into his mouth would have chafed him less intolerably. If the curses he muttered half aloud when he was alone had had no other object than Dunstan's diabolical cunning, he might have shrunk less from the consequences of avowal. But he had something else to curse – his own vicious folly, which now seemed as mad and unaccountable to him as almost all our follies and vices do when their promptings have long passed away. For four years he had thought of Nancy Lammeter, and wooed her with tacit patient worship, as the woman who made him think of the future with joy: she would be his wife, and would make home lovely to him, as his father's home had never been; and it would be easy, when she was always near, to shake off those foolish habits that were no pleasures, but only a feverish way of annulling vacancy. Godfrey's was an essentially domestic nature, bred up in a home where the hearth had no smiles, and where the daily habits were not chastised by the presence of household order. His easy disposition made him fall in unresistingly with the family courses, but the need of some tender permanent affection, the longing for some influence that would make the good he preferred easy to pursue, caused the neatness, purity, and liberal orderliness of the Lammeter household, sunned by the smile of Nancy, to seem like those fresh bright hours of the morning when temptations go to sleep and leave the ear open to the voice of the good angel, inviting to industry, sobriety, and peace. And yet the hope of this paradise had not been enough to save him from a course which shut him out of it for ever. Instead of keeping fast hold of the strong silken rope by which Nancy would have drawn him safe to the green banks where it was easy to step firmly, he had let himself be dragged back into mud and slime, in which it was useless to struggle. He had made ties for himself which robbed him of all wholesome motive and were a constant exasperation.

Still, there was one position worse than the present: it was the position he would be in when the ugly secret was disclosed; and the desire that continually triumphed over every other was that of warding off the evil day, when he would have to bear the consequences of his father's violent resentment for the wound inflicted on his family pride – would have, perhaps, to turn his back on that hereditary ease and dignity which, after all, was a sort of reason for living, and would carry with him the certainty that he was banished for ever from the sight and esteem of Nancy Lammeter. The longer the interval, the more chance there was of deliverance from some, at least, of the hateful consequences to which he had sold himself; the more opportunities remained for him to snatch the strange gratification of seeing Nancy, and gathering some faint indications of her lingering regard. Towards this gratification he was impelled, fitfully, every now and then, after having passed weeks in which he had avoided her as the far-off bright-winged prize that only made him spring forward and find his chain all the more galling. One of those fits of yearning was on him now, and it would have been strong enough to have persuaded him to trust Wildfire to Dunstan rather than disappoint the yearning, even if he had not had another reason for his disinclination towards the morrow's hunt. That other reason was the fact that the morning's meet was near Batherley, the market-town where the unhappy woman lived, whose image became more odious to him every day; and to his thought the whole vicinage[22] was haunted by her. The yoke a man creates for himself by wrong-doing will breed hate in the kindliest nature; and the good-humoured, affectionate-hearted Godfrey Cass was fast becoming a bitter man, visited by cruel wishes, that seemed to enter, and depart, and enter again, like demons who had found in him a ready-garnished home.[23]

What was he to do this evening to pass the time? He might as well go to the Rainbow, and hear the talk about the cock-fighting: everybody was there, and what else was there to be done? Though, for his own part, he did not care a button for cock-fighting. Snuff, the brown spaniel, who had placed herself in front of him, and had been watching him for some time, now jumped up in impatience for the expected caress. But Godfrey thrust her away without looking at her, and left the room, followed humbly by the unresenting Snuff – perhaps because she saw no other career open to her.[24]

Dunstan Cass, setting off in the raw morning, at the judiciously quiet pace of a man who is obliged to ride to cover[1] on his hunter, had to take his way along the lane which, at its farther extremity, passed by the piece of unenclosed ground called the Stone-pit, where stood the cottage, once a stone-cutter's shed, now for fifteen years inhabited by Silas Marner. The spot looked very dreary at this season, with the moist trodden clay about it, and the red, muddy water high up in the deserted quarry. That was Dunstan's first thought as he approached it; the second was, that the old fool of a weaver, whose loom he heard rattling already, had a great deal of money hidden somewhere. How was it that he, Dunstan Cass, who had often heard talk of Marner's miserliness, had never thought of suggesting to Godfrey that he should frighten or persuade the old fellow into lending the money on the excellent security of the young Squire's prospects? The resource occurred to him now as so easy and agreeable, especially as Marner's hoard was likely to be large enough to leave Godfrey a handsome surplus beyond his immediate needs, and enable him to accommodate his faithful brother, that he had almost turned the horse's head towards home again. Godfrey would be ready enough to accept the suggestion: he would snatch eagerly at a plan that might save him from parting with Wildfire. But when Dunstan's meditation reached this point, the inclination to go on grew strong and prevailed. He didn't want to give Godfrey that pleasure: he preferred that Master Godfrey should be vexed. Moreover, Dunstan enjoyed the self-important consciousness of having a horse to sell, and the opportunity of driving a bargain, swaggering, and possibly taking somebody in. He might have all the satisfaction attendant on selling his brother's horse, and not the less have the further satisfaction of setting Godfrey to borrow Marner's money. So he rode on to cover.

Bryce and Keating were there, as Dunstan was quite sure they would be – he was such a lucky fellow.

'Heyday!' said Bryce, who had long had his eye on Wildfire, 'you're on your brother's horse to-day: how's that?'

'Oh, I've swopped with him,' said Dunstan, whose delight in lying, grandly independent of utility, was not to be diminished by the likelihood that his hearer would not believe him – 'Wildfire's mine now.'

'What! has he swopped with you for that big-boned hack of yours?' said Bryce, quite aware that he should get another lie in answer.

'Oh, there was a little account between us,' said Dunsey, carelessly, 'and Wildfire made it even. I accommodated him by taking the horse, though it was against my will, for I'd got an itch for a mare o' Jortin's – as rare a bit o' blood as ever you threw your leg across. But I shall keep Wildfire, now I've got him, though I'd a bid of a hundred and fifty for him the other day, from a man over at Flitton – he's buying for Lord Cromleck – a fellow with a cast in his eye, and a green waistcoat. But I mean to stick to Wildfire: I shan't get a better at a fence in a hurry. The mare's got more blood, but she's a bit too weak in the hind-quarters.'

Bryce of course divined that Dunstan wanted to sell the horse, and Dunstan knew that he divined it (horse-dealing is only one of many human transactions carried on in this ingenious manner); and they both considered that the bargain was in its first stage, when Bryce replied, ironically –

'I wonder at that now; I wonder you mean to keep him; for I never heard of a man who didn't want to sell his horse getting a bid of half as much again as the horse was worth. You'll be lucky if you get a hundred.'

Keating rode up now, and the transaction became more complicated. It ended in the purchase of the horse by Bryce for a hundred and twenty, to be paid on the delivery of Wildfire, safe and sound, at the Batherley stables. It did occur to Dunsey that it might be wise for him to give up the day's hunting, proceed at once to Batherley, and, having waited for Bryce's return, hire a horse to carry him home with the money in his pocket. But the inclination for a run, encouraged by confidence in his luck, and by a draught of brandy from his pocket-pistol² at the conclusion of the bargain, was not easy to overcome, especially with a horse under him that would take the fences to the admiration of the field. Dunstan, however, took one fence too many, and got his horse pierced with a hedge-stake. His own ill-favoured person, which was quite unmarketable, escaped without injury; but poor Wildfire, unconscious of his price, turned on his flank and painfully panted his last. It happened that Dunstan, a short time before, having had to get down to arrange his stirrup, had muttered a good many curses at this interruption, which had thrown him in the rear of the hunt near the moment of glory, and under this exasperation had taken the fences more blindly. He would soon have been up with the hounds again, when the fatal accident happened; and hence he was between eager riders in advance, not troubling themselves about what happened behind them, and far-off stragglers, who were as likely as not to pass quite aloof from the line of road in which Wildfire had fallen. Dunstan, whose nature it was to care more for immediate annoyances than for remote consequences, no sooner recovered his legs, and saw that it was all over with Wildfire, than he felt a satisfaction at the absence of witnesses to a position which no swaggering could make enviable. Reinforcing himself, after his shake, with a little brandy and much swearing, he walked as fast as he could to a coppice on his right hand, through which it occurred to him that he could make his way to Batherley without danger of encountering any member of the hunt. His first intention was to hire a horse there and ride home forthwith, for to walk many miles without a gun in his hand and along an ordinary road, was as much out of the question to him as to other spirited young men of his kind. He did not much mind about taking the bad news to Godfrey, for he had to offer him at the same time the resource of Marner's money; and if Godfrey kicked, as he always did, at the notion of making a fresh debt from which he himself got the smallest share of advantage, why, he wouldn't kick long: Dunstan felt sure he could worry Godfrey into anything. The idea of Marner's money kept growing in vividness, now the want of it had become immediate; the prospect of having to make his appearance with the muddy boots of a pedestrian at Batherley, and to encounter the grinning queries of stablemen, stood unpleasantly in the way of his impatience to be back at Raveloe and carry out his felicitous plan; and a casual visitation of his waistcoat-pocket, as he was ruminating, awakened his memory to the fact that the two or three small coins his fore-finger encountered there, were of too pale a colour to cover that small debt, without payment of which the stable-keeper had declared he would never do any more business with Dunsey Cass. After all, according to the direction in which the run had brought him, he was not so very much farther from home than he was from Batherley; but Dunsey, not being remarkable for clearness of head, was only led to this conclusion by the gradual perception that there were other reasons for choosing the unprecedented course of walking home. It was now nearly four o'clock, and a mist was gathering: the sooner he got into the road the better. He remembered having crossed the road and seen the finger-post only a little while before Wildfire broke down; so, buttoning his coat, twisting the lash of his hunting-whip compactly round the handle, and rapping the tops of his boots with a self-possessed air, as if to assure himself that he was not at all taken by surprise, he set off with the sense that he was undertaking a remarkable feat of bodily exertion, which somehow and at some time he should be able to dress up and magnify to the admiration of a select circle at the Rainbow. When a young gentleman like Dunsey is reduced to so exceptional a mode of locomotion as walking, a whip in his hand is a desirable corrective to a too bewildering dreamy sense of unwontedness in his position; and Dunstan, as he went along through the gathering mist, was always rapping his whip somewhere. It was Godfrey's whip, which he had chosen to take without leave because it had a gold handle; of course no one could see, when Dunstan held it, that the name *Godfrey Cass* was cut in deep letters on that gold handle – they could only see that it was a very handsome whip. Dunsey was not without fear that he might meet some acquaintance in whose eyes he would cut a pitiable figure, for mist is no screen when people get close to each other; but when he at last found himself in the well-known Raveloe lanes without having met a soul, he silently remarked that that was part of his usual good-luck. But now the mist, helped by the evening darkness, was more of a screen than he desired, for it hid the ruts into which his feet were liable to slip – hid everything, so that he had to guide his steps by dragging his whip along the low bushes in advance of the hedgerow. He must soon, he thought, be getting near the opening at the Stone-pits: he should find it out by the break in the hedgerow. He found it out, however, by another circumstance which he had not expected – namely, by certain gleams of light, which he presently guessed to proceed from Silas Marner's cottage. That cottage and the money hidden within it had been in his mind continually during his walk, and he had been imagining ways of cajoling and tempting the weaver to part with the immediate possession of his money for the sake of receiving interest. Dunstan felt as if there must be a little frightening added to the cajolery, for his own arithmetical convictions were not clear enough to afford him any forcible demonstration as to the advantages of interest; and as for security, he regarded it vaguely as a means of cheating a man by making him believe that he would be paid. Altogether, the operation on the miser's mind was a task that Godfrey would be sure to hand over to his more daring and cunning brother: Dunstan had made up his mind to that; and by the time he saw the light gleaming through the chinks of Marner's shutters, the idea of a dialogue with the weaver had become so familiar to him, that it occurred to him as quite a natural thing to make the acquaintance forthwith. There might be several conveniences attending this course: the weaver had possibly got a lantern, and Dunstan was tired of feeling his way. He was still nearly three-quarters of a mile from home, and the lane was becoming unpleasantly slippery, for the mist was passing into rain. He turned up the bank, not without some fear lest he might miss the right way, since he was not certain whether the light were in front or on the side of the cottage. But he felt the ground before him cautiously with his whip-handle, and at last arrived safely at the door. He knocked loudly, rather enjoying the idea that the old fellow would be frightened at the sudden noise. He heard no movement in reply: all was silence in the cottage. Was the weaver gone to bed, then? If so, why had he left a light? That was a strange forgetfulness in a miser. Dunstan knocked still more loudly, and, without pausing for a reply, pushed his fingers through the latch-hole, intending to shake the door and pull the latch-string[3] up and down, not doubting that the door was fastened. But, to his surprise, at this double motion the door opened, and he found himself in front of a bright fire which lit up every corner of the cottage – the bed, the loom, the three chairs, and the table – and showed him that Marner was not there.

Nothing at that moment could be much more inviting to Dunsey than the bright fire on the brick hearth: he walked in and seated himself by it at once. There was something in front of the fire, too, that would have been inviting to a hungry man, if it had been in a different stage of cooking. It was a small bit of pork suspended from the kettle-hanger by a string passed through a large door-key, in a way known to primitive housekeepers unpossessed of jacks.[4] But the pork had been hung at the farthest extremity of the hanger, apparently to prevent the roasting from proceeding too rapidly during the owner's absence. The old staring simpleton had hot meat for his supper, then? thought Dunstan. People had always said he lived on mouldy bread, on purpose to check his appetite. But where could he be at this time, and on such an evening, leaving his supper in this stage of preparation, and his door unfastened? Dunstan's own recent difficulty in making his way suggested to him that the weaver had perhaps gone outside his cottage to fetch in fuel, or for some such brief purpose, and had slipped into the Stone-pit. That was an interesting idea to Dunstan, carrying consequences of entire novelty. If the weaver was dead, who had a right to his money? Who would know where his money was hidden? *Who would know that anybody had come to take it away?* He went no farther into the subtleties of evidence: the pressing question, 'Where *is* the money?' now took such entire possession of him as to make him quite forget that the weaver's death was not a certainty. A dull mind, once arriving at an inference that flatters a desire, is rarely able to retain the impression that the notion from which the inference started was purely problematic. And Dunstan's mind was as dull as the mind of a possible felon usually is. There were only three hiding-places where he had ever heard of cottagers' hoards being found: the thatch, the bed, and a hole in the floor. Marner's cottage had no thatch; and Dunstan's first act, after a train of thought made rapid by the stimulus of cupidity, was to go up to the bed; but while he did so, his eyes travelled eagerly over the floor, where the bricks, distinct in the fire-light, were discernible under the sprinkling of sand. But not everywhere; for there was one spot, and one only, which was quite covered with sand, and sand showing the marks of fingers, which had apparently been careful to spread it over a given space. It was near the treddles' of the loom. In an instant Dunstan darted to that spot, swept away the sand with his whip, and, inserting the thin end of the hook between the bricks, found that they were loose. In haste he lifted up two bricks, and saw what he had no doubt was the object of his search; for what could there be but money in those two leathern bags? And, from their weight, they must be filled with guineas. Dunstan felt round the hole, to be certain that it held no more; then hastily replaced the bricks, and spread the sand over them. Hardly more than five minutes had passed since he entered the cottage, but it seemed to Dunstan like a long while; and though he was without any distinct recognition of the possibility that Marner might be alive, and might re-enter the cottage at any moment, he felt an undefinable dread laying hold on him, as he rose to his feet with the bags in his hand. He would hasten out into the darkness, and then consider what he should do with the bags. He closed the door behind him immediately, that he might shut in the stream of light: a few steps would be enough to carry him beyond betrayal by the gleams from the shutter-chinks and the latch-hole. The rain and darkness had got thicker, and he was glad of it; though it was awkward walking with both hands filled, so that it was as much as he could do to grasp his whip along with one of the bags. But when he had gone a yard or two, he might take his time. So he stepped forward into the darkness.

CHAPTER 5

When Dunstan Cass turned his back on the cottage, Silas Marner was not more than a hundred yards away from it, plodding along from the village with a sack thrown round his shoulders as an over-coat, and with a horn lantern[1] in his hand. His legs were weary, but his mind was at ease, free from the presentiment of change. The sense of security more frequently springs from habit than from conviction, and for this reason it often subsists after such a change in the conditions as might have been expected to suggest alarm. The lapse of time during which a given event has not happened, is, in this logic of habit, constantly alleged as a reason why the event should never happen, even when the lapse of time is precisely the added condition which makes the event imminent. A man will tell you that he has worked in a mine for forty years unhurt by an accident as a reason why he should apprehend no danger, though the roof is beginning to sink; and it is often observable, that the older a man gets, the more difficult it is to him to retain a believing conception of his own death. This influence of habit was necessarily strong in a man whose life was so monotonous as Marner's – who saw no new people and heard of no new events to keep alive in him the idea of the unexpected and the changeful; and it explains simply enough, why his mind could be at ease, though he had left his house and his treasure more defence-less than usual. Silas was thinking with double complacency of his supper: first, because it would be hot and savoury; and secondly, because it would cost him nothing. For the little bit of pork was a present from that excellent housewife, Miss Priscilla Lammeter, to whom he had this day carried home a handsome piece of linen; and it was only on occasion of a present like this, that Silas indulged himself with roast-meat. Supper was his favourite meal, because it came at his time of revelry, when his heart warmed over his gold; whenever he had roast-meat, he always chose to have it for supper. But this evening, he had no sooner ingeniously knotted his string fast round his bit of pork, twisted the string according to rule over his door-key, passed it through the handle, and made it fast on the hanger, than he remembered that a piece of very fine twine was indispensable to his 'setting up' a new piece of work in his loom early in the morning. It had slipped his memory, because, in coming from Mr Lammeter's, he had not had to pass through the village; but to lose time by going on errands in the morning was out of the question. It was a nasty fog to turn out into, but there were things Silas loved better than his own comfort; so, drawing his pork to the extremity of the hanger, and arming himself with his lantern and his old sack, he set out on what, in ordinary weather, would have been a twenty minutes' errand. He could not have locked his door without undoing his well-knotted string and retarding his supper; it was not worth his while to make that sacrifice. What thief would find his way to the Stone-pits on such a night as this? and why should he come on this particular night, when he had never come through all the fifteen years before? These questions were not distinctly present in Silas's mind; they merely serve to represent the vaguely-felt foundation of his freedom from anxiety.

He reached his door in much satisfaction that his errand was done: he opened it, and to his short-sighted eyes everything remained as he had left it, except that the fire sent out a welcome increase of heat. He trod about the floor while putting by his lantern and throwing aside his hat and sack, so as to merge the marks of Dunstan's feet on the sand in the marks of his own nailed boots. Then he moved his pork nearer to the fire, and sat down to the agreeable business of tending the meat and warming himself at the same time.

Any one who had looked at him as the red light shone upon his pale face, strange straining eyes, and meagre form, would perhaps have understood the mixture of contemptuous pity, dread, and suspicion with which he was regarded by his neighbours in Raveloe. Yet few men could be more harmless than poor Marner. In his truthful simple soul, not even the growing greed and worship of gold could beget any vice directly injurious to others. The light of his faith quite put out, and his affections made desolate, he had clung with all the force of his nature to his work and his money; and like all objects to which a man devotes himself, they had fashioned him into correspondence with themselves. His loom, as he wrought in it without ceasing, had in its turn wrought on him, and confirmed more and more the monotonous craving for its monotonous response. His gold, as he hung over it and saw it grow, gathered his power of loving together into a hard isolation like its own.

As soon as he was warm he began to think it would be a long while to wait till after supper before he drew out his guineas, and it would be pleasant to see them on the table before him as he ate his unwonted feast. For joy is the best of wine, and Silas's guineas were a golden wine of that sort.

He rose and placed his candle unsuspectingly on the floor near his loom, swept away the sand without noticing any change, and removed the bricks. The sight of the empty hole made his heart leap violently, but the belief that his gold was gone could not come at once – only terror, and the eager effort to put an end to the terror. He passed his trembling hand all about the hole, trying to think it possible that his eyes had deceived him; then he held the candle in the hole and examined it curiously, trembling more and more. At last he shook so violently that he let fall the candle, and lifted his hands to his head, trying to steady himself, that he might think. Had he put his gold somewhere else, by a sudden resolution last night, and then forgotten it? A man falling into dark waters seeks a momentary footing even on sliding stones; and Silas, by acting as if he believed in false hopes, warded off the moment of despair. He searched in every corner, he turned his bed over, and shook it, and kneaded it; he looked in his brick oven where he laid his sticks. When there was no other place to be searched, he kneeled down again and felt once more all round the hole. There was no untried refuge left for a moment's shelter from the terrible truth.

Yes, there was a sort of refuge which always comes with the prostration of thought under an overpowering passion: it was that expectation of impossibilities, that belief in contradictory images, which is still distinct from madness, because it is capable of being dissipated by the external fact. Silas got up from his knees trembling, and looked round at the table: didn't the gold lie there after all? The table was bare. Then he turned and looked behind him – looked all round his dwelling, seeming to strain his brown eyes after some possible appearance of the bags where he had already sought them in vain. He could see every object in his cottage – and his gold was not there.

Again he put his trembling hands to his head, and gave a wild ringing scream, the cry of desolation. For a few moments after, he stood motionless; but the cry had relieved him from the first maddening pressure of the truth. He turned, and tottered towards his loom, and got into the seat where he worked, instinctively seeking this as the strongest assurance of reality.

And now that all the false hopes had vanished, and the first shock of certainty was past, the idea of a thief began to present itself, and he entertained it eagerly, because a thief might be caught and made to restore the gold. The thought brought some new strength with it, and he started from his loom to the door. As he opened it the rain beat in upon him, for it was falling more and more heavily. There were no footsteps to be tracked on such a night – footsteps? When had the thief come? During Silas's absence in the daytime the door had been locked, and there had been no marks of any inroad on his return by daylight. And in the evening, too, he said to himself, everything was the same as when he had left it. The sand and bricks looked as if they had not been moved. *Was* it a thief who had taken the bags? or was it a cruel power that no hands could reach which had delighted in making him a second time desolate? He shrank from this vaguer dread, and fixed his mind with struggling effort on the robber with hands, who could be reached by hands. His thoughts glanced at all the neighbours who had made any remarks, or asked any questions which he might now regard as a ground of suspicion. There was Jem Rodney, a known poacher, and otherwise disreputable: he had often met Marner in his journeys across the fields, and had said something jestingly about the weaver's money; nay, he had once irritated Marner, by lingering at the fire when he called to light his pipe, instead of going about his business. Jem Rodney was the man – there was ease in the thought. Jem could be found and made to restore the money: Marner did not want to punish him, but only to get back his gold which had gone from him, and left his soul like a forlorn traveller on an unknown desert. The robber must be laid hold of. Marner's ideas of legal authority were confused, but he felt that he must go and proclaim his loss; and the great people in the village – the clergyman, the constable, and Squire Cass – would make Jem Rodney, or somebody else, deliver up the stolen money. He rushed out in the rain, under the stimulus of this hope, forgetting to cover his head, not caring to fasten his door; for he felt as if he had nothing left to lose.

He ran swiftly, till want of breath compelled him to slacken his pace as he was entering the village at the turning close to the Rainbow.

The Rainbow, in Marner's view, was a place of luxurious resort for rich and stout husbands, whose wives had superfluous stores of linen; it was the place where he was likely to find the powers and dignities of Raveloe, and where he could most speedily make his loss public. He lifted the latch, and turned into the bright bar or kitchen on the right hand, where the less lofty customers of the house were in the habit of assembling, the parlour on the left being reserved for the more select society in which Squire Cass frequently enjoyed the double pleasure of conviviality and condescension. But the parlour was dark to-night, the chief personages who ornamented its circle being all at Mrs Osgood's birthday dance, as Godfrey Cass was. And in consequence of this, the party on the high-screened seats in the kitchen was more numerous than usual; several personages, who would otherwise have been admitted into the parlour and enlarged the opportunity of hectoring and condescension for their betters, being content this evening to vary their enjoyment by taking their spirits-and-water where they could themselves hector and condescend in company that called for beer.[2]

CHAPTER 6

The conversation, which was at a high pitch of animation when Silas approached the door of the Rainbow, had, as usual, been slow and intermittent when the company first assembled. The pipes began to be puffed in a silence which had an air of severity; the more important customers, who drank spirits and sat nearest the fire, staring at each other as if a bet were depending on the first man who winked; while the beer-drinkers, chiefly men in fustian¹ jackets and smock-frocks, kept their eyelids down and rubbed their hands across their mouths, as if their draughts of beer were a funereal duty attended with embarrassing sadness. At last, Mr Snell, the landlord, a man of a neutral disposition, accustomed to stand aloof from human differences as those of beings who were all alike in need of liquor, broke silence, by saying in a doubtful tone to his cousin the butcher –

'Some folks 'ud say that was a fine beast you druv in yesterday, Bob?'

The butcher, a jolly, smiling, red-haired man, was not disposed to answer rashly. He gave a few puffs before he spat and replied, 'And they wouldn't be fur wrong, John.'

After this feeble delusive thaw, the silence set in as severely as before.

'Was it a red Durham?'² said the farrier, taking up the thread of discourse after the lapse of a few minutes.

The farrier looked at the landlord, and the landlord looked at the butcher, as the person who must take the responsibility of answering.

'Red it was,' said the butcher, in his good-humoured husky treble – 'and a Durham it was.'

'Then you needn't tell *me* who you bought it of,' said the farrier, looking round with some triumph; 'I know who it is has got the red Durhams o' this country-side. And she'd a white star on her brow, I'll bet a penny?' The farrier leaned forward with his hands on his knees as he put this question, and his eyes twinkled knowingly.

'Well; yes – she might,' said the butcher, slowly, considering that he was giving a decided affirmative. 'I don't say contrary.'

46

'I knew that very well,' said the farrier, throwing himself backward again, and speaking defiantly; 'if *I* don't know Mr Lammeter's cows, I should like to know who does – that's all. And as for the cow you've bought, bargain or no bargain, I've been at the drenching³ of her – contradick me who will.'

The farrier looked fierce, and the mild butcher's conversational spirit was roused a little.

'I'm not for contradicking no man,' he said; 'I'm for peace and quietness. Some are for cutting long ribs – I'm for cutting 'em short myself; but *I* don't quarrel with 'em. All I say is, it's a lovely carkiss – and anybody as was reasonable, it 'ud bring tears into their eyes to look at it.'

'Well, it's the cow as I drenched, whatever it is,' pursued the farrier, angrily; 'and it was Mr Lammeter's cow, else you told a lie when you said it was a red Durham.'

'I tell no lies,' said the butcher, with the same mild huskiness as before, 'and I contradick none – not if a man was to swear himself black: he's no meat o' mine, nor none o' my bargains. All I say is, it's a lovely carkiss. And what I say I'll stick to; but I'll quarrel wi' no man.'

'No,' said the farrier, with bitter sarcasm, looking at the company generally; 'and p'rhaps you arn't pig-headed; and p'rhaps you didn't say the cow was a red Durham; and p'rhaps you didn't say she'd got a star on her brow – stick to that, now you're at it.'

'Come, come,' said the landlord; 'let the cow alone. The truth lies atween you: you're both right and both wrong, as I allays say. And as for the cow's being Mr Lammeter's, I say nothing to that; but this I say, as the Rainbow's the Rainbow. And for the matter o' that, if the talk is to be o' the Lammeters, *you* know the most upo' that head, eh, Mr Macey? You remember when first Mr Lammeter's father come into these parts, and took the Warrens?'

Mr Macey, tailor and parish-clerk, the latter of which functions rheumatism had of late obliged him to share with a small-featured young man who sat opposite him, held his white head on one side, and twirled his thumbs with an air of complacency, slightly seasoned with criticism. He smiled pityingly, in answer to the landlord's appeal, and said –

'Ay, ay; I know, I know; but I let other folks talk. I've laid by now, and gev up to the young uns. Ask them as have been to school at Tarley: they've learnt pernouncing; that's come up since my day.'

'If you're pointing at me, Mr Macey,' said the deputy-clerk, with an air of anxious propriety, 'I'm nowise a man to speak out of my place. As the psalm says –

> "I know what's right, nor only so,
> But also practise what I know." [14]

'Well, then, I wish you'd keep hold o' the tune, when it's set for you; if you're for prac*tis*ing, I wish you'd prac*tise* that,' said a large jocose-looking man, an excellent wheelwright in his week-day capacity, but on Sundays leader of the choir. He winked, as he spoke, at two of the company, who were known officially as the 'bassoon' and the 'key-bugle,'[5] in the confidence that he was expressing the sense of the musical profession in Raveloe.

Mr Tookey, the deputy-clerk, who shared the unpopularity common to deputies, turned very red, but replied, with careful moderation – 'Mr Winthrop, if you'll bring me any proof as I'm in the wrong, I'm not the man to say I won't alter. But there's people set up their own ears for a standard, and expect the whole choir to follow 'em. There may be two opinions, I hope.'

'Ay, ay,' said Mr Macey, who felt very well satisfied with this attack on youthful presumption; 'you're right there, Tookey: there's allays two 'pinions; there's the 'pinion a man has of himsen, and there's the 'pinion other folks have on him. There'd be two 'pinions about a cracked bell, if the bell could hear itself.'

'Well, Mr Macey,' said poor Tookey, serious amidst the general laughter, 'I undertook to partially fill up the office of parish-clerk by Mr Crackenthorp's desire, whenever your infirmities should make you unfitting; and it's one of the rights thereof to sing in the choir – else why have you done the same yourself?'

'Ah! but the old gentleman and you are two folks,' said Ben Winthrop. 'The old gentleman's got a gift. Why, the Squire used to invite him to take a glass, only to hear him sing the "Red Rovier"; didn't he, Mr Macey? It's a nat'ral gift. There's my little lad Aaron, he's got a gift – he can sing a tune off straight, like a throstle. But as for you, Master Tookey, you'd better stick to your "Amens": your voice is well enough when you keep it up in your nose. It's your inside as isn't right made for music: it's no better nor a hollow stalk.'

This kind of unflinching frankness was the most piquant form of joke to the company at the Rainbow, and Ben Winthrop's insult was felt by everybody to have capped Mr Macey's epigram.

'I see what it is plain enough,' said Mr Tookey, unable to keep cool any longer. 'There's a conspceracy to turn me out o' the choir, as I shouldn't share the Christmas money – that's where it is. But I shall speak to Mr Crackenthorp; I'll not be put upon by no man.'

'Nay, nay, Tookey,' said Ben Winthrop. 'We'll pay you your share to keep out of it – that's what we'll do. There's things folks 'ud pay to be rid on, besides varmin.'

'Come, come,' said the landlord, who felt that paying people for their absence was a principle dangerous to society; 'a joke's a joke. We're all good friends here, I hope. We must give and take. You're both right and you're both wrong, as I say. I agree wi' Mr Macey here, as there's two opinions; and if mine was asked, I should say they're both right. Tookey's right and Winthrop's right, and they've only got to split the difference and make themselves even.'

The farrier was puffing his pipe rather fiercely, in some contempt at this trivial discussion. He had no ear for music himself, and never went to church, as being of the medical profession, and likely to be in requisition for delicate cows. But the butcher, having music in his soul, had listened with a divided desire for Tookey's defeat and for the preservation of the peace.

'To be sure,' he said, following up the landlord's conciliatory view, 'we're fond of our old clerk; it's nat'ral, and him used to be such a singer, and got a brother as is known for the first fiddler in this country-side. Eh, it's a pity but what Solomon lived in our village, and could give us a tune when we liked; eh, Mr Macey? I'd keep him in liver and lights[6] for nothing – that I would.'

'Ay, ay,' said Mr Macey, in the height of complacency; 'our family's been known for musicianers as far back as anybody can tell. But them things are dying out, as I tell Solomon every time he comes round; there's no voices like what there used to be, and there's nobody remembers what we remember, if it isn't the old crows.'

'Ay, you remember when first Mr Lammeter's father come into these parts, don't you, Mr Macey?' said the landlord.

'I should think I did,' said the old man, who had now gone through that complimentary process necessary to bring him up to the point of narration; 'and a fine old gentleman he was – as fine, and finer nor the

Mr Lammeter as now is. He came from a bit north'ard, so far as I could ever make out. But there's nobody rightly knows about those parts: only it couldn't be far north'ard, nor much different from this country, for he brought a fine breed o' sheep with him, so there must be pastures there, and everything reasonable. We heared tell as he'd sold his own land to come and take the Warrens, and that seemed odd for a man as had land of his own, to come and rent a farm in a strange place. But they said it was along of his wife's dying; though there's reasons in things as nobody knows on – that's pretty much what I've made out; yet some folks are so wise, they'll find you fifty reasons straight off, and all the while the real reason's winking at 'em in the corner, and they niver see't. Howsomever, it was soon seen as we'd got a new parish'ner as know'd the rights and customs o' things, and kep a good house, and was well looked on by everybody. And the young man – that's the Mr Lammeter as now is, for he'd niver a sister – soon begun to court Miss Osgood, that's the sister o' the Mr Osgood as now is, and a fine handsome lass she was – eh, you can't think – they pretend this young lass is like her, but that's the way wi' people as don't know what come before 'em. *I* should know, for I helped the old rector, Mr Drumlow as was, I helped him marry 'em.'

Here Mr Macey paused; he always gave his narrative in instalments, expecting to be questioned according to precedent.

'Ay, and a partic'lar thing happened, didn't it, Mr Macey, so as you were likely to remember that marriage?' said the landlord, in a congratulatory tone.

'I should think there did – a *very* partic'lar thing,' said Mr Macey, nodding sideways. 'For Mr Drumlow – poor old gentleman, I was fond on him, though he'd got a bit confused in his head, what wi' age and wi' taking a drop o' summat warm when the service come of a cold morning. And young Mr Lammeter he'd have no way but he must be married in Janiwary, which, to be sure, 's a unreasonable time to be married in, for it isn't like a christening or a burying, as you can't help; and so Mr Drumlow – poor old gentleman, I was fond on him – but when he come to put the questions, he put 'em by the rule o' contrairy, like, and he says, "Wilt thou have this man to thy wedded wife?" says he, and then he says, "Wilt thou have this woman to thy wedded husband?" says he. But the partic'larest thing of all is, as nobody took any notice on it but me, and they answered straight off "yes," like as if it had been me saying "Amen" i' the right place, without listening to what went before.'

'But *you* knew what was going on well enough, didn't you, Mr Macey? You were live enough, eh?' said the butcher.

'Lor bless you!' said Mr Macey, pausing, and smiling in pity at the impotence of his hearer's imagination – 'why, I was all of a tremble: it was as if I'd been a coat pulled by the two tails, like; for I couldn't stop the parson, I couldn't take upon me to do that; and yet I said to myself, I says, "Suppose they shouldn't be fast married, 'cause the words are contrairy?" and my head went working like a mill, for I was allays uncommon for turning things over and seeing all round 'em; and I says to myself, "Is't the meanin' or the words as makes folks fast i' wedlock?" For the parson meant right, and the bride and bridegroom meant right. But then, when I come to think on it, meanin' goes but a little way i' most things, for you may mean to stick things together and your glue may be bad, and then where are you? And so I says to mysen, "It isn't the meanin', it's the glue." And I was worreted as if I'd got three bells to pull at once, when we went into the vestry, and they begun to sign their names. But where's the use o' talking? – you can't think what goes on in a 'cute man's inside.'

'But you held in for all that, didn't you, Mr Macey?' said the landlord.

'Ay, I held in tight till I was by mysen wi' Mr Drumlow, and then I out wi' everything, but respectful, as I allays did. And he made light on it, and he says, "Pooh, pooh, Macey, make yourself easy," he says; "it's neither the meaning nor the words – it's the regester does it – that's the glue." So you see he settled it easy; for parsons and doctors know everything by heart, like, so as they aren't worreted wi' think-ing what's the rights and wrongs o' things, as I'n been many and many's the time. And sure enough the wedding turned out all right, on'y poor Mrs Lammeter – that's Miss Osgood as was – died afore the lasses was growed up; but for prosperity and everything respect-able, there's no family more looked on.'

Every one of Mr Macey's audience had heard this story many times, but it was listened to as if it had been a favourite tune, and at certain points the puffing of the pipes was momentarily suspended, that the listeners might give their whole minds to the expected words. But there was more to come; and Mr Snell, the landlord, duly put the leading question.

'Why, old Mr Lammeter had a pretty fortin, didn't they say, when he come into these parts?'

'Well, yes,' said Mr Macey; 'but I daresay it's as much as this Mr Lammeter's done to keep it whole. For there was allays a talk as nobody could get rich on the Warrens: though he holds it cheap, for it's what they call Charity Land.'

'Ay, and there's few folks know so well as you how it come to be Charity Land, eh, Mr Macey?' said the butcher.

'How should they?' said the old clerk, with some contempt. 'Why, my grandfather made the grooms' livery for that Mr Cliff as came and built the big stables at the Warrens. Why, they're stables four times as big as Squire Cass's, for he thought o' nothing but hosses and hunting, Cliff didn't – a Lunnon tailor, some folks said, as had gone mad wi' cheating. For he couldn't ride; lor bless you! they said he'd got no more grip o' the hoss than if his legs had been cross-sticks: my grandfather heared old Squire Cass say so many and many a time. But ride he would as if Old Harry[8] had been a-driving him; and he'd a son, a lad o' sixteen; and nothing would his father have him do, but he must ride and ride – though the lad was frighted, they said. And it was a common saying as the father wanted to ride the tailor out o' the lad, and make a gentleman on him – not but what I'm a tailor myself, but in respect as God made me such, I'm proud on it, for "Macey, tailor," 's been wrote up over our door since afore the Queen's heads[9] went out on the shillings. But Cliff, he was ashamed o' being called a tailor, and he was sore vexed as his riding was laughed at, and nobody o' the gentlefolks hereabout could abide him. Howsomever, the poor lad got sickly and died, and the father didn't live long after him, for he got queerer nor ever, and they said he used to go out i' the dead o' the night, wi' a lantern in his hand, to the stables, and set a lot o' lights burning, for he got as he couldn't sleep; and there he'd stand, cracking his whip and looking at his hosses; and they said it was a mercy as the stables didn't get burnt down wi' the poor dumb creaturs in 'em. But at last he died raving, and they found as he'd left all his property, Warrens and all, to a Lunnon Charity, and that's how the Warrens come to be Charity Land; though, as for the stables, Mr Lammeter never uses 'em – they're out o' all charicter – lor bless you!

if you was to set the doors a-banging in 'em, it 'ud sound like thunder half o'er the parish.'

'Ay, but there's more going on in the stables than what folks see by daylight, eh, Mr Macey?' said the landlord.

'Ay, ay; go that way of a dark night, that's all,' said Mr Macey, winking mysteriously, 'and then make believe, if you like, as you didn't see lights i' the stables, nor hear the stamping o' the hosses, nor the cracking o' the whips, and howling, too, if it's tow'rt daybreak. "Cliff's Holiday" has been the name of it ever sin' I were a boy; that's to say, some said as it was the holiday Old Harry gev him from roasting, like. That's what my father told me, and he was a reasonable man, though there's folks nowadays know what happened afore they were born better nor they know their own business.'

'What do you say to that, eh, Dowlas?' said the landlord, turning to the farrier, who was swelling with impatience for his cue. 'There's a nut for *you* to crack.'

Mr Dowlas was the negative spirit in the company, and was proud of his position.

'Say? I say what a man *should* say as doesn't shut his eyes to look at a finger-post. I say, as I'm ready to wager any man ten pound, if he'll stand out wi' me any dry night in the pasture before the Warren stables, as we shall neither see lights nor hear noises, if it isn't the blowing of our own noses. That's what I say, and I've said it many a time; but there's nobody 'ull ventur a ten-pun' note on their ghos'es as they make so sure of.'

'Why, Dowlas, that's easy betting, that is,' said Ben Winthrop. 'You might as well bet a man as he wouldn't catch the rheumatise if he stood up to's neck in the pool of a frosty night. It 'ud be fine fun for a man to win his bet as he'd catch the rheumatise. Folks as believe in Cliff's Holiday aren't agoing to ventur near it for a matter o' ten pound.'

'If Master Dowlas wants to know the truth on it,' said Mr Macey, with a sarcastic smile, tapping his thumbs together, 'he's no call to lay any bet – let him go and stan' by himself – there's nobody 'ull hinder him; and then he can let the parish'ners know if they're wrong.'

'Thank you! I'm obliged to you,' said the farrier, with a snort of scorn. 'If folks are fools, it's no business o' mine. *I* don't want to make out the truth about ghos'es: I know it a'ready. But I'm not against a bet – everything fair and open. Let any man bet me ten pound as I shall see Cliff's Holiday, and I'll go and stand by myself. I want no company. I'd as lief[10] do it as I'd fill this pipe.'

'Ah, but who's to watch you, Dowlas, and see you do it? That's no fair bet,' said the butcher.

'No fair bet?' replied Mr Dowlas, angrily. 'I should like to hear any man stand up and say I want to bet unfair. Come now, Master Lundy, I should like to hear you say it.'

'Very like you would,' said the butcher. 'But it's no business o' mine. You're none o' my bargains, and I aren't a-going to try and 'bate[11] your price. If anybody 'll bid for you at your own vallying, let him. I'm for peace and quietness, I am.'

'Yes, that's what every yapping cur is, when you hold a stick up at him,' said the farrier. 'But I'm afraid o' neither man nor ghost, and I'm ready to lay a fair bet. *I* aren't a turn-tail cur.'

'Ay, but there's this in it, Dowlas,' said the landlord, speaking in a tone of much candour and tolerance. 'There's folks, i' my opinion, they can't see ghos'es, not if they stood as plain as a pike-staff[12] before 'em. And there's reason i' that. For there's my wife, now, can't smell, not if she'd the strongest o' cheese under her nose. I never see'd a ghost myself; but then I says to myself, "Very like I haven't got the smell for 'em." I mean, putting a ghost for a smell, or else contrairi-ways. And so, I'm for holding with both sides; for, as I say, the truth lies between 'em. And if Dowlas was to go and stand, and say he'd never seen a wink o' Cliff's Holiday all the night through, I'd back him; and if anybody said as Cliff's Holiday was certain sure for all that, I'd back *him* too. For the smell's what I go by.'

The landlord's analogical argument was not well received by the farrier – a man intensely opposed to compromise.

'Tut, tut,' he said, setting down his glass with refreshed irritation; 'what's the smell got to do with it? Did ever a ghost give a man a black eye? That's what I should like to know. If ghos'es want me to believe in 'em, let 'em leave off skulking i' the dark and i' lone places – let 'em come where there's company and candles.'

'As if ghos'es 'ud want to be believed in by anybody so ignirant!' said Mr Macey, in deep disgust at the farrier's crass incompetence to apprehend the conditions of ghostly phenomena.

CHAPTER 7

Yet the next moment there seemed to be some evidence that ghosts had a more condescending disposition than Mr Macey attributed to them; for the pale thin figure of Silas Marner was suddenly seen standing in the warm light, uttering no word, but looking round at the company with his strange unearthly eyes. The long pipes gave a simultaneous movement, like the antennæ of startled insects, and every man present, not excepting even the sceptical farrier, had an impression that he saw, not Silas Marner in the flesh, but an apparition; for the door by which Silas had entered was hidden by the high-screened seats, and no one had noticed his approach. Mr Macey, sitting a long way off the ghost, might be supposed to have felt an argumentative triumph, which would tend to neutralise his share of the general alarm. Had he not always said that when Silas Marner was in that strange trance of his, his soul went loose from his body? Here was the demonstration: nevertheless, on the whole, he would have been as well contented without it. For a few moments there was a dead silence, Marner's want of breath and agitation not allowing him to speak. The landlord, under the habitual sense that he was bound to keep his house open to all company, and confident in the protection of his unbroken neutrality, at last took on himself the task of adjuring the ghost.

'Master Marner,' he said, in a conciliatory tone, 'what's lacking to you? What's your business here?'

'Robbed!' said Silas, gaspingly. 'I've been robbed! I want the constable – and the Justice' – and Squire Cass – and Mr Crackenthorp.'

'Lay hold on him, Jem Rodney,' said the landlord, the idea of a ghost subsiding; 'he's off his head, I doubt. He's wet through.'

Jem Rodney was the outermost man, and sat conveniently near Marner's standing-place; but he declined to give his services.

'Come and lay hold on him yourself, Mr Snell, if you've a mind,' said Jem, rather sullenly. 'He's been robbed, and murdered too, for what I know,' he added, in a muttering tone.

'Jem Rodney!' said Silas, turning and fixing his strange eyes on the suspected man.

'Ay, Master Marner, what do ye want wi' me?' said Jem, trembling a little, and seizing his drinking-can as a defensive weapon.

'If it was you stole my money,' said Silas, clasping his hands entreatingly, and raising his voice to a cry, 'give it me back, – and I won't meddle with you. I won't set the constable on you. Give it me back, and I'll let you – I'll let you have a guinea.'

'Me stole your money!' said Jem, angrily. 'I'll pitch this can at your eye if you talk o' *my* stealing your money.'

'Come, come, Master Marner,' said the landlord, now rising resolutely, and seizing Marner by the shoulder, 'if you've got any information to lay, speak it out sensible, and show as you're in your right mind, if you expect anybody to listen to you. You're as wet as a drownded rat. Sit down and dry yourself, and speak straight forrard.'

'Ah, to be sure, man,' said the farrier, who began to feel that he had not been quite on a par with himself and the occasion. 'Let's have no more staring and screaming, else we'll have you strapped² for a madman. That was why I didn't speak at the first – thinks I, the man's run mad.'

'Ay, ay, make him sit down,' said several voices at once, well pleased that the reality of ghosts remained still an open question.

The landlord forced Marner to take off his coat, and then to sit down on a chair aloof from every one else, in the centre of the circle and in the direct rays of the fire. The weaver, too feeble to have any distinct purpose beyond that of getting help to recover his money, submitted unresistingly. The transient fears of the company were now forgotten in their strong curiosity, and all faces were turned towards Silas, when the landlord, having seated himself again, said –

'Now then, Master Marner, what's this you've got to say – as you've been robbed? Speak out.'

'He'd better not say again as it was me robbed him,' cried Jem Rodney, hastily. 'What could I ha' done with his money? I could as easy steal the parson's surplice, and wear it.'

'Hold your tongue, Jem, and let's hear what he's got to say,' said the landlord. 'Now then, Master Marner.'

Silas now told his story, under frequent questioning as the mysterious character of the robbery became evident.

This strangely novel situation of opening his trouble to his Raveloe neighbours, of sitting in the warmth of a hearth not his own, and feeling the presence of faces and voices which were his nearest promise of help, had doubtless its influence on Marner, in spite of his passionate preoccupation with his loss. Our consciousness rarely registers the beginning of a growth within us any more than without us: there have been many circulations of the sap before we detect the smallest sign of the bud.

The slight suspicion with which his hearers at first listened to him, gradually melted away before the convincing simplicity of his distress: it was impossible for the neighbours to doubt that Marner was telling the truth, not because they were capable of arguing at once from the nature of his statements to the absence of any motive for making them falsely, but because, as Mr Macey observed, 'Folks as had the devil to back 'em were not likely to be so mushed'³ as poor Silas was. Rather, from the strange fact that the robber had left no traces, and had happened to know the nick of time, utterly incalculable by mortal agents, when Silas would go away from home without locking his door, the more probable conclusion seemed to be, that his disreputable intimacy in that quarter, if it ever existed, had been broken up, and that, in consequence, this ill turn had been done to Marner by somebody it was quite in vain to set the constable after. Why this preternatural felon should be obliged to wait till the door was left unlocked, was a question which did not present itself.

'It isn't Jem Rodney as has done this work, Master Marner,' said the landlord. 'You mustn't be a-casting your eye at poor Jem. There may be a bit of a reckoning against Jem for the matter of a hare or so, if anybody was bound to keep their eyes staring open, and niver to wink; but Jem's been a-sitting here drinking his can, like the decentest man i' the parish, since before you left your house, Master Marner, by your own account.'

'Ay, ay,' said Mr Macey; 'let's have no accusing o' the innicent. That isn't the law. There must be folks to swear again' a man before he can be ta'en up. Let's have no accusing o' the innicent, Master Marner.'

Memory was not so utterly torpid in Silas that it could not be wakened by these words. With a movement of compunction as new and strange to him as everything else within the last hour, he started from his chair and went close up to Jem, looking at him as if he wanted to assure himself of the expression in his face.

'I was wrong,' he said – 'yes, yes – I ought to have thought. There's nothing to witness against you, Jem. Only you'd been into my house oftener than anybody else, and so you came into my head. I don't accuse you – I won't accuse anybody – only,' he added, lifting up his hands to his head, and turning away with bewildered misery, 'I try – I try to think where my guineas can be.'

'Ay, ay, they're gone where it's hot enough to melt 'em, I doubt,' said Mr Macey.

'Tchuh!' said the farrier. And then he asked, with a cross-examining air, 'How much money might there be in the bags, Master Marner?'

'Two hundred and seventy-two pounds, twelve and sixpence, last night when I counted it,' said Silas, seating himself again, with a groan.

'Pooh! why, they'd be none so heavy to carry. Some tramp's been in, that's all; and as for the no footmarks, and the bricks and the sand being all right – why, your eyes are pretty much like a insect's, Master Marner; they're obliged to look so close, you can't see much at a time. It's my opinion as, if I'd been you, or you'd been me – for it comes to the same thing – you wouldn't have thought you'd found everything as you left it. But what I vote is, as two of the sensiblest o' the company should go with you to Master Kench, the constable's – he's ill i' bed, I know that much – and get him to appoint one of us his deppity; for that's the law, and I don't think anybody 'ull take upon him to contradick me there. It isn't much of a walk to Kench's; and then, if it's me as is deppity, I'll go back with you, Master Marner, and examine your premises; and if anybody's got any fault to find with that, I'll thank him to stand up and say it out like a man.'

By this pregnant speech the farrier had re-established his self-complacency, and waited with confidence to hear himself named as one of the superlatively sensible men.

'Let us see how the night is, though,' said the landlord, who also considered himself personally concerned in this proposition. 'Why, it rains heavy still,' he said, returning from the door.

'Well, I'm not the man to be afraid o' the rain,' said the farrier. 'For it'll look bad when Justice Malam hears as respectable men like us had a information laid before 'em and took no steps.'

The landlord agreed with this view, and after taking the sense of the company, and duly rehearsing a small ceremony known in high ecclesiastical life as the *nolo episcopari*,[4] he consented to take on himself the chill dignity of going to Kench's. But to the farrier's strong disgust, Mr Macey now started an objection to his proposing himself as a deputy-constable; for that oracular old gentleman, claiming to know the law, stated, as a fact delivered to him by his father, that no doctor could be a constable.

'And you're a doctor, I reckon, though you're only a cow-doctor – for a fly's a fly, though it may be a hoss-fly,' concluded Mr Macey, wondering a little at his own ''cuteness.'

There was a hot debate upon this, the farrier being of course indisposed to renounce the quality of doctor, but contending that a doctor could be a constable if he liked – the law meant, he needn't be one if he didn't like. Mr Macey thought this was nonsense, since the law was not likely to be fonder of doctors than of other folks. Moreover, if it was in the nature of doctors more than of other men not to like being constables, how came Mr Dowlas to be so eager to act in that capacity?

'*I* don't want to act the constable,' said the farrier, driven into a corner by this merciless reasoning; 'and there's no man can say it of me, if he'd tell the truth. But if there's to be any jealousy and envying about going to Kench's in the rain, let them go as like it – you won't get me to go, I can tell you.'

By the landlord's intervention, however, the dispute was accommodated. Mr Dowlas consented to go as a second person disinclined to act officially; and so poor Silas, furnished with some old coverings, turned out with his two companions into the rain again, thinking of the long night-hours before him, not as those do who long to rest, but as those who expect to 'watch for the morning.'[5]

CHAPTER 8

When Godfrey Cass returned from Mrs Osgood's party at midnight, he was not much surprised to learn that Dunsey had not come home. Perhaps he had not sold Wildfire, and was waiting for another chance – perhaps, on that foggy afternoon, he had preferred housing himself at the Red Lion at Batherley for the night, if the run had kept him in that neighbourhood; for he was not likely to feel much concern about leaving his brother in suspense. Godfrey's mind was too full of Nancy Lammeter's looks and behaviour, too full of the exasperation against himself and his lot, which the sight of her always produced in him, for him to give much thought to Wildfire, or to the probabilities of Dunstan's conduct.

The next morning the whole village was excited by the story of the robbery, and Godfrey, like every one else, was occupied in gathering and discussing news about it, and in visiting the Stone-pits. The rain had washed away all possibility of distinguishing foot-marks, but a close investigation of the spot had disclosed, in the direction opposite to the village, a tinder-box,¹ with a flint and steel, half sunk in the mud. It was not Silas's tinder-box, for the only one he had ever had was still standing on his shelf; and the inference generally accepted was, that the tinder-box in the ditch was somehow connected with the robbery. A small minority shook their heads, and intimated their opinion that it was not a robbery to have much light thrown on it by tinder-boxes, that Master Marner's tale had a queer look with it, and that such things had been known as a man's doing himself a mischief, and then setting the justice to look for the doer. But when questioned closely as to their grounds for this opinion, and what Master Marner had to gain by such false pretences, they only shook their heads as before, and observed that there was no knowing what some folks counted gain; moreover, that everybody had a right to their own opinions, grounds or no grounds, and that the weaver, as everybody knew, was partly crazy. Mr Macey, though he joined in the defence of Marner against all suspicions of deceit, also pooh-poohed the tinder-box; indeed, repudiated it as a rather impious suggestion, tending to imply that everything must be done by human hands, and that there was no power which could make away with the guineas without moving the bricks. Nevertheless, he turned round rather sharply on Mr Tookey, when the zealous deputy, feeling that this was a view of the case peculiarly suited to a parish-clerk, carried it still further, and doubted whether it was right to inquire into a robbery at all when the circumstances were so mysterious.

'As if,' concluded Mr Tookey – 'as if there was nothing but what could be made out by justices and constables.'

'Now, don't you be for overshooting the mark, Tookey,' said Mr Macey, nodding his head aside admonishingly. 'That's what you're allays at; if I throw a stone and hit, you think there's summat better than hitting, and you try to throw a stone beyond. What I said was against the tinder-box: I said nothing against justices and constables, for they're o' King George's making, and it 'ud be ill-becoming a man in a parish office to fly out again' King George.'

While these discussions were going on amongst the group outside the Rainbow, a higher consultation was being carried on within, under the presidency of Mr Crackenthorp, the rector, assisted by Squire Cass and other substantial parishioners. It had just occurred to Mr Snell, the landlord – he being, as he observed, a man accustomed to put two and two together – to connect with the tinder-box, which, as deputy-constable, he himself had had the honourable distinction of finding, certain recollections of a pedlar who had called to drink at the house about a month before, and had actually stated that he carried a tinder-box about with him to light his pipe. Here, surely, was a clue to be followed out. And as memory, when duly impregnated with ascertained facts, is sometimes surprisingly fertile, Mr Snell gradually recovered a vivid impression of the effect produced on him by the pedlar's countenance and conversation. He had a 'look with his eye' which fell unpleasantly on Mr Snell's sensitive organism. To be sure, he didn't say anything particular – no, except that about the tinder-box – but it isn't what a man says, it's the way he says it. Moreover, he had a swarthy foreignness of complexion which boded little honesty.

'Did he wear ear-rings?' Mr Crackenthorp wished to know, having some acquaintance with foreign customs.

'Well – stay – let me see,' said Mr Snell, like a docile clairvoyante, who would really not make a mistake if she could help it. After stretching the corners of his mouth and contracting his eyes, as if he were trying to see the ear-rings, he appeared to give up the effort, and said, 'Well, he'd got ear-rings in his box to sell, so it's nat'ral to suppose he might wear 'em. But he called at every house, a'most, in the village; there's somebody else, mayhap, saw 'em in his ears, though I can't take upon me rightly to say.'

Mr Snell was correct in his surmise, that somebody else would remember the pedlar's ear-rings. For on the spread of inquiry among the villagers it was stated with gathering emphasis, that the parson had wanted to know whether the pedlar wore ear-rings in his ears, and an impression was created that a great deal depended on the eliciting of this fact. Of course, every one who heard the question, not having any distinct image of the pedlar as *without* ear-rings, immediately had an image of him *with* ear-rings, larger or smaller, as the case might be; and the image was presently taken for a vivid recollection, so that the glazier's wife, a well-intentioned woman, not given to lying, and whose house was among the cleanest in the village, was ready to declare, as sure as ever she meant to take the sacrament the very next Christmas that was ever coming, that she had seen big ear-rings, in the shape of the young moon, in the pedlar's two ears; while Jinny Oates, the cobbler's daughter, being a more imaginative person, stated not only that she had seen them too, but that they had made her blood creep, as it did at that very moment while there she stood.

Also, by way of throwing further light on this clue of the tinder-box, a collection was made of all the articles purchased from the pedlar at various houses, and carried to the Rainbow to be exhibited there. In fact, there was a general feeling in the village, that for the clearing-up of this robbery there must be a great deal done at the Rainbow, and that no man need offer his wife an excuse for going there while it was the scene of severe public duties.

Some disappointment was felt, and perhaps a little indignation also, when it became known that Silas Marner, on being questioned by the Squire and the parson, had retained no other recollection of the pedlar than that he had called at his door, but had not entered his house, having turned away at once when Silas, holding the door ajar, had said that he wanted nothing. This had been Silas's testimony, though he clutched strongly at the idea of the pedlar's being the culprit, if only because it gave him a definite image of a whereabout for his gold after it had been taken away from its hiding-place: he could see it now in the pedlar's box. But it was observed with some irritation in the village, that anybody but a 'blind creatur' like Marner would have seen the man prowling about, for how came he to leave his tinder-box in the ditch close by, if he hadn't been lingering there? Doubtless, he had made his observations when he saw Marner at the door. Anybody might know – and only look at him – that the weaver was a half-crazy miser. It was a wonder the pedlar hadn't murdered him; men of that sort, with rings in their ears, had been known for murderers often and often; there had been one tried at the 'sizes,[2] not so long ago but what there were people living who remembered it.

Godfrey Cass, indeed, entering the Rainbow during one of Mr Snell's frequently repeated recitals of his testimony, had treated it lightly, stating that he himself had bought a pen-knife of the pedlar, and thought him a merry grinning fellow enough; it was all nonsense, he said, about the man's evil looks. But this was spoken of in the village as the random talk of youth, 'as if it was only Mr Snell who had seen something odd about the pedlar!' On the contrary, there were at least half-a-dozen who were ready to go before Justice Malam, and give in much more striking testimony than any the land-lord could furnish. It was to be hoped Mr Godfrey would not go to Tarley and throw cold water on what Mr Snell said there, and so prevent the justice from drawing up a warrant. He was suspected of intending this, when, after mid-day, he was seen setting off on horse-back in the direction of Tarley.

But by this time Godfrey's interest in the robbery had faded before his growing anxiety about Dunstan and Wildfire, and he was going, not to Tarley, but to Batherley, unable to rest in uncertainty about them any longer. The possibility that Dunstan had played him the ugly trick of riding away with Wildfire, to return at the end of a month, when he had gambled away or otherwise squandered the price of the horse, was a fear that urged itself upon him more, even, than the thought of an accidental injury; and now that the dance at Mrs Osgood's was past, he was irritated with himself that he had trusted his horse to Dunstan. Instead of trying to still his fears he encouraged them, with that superstitious impression which clings to us all, that if we expect evil very strongly it is the less likely to come;

and when he heard a horse approaching at a trot, and saw a hat rising above a hedge beyond an angle of the lane, he felt as if his conjuration had succeeded. But no sooner did the horse come within sight, than his heart sank again. It was not Wildfire; and in a few moments more he discerned that the rider was not Dunstan, but Bryce, who pulled up to speak, with a face that implied something disagreeable.

'Well, Mr Godfrey, that's a lucky brother of yours, that Master Dunsey, isn't he?'

'What do you mean?' said Godfrey, hastily.

'Why, hasn't he been home yet?' said Bryce.

'Home? no. What has happened? Be quick. What has he done with my horse?'

'Ah, I thought it was yours, though he pretended you had parted with it to him.'

'Has he thrown him down and broken his knees?' said Godfrey, flushed with exasperation.

'Worse than that,' said Bryce. 'You see, I'd made a bargain with him to buy the horse for a hundred and twenty – a swinging³ price, but I always liked the horse. And what does he do but go and stake him – fly at a hedge with stakes in it, atop of a bank with a ditch before it. The horse had been dead a pretty good while when he was found. So he hasn't been home since, has he?'

'Home? no,' said Godfrey, 'and he'd better keep away. Confound me for a fool! I might have known this would be the end of it.'

'Well, to tell you the truth,' said Bryce, 'after I'd bargained for the horse, it did come into my head that he might be riding and selling the horse without your knowledge, for I didn't believe it was his own. I knew Master Dunsey was up to his tricks sometimes. But where can he be gone? He's never been seen at Batherley. He couldn't have been hurt, for he must have walked off.'

'Hurt?' said Godfrey, bitterly. 'He'll never be hurt – he's made to hurt other people.'

'And so you *did* give him leave to sell the horse, eh?' said Bryce.

'Yes; I wanted to part with the horse – he was always a little too hard in the mouth for me,' said Godfrey; his pride making him wince under the idea that Bryce guessed the sale to be a matter of necessity. 'I was going to see after him – I thought some mischief had happened. I'll go back now,' he added, turning the horse's head, and wishing he could get rid of Bryce; for he felt that the long-dreaded crisis in his life was close upon him. 'You're coming on to Raveloe, aren't you?'

'Well, no, not now,' said Bryce. 'I *was* coming round there, for I had to go to Flitton, and I thought I might as well take you in my way, and just let you know all I knew myself about the horse. I suppose Master Dunsey didn't like to show himself till the ill news had blown over a bit. He's perhaps gone to pay a visit at the Three Crowns, by Whitbridge – I know he's fond of the house.'

'Perhaps he is,' said Godfrey, rather absently. Then rousing himself, he said, with an effort at carelessness, 'We shall hear of him soon enough, I'll be bound.'

'Well, here's my turning,' said Bryce, not surprised to perceive that Godfrey was rather 'down;' 'so I'll bid you good-day, and wish I may bring you better news another time.'

Godfrey rode along slowly, representing to himself the scene of confession to his father from which he felt that there was now no longer any escape. The revelation about the money must be made the very next morning; and if he withheld the rest, Dunstan would be sure to come back shortly, and, finding that he must bear the brunt of his father's anger, would tell the whole story out of spite, even though he had nothing to gain by it. There was one step, perhaps, by which he might still win Dunstan's silence and put off the evil day: he might tell his father that he had himself spent the money paid to him by Fowler; and as he had never been guilty of such an offence before, the affair would blow over after a little storming. But Godfrey could not bend himself to this. He felt that in letting Dunstan have the money, he had already been guilty of a breach of trust hardly less culpable than that of spending the money directly for his own behoof; and yet there was a distinction between the two acts which made him feel that the one was so much more blackening than the other as to be intolerable to him.

'I don't pretend to be a good fellow,' he said to himself; 'but I'm not a scoundrel – at least, I'll stop short somewhere. I'll bear the consequences of what I *have* done sooner than make believe I've done what I never would have done. I'd never have spent the money for my own pleasure – I was tortured into it.'

Through the remainder of this day Godfrey, with only occasional fluctuations, kept his will bent in the direction of a complete avowal to his father, and he withheld the story of Wildfire's loss till the next morning, that it might serve him as an introduction to heavier matter. The old Squire was accustomed to his son's frequent absence from home, and thought neither Dunstan's nor Wildfire's non-appearance a matter calling for remark. Godfrey said to himself again and again, that if he let slip this one opportunity of confession, he might never have another; the revelation might be made even in a more odious way than by Dunstan's malignity: *she* might come as she had threatened to do. And then he tried to make the scene easier to himself by rehearsal: he made up his mind how he would pass from the admission of his weakness in letting Dunstan have the money to the fact that Dunstan had a hold on him which he had been unable to shake off, and how he would work up his father to expect something very bad before he told him the fact. The old Squire was an implacable man: he made resolutions in violent anger, and he was not to be moved from them after his anger had subsided – as fiery volcanic matters cool and harden into rock. Like many violent and implacable men, he allowed evils to grow under favour of his own heedlessness, till they pressed upon him with exasperating force, and then he turned round with fierce severity and became unrelentingly hard. This was his system with his tenants: he allowed them to get into arrears, neglect their fences, reduce their stock, sell their straw, and otherwise go the wrong way, – and then, when he became short of money in consequence of this indulgence, he took the hardest measures and would listen to no appeal. Godfrey knew all this, and felt it with the greater force because he had constantly suffered annoyance from witnessing his father's sudden fits of unrelentingness, for which his own habitual irresolution deprived him of all sympathy. (He was not critical on the faulty indulgence which preceded these fits; *that* seemed to him natural enough.) Still there was just the chance, Godfrey thought, that his father's pride might see this marriage in a light that would induce him to hush it up, rather than turn his son out and make the family the talk of the country for ten miles round.

This was the view of the case that Godfrey managed to keep before him pretty closely till midnight, and he went to sleep thinking that he had done with inward debating. But when he awoke in the still morning darkness he found it impossible to reawaken his evening thoughts; it was as if they had been tired out and were not to be roused to further work. Instead of arguments for confession, he could now feel the presence of nothing but its evil consequences: the old dread of disgrace came back – the old shrinking from the thought of raising a hopeless barrier between himself and Nancy – the old disposition to rely on chances which might be favourable to him, and save him from betrayal. Why, after all, should he cut off the hope of them by his own act? He had seen the matter in a wrong light yesterday. He had been in a rage with Dunstan, and had thought of nothing but a thorough break-up of their mutual understanding; but what it would be really wisest for him to do, was to try and soften his father's anger against Dunsey, and keep things as nearly as possible in their old condition. If Dunsey did not come back for a few days (and Godfrey did not know but that the rascal had enough money in his pocket to enable him to keep away still longer), everything might blow over.

CHAPTER 9

Godfrey rose and took his own breakfast earlier than usual, but lingered in the wainscoted parlour till his younger brothers had finished their meal and gone out; awaiting his father, who always took a walk with his managing-man¹ before breakfast. Every one breakfasted at a different hour in the Red House, and the Squire was always the latest, giving a long chance to a rather feeble morning appetite before he tried it. The table had been spread with substantial eatables nearly two hours before he presented himself – a tall, stout man of sixty, with a face in which the knit brow and rather hard glance seemed contradicted by the slack and feeble mouth. His person showed marks of habitual neglect, his dress was slovenly; and yet there was something in the presence of the old Squire distinguishable from that of the ordinary farmers in the parish, who were perhaps every whit as refined as he, but, having slouched their way through life with a consciousness of being in the vicinity of their 'betters,' wanted that self-possession and authoritativeness of voice and carriage which belonged to a man who thought of superiors as remote existences with whom he had personally little more to do than with America or the stars. The Squire had been used to parish homage all his life, used to the presupposition that his family, his tankards, and everything that was his, were the oldest and best; and as he never associated with any gentry higher than himself, his opinion was not disturbed by comparison.

He glanced at his son as he entered the room, and said, 'What, sir! haven't *you* had your breakfast yet?' but there was no pleasant morning greeting between them; not because of any unfriendliness, but because the sweet flower of courtesy is not a growth of such homes as the Red House.

'Yes, sir,' said Godfrey, 'I've had my breakfast, but I was waiting to speak to you.'

'Ah! well,' said the Squire, throwing himself indifferently into his chair, and speaking in a ponderous coughing fashion, which was felt in Raveloe to be a sort of privilege of his rank, while he cut a piece of beef, and held it up before the deer-hound that had come in with him. 'Ring the bell for my ale, will you? You youngsters' business is your own pleasure, mostly. There's no hurry about it for anybody but yourselves.'

The Squire's life was quite as idle as his sons', but it was a fiction kept up by himself and his contemporaries in Raveloe that youth was exclusively the period of folly, and that their aged wisdom was constantly in a state of endurance mitigated by sarcasm. Godfrey waited, before he spoke again, until the ale had been brought and the door closed – an interval during which Fleet, the deer-hound, had consumed enough bits of beef to make a poor man's holiday dinner.

'There's been a cursed piece of ill-luck with Wildfire,' he began; 'happened the day before yesterday.'

'What! broke his knees?' said the Squire, after taking a draught of ale. 'I thought you knew how to ride better than that, sir. I never threw a horse down in my life. If I had, I might ha' whistled for another, for *my* father wasn't quite so ready to unstring² as some other fathers I know of. But they must turn over a new leaf – *they* must. What with mortgages and arrears, I'm as short o' cash as a roadside pauper. And that fool Kimble says the newspaper's talking about peace. Why, the country wouldn't have a leg to stand on. Prices 'ud run down like a jack,³ and I should never get my arrears, not if I sold all the fellows up. And there's that damned Fowler, I won't put up with him any longer; I've told Winthrop to go to Cox this very day. The lying scoundrel told me he'd be sure to pay me a hundred last month. He takes advantage because he's on that outlying farm, and thinks I shall forget him.'

The Squire had delivered this speech in a coughing and interrupted manner, but with no pause long enough for Godfrey to make it a pretext for taking up the word again. He felt that his father meant to ward off any request for money on the ground of the misfortune with Wildfire, and that the emphasis he had thus been led to lay on his shortness of cash and his arrears was likely to produce an attitude of mind the most unfavourable for his own disclosure. But he must go on, now he had begun.

'It's worse than breaking the horse's knees – he's been staked and killed,' he said, as soon as his father was silent, and had begun to cut his meat. 'But I wasn't thinking of asking you to buy me another horse; I was only thinking I'd lost the means of paying you with the price of Wildfire, as I'd meant to do. Dunsey took him to the hunt to sell him for me the other day, and after he'd made a bargain for a hundred and twenty with Bryce, he went after the hounds, and took some fool's leap or other that did for the horse at once. If it hadn't been for that, I should have paid you a hundred pounds this morning.'

The Squire had laid down his knife and fork, and was staring at his son in amazement, not being sufficiently quick of brain to form a probable guess as to what could have caused so strange an inversion of the paternal and filial relations as this proposition of his son to pay him a hundred pounds.

'The truth is, sir – I'm very sorry – I was quite to blame,' said Godfrey. 'Fowler did pay that hundred pounds. He paid it to me, when I was over there one day last month. And Dunsey bothered me for the money, and I let him have it, because I hoped I should be able to pay it you before this.'

The Squire was purple with anger before his son had done speaking, and found utterance difficult. 'You let Dunsey have it, sir? And how long have you been so thick with Dunsey that you must *collogue*⁴ with him to embezzle my money? Are you turning out a scamp? I tell you I won't have it. I'll turn the whole pack of you out of the house together, and marry again. I'd have you to remember, sir, my property's got no entail⁵ on it; – since my grandfather's time the Casses can do as they like with their land. Remember that, sir. Let Dunsey have the money! Why should you let Dunsey have the money? There's some lie at the bottom of it.'

'There's no lie, sir,' said Godfrey. 'I wouldn't have spent the money myself, but Dunsey bothered me, and I was a fool, and let him have it. But I meant to pay it, whether he did or not. That's the whole story. I never meant to embezzle money, and I'm not the man to do it. You never knew me do a dishonest trick, sir.'

'Where's Dunsey, then? What do you stand talking there for? Go and fetch Dunsey, as I tell you, and let him give account of what he wanted the money for, and what he's done with it. He shall repent it. I'll turn him out. I said I would, and I'll do it. He shan't brave me. Go and fetch him.'

'Dunsey isn't come back, sir.'

'What! did he break his own neck, then?' said the Squire, with some disgust at the idea that, in that case, he could not fulfil his threat.

'No, he wasn't hurt, I believe, for the horse was found dead, and Dunsey must have walked off. I daresay we shall see him again by-and-by. I don't know where he is.'

'And what must you be letting him have my money for? Answer me that,' said the Squire, attacking Godfrey again, since Dunsey was not within reach.

'Well, sir, I don't know,' said Godfrey, hesitatingly. That was a feeble evasion, but Godfrey was not fond of lying, and, not being sufficiently aware that no sort of duplicity can long flourish without the help of vocal falsehoods, he was quite unprepared with invented motives.

'You don't know? I tell you what it is, sir. You've been up to some trick, and you've been bribing him not to tell,' said the Squire, with a sudden acuteness which startled Godfrey, who felt his heart beat violently at the nearness of his father's guess. The sudden alarm pushed him on to take the next step – a very slight impulse suffices for that on a downward road.

'Why, sir,' he said, trying to speak with careless ease, 'it was a little affair between me and Dunsey; it's no matter to anybody else. It's hardly worth while to pry into young men's fooleries: it wouldn't have made any difference to you, sir, if I'd not had the bad luck to lose Wildfire. I should have paid you the money.'

'Fooleries! Pshaw! it's time you'd done with fooleries. And I'd have you know, sir, you *must* ha' done with 'em,' said the Squire, frowning and casting an angry glance at his son. 'Your goings-on are not what I shall find money for any longer. There's my grandfather had his stables full o' horses, and kept a good house, too, and in worse times, by what I can make out; and so might I, if I hadn't four good-for-nothing fellows to hang on me like horse-leeches. I've been too good a father to you all – that's what it is. But I shall pull up, sir.'

Godfrey was silent. He was not likely to be very penetrating in his judgments, but he had always had a sense that his father's indulgence had not been kindness, and had had a vague longing for some discipline that would have checked his own errant weakness and helped his better will. The Squire ate his bread and meat hastily, took a deep draught of ale, then turned his chair from the table, and began to speak again.

'It'll be all the worse for you, you know – you'd need try and help me keep things together.'

'Well, sir, I've often offered to take the management of things, but you know you've taken it ill always, and seemed to think I wanted to push you out of your place.'

'I know nothing o' your offering or o' my taking it ill,' said the Squire, whose memory consisted in certain strong impressions un- modified by detail; 'but I know, one while you seemed to be thinking o' marrying, and I didn't offer to put any obstacles in your way, as some fathers would. I'd as lieve⁶ you married Lammeter's daughter as anybody. I suppose, if I'd said you nay, you'd ha' kept on with it; but, for want o' contradiction, you've changed your mind. You're a shilly- shally⁷ fellow: you take after your poor mother. She never had a will of her own; a woman has no call for one, if she's got a proper man for her husband. But *your* wife had need have one, for you hardly know your own mind enough to make both your legs walk one way. The lass hasn't said downright she won't have you, has she?'

'No,' said Godfrey, feeling very hot and uncomfortable; 'but I don't think she will.'

'Think! why haven't you the courage to ask her? Do you stick to it, you want to have *her* – that's the thing?'

'There's no other woman I want to marry,' said Godfrey, evasively.

'Well, then, let me make the offer for you, that's all, if you haven't the pluck to do it yourself. Lammeter isn't likely to be loath for his daughter to marry into *my* family, I should think. And as for the pretty lass, she wouldn't have her cousin – and there's nobody else, as I see, could ha' stood in your way.'

'I'd rather let it be, please sir, at present,' said Godfrey, in alarm. 'I think she's a little offended with me just now, and I should like to speak for myself. A man must manage these things for himself.'

'Well, speak, then, and manage it, and see if you can't turn over a new leaf. That's what a man must do when he thinks o' marrying.'

'I don't see how I can think of it at present, sir. You wouldn't like to settle me on one of the farms, I suppose, and I don't think she'd come to live in this house with all my brothers. It's a different sort of life to what she's been used to.'

'Not come to live in this house? Don't tell me. You ask her, that's all,' said the Squire, with a short, scornful laugh.

'I'd rather let the thing be, at present, sir,' said Godfrey. 'I hope you won't try to hurry it on by saying anything.'

'I shall do what I choose,' said the Squire, 'and I shall let you know I'm master; else you may turn out, and find an estate to drop into somewhere else. Go out and tell Winthrop not to go to Cox's, but wait for me. And tell 'em to get my horse saddled. And stop: look out and get that hack o' Dunsey's sold, and hand me the money, will you? He'll keep no more hacks at my expense. And if you know where he's sneaking – I daresay you do – you may tell him to spare himself the journey o' coming back home. Let him turn ostler,[8] and keep himself. He shan't hang on me any more.'

'I don't know where he is; and if I did, it isn't my place to tell him to keep away,' said Godfrey, moving towards the door.

'Confound it, sir, don't stay arguing, but go and order my horse,' said the Squire, taking up a pipe.

Godfrey left the room, hardly knowing whether he were more relieved by the sense that the interview was ended without having made any change in his position, or more uneasy that he had entangled himself still further in prevarication and deceit. What had passed about his proposing to Nancy had raised a new alarm, lest by some after-dinner words of his father's to Mr Lammeter he should be thrown into the embarrassment of being obliged absolutely to decline her when she seemed to be within his reach. He fled to his usual refuge, that of hoping for some unforeseen turn of fortune, some favourable chance which would save him from unpleasant consequences – perhaps even justify his insincerity by manifesting its prudence.

In this point of trusting to some throw of fortune's dice, Godfrey can hardly be called old-fashioned. Favourable Chance is the god of all men who follow their own devices instead of obeying a law they believe in. Let even a polished man of these days get into a position he is ashamed to avow, and his mind will be bent on all the possible issues that may deliver him from the calculable results of that position. Let him live outside his income, or shirk the resolute honest work that brings wages, and he will presently find himself dreaming of a possible benefactor, a possible simpleton who may be cajoled into using his interest, a possible state of mind in some possible person not yet forthcoming. Let him neglect the responsibilities of his office, and he will inevitably anchor himself on the chance, that the thing left undone may turn out not to be of the supposed importance. Let him betray his friend's confidence, and he will adore that same cunning complexity called Chance, which gives him the hope that his friend will never know. Let him forsake a decent craft that he may pursue the gentilities of a profession to which nature never called him, and his religion will infallibly be the worship of blessed Chance, which he will believe in as the mighty creator of success. The evil principle deprecated in that religion, is the orderly sequence by which the seed brings forth a crop after its kind.[9]

CHAPTER 10

Justice Malam was naturally regarded in Tarley and Raveloe as a man of capacious mind, seeing that he could draw much wider conclusions without evidence than could be expected of his neighbours who were not on the Commission of the Peace.[1] Such a man was not likely to neglect the clue of the tinder-box, and an inquiry was set on foot concerning a pedlar, name unknown, with curly black hair and a foreign complexion, carrying a box of cutlery and jewellery, and wearing large rings in his ears. But either because inquiry was too slow-footed to overtake him, or because the description applied to so many pedlars that inquiry did not know how to choose among them, weeks passed away, and there was no other result concerning the robbery than a gradual cessation of the excitement it had caused in Raveloe. Dunstan Cass's absence was hardly a subject of remark: he had once before had a quarrel with his father, and had gone off, nobody knew whither, to return at the end of six weeks, take up his old quarters unforbidden and swagger as usual. His own family, who equally expected this issue, with the sole difference that the Squire was determined this time to forbid him the old quarters, never mentioned his absence; and when his uncle Kimble or Mr Osgood noticed it, the story of his having killed Wildfire and committed some offence against his father was enough to prevent surprise. To connect the fact of Dunsey's disappearance with that of the robbery occurring on the same day, lay quite away from the track of every one's thought – even Godfrey's, who had better reason than any one else to know what his brother was capable of. He remembered no mention of the weaver between them since the time, twelve years ago, when it was their boyish sport to deride him; and, besides, his imagination constantly created an *alibi* for Dunstan: he saw him continually in some congenial haunt, to which he had walked off on leaving Wildfire – saw him sponging on chance acquaintances, and meditating a return home to the old amusement of tormenting his elder brother. Even if any brain in Raveloe had put the said two facts together, I doubt whether a combination so injurious to the prescriptive respectability of a family with a mural monument and venerable tankards, would not have been suppressed as of unsound tendency. But Christmas puddings, brawn,[2] and abundance of spirituous liquors, throwing the mental originality into the channel of nightmare, are great preservatives against a dangerous spontaneity of waking thought.

When the robbery was talked of at the Rainbow and elsewhere, in good company, the balance continued to waver between the rational explanation founded on the tinder-box, and the theory of an impenetrable mystery that mocked investigation. The advocates of the tinder-box-and-pedlar view considered the other side a muddle-headed and credulous set, who, because they themselves were wall-eyed,[3] supposed everybody else to have the same blank outlook; and the adherents of the inexplicable more than hinted that their antagonists were animals inclined to crow before they had found any corn – mere skimming-dishes[4] in point of depth – whose clear-sightedness consisted in supposing there was nothing behind a barn-door because they couldn't see through it; so that, though their controversy did not serve to elicit the fact concerning the robbery, it elicited some true opinions of collateral importance.

But while poor Silas's loss served thus to brush the slow current of Raveloe conversation, Silas himself was feeling the withering desolation of that bereavement about which his neighbours were arguing at their ease. To any one who had observed him before he lost his gold, it might have seemed that so withered and shrunken a life as his could hardly be susceptible of a bruise, could hardly endure any subtraction but such as would put an end to it altogether. But in reality it had been an eager life, filled with immediate purpose which fenced him in from the wide, cheerless unknown. It had been a clinging life; and though the object round which its fibres had clung was a dead disrupted thing, it satisfied the need for clinging. But now the fence was broken down – the support was snatched away. Marner's thoughts could no longer move in their old round, and were baffled by a blank like that which meets a plodding ant when the earth has broken away on its homeward path. The loom was there, and the weaving, and the growing pattern in the cloth; but the bright treasure in the hole under his feet was gone; the prospect of handling and counting it was gone: the evening had no phantasm of delight to still the poor soul's craving. The thought of the money he would get by

his actual work could bring no joy, for its meagre image was only a
fresh reminder of his loss; and hope was too heavily crushed by the
sudden blow, for his imagination to dwell on the growth of a new
hoard from that small beginning.

He filled up the blank with grief. As he sat weaving, he every now
and then moaned low, like one in pain: it was the sign that his
thoughts had come round again to the sudden chasm – to the empty
evening time. And all the evening, as he sat in his loneliness by his
dull fire, he leaned his elbows on his knees, and clasped his head with
his hands, and moaned very low – not as one who seeks to be heard.

And yet he was not utterly forsaken in his trouble. The repulsion
Marner had always created in his neighbours was partly dissipated by
the new light in which this misfortune had shown him. Instead of a
man who had more cunning than honest folks could come by, and,
what was worse, had not the inclination to use that cunning in a
neighbourly way, it was now apparent that Silas had not cunning
enough to keep his own. He was generally spoken of as a 'poor
mushed creatur;' and that avoidance of his neighbours, which had
before been referred to his ill-will and to a probable addiction to
worse company, was now considered mere craziness.

This change to a kindlier feeling was shown in various ways. The
odour of Christmas cooking being on the wind, it was the season
when superfluous pork and black puddings are suggestive of charity
in well-to-do families; and Silas's misfortune had brought him uppermost in the memory of housekeepers like Mrs Osgood. Mr Crackenthorp, too, while he admonished Silas that his money had probably
been taken from him because he thought too much of it and never
came to church, enforced the doctrine by a present of pigs' pettitoes,⁵
well calculated to dissipate unfounded prejudices against the clerical
character. Neighbours who had nothing but verbal consolation to give
showed a disposition not only to greet Silas and discuss his misfortune at some length when they encountered him in the village, but
also to take the trouble of calling at his cottage and getting him to
repeat all the details on the very spot; and then they would try to
cheer him by saying, 'Well, Master Marner, you're no worse off nor
other poor folks, after all; and if you was to be crippled, the parish 'ud
give you a 'lowance.'

I suppose one reason why we are seldom able to comfort our

neighbours with our words is that our goodwill gets adulterated, in spite of ourselves, before it can pass our lips. We can send black puddings and pettitoes without giving them a flavour of our own egoism; but language is a stream that is almost sure to smack of a mingled soil. There was a fair proportion of kindness in Raveloe; but it was often of a beery and bungling sort, and took the shape least allied to the complimentary and hypocritical.

Mr Macey, for example, coming one evening expressly to let Silas know that recent events had given him the advantage of standing more favourably in the opinion of a man whose judgment was not formed lightly, opened the conversation by saying, as soon as he had seated himself and adjusted his thumbs –

'Come, Master Marner, why, you've no call to sit a-moaning. You're a deal better off to ha' lost your money, nor to ha' kep it by foul means. I used to think, when you first come into these parts, as you were no better nor you should be; you were younger a deal than what you are now; but you were allays a staring, white-faced creatur, partly like a bald-faced calf, as I may say. But there's no knowing: it isn't every queer-looksed thing as Old Harry's had the making of – I mean, speaking o' toads and such; for they're often harmless, and useful against varmin. And it's pretty much the same wi' you, as fur as I can see. Though as to the yarbs⁶ and stuff to cure the breathing, if you brought that sort o' knowledge from distant parts, you might ha' been a bit freer of it. And if the knowledge wasn't well come by, why, you might ha' made up for it by coming to church reg'lar; for as for the children as the Wise Woman charmed, I've been at the christening of 'em again and again, and they took the water⁷ just as well. And that's reasonable; for if Old Harry's a mind to do a bit o' kindness for a holiday, like, who's got anything against it? That's my thinking; and I've been clerk o' this parish forty year, and I know, when the parson and me does the cussing of a Ash Wednesday,⁸ there's no cussing o' folks as have a mind to be cured without a doctor, let Kimble say what he will. And so, Master Marner, as I was saying – for there's windings i' things as they may carry you to the fur end o' the prayer-book afore you get back to 'em – my advice is, as you keep up your sperrits; for as for thinking you're a deep un, and ha' got more inside you nor 'ull bear daylight, I'm not o' that opinion at all, and so I tell the neighbours. For, says I, you talk o' Master Marner making out a tale – why, it's nonsense, that is: it 'ud take a 'cute man to make a tale like that; and, says I, he looked as scared as a rabbit.'

During this discursive address Silas had continued motionless in his previous attitude, leaning his elbows on his knees, and pressing his hands against his head. Mr Macey, not doubting that he had been listened to, paused, in the expectation of some appreciatory reply, but Marner remained silent. He had a sense that the old man meant to be good-natured and neighbourly; but the kindness fell on him as sunshine falls on the wretched – he had no heart to taste it, and felt that it was very far off him.

'Come, Master Marner, have you got nothing to say to that?' said Mr Macey at last, with a slight accent of impatience.

'Oh,' said Marner, slowly, shaking his head between his hands, 'I thank you – thank you – kindly.'

'Ay, ay, to be sure: I thought you would,' said Mr Macey; 'and my advice is – have you got a Sunday suit?'

'No,' said Marner.

'I doubted it was so,' said Mr Macey. 'Now, let me advise you to get a Sunday suit: there's Tookey, he's a poor creatur, but he's got my tailoring business, and some o' my money in it, and he shall make a suit at a low price, and give you trust,' and then you can come to church, and be a bit neighbourly. Why, you've never heared me say "Amen" since you come into these parts, and I recommend you to lose no time, for it'll be poor work when Tookey has it all to himself, for I mayn't be equil to stand i' the desk at all, come another winter.' Here Mr Macey paused, perhaps expecting some sign of emotion in his hearer; but not observing any, he went on. 'And as for the money for the suit o' clothes, why, you get a matter of a pound a-week at your weaving, Master Marner, and you're a young man, eh, for all you look so mushed. Why, you couldn't ha' been five-and-twenty when you come into these parts, eh?'

Silas started a little at the change to a questioning tone, and answered mildly, 'I don't know; I can't rightly say – it's a long while since.'

After receiving such an answer as this, it is not surprising that Mr Macey observed, later on in the evening at the Rainbow, that Marner's head was 'all of a muddle,' and that it was to be doubted if he ever knew when Sunday came round, which showed him a worse heathen than many a dog.

Another of Silas's comforters,[10] besides Mr Macey, came to him with a mind highly charged on the same topic. This was Mrs Winthrop, the wheelwright's wife. The inhabitants of Raveloe were not severely regular in their church-going, and perhaps there was hardly a person in the parish who would not have held that to go to church every Sunday in the calendar would have shown a greedy desire to stand well with Heaven, and get an undue advantage over their neighbours – a wish to be better than the 'common run,' that would have implied a reflection on those who had had godfathers and godmothers as well as themselves, and had an equal right to the burying-service. At the same time, it was understood to be requisite for all who were not household servants, or young men, to take the sacrament[11] at one of the great festivals: Squire Cass himself took it on Christmas-day; while those who were held to be 'good livers' went to church with greater, though still with moderate, frequency.

Mrs Winthrop was one of these: she was in all respects a woman of scrupulous conscience, so eager for duties that life seemed to offer them too scantily unless she rose at half-past four, though this threw a scarcity of work over the more advanced hours of the morning, which it was a constant problem with her to remove. Yet she had not the vixenish temper which is sometimes supposed to be a necessary condition of such habits: she was a very mild, patient woman, whose nature it was to seek out all the sadder and more serious elements of life, and pasture her mind upon them. She was the person always first thought of in Raveloe when there was illness or death in a family, when leeches were to be applied, or there was a sudden disappointment in a monthly nurse.[12] She was a 'comfortable woman' – good-looking, fresh-complexioned, having her lips always slightly screwed, as if she felt herself in a sick-room with the doctor or the clergyman present. But she was never whimpering; no one had seen her shed tears; she was simply grave and inclined to shake her head and sigh, almost imperceptibly, like a funereal mourner who is not a relation. It seemed surprising that Ben Winthrop, who loved his quart-pot and his joke, got along so well with Dolly; but she took her husband's jokes and joviality as patiently as everything else, considering that 'men *would* be so,' and viewing the stronger sex in the light of animals whom it had pleased Heaven to make naturally troublesome, like bulls and turkey-cocks.

This good wholesome woman could hardly fail to have her mind drawn strongly towards Silas Marner, now that he appeared in the light of a sufferer; and one Sunday afternoon she took her little boy Aaron with her, and went to call on Silas, carrying in her hand some small lard-cakes,[13] flat paste-like articles much esteemed in Raveloe. Aaron, an apple-cheeked youngster of seven, with a clean starched frill which looked like a plate for the apples, needed all his adventurous curiosity to embolden him against the possibility that the big-eyed weaver might do him some bodily injury; and his dubiety was much increased when, on arriving at the Stone-pits, they heard the mysterious sound of the loom.

'Ah, it is as I thought,' said Mrs Winthrop, sadly.

They had to knock loudly before Silas heard them; but when he did come to the door he showed no impatience, as he would once have done, at a visit that had been unasked for and unexpected. Formerly, his heart had been as a locked casket with its treasure inside; but now the casket was empty, and the lock was broken. Left groping in darkness, with his prop utterly gone, Silas had inevitably a sense, though a dull and half-despairing one, that if any help came to him it must come from without; and there was a slight stirring of expectation at the sight of his fellow-men, a faint consciousness of dependence on their goodwill. He opened the door wide to admit Dolly, but without otherwise returning her greeting than by moving the armchair a few inches as a sign that she was to sit down in it. Dolly, as soon as she was seated, removed the white cloth that covered her lard-cakes, and said in her gravest way –

'I'd a baking yesterday, Master Marner, and the lard-cakes turned out better nor common, and I'd ha' asked you to accept some, if you'd thought well. I don't eat such things myself, for a bit o' bread's what I like from one year's end to the other; but men's stomichs are made so comical, they want a change – they do, I know, God help 'em.'

Dolly sighed gently as she held out the cakes to Silas, who thanked her kindly and looked very close at them, absently, being accustomed to look so at everything he took into his hand – eyed all the while by the wondering bright orbs of the small Aaron, who had made an outwork of his mother's chair, and was peeping round from behind it.

'There's letters pricked on 'em,' said Dolly. 'I can't read 'em myself, and there's nobody, not Mr Macey himself, rightly knows what they mean; but they've a good meaning, for they're the same as is on the pulpit-cloth at church. What are they, Aaron, my dear?'

Aaron retreated completely behind his outwork.

'Oh go, that's naughty,' said his mother, mildly. 'Well, whativer the letters are, they've a good meaning; and it's a stamp as has been in our house, Ben says, ever since he was a little un, and his mother used to put it on the cakes, and I've allays put it on too; for if there's any good, we've need of it i' this world.'

'It's I. H. S.,'[4] said Silas, at which proof of learning Aaron peeped round the chair again.

'Well, to be sure, you can read 'em off,' said Dolly. 'Ben's read 'em to me many and many a time, but they slip out o' my mind again; the more's the pity, for they're good letters, else they wouldn't be in the church; and so I prick 'em on all the loaves and all the cakes, though sometimes they won't hold, because o' the rising – for, as I said, if there's any good to be got we've need of it i' this world – that we have; and I hope they'll bring good to you, Master Marner, for it's wi' that will I brought you the cakes; and you see the letters have held better nor common.'

Silas was as unable to interpret the letters as Dolly, but there was no possibility of misunderstanding the desire to give comfort that made itself heard in her quiet tones. He said, with more feeling than before – 'Thank you – thank you kindly.' But he laid down the cakes and seated himself absently – drearily unconscious of any distinct benefit towards which the cakes and the letters, or even Dolly's kindness, could tend for him.

'Ah, if there's good anywhere, we've need of it,' repeated Dolly, who did not lightly forsake a serviceable phrase. She looked at Silas pityingly as she went on. 'But you didn't hear the church-bells this morning, Master Marner? I doubt you didn't know it was Sunday. Living so lone here, you lose your count, I daresay; and then, when your loom makes a noise, you can't hear the bells, more partic'lar now the frost kills the sound.'

'Yes, I did; I heard 'em,' said Silas, to whom Sunday bells were a mere accident of the day, and not part of its sacredness. There had been no bells in Lantern Yard.

'Dear heart!' said Dolly, pausing before she spoke again. 'But what a pity it is you should work of a Sunday, and not clean yourself – if you *didn't* go to church; for if you'd a roasting bit, it might be as you couldn't leave it, being a lone man. But there's the bakehus,[15] if you could make up your mind to spend a twopence on the oven now and then, – not every week, in course – I shouldn't like to do that myself, – you might carry your bit o' dinner there, for it's nothing but right to have a bit o' summat hot of a Sunday, and not to make it as you can't know your dinner from Saturday. But now, upo' Christmas-day, this blessed Christmas as is ever coming, if you was to take your dinner to the bakehus, and go to church, and see the holly and the yew, and hear the anthim, and then take the sacramen', you'd be a deal the better, and you'd know which end you stood on, and you could put your trust i' Them as knows better nor we do, seein' you'd ha' done what it lies on us all to do.'

Dolly's exhortation, which was an unusually long effort of speech for her, was uttered in the soothing persuasive tone with which she would have tried to prevail on a sick man to take his medicine, or a basin of gruel for which he had no appetite. Silas had never before been closely urged on the point of his absence from church, which had only been thought of as a part of his general queerness; and he was too direct and simple to evade Dolly's appeal.

'Nay, nay,' he said, 'I know nothing o' church. I've never been to church.'

'No!' said Dolly, in a low tone of wonderment. Then bethinking herself of Silas's advent from an unknown country, she said, 'Could it ha' been as they'd no church where you was born?'

'Oh yes,' said Silas, meditatively, sitting in his usual posture of leaning on his knees, and supporting his head. 'There was churches – a many – it was a big town. But I knew nothing of 'em – I went to chapel.'

Dolly was much puzzled at this new word, but she was rather afraid of inquiring further, lest 'chapel' might mean some haunt of wickedness. After a little thought, she said –

'Well, Master Marner, it's niver too late to turn over a new leaf, and if you've niver had no church, there's no telling the good it 'll do you. For I feel so set up and comfortable as niver was, when I've been and heard the prayers, and the singing to the praise and glory o' God, as Mr Macey gives out – and Mr Crackenthorp saying good words, and more partic'lar on Sacramen' Day;[16] and if a bit o' trouble comes, I feel as I can put up wi' it, for I've looked for help i' the right quarter, and gev myself up to Them as we must all give ourselves up to at the last; and if we 'n done our part, it isn't to be believed as Them as are above us 'ull be worse nor we are, and come short o' Their'n.'

Poor Dolly's exposition of her simple Raveloe theology fell rather unmeaningly on Silas's ears, for there was no word in it that could rouse a memory of what he had known as religion, and his comprehension was quite baffled by the plural pronoun, which was no heresy of Dolly's, but only her way of avoiding a presumptuous familiarity. He remained silent, not feeling inclined to assent to the part of Dolly's speech which he fully understood – her recommendation that he should go to church. Indeed, Silas was so unaccustomed to talk beyond the brief questions and answers necessary for the transaction of his simple business, that words did not easily come to him without the urgency of a distinct purpose.

But now, little Aaron, having become used to the weaver's awful presence, had advanced to his mother's side, and Silas, seeming to notice him for the first time, tried to return Dolly's signs of good-will by offering the lad a bit of lard-cake. Aaron shrank back a little, and rubbed his head against his mother's shoulder, but still thought the piece of cake worth the risk of putting his hand out for it.

'Oh, for shame, Aaron,' said his mother, taking him on her lap, however; 'why, you don't want cake again yet awhile. He's wonderful hearty,' she went on, with a little sigh – 'that he is, God knows. He's my youngest, and we spoil him sadly, for either me or the father must allays hev him in our sight – that we must.'

She stroked Aaron's brown head, and thought it must do Master Marner good to see such a 'pictur of a child.' But Marner, on the other side of the hearth, saw the neat-featured rosy face as a mere dim round, with two dark spots in it.

'And he's got a voice like a bird – you wouldn't think,' Dolly went on; 'he can sing a Christmas carril as his father's taught him; and I take it for a token as he'll come to good, as he can learn the good tunes so quick. Come, Aaron, stan' up and sing the carril to Master Marner, come.'

Aaron replied by rubbing his forehead against his mother's shoulder.

'Oh, that's naughty,' said Dolly, gently. 'Stan' up, when mother tells you, and let me hold the cake till you've done.'

Aaron was not indisposed to display his talents, even to an ogre, under protecting circumstances; and after a few more signs of coyness, consisting chiefly in rubbing the backs of his hands over his eyes, and then peeping between them at Master Marner, to see if he looked anxious for the 'carril,' he at length allowed his head to be duly adjusted, and standing behind the table, which let him appear above it only as far as his broad frill, so that he looked like a cherubic head untroubled with a body, he began with a clear chirp, and in a melody that had the rhythm of an industrious hammer –

> 'God rest you, merry gentlemen,
> Let nothing you dismay,
> For Jesus Christ our Saviour
> Was born on Christmas-day.'[7]

Dolly listened with a devout look, glancing at Marner in some confidence that this strain would help to allure him to church.

'That's Christmas music,' she said, when Aaron had ended, and had secured his piece of cake again. 'There's no other music equil to the Christmas music – "Hark the erol angils sing."[18] And you may judge what it is at church, Master Marner, with the bassoon and the voices, as you can't help thinking you've got to a better place a'ready – for I wouldn't speak ill o' this world, seeing as Them put us in it as knows best – but what wi' the drink, and the quarrelling, and the bad illness-es, and the hard dying, as I've seen times and times, one's thankful to hear of a better. The boy sings pretty, don't he, Master Marner?'

'Yes,' said Silas, absently, 'very pretty.'

The Christmas carol, with its hammer-like rhythm, had fallen on his ears as strange music, quite unlike a hymn, and could have none of the effect Dolly contemplated. But he wanted to show her that he was grateful, and the only mode that occurred to him was to offer Aaron a bit more cake.

'Oh no, thank you, Master Marner,' said Dolly, holding down Aaron's willing hands. 'We must be going home now. And so I wish you good-bye, Master Marner; and if you ever feel anyways bad in your inside, as you can't fend for yourself, I'll come and clean up for you, and get you a bit o' victual, and willing. But I beg and pray of you to leave off weaving of a Sunday, for it's bad for soul and body – and the money as comes i' that way 'ull be a bad bed to lie down on at the last, if it doesn't fly away, nobody knows where, like the white frost. And you'll excuse me being that free with you, Master Marner, for I wish you well – I do. Make your bow, Aaron.'

Silas said 'Good-bye, and thank you kindly,' as he opened the door for Dolly, but he couldn't help feeling relieved when she was gone – relieved that he might weave again and moan at his ease. Her simple view of life and its comforts, by which she had tried to cheer him, was only like a report of unknown objects, which his imagination could not fashion. The fountains of human love and of faith in a divine love had not yet been unlocked, and his soul was still the shrunken rivulet, with only this difference, that its little groove of sand was blocked up, and it wandered confusedly against dark obstruction.

And so, notwithstanding the honest persuasions of Mr Macey and Dolly Winthrop, Silas spent his Christmas-day in loneliness, eating his meat in sadness of heart, though the meat had come to him as a neighbourly present. In the morning he looked out on the black frost that seemed to press cruelly on every blade of grass, while the half-icy red pool shivered under the bitter wind; but towards evening the snow began to fall, and curtained from him even that dreary outlook, shutting him close up with his narrow grief. And he sat in his robbed home through the livelong evening, not caring to close his shutters or lock his door, pressing his head between his hands and moaning, till the cold grasped him and told him that his fire was grey.

Nobody in this world but himself knew that he was the same Silas Marner who had once loved his fellow with tender love, and trusted in an unseen goodness. Even to himself that past experience had become dim.

But in Raveloe village the bells rang merrily, and the church was fuller than all through the rest of the year, with red faces among the abundant dark-green boughs – faces prepared for a longer service than usual by an odorous breakfast of toast and ale.[19] Those green boughs, the hymn and anthem never heard but at Christmas – even the Athanasian Creed,[20] which was discriminated from the others only as being longer and of exceptional virtue, since it was only read on rare occasions – brought a vague exulting sense, for which the grown men could as little have found words as the children, that something great and mysterious had been done for them in heaven above and in earth below, which they were appropriating by their presence. And then the red faces made their way through the black biting frost to their own homes, feeling themselves free for the rest of the day to eat, drink, and be merry, and using that Christian freedom without diffidence.

At Squire Cass's family party that day nobody mentioned Dunstan – nobody was sorry for his absence, or feared it would be too long. The doctor and his wife, uncle and aunt Kimble, were there, and the annual Christmas talk was carried through without any omissions, rising to the climax of Mr Kimble's experience when he walked the London hospitals thirty years back, together with striking professional anecdotes then gathered. Whereupon cards followed, with aunt Kimble's annual failure to follow suit, and uncle Kimble's irascibility concerning the odd trick which was rarely explicable to him, when it was not on his side, without a general visitation of tricks to see that they were formed on sound principles: the whole being accompanied by a strong steaming odour of spirits-and-water.

But the party on Christmas-day, being a strictly family party, was not the pre-eminently brilliant celebration of the season at the Red House. It was the great dance on New Year's Eve that made the glory of Squire Cass's hospitality, as of his forefathers', time out of mind. This was the occasion when all the society of Raveloe and Tarley, whether old acquaintances separated by long rutty distances, or cooled acquaintances separated by misunderstandings concerning runaway calves, or acquaintances founded on intermittent condescension, counted on meeting and on comporting themselves with mutual appropriateness. This was the occasion on which fair dames who came on pillions sent their bandboxes before them, supplied with more than their evening costume; for the feast was not to end with a single evening, like a paltry town entertainment, where the whole supply of eatables is put on the table at once, and bedding is scanty. The Red House was provisioned as if for a siege; and as for the spare feather-beds ready to be laid on floors, they were as plentiful as might naturally be expected in a family that had killed its own geese for many generations.

Godfrey Cass was looking forward to this New Year's Eve with a foolish reckless longing, that made him half deaf to his importunate companion, Anxiety.

'Dunsey will be coming home soon: there will be a great blow-up, and how will you bribe his spite to silence?' said Anxiety.

'Oh, he won't come home before New Year's Eve, perhaps,' said Godfrey; 'and I shall sit by Nancy then, and dance with her, and get a kind look from her in spite of herself.'

'But money is wanted in another quarter,' said Anxiety, in a louder voice, 'and how will you get it without selling your mother's diamond pin? And if you don't get it . . .?'

'Well, but something may happen to make things easier. At any rate, there's one pleasure for me close at hand: Nancy is coming.'

'Yes, and suppose your father should bring matters to a pass that will oblige you to decline marrying her – and to give your reasons?'

'Hold your tongue, and don't worry me. I can see Nancy's eyes, just as they will look at me, and feel her hand in mine already.'

But Anxiety went on, though in noisy Christmas company; refusing to be utterly quieted even by much drinking.

Some women, I grant, would not appear to advantage seated on a pillion, and attired in a drab joseph[1] and a drab beaver-bonnet, with a crown resembling a small stew-pan; for a garment suggesting a coachman's greatcoat, cut out under an exiguity of cloth that would only allow of miniature capes, is not well adapted to conceal deficiencies of contour, nor is drab a colour that will throw sallow cheeks into lively contrast. It was all the greater triumph to Miss Nancy Lammeter's beauty that she looked thoroughly bewitching in that costume, as, seated on the pillion behind her tall, erect father, she held one arm round him, and looked down, with open-eyed anxiety, at the treacherous snow-covered pools and puddles, which sent up formidable splashings of mud under the stamp of Dobbin's foot. A painter would, perhaps, have preferred her in those moments when she was free from self-consciousness; but certainly the bloom on her cheeks was at its highest point of contrast with the surrounding drab when she arrived at the door of the Red House, and saw Mr Godfrey Cass ready to lift her from the pillion. She wished her sister Priscilla had come up at the same time behind the servant, for then she would have contrived that Mr Godfrey should have lifted off Priscilla first, and, in the meantime, she would have persuaded her father to go round to the horseblock instead of alighting at the door-steps. It was very painful, when you had made it quite clear to a young man that you were determined not to marry him, however much he might wish it, that he would still continue to pay you marked attentions; besides, why didn't he always show the same attentions, if he meant them sincerely, instead of being so strange as Mr Godfrey Cass was, sometimes behaving as if he didn't want to speak to her, and taking no notice of her for weeks and weeks, and then, all on a sudden, almost making love again? Moreover, it was quite plain he had no real love for her, else he would not let people have *that* to say of him which they did say. Did he suppose that Miss Nancy Lammeter was to be won by any man, squire or no squire, who led a bad life? That was not what she had been used to see in her own father, who was the soberest and best man in that country-side, only a little hot and hasty now and then, if things were not done to the minute.

All these thoughts rushed through Miss Nancy's mind, in their habitual succession, in the moments between her first sight of Mr Godfrey Cass standing at the door and her own arrival there. Happily, the Squire came out too and gave a loud greeting to her father, so that, somehow, under cover of this noise she seemed to find concealment for her confusion and neglect of any suitably formal behaviour, while she was being lifted from the pillion by strong arms which seemed to find her ridiculously small and light. And there was the best reason for hastening into the house at once, since the snow was beginning to fall again, threatening an unpleasant journey for such guests as were still on the road. These were a small minority; for already the afternoon was beginning to decline, and there would not be too much time for the ladies who came from a distance to attire themselves in readiness for the early tea which was to inspirit them for the dance.

There was a buzz of voices through the house, as Miss Nancy entered, mingled with the scrape of a fiddle preluding in the kitchen; but the Lammeters were guests whose arrival had evidently been thought of so much that it had been watched for from the windows, for Mrs Kimble, who did the honours at the Red House on these great occasions, came forward to meet Miss Nancy in the hall, and conduct her up-stairs. Mrs Kimble was the Squire's sister, as well as the doctor's wife – a double dignity, with which her diameter was in direct proportion; so that, a journey up-stairs being rather fatiguing to her, she did not oppose Miss Nancy's request to be allowed to find her way alone to the Blue Room, where the Miss Lammeters' bandboxes had been deposited on their arrival in the morning.

There was hardly a bedroom in the house where feminine compliments were not passing and feminine toilettes going forward, in various stages, in space made scanty by extra beds spread upon the floor; and Miss Nancy, as she entered the Blue Room, had to make her little formal curtsy to a group of six. On the one hand, there were ladies no less important than the two Miss Gunns, the wine merchant's daughters from Lytherly, dressed in the height of fashion, with the tightest skirts and the shortest waists, and gazed at by Miss Ladbrook (of the Old Pastures) with a shyness not unsustained by inward criticism.

Partly, Miss Ladbrook felt that her own skirt must be regarded as unduly lax by the Miss Gunns, and partly, that it was a pity the Miss Gunns did not show that judgment which she herself would show if she were in their place, by stopping a little on this side of the fashion. On the other hand, Mrs Ladbrook was standing in skullcap and front, with her turban in her hand, curtsying and smiling blandly and saying, 'After you, ma'am,' to another lady in similar circumstances, who had politely offered the precedence at the looking-glass.

But Miss Nancy had no sooner made her curtsy than an elderly lady came forward, whose full white muslin kerchief, and mob-cap[2] round her curls of smooth grey hair, were in daring contrast with the puffed yellow satins and top-knotted caps[3] of her neighbours. She approached Miss Nancy with much primness, and said, with a slow, treble suavity –

'Niece, I hope I see you well in health.' Miss Nancy kissed her aunt's cheek dutifully, and answered, with the same sort of amiable primness, 'Quite well, I thank you, aunt; and I hope I see you the same.'

'Thank you, niece; I keep my health for the present. And how is my brother-in-law?'

These dutiful questions and answers were continued until it was ascertained in detail that the Lammeters were all as well as usual, and the Osgoods likewise, also that niece Priscilla must certainly arrive shortly, and that travelling on pillions in snowy weather was unpleasant, though a joseph was a great protection. Then Nancy was formally introduced to her aunt's visitors, the Miss Gunns, as being the daughters of a mother known to *their* mother, though now for the first time induced to make a journey into these parts; and these ladies were so taken by surprise at finding such a lovely face and figure in an out-of-the-way country place, that they began to feel some curiosity about the dress she would put on when she took off her joseph. Miss Nancy, whose thoughts were always conducted with the propriety and moderation conspicuous in her manners, remarked to herself that the Miss Gunns were rather hard-featured than otherwise, and that such very low dresses as they wore might have been attributed to vanity if their shoulders had been pretty, but that, being as they were, it was not reasonable to suppose that they showed their necks from a love of display, but rather from some obligation not inconsistent with sense and modesty. She felt convinced, as she opened her box, that this must be her aunt Osgood's opinion, for Miss Nancy's mind resembled her aunt's to a degree that everybody said was surprising, considering the kinship was on Mr Osgood's side; and though you might not have supposed it from the formality of their greeting, there was a devoted attachment and mutual admiration between aunt and niece. Even Miss Nancy's refusal of her cousin Gilbert Osgood (on the ground solely that he was her cousin), though it had grieved her aunt greatly, had not in the least cooled the preference which had determined her to leave Nancy several of her hereditary ornaments, let Gilbert's future wife be whom she might.

Three of the ladies quickly retired, but the Miss Gunns were quite content that Mrs Osgood's inclination to remain with her niece gave them also a reason for staying to see the rustic beauty's toilette. And it was really a pleasure – from the first opening of the bandbox, where everything smelt of lavender and rose-leaves, to the clasping of the small coral necklace that fitted closely round her little white neck. Everything belonging to Miss Nancy was of delicate purity and nattiness: not a crease was where it had no business to be, not a bit of her linen professed whiteness without fulfilling its profession; the very pins on her pincushion were stuck in after a pattern from which she was careful to allow no aberration; and as for her own person, it gave the same idea of perfect unvarying neatness as the body of a little bird. It is true that her light-brown hair was cropped behind like a boy's, and was dressed in front in a number of flat rings, that lay quite away from her face; but there was no sort of coiffure that could make Miss Nancy's cheek and neck look otherwise than pretty; and when at last she stood complete in her silvery twilled silk, her lace tucker,[4] her coral necklace, and coral ear-drops, the Miss Gunns could see nothing to criticise except her hands, which bore the traces of butter-making, cheese-crushing, and even still coarser work. But Miss Nancy was not ashamed of that, for while she was dressing she narrated to her aunt how she and Priscilla had packed their boxes yesterday, because this morning was baking morning, and since they were leaving home, it was desirable to make a good supply of meat-pies for the kitchen; and as she concluded this judicious remark, she turned to the Miss Gunns that she might not commit the rudeness of not including them in the conversation. The Miss Gunns smiled stiffly, and thought what a pity it was that these rich country people, who could afford to buy such good clothes (really Miss Nancy's lace and silk were very costly), should be brought up in utter ignorance and vulgarity. She actually said 'mate' for 'meat,' ''appen' for 'perhaps,' and 'oss' for 'horse,' which, to young ladies living in good Lytherly society, who habitually said 'orse, even in domestic privacy, and only said 'appen on the right occasions, was necessarily shocking. Miss Nancy, indeed, had never been to any school higher than Dame Tedman's: her acquaintance with profane literature hardly went beyond the rhymes she had worked in her large sampler under the lamb and the shepherdess; and in order to balance an account, she was obliged to effect her subtraction by removing visible metallic shillings and sixpences from a visible metallic total. There is hardly a servant-maid in these days who is not better informed than Miss Nancy; yet she had the essential attributes of a lady – high veracity, delicate honour in her dealings, deference to others, and refined personal habits, – and lest these should not suffice to convince grammatical fair ones that her feelings can at all resemble theirs, I will add that she was slightly proud and exacting, and as constant in her affection towards a baseless opinion as towards an erring lover.

The anxiety about sister Priscilla, which had grown rather active by the time the coral necklace was clasped, was happily ended by the entrance of that cheerful-looking lady herself, with a face made blowsy by cold and damp. After the first questions and greetings, she turned to Nancy, and surveyed her from head to foot – then wheeled her round, to ascertain that the back view was equally faultless.

'What do you think o' *these* gowns, aunt Osgood?' said Priscilla, while Nancy helped her to unrobe.

'Very handsome indeed, niece,' said Mrs Osgood, with a slight increase of formality. She always thought niece Priscilla too rough.

'I'm obliged to have the same as Nancy, you know, for all I'm five years older, and it makes me look yellow; for she never *will* have anything without I have mine just like it, because she wants us to look like sisters. And I tell her, folks 'ull think it's my weakness makes me fancy as I shall look pretty in what she looks pretty in. For I *am* ugly – there's no denying that: I feature my father's family. But, law! I don't mind, do you?' Priscilla here turned to the Miss Gunns, rattling on in too much preoccupation with the delight of talking, to notice that her candour was not appreciated. 'The pretty uns do for fly-catchers – they keep the men off us. I've no opinion o' the men, Miss Gunn – I don't know what *you* have. And as for fretting and stewing about what *they*'ll think of you from morning till night, and making your life uneasy about what they're doing when they're out o' your sight – as I tell Nancy, it's a folly no woman need be guilty of, if she's got a good father and a good home: let her leave it to them as have got no fortin,[5] and can't help themselves. As I say, Mr Have-your-own-way is the best husband, and the only one I'd ever promise to obey. I know it isn't pleasant, when you've been used to living in a big way, and managing hogsheads[6] and all that, to go and put your nose in by somebody else's fireside, or to sit down by yourself to a scrag or a knuckle;[7] but, thank God! my father's a sober man and likely to live; and if you've got a man by the chimney-corner, it doesn't matter if he's childish – the business needn't be broke up.'

The delicate process of getting her narrow gown over her head without injury to her smooth curls, obliged Miss Priscilla to pause in this rapid survey of life, and Mrs Osgood seized the opportunity of rising and saying –

'Well, niece, you'll follow us. The Miss Gunns will like to go down.'

'Sister,' said Nancy, when they were alone, 'you've offended the Miss Gunns, I'm sure.'

'What have I done, child?' said Priscilla, in some alarm.

'Why, you asked them if they minded about being ugly – you're so very blunt.'

'Law, did I? Well, it popped out: it's a mercy I said no more, for I'm a bad un to live with folks when they don't like the truth. But as for being ugly, look at me, child, in this silver-coloured silk – I told you how it 'ud be – I look as yellow as a daffadil. Anybody 'ud say you wanted to make a mawkin[8] of me.'

'No, Priscy, don't say so. I begged and prayed of you not to let us have this silk if you'd like another better. I was willing to have *your* choice, you know I was,' said Nancy, in anxious self-vindication.

'Nonsense, child! you know you'd set your heart on this; and reason good, for you're the colour o' cream. It 'ud be fine doings for you to dress yourself to suit *my* skin. What I find fault with, is that notion o' yours as I must dress myself just like you. But you do as you like with me – you always did, from when first you begun to walk. If you wanted to go the field's length, the field's length you'd go; and there was no whipping you, for you looked as prim and innicent as a daisy all the while.'

'Priscy,' said Nancy, gently, as she fastened a coral necklace, exactly like her own, round Priscilla's neck, which was very far from being like her own, 'I'm sure I'm willing to give way as far as is right, but who shouldn't dress alike if it isn't sisters? Would you have us go about looking as if we were no kin to one another – us that have got no mother and not another sister in the world? I'd do what was right, if I dressed in a gown dyed with cheese-colouring; and I'd rather you'd choose, and let me wear what pleases you.'

'There you go again! You'd come round to the same thing if one talked to you from Saturday night till Saturday morning. It'll be fine fun to see how you'll master your husband and never raise your voice above the singing o' the kettle all the while. I like to see the men mastered!'

'Don't talk *so*, Priscy,' said Nancy, blushing. 'You know I don't mean ever to be married.'

'Oh, you never mean a fiddlestick's end!' said Priscilla, as she arranged her discarded dress, and closed her bandbox. 'Who shall *I* have to work for when father's gone, if you are to go and take notions in your head and be an old maid, because some folks are no better than they should be? I haven't a bit o' patience with you – sitting on an addled egg for ever, as if there was never a fresh un in the world. One old maid's enough out o' two sisters; and I shall do credit to a single life, for God A'mighty meant me for it. Come, we can go down now. I'm as ready as a mawkin *can* be – there's nothing awanting to frighten the crows, now I've got my ear-droppers in.'

As the two Miss Lammeters walked into the large parlour together, any one who did not know the character of both might certainly have supposed that the reason why the square-shouldered, clumsy, high-featured Priscilla wore a dress the facsimile of her pretty sister's, was either the mistaken vanity of the one, or the malicious contrivance of the other in order to set off her own rare beauty. But the good-natured self-forgetful cheeriness and common-sense of Priscilla would soon have dissipated the one suspicion; and the modest calm of Nancy's speech and manners told clearly of a mind free from all disavowed devices.

Places of honour had been kept for the Miss Lammeters near the head of the principal tea-table in the wainscoted parlour, now looking fresh and pleasant with handsome branches of holly, yew, and laurel, from the abundant growths of the old garden; and Nancy felt an inward flutter, that no firmness of purpose could prevent, when she saw Mr Godfrey Cass advancing to lead her to a seat between himself and Mr Crackenthorp, while Priscilla was called to the opposite side between her father and the Squire. It certainly did make some difference to Nancy that the lover she had given up was the young man of quite the highest consequence in the parish – at home in a venerable and unique parlour, which was the extremity of grandeur in her experience, a parlour where *she* might one day have been mistress, with the consciousness that she was spoken of as 'Madam Cass,' the Squire's wife. These circumstances exalted her inward drama in her own eyes, and deepened the emphasis with which she declared to herself that not the most dazzling rank should induce her to marry a man whose conduct showed him careless of his character, but that, 'love once, love always,' was the motto of a true and pure woman, and no man should ever have any right over her which would be a call on her to destroy the dried flowers that she treasured, and always would treasure, for Godfrey Cass's sake. And Nancy was capable of keeping her word to herself under very trying conditions. Nothing but a becoming blush betrayed the moving thoughts that urged themselves upon her as she accepted the seat next to Mr Crackenthorp; for she was so instinctively neat and adroit in all her actions, and her pretty lips met each other with such quiet firmness, that it would have been difficult for her to appear agitated.

It was not the Rector's practice to let a charming blush pass without an appropriate compliment. He was not in the least lofty or aristocratic, but simply a merry-eyed, small-featured, grey-haired man, with his chin propped by an ample many-creased white neck-cloth which seemed to predominate over every other point in his person, and somehow to impress its peculiar character on his remarks; so that to have considered his amenities apart from his cravat would have been a severe, and perhaps a dangerous, effort of abstraction.

'Ha, Miss Nancy,' he said, turning his head within his cravat and smiling down pleasantly upon her, 'when anybody pretends this has been a severe winter, I shall tell them I saw the roses blooming on New Year's Eve – eh, Godfrey, what do *you* say?'

Godfrey made no reply, and avoided looking at Nancy very markedly; for though these complimentary personalities were held to be in excellent taste in old-fashioned Raveloe society, reverent love has a politeness of its own which it teaches to men otherwise of small schooling. But the Squire was rather impatient at Godfrey's showing himself a dull spark in this way. By this advanced hour of the day, the Squire was always in higher spirits than we have seen him in at the breakfast-table, and felt it quite pleasant to fulfil the hereditary duty of being noisily jovial and patronising: the large silver snuff-box was in active service and was offered without fail to all neighbours from time to time, however often they might have declined the favour. At present, the Squire had only given an express welcome to the heads of families as they appeared; but always as the evening deepened, his hospitality rayed out more widely, till he had tapped the youngest guests on the back and shown a peculiar fondness for their presence, in the full belief that they must feel their lives made happy by their belonging to a parish where there was such a hearty man as Squire Cass to invite them and wish them well. Even in this early stage of the jovial mood, it was natural that he should wish to supply his son's deficiencies by looking and speaking for him.

'Ay, ay,' he began, offering his snuff-box to Mr Lammeter, who for the second time bowed his head and waved his hand in stiff rejection of the offer, 'us old fellows may wish ourselves young to-night, when we see the mistletoe-bough in the White Parlour. It's true, most things are gone back'ard in these last thirty years – the country's going down since the old king fell ill.[10] But when I look at Miss Nancy here, I begin to think the lasses keep up their quality; – ding me if I remember a sample to match her, not when I was a fine young fellow, and thought a deal about my pigtail. No offence to you, madam,' he added, bending to Mrs Crackenthorp, who sat by him, 'I didn't know *you* when you were as young as Miss Nancy here.'

Mrs Crackenthorp – a small blinking woman, who fidgeted incessantly with her lace, ribbons, and gold chain, turning her head about and making subdued noises, very much like a guinea-pig that twitches its nose and soliloquises in all company indiscriminately – now blinked and fidgeted towards the Squire, and said, 'Oh no – no offence.'

This emphatic compliment of the Squire's to Nancy was felt by others besides Godfrey to have a diplomatic significance; and her father gave a slight additional erectness to his back, as he looked across the table at her with complacent gravity. That grave and orderly senior was not going to bate a jot of his dignity by seeming elated at the notion of a match between his family and the Squire's: he was gratified by any honour paid to his daughter; but he must see an alteration in several ways before his consent would be vouchsafed. His spare but healthy person, and high-featured firm face, that looked as if it had never been flushed by excess, was in strong contrast, not only with the Squire's, but with the appearance of the Raveloe farmers generally – in accordance with a favourite saying of his own, that 'breed was stronger than pasture.'

'Miss Nancy's wonderful like what her mother was, though; isn't she, Kimble?' said the stout lady of that name, looking round for her husband.

But Doctor Kimble (country apothecaries in old days enjoyed that title without authority of diploma), being a thin and agile man, was flitting about the room with his hands in his pockets, making himself agreeable to his feminine patients, with medical impartiality, and being welcomed everywhere as a doctor by hereditary right – not one of those miserable apothecaries who canvass for practice in strange neighbourhoods, and spend all their income in starving their one horse, but a man of substance, able to keep an extravagant table like the best of his patients. Time out of mind the Raveloe doctor had been a Kimble; Kimble was inherently a doctor's name; and it was difficult to contemplate firmly the melancholy fact that the actual Kimble had no son, so that his practice might one day be handed over to a successor with the incongruous name of Taylor or Johnson. But in that case the wiser people in Raveloe would employ Dr Blick of Flitton – as less unnatural.

'Did you speak to me, my dear?' said the authentic doctor, coming quickly to his wife's side; but, as if foreseeing that she would be too much out of breath to repeat her remark, he went on immediately –

'Ha, Miss Priscilla, the sight of you revives the taste of that super-excellent pork-pie. I hope the batch isn't near an end.'

'Yes, indeed, it is, doctor,' said Priscilla; 'but I'll answer for it the next shall be as good. My pork-pies don't turn out well by chance.'

'Not as your doctoring does, eh, Kimble? – because folks forget to take your physic, eh?' said the Squire, who regarded physic and doctors as many loyal churchmen regard the church and the clergy – tasting a joke against them when he was in health, but impatiently eager for their aid when anything was the matter with him. He tapped his box, and looked round with a triumphant laugh.

'Ah, she has a quick wit, my friend Priscilla has,' said the doctor, choosing to attribute the epigram to a lady rather than allow a brother-in-law that advantage over him. 'She saves a little pepper to sprinkle over her talk – that's the reason why she never puts too much into her pies. There's my wife, now, she never has an answer at her tongue's end; but if I offend her, she's sure to scarify my throat with black pepper the next day, or else give me the colic with watery greens. That's an awful tit-for-tat.' Here the vivacious doctor made a pathetic grimace.

'Did you ever hear the like?' said Mrs Kimble, laughing above her double chin with much good-humour, aside to Mrs Crackenthorp, who blinked and nodded, and amiably intended to smile, but the intention lost itself in small twitchings and noises.

'I suppose that's the sort of tit-for-tat adopted in your profession, Kimble, if you've a grudge against a patient,' said the rector.

'Never do have a grudge against our patients,' said Mr Kimble, 'except when they leave us: and then, you see, we haven't the chance of prescribing for 'em. Ha, Miss Nancy,' he continued, suddenly skipping to Nancy's side, 'you won't forget your promise? You're to save a dance for me, you know.'

'Come, come, Kimble, don't you be too for'ard,' said the Squire. 'Give the young uns fair-play. There's my son Godfrey 'll be wanting to have a round with you if you run off with Miss Nancy. He's bespoke her for the first dance, I'll be bound. Eh, sir! what do you say?' he continued, throwing himself backward, and looking at Godfrey. 'Haven't you asked Miss Nancy to open the dance with you?'

Godfrey, sorely uncomfortable under this significant insistance about Nancy, and afraid to think where it would end by the time his father had set his usual hospitable example of drinking before and after supper, saw no course open but to turn to Nancy and say, with as little awkwardness as possible –

'No; I've not asked her yet, but I hope she'll consent – if somebody else hasn't been before me.'

'No, I've not engaged myself,' said Nancy, quietly, though blushingly. (If Mr Godfrey founded any hopes on her consenting to dance with him, he would soon be undeceived; but there was no need for her to be uncivil.)

'Then I hope you've no objections to dancing with me,' said Godfrey, beginning to lose the sense that there was anything uncomfortable in this arrangement.

'No, no objections,' said Nancy, in a cold tone.

'Ah, well, you're a lucky fellow, Godfrey,' said uncle Kimble; 'but you're my godson, so I won't stand in your way. Else I'm not so very old, eh, my dear?' he went on, skipping to his wife's side again. 'You wouldn't mind my having a second after you were gone – not if I cried a good deal first?'

'Come, come, take a cup o' tea and stop your tongue, do,' said good-humoured Mrs Kimble, feeling some pride in a husband who must be regarded as so clever and amusing by the company generally. If he had only not been irritable at cards!

While safe, well-tested personalities were enlivening the tea in this way, the sound of the fiddle approaching within a distance at which it could be heard distinctly, made the young people look at each other with sympathetic impatience for the end of the meal.

'Why, there's Solomon in the hall,' said the Squire, 'and playing my fav'rite tune, I believe – "The flaxen-headed ploughboy"" – he's for giving us a hint as we aren't enough in a hurry to hear him play. Bob,' he called out to his third long-legged son, who was at the other end of the room, 'open the door, and tell Solomon to come in. He shall give us a tune here.'

Bob obeyed, and Solomon walked in, fiddling as he walked, for he would on no account break off in the middle of a tune.

'Here, Solomon,' said the Squire, with loud patronage. 'Round here, my man. Ah, I knew it was "The flaxen-headed ploughboy:" there's no finer tune.'

Solomon Macey, a small hale old man, with an abundant crop of long white hair reaching nearly to his shoulders, advanced to the indicated spot, bowing reverently while he fiddled, as much as to say that he respected the company though he respected the key-note more. As soon as he had repeated the tune and lowered his fiddle, he bowed again to the Squire and the Rector, and said, 'I hope I see your honour and your reverence well, and wishing you health and long life and a happy New Year. And wishing the same to you, Mr Lammeter, sir; and to the other gentlemen, and the madams, and the young lasses.'

As Solomon uttered the last words, he bowed in all directions solicitously, lest he should be wanting in due respect. But thereupon he immediately began to prelude, and fell into the tune which he knew would be taken as a special compliment by Mr Lammeter.

'Thank ye, Solomon, thank ye,' said Mr Lammeter when the fiddle paused again. 'That's "Over the hills and far away,"[12] that is. My father used to say to me, whenever we heard that tune, "Ah, lad, *I* come from over the hills and far away." There's a many tunes I don't make head or tail of; but that speaks to me like the blackbird's whistle. I suppose it's the name: there's a deal in the name of a tune.'

But Solomon was already impatient to prelude again, and presently broke with much spirit into 'Sir Roger de Coverley,'[13] at which there was a sound of chairs pushed back, and laughing voices.

'Ay, ay, Solomon, we know what that means,' said the Squire, rising. 'It's time to begin the dance, eh? Lead the way, then, and we'll all follow you.'

So Solomon, holding his white head on one side, and playing vigorously, marched forward at the head of the gay procession into the White Parlour, where the mistletoe-bough was hung, and multitudinous tallow candles made rather a brilliant effect, gleaming from among the berried holly-boughs, and reflected in the old-fashioned oval mirrors fastened in the panels of the white wainscot. A quaint procession! Old Solomon, in his seedy clothes and long white locks, seemed to be luring that decent company by the magic scream of his fiddle – luring discreet matrons in turban-shaped caps, nay, Mrs Crackenthorp herself, the summit of whose perpendicular feather was on a level with the Squire's shoulder – luring fair lasses complacently conscious of very short waists and skirts blameless of front-folds – luring burly fathers in large variegated waistcoats, and ruddy sons, for the most part shy and sheepish, in short nether garments and very long coat-tails.

Already Mr Macey and a few other privileged villagers, who were allowed to be spectators on these great occasions, were seated on benches placed for them near the door; and great was the admiration and satisfaction in that quarter when the couples had formed themselves for the dance, and the Squire led off with Mrs Crackenthorp, joining hands with the Rector and Mrs Osgood. That was as it should be – that was what everybody had been used to – and the charter of Raveloe seemed to be renewed by the ceremony. It was not thought of as an unbecoming levity for the old and middle-aged people to dance a little before sitting down to cards, but rather as part of their social duties. For what were these if not to be merry at appropriate times, interchanging visits and poultry with due frequency, paying each other old-established compliments in sound traditional phrases, passing well-tried personal jokes, urging your guests to eat and drink too much out of hospitality, and eating and drinking too much in your neighbour's house to show that you liked your cheer? And the parson naturally set an example in these social duties. For it would not have been possible for the Raveloe mind, without a peculiar revelation, to know that a clergyman should be a pale-faced memento of solemnities, instead of a reasonably faulty man whose exclusive authority to read prayers and preach, to christen, marry, and bury you, necessarily coexisted with the right to sell you the ground to be buried in and to take tithe in kind;[4] on which last point, of course, there was a little grumbling, but not to the extent of irreligion – not of deeper significance than the grumbling at the rain, which was by no means accompanied with a spirit of impious defiance, but with a desire that the prayer for fine weather might be read forthwith.

There was no reason, then, why the rector's dancing should not be received as part of the fitness of things quite as much as the Squire's, or why, on the other hand, Mr Macey's official respect should restrain him from subjecting the parson's performance to that criticism with which minds of extraordinary acuteness must necessarily contemplate the doings of their fallible fellow-men.

'The Squire's pretty springe,[5] considering his weight,' said Mr Macey, 'and he stamps uncommon well. But Mr Lammeter beats 'em all for shapes: you see he holds his head like a sodger, and he isn't so cushiony as most o' the oldish gentlefolks – they run fat in general; and he's got a fine leg. The parson's nimble enough, but he hasn't got much of a leg: it's a bit too thick down'ard, and his knees might be a bit nearer wi'out damage; but he might do worse, he might do worse. Though he hasn't that grand way o' waving his hand as the Squire has.'

'Talk o' nimbleness, look at Mrs Osgood,' said Ben Winthrop, who was holding his son Aaron between his knees. 'She trips along with her little steps, so as nobody can see how she goes – it's like as if she had little wheels to her feet. She doesn't look a day older nor last year: she's the finest-made woman as is, let the next be where she will.'

'I don't heed how the women are made,' said Mr Macey, with some contempt. 'They wear nayther coat nor breeches: you can't make much out o' their shapes.'

'Fayder,' said Aaron, whose feet were busy beating out the tune, 'how does that big cock's-feather stick in Mrs Crackenthorp's yead? Is there a little hole for it, like in my shuttle-cock?'

'Hush, lad, hush; that's the way the ladies dress theirselves, that is,' said the father, adding, however, in an under-tone to Mr Macey, 'It does make her look funny, though – partly like a short-necked bottle wi' a long quill in it. Hey, by jingo, there's the young Squire leading off now, wi' Miss Nancy for partners! There's a lass for you! – like a pink-and-white posy – there's nobody 'ud think as anybody could be so pritty. I shouldn't wonder if she's Madam Cass some day, arter all – and nobody more rightfuller, for they'd make a fine match. You can find nothing against Master Godfrey's shapes, Macey, I'll bet a penny.'

Mr Macey screwed up his mouth, leaned his head further on one side, and twirled his thumbs with a presto movement[16] as his eyes followed Godfrey up the dance. At last he summed up his opinion.

'Pretty well down'ard, but a bit too round i' the shoulder-blades. And as for them coats as he gets from the Flitton tailor, they're a poor cut to pay double money for.'

'Ah, Mr Macey, you and me are two folks,' said Ben, slightly indignant at this carping. 'When I've got a pot o' good ale, I like to swaller it, and do my inside good, i'stead o' smelling and staring at it to see if I can't find faut wi' the brewing. I should like you to pick me out a finer-limbed young fellow nor Master Godfrey – one as 'ud knock you down easier, or 's more pleasanter looksed when he's piert[17] and merry.'

'Tchuh!' said Mr Macey, provoked to increased severity, 'he isn't come to his right colour yet: he's partly like a slack-baked[18] pie. And I doubt he's got a soft place in his head, else why should he be turned round the finger by that offal[19] Dunsey as nobody's seen o' late, and let him kill that fine hunting hoss as was the talk o' the country? And one while he was allays after Miss Nancy, and then it all went off again, like a smell o' hot porridge, as I may say. That wasn't my way when *I* went a-coorting.'

'Ah, but mayhap Miss Nancy hung off like, and your lass didn't,' said Ben.

'I should say she didn't,' said Mr Macey, significantly. 'Before I said "sniff," I took care to know as she'd say "snaff," and pretty quick too. I wasn't a-going to open *my* mouth, like a dog at a fly, and snap it to again, wi' nothing to swaller.'

'Well, I think Miss Nancy's a-coming round again,' said Ben, 'for Master Godfrey doesn't look so down-hearted to-night. And I see he's for taking her away to sit down, now they're at the end o' the dance: that looks like sweethearting, that does.'

The reason why Godfrey and Nancy had left the dance was not so tender as Ben imagined. In the close press of couples a slight accident had happened to Nancy's dress, which, while it was short enough to show her neat ankle in front, was long enough behind to be caught under the stately stamp of the Squire's foot, so as to rend certain stitches at the waist, and cause much sisterly agitation in Priscilla's mind, as well as serious concern in Nancy's. One's thoughts may be much occupied with love-struggles, but hardly so as to be insensible to a disorder in the general framework of things. Nancy had no sooner completed her duty in the figure they were dancing than she said to Godfrey, with a deep blush, that she must go and sit down till Priscilla could come to her; for the sisters had already exchanged a short whisper and an open-eyed glance full of meaning. No reason less urgent than this could have prevailed on Nancy to give Godfrey this opportunity of sitting apart with her. As for Godfrey, he was feeling so happy and oblivious under the long charm of the country-dance with Nancy, that he got rather bold on the strength of her confusion, and was capable of leading her straight away, without leave asked, into the adjoining small parlour, where the card-tables were set.

'Oh no, thank you,' said Nancy, coldly, as soon as she perceived where he was going, 'not in there. I'll wait here till Priscilla's ready to come to me. I'm sorry to bring you out of the dance and make myself troublesome.'

'Why, you'll be more comfortable here by yourself,' said the artful Godfrey: 'I'll leave you here till your sister can come.' He spoke in an indifferent tone.

That was an agreeable proposition, and just what Nancy desired; why, then, was she a little hurt that Mr Godfrey should make it? They entered, and she seated herself on a chair against one of the card-tables, as the stiffest and most unapproachable position she could choose.

'Thank you, sir,' she said immediately. 'I needn't give you any more trouble. I'm sorry you've had such an unlucky partner.'

'That's very ill-natured of you,' said Godfrey, standing by her without any sign of intended departure, 'to be sorry you've danced with me.'

'Oh no, sir, I don't mean to say what's ill-natured at all,' said Nancy, looking distractingly prim and pretty. 'When gentlemen have so many pleasures, one dance can matter but very little.'

'You know that isn't true. You know one dance with you matters more to me than all the other pleasures in the world.'

It was a long, long while since Godfrey had said anything so direct as that, and Nancy was startled. But her instinctive dignity and repugnance to any show of emotion made her sit perfectly still, and only throw a little more decision into her voice, as she said –

'No, indeed, Mr Godfrey, that's not known to me, and I have very good reasons for thinking different. But if it's true, I don't wish to hear it.'

'Would you never forgive me, then, Nancy – never think well of me, let what would happen – would you never think the present made amends for the past? Not if I turned a good fellow, and gave up everything you didn't like?'

Godfrey was half conscious that this sudden opportunity of speaking to Nancy alone had driven him beside himself; but blind feeling had got the mastery of his tongue. Nancy really felt much agitated by the possibility Godfrey's words suggested, but this very pressure of emotion that she was in danger of finding too strong for her, roused all her power of self-command.

'I should be glad to see a good change in anybody, Mr Godfrey,' she answered, with the slightest discernible difference of tone, 'but it 'ud be better if no change was wanted.'

'You're very hard-hearted, Nancy,' said Godfrey, pettishly. 'You might encourage me to be a better fellow. I'm very miserable – but you've no feeling.'

'I think those have the least feeling that act wrong to begin with,' said Nancy, sending out a flash in spite of herself. Godfrey was delighted with that little flash, and would have liked to go on and make her quarrel with him; Nancy was so exasperatingly quiet and firm. But she was not indifferent to him *yet*.

The entrance of Priscilla, bustling forward and saying, 'Dear heart alive, child, let us look at this gown,' cut off Godfrey's hopes of a quarrel.

'I suppose I must go now,' he said to Priscilla.

'It's no matter to me whether you go or stay,' said that frank lady, searching for something in her pocket, with a preoccupied brow.

'Do *you* want me to go?' said Godfrey, looking at Nancy, who was now standing up by Priscilla's order.

'As you like,' said Nancy, trying to recover all her former coldness, and looking down carefully at the hem of her gown.

'Then I like to stay,' said Godfrey, with a reckless determination to get as much of this joy as he could to-night, and think nothing of the morrow.

CHAPTER 12

While Godfrey Cass was taking draughts of forgetfulness from the sweet presence of Nancy, willingly losing all sense of that hidden bond which at other moments galled and fretted him so as to mingle irritation with the very sunshine, Godfrey's wife was walking with slow uncertain steps through the snow-covered Raveloe lanes, carrying her child in her arms.

This journey on New Year's Eve was a premeditated act of vengeance which she had kept in her heart ever since Godfrey, in a fit of passion, had told her he would sooner die than acknowledge her as his wife. There would be a great party at the Red House on New Year's Eve, she knew: her husband would be smiling and smiled upon, hiding *her* existence in the darkest corner of his heart. But she would mar his pleasure: she would go in her dingy rags, with her faded face, once as handsome as the best, with her little child that had its father's hair and eyes, and disclose herself to the Squire as his eldest son's wife. It is seldom that the miserable can help regarding their misery as a wrong inflicted by those who are less miserable. Molly knew that the cause of her dingy rags was not her husband's neglect, but the demon Opium to whom she was enslaved, body and soul, except in the lingering mother's tenderness that refused to give him her hungry child. She knew this well; and yet, in the moments of wretched unbe-numbed consciousness, the sense of her want and degradation trans-formed itself continually into bitterness towards Godfrey. *He* was well off; and if she had her rights she would be well off too. The belief that he repented his marriage, and suffered from it, only aggravated her vindictiveness. Just and self-reproving thoughts do not come to us too thickly, even in the purest air and with the best lessons of heaven and earth; how should those white-winged delicate messengers make their way to Molly's poisoned chamber, inhabited by no higher memor-ies than those of a barmaid's paradise of pink ribbons and gentlemen's jokes?

She had set out at an early hour, but had lingered on the road, inclined by her indolence to believe that if she waited under a warm shed the snow would cease to fall. She had waited longer than she knew, and now that she found herself belated in the snow-hidden ruggedness of the long lanes, even the animation of a vindictive purpose could not keep her spirit from failing. It was seven o'clock, and by this time she was not very far from Raveloe, but she was not familiar enough with those monotonous lanes to know how near she was to her journey's end. She needed comfort, and she knew but one comforter – the familiar demon in her bosom; but she hesitated a moment, after drawing out the black remnant, before she raised it to her lips. In that moment the mother's love pleaded for painful consciousness rather than oblivion – pleaded to be left in aching weariness, rather than to have the encircling arms benumbed so that they could not feel the dear burden. In another moment Molly had flung something away, but it was not the black remnant – it was an empty phial. And she walked on again under the breaking cloud, from which there came now and then the light of a quickly veiled star, for a freezing wind had sprung up since the snowing had ceased. But she walked always more and more drowsily, and clutched more and more automatically the sleeping child at her bosom.

Slowly the demon was working his will, and cold and weariness were his helpers. Soon she felt nothing but a supreme immediate longing that curtained off all futurity – the longing to lie down and sleep. She had arrived at a spot where her footsteps were no longer checked by a hedgerow, and she had wandered vaguely, unable to distinguish any objects, notwithstanding the wide whiteness around her, and the growing starlight. She sank down against a straggling furze bush, an easy pillow enough; and the bed of snow, too, was soft. She did not feel that the bed was cold, and did not heed whether the child would wake and cry for her. But her arms had not yet relaxed their instinctive clutch; and the little one slumbered on as gently as if it had been rocked in a lace-trimmed cradle.

But the complete torpor came at last: the fingers lost their tension, the arms unbent; then the little head fell away from the bosom, and the blue eyes opened wide on the cold starlight. At first there was a little peevish cry of 'mammy,' and an effort to regain the pillowing arm and bosom; but mammy's ear was deaf, and the pillow seemed to be slipping away backward. Suddenly, as the child rolled downward on its mother's knees, all wet with snow, its eyes were caught by a bright glancing light on the white ground, and, with the ready transition of infancy, it was immediately absorbed in watching the bright living thing running towards it, yet never arriving. That bright living thing must be caught; and in a instant the child had slipped on all fours, and held out one little hand to catch the gleam. But the gleam would not be caught in that way, and now the head was held up to see where the cunning gleam came from. It came from a very bright place; and the little one, rising on its legs, toddled through the snow, the old grimy shawl in which it was wrapped trailing behind it, and the queer little bonnet dangling at its back – toddled on to the open door of Silas Marner's cottage, and right up to the warm hearth, where there was a bright fire of logs and sticks, which had thoroughly warmed the old sack (Silas's greatcoat) spread out on the bricks to dry. The little one, accustomed to be left to itself for long hours without notice from its mother, squatted down on the sack, and spread its tiny hands towards the blaze, in perfect contentment, gurgling and making many inarticulate communications to the cheerful fire, like a new-hatched gosling beginning to find itself comfortable. But presently the warmth had a lulling effect, and the little golden head sank down on the old sack, and the blue eyes were veiled by their delicate half-transparent lids.

But where was Silas Marner while this strange visitor had come to his hearth? He was in the cottage, but he did not see the child. During the last few weeks, since he had lost his money, he had contracted the habit of opening his door and looking out from time to time, as if he thought that his money might be somehow coming back to him, or that some trace, some news of it, might be mysteriously on the road, and be caught by the listening ear or the straining eye. It was chiefly at night, when he was not occupied in his loom, that he fell into this repetition of an act for which he could have assigned no definite purpose, and which can hardly be understood except by those who have undergone a bewildering separation from a supremely loved object. In the evening twilight, and later whenever the night was not dark, Silas looked out on that narrow prospect round the Stone-pits, listening and gazing, not with hope, but with mere yearning and unrest.

This morning he had been told by some of his neighbours that it was New Year's Eve, and that he must sit up and hear the old year rung out and the new rung in, because that was good luck, and might bring his money back again. This was only a friendly Raveloe-way of jesting with the half-crazy oddities of a miser, but it had perhaps helped to throw Silas into a more than usually excited state. Since the on-coming of twilight he had opened his door again and again, though only to shut it immediately at seeing all distance veiled by the falling snow. But the last time he opened it the snow had ceased, and the clouds were parting here and there. He stood and listened, and gazed for a long while – there was really something on the road coming towards him then, but he caught no sign of it; and the stillness and the wide trackless snow seemed to narrow his solitude, and touched his yearning with the chill of despair. He went in again, and put his right hand on the latch of the door to close it – but he did not close it: he was arrested, as he had been already since his loss, by the invisible wand of catalepsy, and stood like a graven image, with wide but sightless eyes, holding open his door, powerless to resist either the good or evil that might enter there.

When Marner's sensibility returned, he continued the action which had been arrested, and closed his door, unaware of the chasm in his consciousness, unaware of any intermediate change, except that the light had grown dim, and that he was chilled and faint. He thought he had been too long standing at the door and looking out. Turning towards the hearth, where the two logs had fallen apart, and sent forth only a red uncertain glimmer, he seated himself on his fireside chair, and was stooping to push his logs together, when, to his blurred vision, it seemed as if there were gold on the floor in front of the hearth. Gold! – his own gold – brought back to him as mysteriously as it had been taken away! He felt his heart begin to beat violently, and for a few moments he was unable to stretch out his hand and grasp the restored treasure. The heap of gold seemed to glow and get larger beneath his agitated gaze. He leaned forward at last, and stretched forth his hand; but instead of the hard coin with the familiar resisting outline, his fingers encountered soft warm curls. In utter amazement, Silas fell on his knees and bent his head low to examine the marvel: it was a sleeping child – a round, fair thing, with soft yellow rings all over its head. Could this be his little sister come back to him in a dream – his little sister whom he had carried about in his arms for a year before she died, when he was a small boy without shoes or stockings? That was the first thought that darted across Silas's blank wonderment. *Was* it a dream? He rose to his feet again, pushed his logs together, and, throwing on some dried leaves and sticks, raised a flame; but the flame did not disperse the vision – it only lit up more distinctly the little round form of the child, and its shabby clothing. It was very much like his little sister. Silas sank into his chair, powerless under the double presence of an inexplicable surprise and a hurrying influx of memories. How and when had the child come in without his knowledge? He had never been beyond the door. But along with that question, and almost thrusting it away, there was a vision of the old home and the old streets leading to Lantern Yard – and within that vision another, of the thoughts which had been present with him in those far-off scenes. The thoughts were strange to him now, like old friendships impossible to revive; and yet he had a dreamy feeling that this child was somehow a message come to him from that far-off life: it stirred fibres that had never been moved in Raveloe – old quiverings of tenderness – old impressions of awe at the presentiment of some Power presiding over his life; for his imagination had not yet extricated itself from the sense of mystery in the child's sudden presence, and had formed no conjectures of ordinary natural means by which the event could have been brought about.

But there was a cry on the hearth: the child had awaked, and Marner stooped to lift it on his knee. It clung round his neck, and burst louder and louder into that mingling of inarticulate cries with 'mammy' by which little children express the bewilderment of waking. Silas pressed it to him, and almost unconsciously uttered sounds of hushing tenderness, while he bethought himself that some of his porridge, which had got cool by the dying fire, would do to feed the child with if it were only warmed up a little.

He had plenty to do through the next hour. The porridge, sweetened with some dry brown sugar from an old store which he had refrained from using for himself, stopped the cries of the little one, and made her lift her blue eyes with a wide quiet gaze at Silas, as he put the spoon into her mouth. Presently she slipped from his knee and began to toddle about, but with a pretty stagger that made Silas jump up and follow her lest she should fall against anything that would hurt her. But she only fell in a sitting posture on the ground, and began to pull at her boots, looking up at him with a crying face as if the boots hurt her. He took her on his knee again, but it was some time before it occurred to Silas's dull bachelor mind that the wet boots were the grievance, pressing on her warm ankles. He got them off with difficulty, and Baby was at once happily occupied with the primary mystery of her own toes, inviting Silas, with much chuckling, to consider the mystery too. But the wet boots had at last suggested to Silas that the child had been walking on the snow, and this roused him from his entire oblivion of any ordinary means by which it could have entered or been brought into his house. Under the prompting of this new idea, and without waiting to form conjectures, he raised the child in his arms, and went to the door. As soon as he had opened it, there was the cry of 'mammy' again, which Silas had not heard since the child's first hungry waking. Bending forward, he could just discern the marks made by the little feet on the virgin snow, and he followed their track to the furze bushes. 'Mammy!' the little one cried again and again, stretching itself forward so as almost to escape from Silas's arms, before he himself was aware that there was something more than the bush before him – that there was a human body, with the head sunk low in the furze, and half-covered with the shaken snow.

CHAPTER 13

It was after the early supper-time at the Red House, and the entertainment was in that stage when bashfulness itself had passed into easy jollity, when gentlemen, conscious of unusual accomplishments, could at length be prevailed on to dance a hornpipe, and when the Squire preferred talking loudly, scattering snuff, and patting his visitors' backs, to sitting longer at the whist-table – a choice exasperating to uncle Kimble, who, being always volatile in sober business hours, became intense and bitter over cards and brandy, shuffled before his adversary's deal with a glare of suspicion, and turned up a mean trump-card with an air of inexpressible disgust, as if in a world where such things could happen one might as well enter on a course of reckless profligacy. When the evening had advanced to this pitch of freedom and enjoyment, it was usual for the servants, the heavy duties of supper being well over, to get their share of amusement by coming to look on at the dancing; so that the back regions of the house were left in solitude.

There were two doors by which the White Parlour was entered from the hall, and they were both standing open for the sake of air; but the lower one was crowded with the servants and villagers, and only the upper doorway was left free. Bob Cass was figuring in a hornpipe, and his father, very proud of this lithe son, whom he repeatedly declared to be just like himself in his young days in a tone that implied this to be the very highest stamp of juvenile merit, was the centre of a group who had placed themselves opposite the performer, not far from the upper door. Godfrey was standing a little way off, not to admire his brother's dancing, but to keep sight of Nancy, who was seated in the group, near her father. He stood aloof, because he wished to avoid suggesting himself as a subject for the Squire's fatherly jokes in connection with matrimony and Miss Nancy Lammeter's beauty, which were likely to become more and more explicit. But he had the prospect of dancing with her again when the hornpipe was concluded, and in the meanwhile it was very pleasant to get long glances at her quite unobserved.

But when Godfrey was lifting his eyes from one of those long glances, they encountered an object as startling to him at that moment as if it had been an apparition from the dead. It *was* an apparition from that hidden life which lies, like a dark by-street, behind the goodly ornamented façade that meets the sunlight and the gaze of respectable admirers. It was his own child carried in Silas Marner's arms. That was his instantaneous impression, unaccompanied by doubt, though he had not seen the child for months past; and when the hope was rising that he might possibly be mistaken, Mr Crackenthorp and Mr Lammeter had already advanced to Silas, in astonishment at this strange advent. Godfrey joined them immediately, unable to rest without hearing every word – trying to control himself, but conscious that if any one noticed him, they must see that he was white-lipped and trembling.

But now all eyes at that end of the room were bent on Silas Marner; the Squire himself had risen, and asked angrily, 'How's this? – what's this? – what do you do coming in here in this way?'

'I'm come for the doctor – I want the doctor,' Silas had said, in the first moment, to Mr Crackenthorp.

'Why, what's the matter, Marner?' said the rector. 'The doctor's here; but say quietly what you want him for.'

'It's a woman,' said Silas, speaking low, and half-breathlessly, just as Godfrey came up. 'She's dead, I think – dead in the snow at the Stone-pits – not far from my door.'

Godfrey felt a great throb: there was one terror in his mind at that moment: it was, that the woman might *not* be dead. That was an evil terror – an ugly inmate to have found a nestling-place in Godfrey's kindly disposition; but no disposition is a security from evil wishes to a man whose happiness hangs on duplicity.

'Hush, hush!' said Mr Crackenthorp. 'Go out into the hall there. I'll fetch the doctor to you. Found a woman in the snow – and thinks she's dead,' he added, speaking low, to the Squire. 'Better say as little about it as possible: it will shock the ladies. Just tell them a poor woman is ill from cold and hunger. I'll go and fetch Kimble.'

By this time, however, the ladies had pressed forward, curious to know what could have brought the solitary linen-weaver there under such strange circumstances, and interested in the pretty child, who, half alarmed and half attracted by the brightness and the numerous company, now frowned and hid her face, now lifted up her head again and looked round placably, until a touch or a coaxing word brought back the frown, and made her bury her face with new determination.

'What child is it?' said several ladies at once, and, among the rest, Nancy Lammeter, addressing Godfrey.

'I don't know – some poor woman's who has been found in the snow, I believe,' was the answer Godfrey wrung from himself with a terrible effort. ('After all, *am* I certain?' he hastened to add, in anticipation of his own conscience.)

'Why, you'd better leave the child here, then, Master Marner,' said good-natured Mrs Kimble, hesitating, however, to take those dingy clothes into contact with her own ornamented satin boddice. 'I'll tell one o' the girls to fetch it.'

'No – no – I can't part with it, I can't let it go,' said Silas, abruptly. 'It's come to me – I've a right to keep it.'

The proposition to take the child from him had come to Silas quite unexpectedly, and his speech, uttered under a strong sudden impulse, was almost like a revelation to himself: a minute before, he had no distinct intention about the child.

'Did you ever hear the like?' said Mrs Kimble, in mild surprise, to her neighbour.

'Now, ladies, I must trouble you to stand aside,' said Mr Kimble, coming from the card-room, in some bitterness at the interruption, but drilled by the long habit of his profession into obedience to unpleasant calls, even when he was hardly sober.

'It's a nasty business turning out now, eh, Kimble?' said the Squire. 'He might ha' gone for your young fellow – the 'prentice, there – what's his name?'

'Might? ay – what's the use of talking about might?' growled uncle Kimble, hastening out with Marner, and followed by Mr Crackenthorp and Godfrey. 'Get me a pair of thick boots, Godfrey, will you? And stay, let somebody run to Winthrop's and fetch Dolly – she's the best woman to get. Ben was here himself before supper; is he gone?'

'Yes, sir, I met him,' said Marner; 'but I couldn't stop to tell him anything, only I said I was going for the doctor, and he said the doctor was at the Squire's. And I made haste and ran, and there was nobody to be seen at the back o' the house, and so I went in to where the company was.'

The child, no longer distracted by the bright light and the smiling women's faces, began to cry and call for 'mammy,' though always clinging to Marner, who had apparently won her thorough confidence. Godfrey had come back with the boots, and felt the cry as if some fibre were drawn tight within him.

'I'll go,' he said, hastily, eager for some movement; 'I'll go and fetch the woman – Mrs Winthrop.'

'Oh, pooh – send somebody else,' said uncle Kimble, hurrying away with Marner.

'You'll let me know if I can be of any use, Kimble,' said Mr Crackenthorp. But the doctor was out of hearing.

Godfrey, too, had disappeared: he was gone to snatch his hat and coat, having just reflection enough to remember that he must not look like a madman; but he rushed out of the house into the snow without heeding his thin shoes.

In a few minutes he was on his rapid way to the Stone-pits by the side of Dolly, who, though feeling that she was entirely in her place in encountering cold and snow on an errand of mercy, was much concerned at a young gentleman's getting his feet wet under a like impulse.

'You'd a deal better go back, sir,' said Dolly, with respectful compassion. 'You've no call to catch cold; and I'd ask you if you'd be so good as tell my husband to come, on your way back – he's at the Rainbow, I doubt – if you found him anyway sober enough to be o' use. Or else, there's Mrs Snell 'ud happen send the boy up to fetch and carry, for there may be things wanted from the doctor's.'

'No, I'll stay, now I'm once out – I'll stay outside here,' said Godfrey, when they came opposite Marner's cottage. 'You can come and tell me if I can do anything.'

'Well, sir, you're very good: you've a tender heart,' said Dolly, going to the door.

Godfrey was too painfully preoccupied to feel a twinge of self-reproach at this undeserved praise. He walked up and down, unconscious that he was plunging ankle-deep in snow, unconscious of everything but trembling suspense about what was going on in the cottage, and the effect of each alternative on his future lot. No, not quite unconscious of everything else. Deeper down, and half-smothered by passionate desire and dread, there was the sense that he ought not to be waiting on these alternatives; that he ought to accept the consequences of his deeds, own the miserable wife, and fulfil the claims of the helpless child. But he had not moral courage enough to contemplate that active renunciation of Nancy as possible for him: he had only conscience and heart enough to make him for ever uneasy under the weakness that forbade the renunciation. And at this moment his mind leaped away from all restraint toward the sudden prospect of deliverance from his long bondage.

'Is she dead?' said the voice that predominated over every other within him. 'If she is, I may marry Nancy; and then I shall be a good fellow in future, and have no secrets, and the child – shall be taken care of somehow.' But across that vision came the other possibility – 'She may live, and then it's all up with me.'

Godfrey never knew how long it was before the door of the cottage opened and Mr Kimble came out. He went forward to meet his uncle, prepared to suppress the agitation he must feel, whatever news he was to hear.

'I waited for you, as I'd come so far,' he said, speaking first.

'Pooh, it was nonsense for you to come out: why didn't you send one of the men? There's nothing to be done. She's dead – has been dead for hours, I should say.'

'What sort of woman is she?' said Godfrey, feeling the blood rush to his face.

'A young woman, but emaciated, with long black hair. Some vagrant – quite in rags. She's got a wedding-ring on, however. They must fetch her away to the workhouse to-morrow. Come, come along.'

'I want to look at her,' said Godfrey. 'I think I saw such a woman yesterday. I'll overtake you in a minute or two.'

Mr Kimble went on, and Godfrey turned back to the cottage. He cast only one glance at the dead face on the pillow, which Dolly had smoothed with decent care; but he remembered that last look at his unhappy hated wife so well, that at the end of sixteen years every line in the worn face was present to him when he told the full story of this night.

He turned immediately towards the hearth, where Silas Marner sat lulling the child. She was perfectly quiet now, but not asleep – only soothed by sweet porridge and warmth into that wide-gazing calm which makes us older human beings, with our inward turmoil, feel a certain awe in the presence of a little child, such as we feel before some quiet majesty or beauty in the earth or sky – before a steady glowing planet, or a full-flowered eglantine, or the bending trees over a silent pathway. The wide-open blue eyes looked up at Godfrey's without any uneasiness or sign of recognition: the child could make no visible [or] audible claim on its father; and the father felt a strange mixture of feelings, a conflict of regret and joy, that the pulse of that little heart had no response for the half-jealous yearning in his own, when the blue eyes turned away from him slowly, and fixed themselves on the weaver's queer face, which was bent low down to look at them, while the small hand began to pull Marner's withered cheek with loving disfiguration.

'You'll take the child to the parish to-morrow?' asked Godfrey, speaking as indifferently as he could.

'Who says so?' said Marner, sharply. 'Will they make me take her?'

'Why, you wouldn't like to keep her, should you – an old bachelor like you?'

'Till anybody shows they've a right to take her away from me,' said Marner. 'The mother's dead, and I reckon it's got no father: it's a lone thing – and I'm a lone thing. My money's gone, I don't know where – and this is come from I don't know where. I know nothing – I'm partly mazed.'

'Poor little thing!' said Godfrey. 'Let me give something towards finding it clothes.'

He had put his hand in his pocket and found half-a-guinea, and, thrusting it into Silas's hand, he hurried out of the cottage to overtake Mr Kimble.

'Ah, I see it's not the same woman I saw,' he said, as he came up. 'It's a pretty little child: the old fellow seems to want to keep it; that's strange for a miser like him. But I gave him a trifle to help him out: the parish isn't likely to quarrel with him for the right to keep the child.'

'No; but I've seen the time when I might have quarrelled with him for it myself. It's too late now, though. If the child ran into the fire, your aunt's too fat to overtake it: she could only sit and grunt like an alarmed sow. But what a fool you are, Godfrey, to come out in your dancing shoes and stockings in this way – and you one of the beaux of the evening, and at your own house! What do you mean by such freaks, young fellow? Has Miss Nancy been cruel, and do you want to spite her by spoiling your pumps?'

'Oh, everything has been disagreeable to-night. I was tired to death of jigging and gallanting,' and that bother about the hornpipes. And I'd got to dance with the other Miss Gunn,' said Godfrey, glad of the subterfuge his uncle had suggested to him.

The prevarication and white lies which a mind that keeps itself ambitiously pure is as uneasy under as a great artist under the false touches that no eye detects but his own, are worn as lightly as mere trimmings when once the actions have become a lie.

Godfrey reappeared in the White Parlour with dry feet, and, since the truth must be told, with a sense of relief and gladness that was too strong for painful thoughts to struggle with. For could he not venture now, whenever opportunity offered, to say the tenderest things to Nancy Lammeter – to promise her and himself that he would always be just what she would desire to see him? There was no danger that his dead wife would be recognised: those were not days of active inquiry and wide report; and as for the registry of their marriage, that was a long way off, buried in unturned pages, away from every one's interest but his own. Dunsey might betray him if he came back; but Dunsey might be won to silence.

And when events turn out so much better for a man than he has had reason to dread, is it not a proof that his conduct has been less foolish and blameworthy than it might otherwise have appeared? When we are treated well, we naturally begin to think that we are not altogether unmeritorious, and that it is only just we should treat ourselves well, and not mar our own good fortune. Where, after all, would be the use of his confessing the past to Nancy Lammeter, and throwing away his happiness? – nay, hers? for he felt some confidence that she loved him. As for the child, he would see that it was cared for: he would never forsake it; he would do everything but own it. Perhaps it would be just as happy in life without being owned by its father, seeing that nobody could tell how things would turn out, and that – is there any other reason wanted? – well, then, that the father would be much happier without owning the child.

CHAPTER 14

There was a pauper's burial that week in Raveloe, and up Kench Yard at Batherley it was known that the dark-haired woman with the fair child, who had lately come to lodge there, was gone away again. That was all the express note taken that Molly had disappeared from the eyes of men. But the unwept death which, to the general lot, seemed as trivial as the summer-shed leaf, was charged with the force of destiny to certain human lives that we know of, shaping their joys and sorrows even to the end.

Silas Marner's determination to keep the 'tramp's child' was matter of hardly less surprise and iterated talk in the village than the robbery of his money. That softening of feeling towards him which dated from his misfortune, that merging of suspicion and dislike in a rather contemptuous pity for him as lone and crazy, was now accompanied with a more active sympathy, especially amongst the women. Notable mothers, who knew what it was to keep children 'whole and sweet;' lazy mothers, who knew what it was to be interrupted in folding their arms and scratching their elbows by the mischievous propensities of children just firm on their legs, were equally interested in conjecturing how a lone man would manage with a two-year-old child on his hands, and were equally ready with their suggestions: the notable chiefly telling him what he had better do, and the lazy ones being emphatic in telling him what he would never be able to do.

Among the notable mothers, Dolly Winthrop was the one whose neighbourly offices were the most acceptable to Marner, for they were rendered without any show of bustling instruction. Silas had shown her the half-guinea given to him by Godfrey, and had asked her what he should do about getting some clothes for the child.

'Eh, Master Marner,' said Dolly, 'there's no call to buy, no more nor a pair o' shoes; for I've got the little petticoats as Aaron wore five years ago, and it's ill spending the money on them baby-clothes, for the child 'ull grow like grass i' May, bless it – that it will.'

And the same day Dolly brought her bundle, and displayed to Marner, one by one, the tiny garments in their due order of succession, most of them patched and darned, but clean and neat as fresh-sprung herbs. This was the introduction to a great ceremony with soap and water, from which Baby came out in new beauty, and sat on Dolly's knee, handling her toes and chuckling and patting her palms together with an air of having made several discoveries about herself, which she communicated by alternate sounds of 'gug-gug-gug,' and 'mammy.' The 'mammy' was not a cry of need or uneasiness: Baby had been used to utter it without expecting either tender sound or touch to follow.

'Anybody 'ud think the angils in heaven couldn't be prettier,' said Dolly, rubbing the golden curls and kissing them. 'And to think of its being covered wi' them dirty rags – and the poor mother – froze to death; but there's Them as took care of it, and brought it to your door, Master Marner. The door was open, and it walked in over the snow, like as if it had been a little starved robin. Didn't you say the door was open?'

'Yes,' said Silas, meditatively. 'Yes – the door was open. The money's gone I don't know where, and this is come from I don't know where.'

He had not mentioned to any one his unconsciousness of the child's entrance, shrinking from questions which might lead to the fact he himself suspected – namely, that he had been in one of his trances.

'Ah,' said Dolly, with soothing gravity, 'it's like the night and the morning, and the sleeping and the waking, and the rain and the harvest' – one goes and the other comes, and we know nothing how nor where. We may strive and scrat and fend,² but it's little we can do arter all the big things come and go wi' no striving o' our'n – they do, that they do; and I think you're in the right on it to keep the little un, Master Marner, seeing as it's been sent to you, though there's folks as thinks different. You'll happen be a bit moithered³ with it while it's so little; but I'll come, and welcome, and see to it for you: I've a bit o' time to spare most days, for when one gets up betimes i' the morning, the clock seems to stan' still tow'rt ten, afore it's time to go about the victual. So, as I say, I'll come and see to the child for you, and welcome.'

'Thank you ... kindly,' said Silas, hesitating a little. 'I'll be glad if you'll tell me things. But,' he added, uneasily, leaning forward to look at Baby with some jealousy, as she was resting her head backward against Dolly's arm, and eyeing him contentedly from a distance – 'But I want to do things for it myself, else it may get fond o' some-body else, and not fond o' me. I've been used to fending for myself in the house – I can learn, I can learn.'

'Eh, to be sure,' said Dolly, gently. 'I've seen men as are wonderful handy wi' children. The men are awk'ard and contrairy mostly, God help 'em – but when the drink's out of 'em, they aren't unsensible, though they're bad for leeching and bandaging – so fiery and un-patient. You see this goes first, next the skin,' proceeded Dolly, taking up the little shirt, and putting it on.

'Yes,' said Marner, docilely, bringing his eyes very close, that they might be initiated in the mysteries; whereupon Baby seized his head with both her small arms, and put her lips against his face with purring noises.

'See there,' said Dolly, with a woman's tender tact, 'she's fondest o' you. She wants to go o' your lap, I'll be bound. Go, then: take her, Master Marner; you can put the things on, and then you can say as you've done for her from the first of her coming to you.'

Marner took her on his lap, trembling with an emotion mysterious to himself, at something unknown dawning on his life. Thought and feeling were so confused within him, that if he had tried to give them utterance, he could only have said that the child was come instead of the gold – that the gold had turned into the child. He took the garments from Dolly, and put them on under her teaching; inter-rupted, of course, by Baby's gymnastics.

'There, then! why, you take to it quite easy, Master Marner,' said Dolly; 'but what shall you do when you're forced to sit in your loom? For she'll get busier and mischievouser every day – she will, bless her. It's lucky as you've got that high hearth i'stead of a grate, for that keeps the fire more out of her reach: but if you've got anything as can be spilt or broke, or as is fit to cut her fingers off, she'll be at it – and it is but right you should know.'

Silas meditated a little while in some perplexity. 'I'll tie her to the leg o' the loom,' he said at last – 'tie her with a good long strip o' something.'

'Well, mayhap that'll do, as it's a little gell, for they're easier per-suaded to sit i' one place nor the lads. I know what the lads are; for

I've had four – four I've had, God knows – and if you was to take and tie 'em up, they'd make a fighting and a crying as if you was ringing the pigs.[4] But I'll bring you my little chair, and some bits o' red rag and things for her to play wi'; an' she'll sit and chatter to 'em as if they was alive. Eh, if it wasn't a sin to the lads to wish 'em made different, bless 'em, I should ha' been glad for one of 'em to be a little gell; and to think as I could ha' taught her to scour, and mend, and the knitting, and everything. But I can teach 'em this little un, Master Marner, when she gets old enough.'

'But she'll be *my* little un,' said Marner, rather hastily. 'She'll be nobody else's.'

'No, to be sure; you'll have a right to her, if you're a father to her, and bring her up according. But,' added Dolly, coming to a point which she had determined beforehand to touch upon, 'you must bring her up like christened folks's children, and take her to church, and let her learn her catechise, as my little Aaron can say off – the "I believe," and everything, and "hurt nobody by word or deed,"[5] – as well as if he was the clerk. That's what you must do, Master Marner, if you'd do the right thing by the orphin child.'

Marner's pale face flushed suddenly under a new anxiety. His mind was too busy trying to give some definite bearing to Dolly's words for him to think of answering her.

'And it's my belief,' she went on, 'as the poor little creature has never been christened, and it's nothing but right as the parson should be spoke to; and if you was noways unwilling, I'd talk to Mr Macey about it this very day. For if the child ever went anyways wrong, and you hadn't done your part by it, Master Marner – 'noculation, and everything to save it from harm – it 'ud be a thorn i' your bed for ever o' this side the grave; and I can't think as it 'ud be easy lying down for anybody when they'd got to another world, if they hadn't done their part by the helpless children as come wi'out their own asking.'

Dolly herself was disposed to be silent for some time now, for she had spoken from the depths of her own simple belief, and was much concerned to know whether her words would produce the desired effect on Silas. He was puzzled and anxious, for Dolly's word 'christened'[6] conveyed no distinct meaning to him. He had only heard of baptism, and had only seen the baptism of grown-up men and women.

'What is it as you mean by "christened"?' he said at last, timidly. 'Won't folks be good to her without it?'

'Dear, dear! Master Marner,' said Dolly, with gentle distress and compassion. 'Had you never no father nor mother as taught you to say your prayers, and as there's good words and good things to keep us from harm?'

'Yes,' said Silas, in a low voice; 'I know a deal about that – used to, used to. But your ways are different: my country was a good way off.' He paused a few moments, and then added, more decidedly, 'But I want to do everything as can be done for the child. And whatever's right for it i' this country, and you think 'ull do it good, I'll act according, if you'll tell me.'

'Well, then, Master Marner,' said Dolly, inwardly rejoiced, 'I'll ask Mr Macey to speak to the parson about it; and you must fix on a name for it, because it must have a name giv' it when it's christened.'

'My mother's name was Hephzibah,[7] said Silas, 'and my little sister was named after her.'

'Eh, that's a hard name,' said Dolly. 'I partly think it isn't a christened name.'

'It's a Bible name,' said Silas, old ideas recurring.

'Then I've no call to speak again' it,' said Dolly, rather startled by Silas's knowledge on this head; 'but you see I'm no scholard, and I'm slow at catching the words. My husband says I'm allays like as if I was putting the haft for the handle[8] – that's what he says – for he's very sharp, God help him. But it was awk'ard calling your little sister by such a hard name, when you'd got nothing big to say, like – wasn't it, Master Marner?'

'We called her Eppie,' said Silas.

'Well, if it was noways wrong to shorten the name, it 'ud be a deal handier. And so I'll go now, Master Marner, and I'll speak about the christening afore dark; and I wish you the best o' luck, and it's my belief as it'll come to you, if you do what's right by the orphin child; – and there's the 'noculation to be seen to; and as to washing its bits o' things, you need look to nobody but me, for I can do 'em wi' one hand when I've got my suds about. Eh, the blessed angil! You'll let me bring my Aaron one o' these days, and he'll show her his little cart as his father's made for him, and the black-and-white pup as he's got a-rearing.'

Baby *was* christened, the rector deciding that a double baptism was the lesser risk to incur; and on this occasion Silas, making himself as clean and tidy as he could, appeared for the first time within the church, and shared in the observances held sacred by his neighbours. He was quite unable, by means of anything he heard or saw, to identify the Raveloe religion with his old faith; if he could at any time in his previous life have done so, it must have been by the aid of a strong feeling ready to vibrate with sympathy, rather than by a comparison of phrases and ideas: and now for long years that feeling had been dormant. He had no distinct idea about the baptism and the church-going, except that Dolly had said it was for the good of the child; and in this way, as the weeks grew to months, the child created fresh and fresh links between his life and the lives from which he had hitherto shrunk continually into narrower isolation. Unlike the gold which needed nothing, and must be worshipped in close-locked solitude – which was hidden away from the daylight, was deaf to the song of birds, and started to no human tones – Eppie was a creature of endless claims and ever-growing desires, seeking and loving sunshine, and living sounds, and living movements; making trial of everything, with trust in new joy, and stirring the human kindness in all eyes that looked on her. The gold had kept his thoughts in an ever-repeated circle, leading to nothing beyond itself; but Eppie was an object compacted of changes and hopes that forced his thoughts onward, and carried them far away from their old eager pacing towards the same blank limit – carried them away to the new things that would come with the coming years, when Eppie would have learned to understand how her father Silas cared for her; and made him look for images of that time in the ties and charities that bound together the families of his neighbours. The gold had asked that he should sit weaving longer and longer, deafened and blinded more and more to all things except the monotony of his loom and the repetition of his web; but Eppie called him away from his weaving, and made him think all its pauses a holiday, reawakening his senses with her fresh life, even to the old winter-flies that came crawling forth in the early spring sunshine, and warming him into joy because *she* had joy.

And when the sunshine grew strong and lasting, so that the buttercups were thick in the meadows, Silas might be seen in the sunny mid-day, or in the late afternoon when the shadows were lengthening under the hedgerows, strolling out with uncovered head to carry Eppie beyond the Stone-pits to where the flowers grew, till they reached some favourite bank where he could sit down, while Eppie toddled to pluck the flowers, and make remarks to the winged things that murmured happily above the bright petals, calling 'Dad-dad's' attention continually by bringing him the flowers. Then she would turn her ear to some sudden bird-note, and Silas learned to please her by making signs of hushed stillness, that they might listen for the note to come again: so that when it came, she set up[9] her small back and laughed with gurgling triumph. Sitting on the banks in this way, Silas began to look for the once familiar herbs again; and as the leaves, with their unchanged outline and markings, lay on his palm, there was a sense of crowding remembrances from which he turned away timidly, taking refuge in Eppie's little world, that lay lightly on his enfeebled spirit.

As the child's mind was growing into knowledge, his mind was growing into memory: as her life unfolded, his soul, long stupefied in a cold narrow prison, was unfolding too, and trembling gradually into full consciousness.

It was an influence which must gather force with every new year: the tones that stirred Silas's heart grew articulate, and called for more distinct answers; shapes and sounds grew clearer for Eppie's eyes and ears, and there was more that 'Dad-dad' was imperatively required to notice and account for. Also, by the time Eppie was three years old, she developed a fine capacity for mischief, and for devising ingenious ways of being troublesome, which found much exercise, not only for Silas's patience, but for his watchfulness and penetration. Sorely was poor Silas puzzled on such occasions by the incompatible demands of love. Dolly Winthrop told him that punishment was good for Eppie, and that, as for rearing a child without making it tingle a little in soft and safe places now and then, it was not to be done.

'To be sure, there's another thing you might do, Master Marner,' added Dolly, meditatively: 'you might shut her up once i' the coal-hole. That was what I did wi' Aaron; for I was that silly wi' the youngest lad, as I could never bear to smack him. Not as I could find i' my heart to let him stay i' the coal-hole more nor a minute, but it was enough to colly[10] him all over, so as he must be new washed and dressed, and it was as good as a rod to him – that was. But I put it upo' your conscience, Master Marner, as there's one of 'em you must choose – ayther smacking or the coal-hole – else she'll get so masterful, there'll be no holding her.'

Silas was impressed with the melancholy truth of this last remark; but his force of mind failed before the only two penal methods open to him, not only because it was painful to him to hurt Eppie, but because he trembled at a moment's contention with her, lest she should love him the less for it. Let even an affectionate Goliath[II] get himself tied to a small tender thing, dreading to hurt it by pulling, and dreading still more to snap the cord, and which of the two, pray, will be master? It was clear that Eppie, with her short toddling steps, must lead father Silas a pretty dance on any fine morning when circumstances favoured mischief.

For example. He had wisely chosen a broad strip of linen as a means of fastening her to his loom when he was busy: it made a broad belt round her waist, and was long enough to allow of her reaching the truckle-bed and sitting down on it, but not long enough for her to attempt any dangerous climbing. One bright summer's morning Silas had been more engrossed than usual in 'setting up' a new piece of work, an occasion on which his scissors were in requisition. These scissors, owing to an especial warning of Dolly's, had been kept carefully out of Eppie's reach; but the click of them had had a peculiar attraction for her ear, and watching the results of that click, she had derived the philosophic lesson that the same cause would produce the same effect. Silas had seated himself in his loom, and the noise of weaving had begun; but he had left his scissors on a ledge which Eppie's arm was long enough to reach; and now, like a small mouse, watching her opportunity, she stole quietly from her corner, secured the scissors, and toddled to the bed again, setting up her back as a mode of concealing the fact. She had a distinct intention as to the use of the scissors; and having cut the linen strip in a jagged but effectual manner, in two moments she had run out at the open door where the sunshine was inviting her, while poor Silas believed her to be a better child than usual. It was not until he happened to need his scissors that the terrible fact burst upon him: Eppie had run out by herself – had perhaps fallen into the Stone-pit. Silas, shaken by the worst fear that could have befallen him, rushed out, calling 'Eppie!' and ran eagerly about the unenclosed space, exploring the dry cavities into which she might have fallen, and then gazing with questioning dread at the smooth red surface of the water. The cold drops stood on his brow. How long had she been out? There was one hope – that she had crept through the stile and got into the fields, where he habitually took her to stroll. But the grass was high in the meadow, and there was no descrying her, if she were there, except by a close search that would be a trespass on Mr Osgood's crop. Still, that misdemeanour must be committed; and poor Silas, after peering all round the hedge-rows, traversed the grass, beginning with perturbed vision to see Eppie behind every group of red sorrel, and to see her moving always farther off as he approached. The meadow was searched in vain; and he got over the stile into the next field, looking with dying hope towards a small pond which was now reduced to its summer shallow-ness, so as to leave a wide margin of good adhesive mud. Here, however, sat Eppie, discoursing cheerfully to her own small boot, which she was using as a bucket to convey the water into a deep hoof-mark, while her little naked foot was planted comfortably on a cush-ion of olive-green mud. A red-headed calf was observing her with alarmed doubt through the opposite hedge.

Here was clearly a case of aberration in a christened child which demanded severe treatment; but Silas, overcome with convulsive joy at finding his treasure again, could do nothing but snatch her up, and cover her with half-sobbing kisses. It was not until he had carried her home, and had begun to think of the necessary washing, that he recollected the need that he should punish Eppie, and 'make her remember.' The idea that she might run away again and come to harm, gave him unusual resolution, and for the first time he deter-mined to try the coal-hole – a small closet near the hearth.

'Naughty, naughty Eppie,' he suddenly began, holding her on his knee, and pointing to her muddy feet and clothes – 'naughty to cut with the scissors and run away. Eppie must go into the coal-hole for being naughty. Daddy must put her in the coal-hole.'

He half-expected that this would be shock enough, and that Eppie would begin to cry. But instead of that, she began to shake herself on his knee, as if the proposition opened a pleasing novelty. Seeing that he must proceed to extremities, he put her into the coal-hole, and held the door closed, with a trembling sense that he was using a strong measure. For a moment there was silence, but then came a little cry, 'Opy, opy!' and Silas let her out again, saying, 'Now Eppie 'ull never be naughty again, else she must go in the coal-hole – a black naughty place.'

The weaving must stand still a long while this morning, for now Eppie must be washed, and have clean clothes on; but it was to be hoped that this punishment would have a lasting effect, and save time in future – though, perhaps, it would have been better if Eppie had cried more.

In half an hour she was clean again, and Silas having turned his back to see what he could do with the linen band, threw it down again, with the reflection that Eppie would be good without fastening for the rest of the morning. He turned round again, and was going to place her in her little chair near the loom, when she peeped out at him with black face and hands again, and said, 'Eppie in de toal-hole!'

This total failure of the coal-hole discipline shook Silas's belief in the efficacy of punishment. 'She'd take it all for fun,' he observed to Dolly, 'if I didn't hurt her, and that I can't do, Mrs Winthrop. If she makes me a bit o' trouble, I can bear it. And she's got no tricks but what she'll grow out of.'

'Well, that's partly true, Master Marner,' said Dolly, sympathetically; 'and if you can't bring your mind to frighten her off touching things, you must do what you can to keep 'em out of her way. That's what I do wi' the pups as the lads are allays a-rearing. They *will* worry and gnaw – worry and gnaw they will, if it was one's Sunday cap as hung anywhere so as they could drag it. They know no difference, God help 'em: it's the pushing o' the teeth as sets 'em on, that's what it is.'

So Eppie was reared without punishment, the burden of her misdeeds being borne vicariously by father Silas. The stone hut was made a soft nest for her, lined with downy patience: and also in the world that lay beyond the stone hut she knew nothing of frowns and denials.

Notwithstanding the difficulty of carrying her and his yarn or linen at the same time, Silas took her with him in most of his journeys to the farm-houses, unwilling to leave her behind at Dolly Winthrop's, who was always ready to take care of her; and little curly-headed Eppie, the weaver's child, became an object of interest at several outlying homesteads, as well as in the village. Hitherto he had been treated very much as if he had been a useful gnome or brownie[12] – a queer and unaccountable creature, who must necessarily be looked at with wondering curiosity and repulsion, and with whom one would be glad to make all greetings and bargains as brief as possible, but who must be dealt with in a propitiatory way, and occasionally have a present of pork or garden stuff to carry home with him, seeing that without him there was no getting the yarn woven. But now Silas met with open smiling faces and cheerful questioning, as a person whose satisfactions and difficulties could be understood. Everywhere he must sit a little and talk about the child, and words of interest were always ready for him: 'Ah, Master Marner, you'll be lucky if she takes the measles soon and easy!' – or, 'Why, there isn't many lone men 'ud ha' been wishing to take up with a little un like that: but I reckon the weaving makes you handier than men as do out-door work – you're partly as handy as a woman, for weaving comes next to spinning.' Elderly masters and mistresses, seated observantly in large kitchen arm-chairs, shook their heads over the difficulties attendant on rearing children, felt Eppie's round arms and legs, and pronounced them remarkably firm, and told Silas that, if she turned out well (which, however, there was no telling), it would be a fine thing for him to have a steady lass to do for him when he got helpless. Servant maidens were fond of carrying her out to look at the hens and chickens, or to see if any cherries could be shaken down in the orchard; and the small boys and girls approached her slowly, with cautious movement and steady gaze, like little dogs face to face with one of their own kind, till attraction had reached the point at which the soft lips were put out for a kiss. No child was afraid of approaching Silas when Eppie was near him: there was no repulsion around him now, either for young or old; for the little child had come to link him once more with the whole world. There was love between him and the child that blent them into one, and there was love between the child and the world – from men and women with parental looks and tones, to the red lady-birds and the round pebbles.

Silas began now to think of Raveloe life entirely in relation to Eppie: she must have everything that was a good in Raveloe; and he listened docilely, that he might come to understand better what this life was, from which, for fifteen years, he had stood aloof as from a strange thing, wherewith he could have no communion: as some man who has a precious plant to which he would give a nurturing home in a new soil, thinks of the rain, and the sunshine, and all influences, in relation to his nursling, and asks industriously for all knowledge that will help him to satisfy the wants of the searching roots, or to guard leaf and bud from invading harm. The disposition to hoard had been utterly crushed at the very first by the loss of his long-stored gold: the coins he earned afterwards seemed as irrelevant as stones brought to complete a house suddenly buried by an earthquake; the sense of bereavement was too heavy upon him for the old thrill of satisfaction to arise again at the touch of the newly-earned coin. And now something had come to replace his hoard which gave a growing purpose to the earnings, drawing his hope and joy continually onward beyond the money.

In old days there were angels who came and took men by the hand and led them away from the city of destruction.[13] We see no white-winged angels now. But yet men are led away from threatening destruction: a hand is put into theirs, which leads them forth gently towards a calm and bright land, so that they look no more backward; and the hand may be a little child's.

CHAPTER 15

There was one person, as you will believe, who watched with keener though more hidden interest than any other, the prosperous growth of Eppie under the weaver's care. He dared not do anything that would imply a stronger interest in a poor man's adopted child than could be expected from the kindliness of the young Squire, when a chance meeting suggested a little present to a simple old fellow whom others noticed with goodwill; but he told himself that the time would come when he might do something towards furthering the welfare of his daughter without incurring suspicion. Was he very uneasy in the meantime at his inability to give his daughter her birthright? I cannot say that he was. The child was being taken care of, and would very likely be happy, as people in humble stations often were – happier, perhaps, than those brought up in luxury.

That famous ring' that pricked its owner when he forgot duty and followed desire – I wonder if it pricked very hard when he set out on the chase, or whether it pricked but lightly then, and only pierced to the quick when the chase had long been ended, and hope, folding her wings, looked backward and became regret?

Godfrey Cass's cheek and eye were brighter than ever now. He was so undivided in his aims, that he seemed like a man of firmness. No Dunsey had come back: people had made up their minds that he was gone for a soldier, or gone 'out of the country,' and no one cared to be specific in their inquiries on a subject delicate to a respectable family. Godfrey had ceased to see the shadow of Dunsey across his path; and the path now lay straight forward to the accomplishment of his best, longest-cherished wishes. Everybody said Mr Godfrey had taken the right turn; and it was pretty clear what would be the end of things, for there were not many days in the week that he was not seen riding to the Warrens. Godfrey himself, when he was asked jocosely if the day had been fixed, smiled with the pleasant consciousness of a lover who could say 'yes,' if he liked. He felt a reformed man, delivered from temptation; and the vision of his future life seemed to him as a promised land for which he had no cause to fight. He saw himself with all his happiness centred on his own hearth, while Nancy would smile on him as he played with the children.

And that other child, not on the hearth – he would not forget it; he would see that it was well provided for. That was a father's duty.

PART II

CHAPTER 16

It was a bright autumn Sunday, sixteen years after Silas Marner had found his new treasure on the hearth. The bells of the old Raveloe church were ringing the cheerful peal which told that the morning service was ended; and out of the arched doorway in the tower came slowly, retarded by friendly greetings and questions, the richer parishioners who had chosen this bright Sunday morning as eligible for church-going. It was the rural fashion of that time for the more important members of the congregation to depart first, while their humbler neighbours waited and looked on, stroking their bent heads or dropping their curtsies to any large ratepayer who turned to notice them.

Foremost among these advancing groups of well-clad people, there are some whom we shall recognise, in spite of Time, who has laid his hand on them all. The tall blond man of forty is not much changed in feature from the Godfrey Cass of six-and-twenty: he is only fuller in flesh, and has only lost the indefinable look of youth – a loss which is marked even when the eye is undulled and the wrinkles are not yet come. Perhaps the pretty woman, not much younger than he, who is leaning on his arm, is more changed than her husband: the lovely bloom that used to be always on her cheek now comes but fitfully, with the fresh morning air or with some strong surprise; yet to all who love human faces best for what they tell of human experience, Nancy's beauty has a heightened interest. Often the soul is ripened into fuller goodness while age has spread an ugly film, so that mere glances can never divine the preciousness of the fruit. But the years have not been so cruel to Nancy. The firm yet placid mouth, the clear veracious glance of the brown eyes, speak now of a nature that has been tested and has kept its highest qualities; and even the costume, with its dainty neatness and purity, has more significance now the coquetries of youth can have nothing to do with it.

Mr and Mrs Godfrey Cass (any higher title has died away from Raveloe lips since the old Squire was gathered to his fathers and his inheritance was divided) have turned round to look for the tall aged

man and the plainly dressed woman who are a little behind – Nancy
having observed that they must wait for 'father and Priscilla' – and
now they all turn into a narrower path leading across the churchyard
to a small gate opposite the Red House. We will not follow them now;
for may there not be some others in this departing congregation
whom we should like to see again – some of those who are not likely
to be handsomely clad, and whom we may not recognise so easily as
the master and mistress of the Red House?

But it is impossible to mistake Silas Marner. His large brown eyes
seem to have gathered a longer vision, as is the way with eyes that have
been short-sighted in early life, and they have a less vague, a more
answering gaze; but in everything else one sees signs of a frame much
enfeebled by the lapse of the sixteen years. The weaver's bent shoulders and white hair give him almost the look of advanced age, though
he is not more than five-and-fifty; but there is the freshest blossom of
youth close by his side – a blond dimpled girl of eighteen, who has
vainly tried to chastise her curly auburn hair into smoothness under
her brown bonnet: the hair ripples as obstinately as a brooklet under
the March breeze, and the little ringlets burst away from the restrain-
ing comb behind and show themselves below the bonnet-crown. Eppie
cannot help being rather vexed about her hair, for there is no other girl
in Raveloe who has hair at all like it, and she thinks hair ought to be
smooth. She does not like to be blameworthy even in small things: you
see how neatly her prayer-book is folded in her spotted handkerchief.

That good-looking young fellow, in a new fustian suit, who walks
behind her, is not quite sure upon the question of hair in the abstract,
when Eppie puts it to him, and thinks that perhaps straight hair is the
best in general, but he doesn't want Eppie's hair to be different. She
surely divines that there is some one behind her who is thinking
about her very particularly, and mustering courage to come to her
side as soon as they are out in the lane, else why should she look
rather shy, and take care not to turn away her head from her father
Silas, to whom she keeps murmuring little sentences as to who was at
church, and who was not at church, and how pretty the red
mountain-ash is over the Rectory wall!

'I wish *we* had a little garden, father, with double daisies in, like
Mrs Winthrop's,' said Eppie, when they were out in the lane; 'only
they say it 'ud take a deal of digging and bringing fresh soil – and you

couldn't do that, could you, father? Anyhow, I shouldn't like you to do it, for it 'ud be too hard work for you.'

'Yes, I could do it, child, if you want a bit o' garden: these long evenings, I could work at taking in a little bit o' the waste, just enough for a root or two o' flowers for you; and again, i' the morning, I could have a turn wi' the spade before I sat down to the loom. Why didn't you tell me before as you wanted a bit o' garden?'

'*I* can dig it for you, Master Marner,' said the young man in fustian, who was now by Eppie's side, entering into the conversation without the trouble of formalities. 'It'll be play to me after I've done my day's work, or any odd bits o' time when the work's slack. And I'll bring you some soil from Mr Cass's garden – he'll let me, and willing.'

'Eh, Aaron, my lad, are you there?' said Silas; 'I wasn't aware of you; for when Eppie's talking o' things, I see nothing but what she's a-saying. Well, if you could help me with the digging, we might get her a bit o' garden all the sooner.'

'Then, if you think well and good,' said Aaron, 'I'll come to the Stone-pits this afternoon, and we'll settle what land's to be taken in, and I'll get up an hour earlier i' the morning, and begin on it.'

'But not if you don't promise me not to work at the hard digging, father,' said Eppie. 'For I shouldn't ha' said anything about it,' she added, half-bashfully half-roguishly, 'only Mrs Winthrop said as Aaron 'ud be so good, and—'

'And you might ha' known it without mother telling you,' said Aaron. 'And Master Marner knows too, I hope, as I'm able and willing to do a turn o' work for him, and he won't do me the unkindness to anyways take it out o' my hands.'

'There, now, father, you won't work in it till it's all easy,' said Eppie, 'and you and me can mark out the beds, and make holes and plant the roots. It'll be a deal livelier at the Stone-pits when we've got some flowers, for I always think the flowers can see us and know what we're talking about. And I'll have a bit o' rosemary, and bergamot, and thyme, because they're so sweet-smelling; but there's no lavender only in the gentlefolks' gardens, I think.'

'That's no reason why you shouldn't have some,' said Aaron, 'for I can bring you slips of anything; I'm forced to cut no end of 'em when I'm gardening, and throw 'em away mostly. There's a big bed o' lavender at the Red House: the missis is very fond of it.'

'Well,' said Silas, gravely, 'so as you don't make free for us, or ask for anything as is worth much at the Red House: for Mr Cass's been so good to us, and built us up the new end o' the cottage, and given us beds and things, as I couldn't abide to be imposin' for garden-stuff or anything else.'

'No, no, there's no imposin',' said Aaron; 'there's never a garden in all the parish but what there's endless waste in it for want o' somebody as could use everything up. It's what I think to myself sometimes, as there need nobody run short o' victuals if the land was made the most on, and there was never a morsel but what could find its way to a mouth. It sets one thinking o' that – gardening does. But I must go back now, else mother 'ull be in trouble as I aren't there.'

'Bring her with you this afternoon, Aaron,' said Eppie; 'I shouldn't like to fix about the garden, and her not know everything from the first – should *you*, father?'

'Ay, bring her if you can, Aaron,' said Silas; 'she's sure to have a word to say as 'll help us to set things on their right end.'

Aaron turned back up the village, while Silas and Eppie went on up the lonely sheltered lane.

'Oh daddy!' she began, when they were in privacy, clasping and squeezing Silas's arm, and skipping round to give him an energetic kiss. 'My little old daddy! I'm so glad. I don't think I shall want anything else when we've got a little garden; and I knew Aaron would dig it for us,' she went on with roguish triumph – 'I knew that very well.'

'You're a deep little puss, you are,' said Silas, with the mild passive happiness of love-crowned age in his face; 'but you'll make yourself fine and beholden to Aaron.'

'Oh no, I shan't,' said Eppie, laughing and frisking; 'he likes it.'

'Come, come, let me carry your prayer-book, else you'll be dropping it, jumping i' that way.'

Eppie was now aware that her behaviour was under observation, but it was only the observation of a friendly donkey, browsing with a log fastened to his foot – a meek donkey, not scornfully critical of human trivialities, but thankful to share in them, if possible, by getting his nose scratched; and Eppie did not fail to gratify him with her usual notice, though it was attended with the inconvenience of his following them, painfully, up to the very door of their home.

But the sound of a sharp bark inside, as Eppie put the key in the door, modified the donkey's views, and he limped away again without bidding. The sharp bark was the sign of an excited welcome that was awaiting them from a knowing brown terrier, who, after dancing at their legs in a hysterical manner, rushed with a worrying noise at a tortoise-shell kitten under the loom, and then rushed back with a sharp bark again, as much as to say, 'I have done my duty by this feeble creature, you perceive;' while the lady-mother of the kitten sat sunning her white bosom in the window, and looked round with a sleepy air of expecting caresses, though she was not going to take any trouble for them.

The presence of this happy animal life was not the only change which had come over the interior of the stone cottage. There was no bed now in the living-room, and the small space was well filled with decent furniture, all bright and clean enough to satisfy Dolly Winthrop's eye. The oaken table and three-cornered oaken chair were hardly what was likely to be seen in so poor a cottage: they had come, with the beds and other things, from the Red House; for Mr Godfrey Cass, as every one said in the village, did very kindly by the weaver; and it was nothing but right a man should be looked on and helped by those who could afford it, when he had brought up an orphan child, and been father and mother to her – and had lost his money too, so as he had nothing but what he worked for week by week, and when the weaving was going down² too – for there was less and less flax spun – and Master Marner was none so young. Nobody was jealous of the weaver, for he was regarded as an exceptional person, whose claims on neighbourly help were not to be matched in Raveloe. Any superstition that remained concerning him had taken an entirely new colour; and Mr Macey, now a very feeble old man of fourscore and six, never seen except in his chimney-corner or sitting in the sunshine at his door-sill, was of opinion that when a man had done what Silas had done by an orphan child, it was a sign that his money would come to light again, or leastwise that the robber would be made to answer for it – for, as Mr Macey observed of himself, his faculties were as strong as ever.

Silas sat down now and watched Eppie with a satisfied gaze as she spread the clean cloth, and set on it the potato-pie, warmed up slowly in a safe Sunday fashion, by being put into a dry pot over a slowly-dying fire, as the best substitute for an oven. For Silas would not consent to have a grate and oven added to his conveniences: he loved the old brick hearth as he had loved his brown pot – and was it not there, when he had found Eppie? The gods of the hearth exist for us still; and let all new faith be tolerant of that fetishism, lest it bruise its own roots.

Silas ate his dinner more silently than usual, soon laying down his knife and fork, and watching half-abstractedly Eppie's play with Snap and the cat, by which her own dining was made rather a lengthy business. Yet it was a sight that might well arrest wandering thoughts: Eppie, with the rippling radiance of her hair and the whiteness of her rounded chin and throat set off by the dark-blue cotton gown, laughing merrily as the kitten held on with her four claws to one shoulder, like a design for a jug-handle, while Snap on the right hand and Puss on the other put up their paws towards a morsel which she held out of the reach of both – Snap occasionally desisting in order to remonstrate with the cat by a cogent worrying growl on the greediness and futility of her conduct; till Eppie relented, caressed them both, and divided the morsel between them.

But at last Eppie, glancing at the clock, checked the play, and said, 'Oh daddy, you're wanting to go into the sunshine to smoke your pipe. But I must clear away first, so as the house may be tidy when godmother comes. I'll make haste – I won't be long.'

Silas had taken to smoking a pipe daily during the last two years, having been strongly urged to it by the sages of Raveloe, as a practice 'good for the fits;' and this advice was sanctioned by Dr Kimble, on the ground that it was as well to try what could do no harm – a principle which was made to answer for a great deal of work in that gentleman's medical practice. Silas did not highly enjoy smoking, and often wondered how his neighbours could be so fond of it; but a humble sort of acquiescence in what was held to be good, had become a strong habit of that new self which had been developed in him since he had found Eppie on his hearth: it had been the only clue his bewildered mind could hold by in cherishing this young life that had been sent to him out of the darkness into which his gold had departed. By seeking what was needful for Eppie, by sharing the effect that everything produced on her, he had himself come to appro-priate the forms of custom and belief which were the mould of Raveloe life; and as, with reawakening sensibilities, memory also reawakened, he had begun to ponder over the elements of his old faith, and blend them with his new impressions, till he recovered a consciousness of unity between his past and present. The sense of presiding goodness and the human trust which come with all pure peace and joy, had given him a dim impression that there had been some error, some mistake, which had thrown that dark shadow over the days of his best years; and as it grew more and more easy to him to open his mind to Dolly Winthrop, he gradually communicated to her all he could describe of his early life. The communication was necessarily a slow and difficult process, for Silas's meagre power of explanation was not aided by any readiness of interpretation in Dolly, whose narrow outward experience gave her no key to strange customs, and made every novelty a source of wonder that arrested them at every step of the narrative. It was only by fragments, and at intervals which left Dolly time to revolve what she had heard till it acquired some familiarity for her, that Silas at last arrived at the climax of the sad story – the drawing of lots, and its false testimony concerning him; and this had to be repeated in several interviews, under new questions on her part as to the nature of this plan for detecting the guilty and clearing the innocent.

'And yourn's the same Bible, you're sure o' that, Master Marner – the Bible as you brought wi' you from that country – it's the same as what they've got at church, and what Eppie's a-learning to read in?'

'Yes,' said Silas, 'every bit the same; and there's drawing o' lots in the Bible,' mind you,' he added in a lower tone.

'Oh dear, dear,' said Dolly in a grieved voice, as if she were hearing an unfavourable report of a sick man's case. She was silent for some minutes; at last she said –

'There's wise folks, happen, as know how it all is; the parson knows, I'll be bound; but it takes big words to tell them things, and such as poor folks can't make much out on. I can never rightly know the meaning o' what I hear at church, only a bit here and there, but I know it's good words – I do. But what lies upo' your mind – it's this, Master Marner: as, if Them above had done the right thing by you, They'd never ha' let you be turned out for a wicked thief when you was innicent.'

'Ah!' said Silas, who had now come to understand Dolly's phraseology, 'that was what fell on me like as if it had been red-hot iron;

because, you see, there was nobody as cared for me or clave to me above nor below. And him as I'd gone out and in wi' for ten year and more, since when we was lads and went halves – mine own famil'ar friend in whom I trusted, had lifted up his heel again' me,[4] and worked to ruin me.'

'Eh, but he was a bad 'un – I can't think as there's another such,' said Dolly. 'But I'm o'ercome, Master Marner; I'm like as if I'd waked and didn't know whether it was night or morning. I feel somehow as sure as I do when I've laid something up though I can't justly put my hand on it, as there was a rights in what happened to you, if one could but make it out; and you'd no call to lose heart as you did. But we'll talk on it again; for sometimes things come into my head when I'm leeching or poulticing, or such, as I could never think on when I was sitting still.'

Dolly was too useful a woman not to have many opportunities of illumination of the kind she alluded to, and she was not long before she recurred to the subject.

'Master Marner,' she said, one day that she came to bring home Eppie's washing, 'I've been sore puzzled for a good bit wi' that trouble o' yourn and the drawing o' lots; and it got twisted back'ards and for'ards, as I didn't know which end to lay hold on. But it come to me all clear like, that night when I was sitting up wi' poor Bessy Fawkes, as is dead and left her children behind, God help 'em – it come to me as clear as daylight; but whether I've got hold on it now, or can anyways bring it to my tongue's end, that I don't know. For I've often a deal inside me as 'll never come out; and for what you talk o' your folks in your old country niver saying prayers by heart nor saying 'em out of a book, they must be wonderful cliver; for if I didn't know "Our Father," and little bits o' good words as I can carry out o' church wi' me, I might down o' my knees every night, but nothing could I say.'

'But you can mostly say something as I can make sense on, Mrs Winthrop,' said Silas.

'Well, then, Master Marner, it come to me summat like this: I can make nothing o' the drawing o' lots and the answer coming wrong; it 'ud mayhap take the parson to tell that, and he could only tell us i' big words. But what come to me as clear as the daylight, it was when I was troubling over poor Bessy Fawkes, and it allays comes into my

head when I'm sorry for folks, and feel as I can't do a power to help
'em, not if I was to get up i' the middle o' the night – it comes into
my head as Them above has got a deal tenderer heart nor what I've
got – for I can't be anyways better nor Them as made me; and if
anything looks hard to me, it's because there's things I don't know on;
and for the matter o' that, there may be plenty o' things I don't know
on, for it's little as I know – that it is. And so, while I was thinking o'
that, you come into my mind, Master Marner, and it all come pouring in: – if *I* felt i' my inside what was the right and just thing by you,
and them as prayed and drawed the lots, all but that wicked un, if
they'd ha' done the right thing by you if they could, isn't there Them
as was at the making on us, and knows better and has a better will?
And that's all as ever I can be sure on, and everything else is a big
puzzle to me when I think on it. For there was the fever come and
took off them as were full-growed, and left the helpless children; and
there's the breaking o' limbs; and them as 'ud do right and be sober
have to suffer by them as are contrary – eh, there's trouble i' this
world, and there's things as we can niver make out the rights on. And
all as we've got to do is to trusten, Master Marner – to do the right
thing as fur as we know, and to trusten. For if us as knows so little can
see a bit o' good and rights, we may be sure as there's a good and a
rights bigger nor what we can know – I feel it i' my own inside as it
must be so. And if you could but ha' gone on trustening, Master
Marner, you wouldn't ha' run away from your fellow-creaturs and
been so lone.'

'Ah, but that 'ud ha' been hard,' said Silas, in an under-tone; 'it 'ud
ha' been hard to trusten then.'

'And so it would,' said Dolly, almost with compunction; 'them
things are easier said nor done; and I'm partly ashamed o' talking.'

'Nay, nay,' said Silas, 'you're i' the right, Mrs Winthrop – you're i'
the right. There's good i' this world – I've a feeling o' that now; and it
makes a man feel as there's a good more nor he can see, i' spite o' the
trouble and the wickedness. That drawing o' the lots is dark; but the
child was sent to me: there's dealings with us – there's dealings.'

This dialogue took place in Eppie's earlier years, when Silas had to
part with her for two hours every day, that she might learn to read at
the dame school,⁵ after he had vainly tried himself to guide her in
that first step to learning. Now that she was grown up, Silas had often

been led, in those moments of quiet outpouring which come to people who live together in perfect love, to talk with *her* too of the past, and how and why he had lived a lonely man until she had been sent to him. For it would have been impossible for him to hide from Eppie that she was not his own child: even if the most delicate reticence on the point could have been expected from Raveloe gossips in her presence, her own questions about her mother could not have been parried, as she grew up, without that complete shrouding of the past which would have made a painful barrier between their minds. So Eppie had long known how her mother had died on the snowy ground, and how she herself had been found on the hearth by father Silas, who had taken her golden curls for his lost guineas brought back to him. The tender and peculiar love with which Silas had reared her in almost inseparable companionship with himself, aided by the seclusion of their dwelling, had preserved her from the lowering influences of the village talk and habits, and had kept her mind in that freshness which is sometimes falsely supposed to be an invariable attribute of rusticity. Perfect love has a breath of poetry which can exalt the relations of the least-instructed human beings;[6] and this breath of poetry had surrounded Eppie from the time when she had followed the bright gleam that beckoned her to Silas's hearth; so that it is not surprising if, in other things besides her delicate prettiness, she was not quite a common village maiden, but had a touch of refinement and fervour which came from no other teaching than that of tenderly-nurtured unvitiated feeling. She was too childish and simple for her imagination to rove into questions about her unknown father; for a long while it did not even occur to her that she must have had a father; and the first time that the idea of her mother having had a husband presented itself to her, was when Silas showed her the wedding-ring which had been taken from the wasted finger, and had been carefully preserved by him in a little lackered box shaped like a shoe. He delivered this box into Eppie's charge when she had grown up, and she often opened it to look at the ring: but still she thought hardly at all about the father of whom it was the symbol. Had she not a father very close to her, who loved her better than any real fathers in the village seemed to love their daughters? On the contrary, who her mother was, and how she came to die in that forlornness, were questions that often pressed on Eppie's mind. Her knowledge of Mrs Winthrop, who was her nearest friend next to Silas, made her feel that a mother must be very precious; and she had again and again asked Silas to tell her how her mother looked, whom she was like, and how he had found her against the furze bush, led towards it by the little footsteps and the outstretched arms. The furze bush was there still; and this afternoon, when Eppie came out with Silas into the sunshine, it was the first object that arrested her eyes and thoughts.

'Father,' she said, in a tone of gentle gravity, which sometimes came like a sadder, slower cadence across her playfulness, 'we shall take the furze bush into the garden; it 'll come into the corner, and just against it I'll put snowdrops and crocuses, 'cause Aaron says they won't die out, but 'll always get more and more.'

'Ah, child,' said Silas, always ready to talk when he had his pipe in his hand, apparently enjoying the pauses more than the puffs, 'it wouldn't do to leave out the furze bush; and there's nothing prettier to my thinking, when it's yallow with flowers. But it's just come into my head what we're to do for a fence – mayhap Aaron can help us to a thought; but a fence we must have, else the donkeys and things 'ull come and trample everything down. And fencing's hard to be got at, by what I can make out.'

'Oh, I'll tell you, daddy,' said Eppie, clasping her hands suddenly, after a minute's thought. 'There's lots o' loose stones about, some of 'em not big, and we might lay 'em atop of one another, and make a wall. You and me could carry the smallest, and Aaron 'ud carry the rest – I know he would.'

'Eh, my precious un,' said Silas, 'there isn't enough stones to go all round; and as for you carrying, why, wi' your little arms you couldn't carry a stone no bigger than a turnip. You're dillicate made, my dear,' he added, with a tender intonation – 'that's what Mrs Winthrop says.'

'Oh, I'm stronger than you think, daddy,' said Eppie; 'and if there wasn't stones enough to go all round, why they'll go part o' the way, and then it 'll be easier to get sticks and things for the rest. See here, round the big pit, what a many stones!'

She skipped forward to the pit, meaning to lift one of the stones and exhibit her strength, but she started back in surprise.

'Oh, father, just come and look here,' she exclaimed – 'come and see how the water's gone down since yesterday. Why, yesterday the pit was ever so full!'

'Well, to be sure,' said Silas, coming to her side. 'Why, that's the draining they've begun on, since harvest, i' Mr Osgood's fields, I reckon. The foreman said to me the other day, when I passed by 'em, "Master Marner," he said, "I shouldn't wonder if we lay your bit o' waste as dry as a bone." It was Mr Godfrey Cass, he said, had gone into the draining: he'd been taking these fields o' Mr Osgood.'

'How odd it 'll seem to have the old pit dried up!' said Eppie, turning away, and stooping to lift rather a large stone. 'See, daddy, I can carry this quite well,' she said, going along with much energy for a few steps, but presently letting it fall.

'Ah, you're fine and strong, arn't you?' said Silas, while Eppie shook her aching arms and laughed. 'Come, come, let us go and sit down on the bank against the stile there, and have no more lifting. You might hurt yourself, child. You'd need have somebody to work for you – and my arm isn't overstrong.'

Silas uttered the last sentence slowly, as if it implied more than met the ear; and Eppie, when they sat down on the bank, nestled close to his side, and, taking hold caressingly of the arm that was not over strong, held it on her lap, while Silas puffed again dutifully at the pipe, which occupied his other arm. An ash in the hedgerow behind made a fretted screen from the sun, and threw happy playful shadows all about them.

'Father,' said Eppie, very gently, after they had been sitting in silence a little while, 'if I was to be married, ought I to be married with my mother's ring?'

Silas gave an almost imperceptible start, though the question fell in with the under-current of thought in his own mind, and then said, in a subdued tone, 'Why, Eppie, have you been a-thinking on it?'

'Only this last week, father,' said Eppie, ingenuously, 'since Aaron talked to me about it.'

'And what did he say?' said Silas, still in the same subdued way, as if he were anxious lest he should fall into the slightest tone that was not for Eppie's good.

'He said he should like to be married, because he was a-going in four-and-twenty, and had got a deal of gardening work, now Mr Mott's given up; and he goes twice a-week regular to Mr Cass's, and once to Mr Osgood's, and they're going to take him on at the Rectory.'

'And who is it as he's wanting to marry?' said Silas, with rather a sad smile.

'Why, me, to be sure, daddy,' said Eppie, with dimpling laughter, kissing her father's cheek; 'as if he'd want to marry anybody else!'

'And you mean to have him, do you?' said Silas.

'Yes, some time,' said Eppie, 'I don't know when. Everybody's married some time, Aaron says. But I told him that wasn't true: for, I said, look at father – he's never been married.'

'No, child,' said Silas, 'your father was a lone man till you was sent to him.'

'But you'll never be lone again, father,' said Eppie, tenderly. 'That was what Aaron said – "I could never think o' taking you away from Master Marner, Eppie." And I said, "It 'ud be no use if you did, Aaron." And he wants us all to live together, so as you needn't work a bit, father, only what's for your own pleasure; and he'd be as good as a son to you – that was what he said.'

'And should you like that, Eppie?' said Silas, looking at her.

'I shouldn't mind it, father,' said Eppie, quite simply. 'And I should like things to be so as you needn't work much. But if it wasn't for that, I'd sooner things didn't change. I'm very happy: I like Aaron to be fond of me, and come and see us often, and behave pretty to you – he always *does* behave pretty to you, doesn't he, father?'

'Yes, child, nobody could behave better,' said Silas, emphatically. 'He's his mother's lad.'

'But I don't want any change,' said Eppie. 'I should like to go on a long, long while, just as we are. Only Aaron does want a change; and he made me cry a bit – only a bit – because he said I didn't care for him, for if I cared for him I should want us to be married, as he did.'

'Eh, my blessed child,' said Silas, laying down his pipe as if it were useless to pretend to smoke any longer, 'you're o'er young to be married. We'll ask Mrs Winthrop – we'll ask Aaron's mother what *she* thinks: if there's a right thing to do, she'll come at it. But there's this to be thought on, Eppie: things *will* change, whether we like it or no; things won't go on for a long while just as they are and no difference. I shall get older and helplesser, and be a burden on you, belike, if I don't go away from you altogether. Not as I mean you'd think me a burden – I know you wouldn't – but it 'ud be hard upon you; and when I look for'ard to that, I like to think as you'd have somebody else besides me – somebody young and strong, as 'll outlast your own life, and take care on you to the end.' Silas paused, and, resting his wrists on his knees, lifted his hands up and down meditatively as he looked on the ground.

'Then, would you like me to be married, father?' said Eppie, with a little trembling in her voice.

'I'll not be the man to say no, Eppie,' said Silas, emphatically; 'but we'll ask your god-mother. She'll wish the right thing by you and her son too.'

'There they come then,' said Eppie. 'Let us go and meet 'em. Oh the pipe! won't you have it lit again, father?' said Eppie, lifting that medicinal appliance from the ground.

'Nay, child,' said Silas, 'I've done enough for to-day. I think, mayhap, a little of it does me more good than so much at once.'

CHAPTER 17

While Silas and Eppie were seated on the bank discoursing in the fleckered shade of the ash-tree, Miss Priscilla Lammeter was resisting her sister's arguments, that it would be better to take tea at the Red House, and let her father have a long nap, than drive home to the Warrens so soon after dinner. The family party (of four only) were seated round the table in the dark wainscoted parlour, with the Sunday dessert before them, of fresh filberts,¹ apples, and pears, duly ornamented with leaves by Nancy's own hand before the bells had rung for church.

A great change has come over the dark wainscoted parlour since we saw it in Godfrey's bachelor days, and under the wifeless reign of the old Squire. Now all is polish, on which no yesterday's dust is ever allowed to rest, from the yard's width of oaken boards round the carpet, to the old Squire's gun and whips and walking-sticks, ranged on the stag's antlers above the mantelpiece. All other signs of sporting and outdoor occupation Nancy has removed to another room; but she has brought into the Red House the habit of filial reverence, and preserves sacredly in a place of honour these relics of her husband's departed father. The tankards are on the side-table still, but the bossed silver is undimmed by handling, and there are no dregs to send forth unpleasant suggestions: the only prevailing scent is of the lavender and rose-leaves that fill the vases of Derbyshire spar.² All is purity and order in this once dreary room, for, fifteen years ago, it was entered by a new presiding spirit.

'Now, father,' said Nancy, '*is* there any call for you to go home to tea? Mayn't you just as well stay with us? – such a beautiful evening as it's likely to be.'

The old gentleman had been talking with Godfrey about the increasing poor-rate³ and the ruinous times, and had not heard the dialogue between his daughters.

'My dear, you must ask Priscilla,' he said, in the once firm voice, now become rather broken. 'She manages me and the farm too.'

'And reason good as I should manage you, father,' said Priscilla,

151

'else you'd be giving yourself your death with rheumatism. And as for the farm, if anything turns out wrong, as it can't but do in these times, there's nothing kills a man so soon as having nobody to find fault with but himself. It's a deal the best way o' being master, to let somebody else do the ordering, and keep the blaming in your own hands. It 'ud save many a man a stroke, *I* believe.'

'Well, well, my dear,' said her father, with a quiet laugh, 'I didn't say you don't manage for everybody's good.'

'Then manage so as you may stay tea, Priscilla,' said Nancy, putting her hand on her sister's arm affectionately. 'Come now; and we'll go round the garden while father has his nap.'

'My dear child, he'll have a beautiful nap in the gig, for I shall drive. And as for staying tea, I can't hear of it; for there's this dairy-maid, now she knows she's to be married, turned Michaelmas,[4] she'd as lief pour the new milk into the pig-trough as into the pans. That's the way with 'em all: it's as if they thought the world 'ud be new-made because they're to be married. So come and let me put my bonnet on, and there'll be time for us to walk round the garden while the horse is being put in.'

When the sisters were treading the neatly-swept garden-walks, between the bright turf that contrasted pleasantly with the dark cones and arches and wall-like hedges of yew, Priscilla said –

'I'm as glad as anything at your husband's making that exchange o' land with cousin Osgood, and beginning the dairying. It's a thousand pities you didn't do it before; for it'll give you something to fill your mind. There's nothing like a dairy if folks want a bit o' worrit to make the days pass. For as for rubbing furniture, when you can once see your face in a table there's nothing else to look for; but there's always something fresh with the dairy; for even in the depths o' winter there's some pleasure in conquering the butter, and making it come whether or no. My dear,' added Priscilla, pressing her sister's hand affectionately as they walked side by side, 'you'll never be low when you've got a dairy.'

'Ah, Priscilla,' said Nancy, returning the pressure with a grateful glance of her clear eyes, 'but it won't make up to Godfrey: a dairy's not so much to a man. And it's only what he cares for that ever makes me low. I'm contented with the blessings we have, if he could be contented.'

'It drives me past patience,' said Priscilla, impetuously, 'that way o' the men – always wanting and wanting, and never easy with what they've got: they can't sit comfortable in their chairs when they've neither ache nor pain, but either they must stick a pipe in their mouths, to make 'em better than well, or else they must be swallowing something strong, though they're forced to make haste before the next meal comes in. But joyful be it spoken, our father was never that sort o' man. And if it had pleased God to make you ugly, like me, so as the men wouldn't ha' run after you, we might have kept to our own family, and had nothing to do with folks as have got uneasy blood in their veins.'

'Oh don't say so, Priscilla,' said Nancy, repenting that she had called forth this outburst; 'nobody has any occasion to find fault with Godfrey. It's natural he should be disappointed at not having any children: every man likes to have somebody to work for and lay by for, and he always counted so on making a fuss with 'em when they were little. There's many another man 'ud hanker more than he does. He's the best of husbands.'

'Oh, I know,' said Priscilla, smiling sarcastically, 'I know the way o' wives; they set one on to abuse their husbands, and then they turn round on one and praise 'em as if they wanted to sell 'em. But father 'll be waiting for me; we must turn now.'

The large gig with the steady old grey was at the front door, and Mr Lammeter was already on the stone steps, passing the time in recalling to Godfrey what very fine points Speckle had when his master used to ride him.

'I always *would* have a good horse, you know,' said the old gentleman, not liking that spirited time to be quite effaced from the memory of his juniors.

'Mind you bring Nancy to the Warrens before the week's out, Mr Cass,' was Priscilla's parting injunction, as she took the reins, and shook them gently, by way of friendly incitement to Speckle.

'I shall just take a turn to the fields against the Stone-pits, Nancy, and look at the draining,' said Godfrey.

'You'll be in again by tea-time, dear?'

'Oh yes, I shall be back in an hour.'

It was Godfrey's custom on a Sunday afternoon to do a little contemplative farming in a leisurely walk. Nancy seldom accompanied him;

for the women of her generation – unless, like Priscilla, they took to outdoor management – were not given to much walking beyond their own house and garden, finding sufficient exercise in domestic duties. So, when Priscilla was not with her, she usually sat with Mant's Bible⁵ before her, and after following the text with her eyes for a little while, she would gradually permit them to wander as her thoughts had already insisted on wandering.

But Nancy's Sunday thoughts were rarely quite out of keeping with the devout and reverential intention implied by the book spread open before her. She was not theologically instructed enough to discern very clearly the relation between the sacred documents of the past which she opened without method, and her own obscure, simple life; but the spirit of rectitude, and the sense of responsibility for the effect of her conduct on others, which were strong elements in Nancy's character, had made it a habit with her to scrutinise her past feelings and actions with self-questioning solicitude. Her mind not being courted by a great variety of subjects, she filled the vacant moments by living inwardly, again and again, through all her remembered experience, especially through the fifteen years of her married time, in which her life and its significance had been doubled. She recalled the small details, the words, tones, and looks, in the critical scenes which had opened a new epoch for her by giving her a deeper insight into the relations and trials of life, or which had called on her for some little effort of forbearance, or of painful adherence to an imagined or real duty – asking herself continually whether she had been in any respect blamable. This excessive rumination and self-questioning is perhaps a morbid habit inevitable to a mind of much moral sensibility when shut out from its due share of outward activity and of practical claims on its affections – inevitable to a noble-hearted, childless woman, when her lot is narrow. 'I can do so little – have I done it all well?' is the perpetually recurring thought; and there are no voices calling her away from that soliloquy, no peremptory demands to divert energy from vain regret or superfluous scruple.

There was one main thread of painful experience in Nancy's married life, and on it hung certain deeply-felt scenes, which were the oftenest revived in retrospect. The short dialogue with Priscilla in the garden had determined the current of retrospect in that frequent direction this particular Sunday afternoon. The first wandering of her thought from the text, which she still attempted dutifully to follow with her eyes and silent lips, was into an imaginary enlargement of the defence she had set up for her husband against Priscilla's implied blame. The vindication of the loved object is the best balm affection can find for its wounds: – 'A man must have so much on his mind,' is the belief by which a wife often supports a cheerful face under rough answers and unfeeling words. And Nancy's deepest wounds had all come from the perception that the absence of children from their hearth was dwelt on in her husband's mind as a privation to which he could not reconcile himself.

Yet sweet Nancy might have been expected to feel still more keenly the denial of a blessing to which she had looked forward with all the varied expectations and preparations, solemn and prettily trivial, which fill the mind of a loving woman when she expects to become a mother. Was there not a drawer filled with the neat work of her hands, all unworn and untouched, just as she had arranged it there fourteen years ago – just, but for one little dress, which had been made the burial-dress? But under this immediate personal trial Nancy was so firmly unmurmuring, that years ago she had suddenly renounced the habit of visiting this drawer, lest she should in this way be cherishing a longing for what was not given.

Perhaps it was this very severity towards any indulgence of what she held to be sinful regret in herself, that made her shrink from applying her own standard to her husband. 'It is very different – it is much worse for a man to be disappointed in that way: a woman can always be satisfied with devoting herself to her husband, but a man wants something that will make him look forward more – and sitting by the fire is so much duller to him than to a woman.' And always, when Nancy reached this point in her meditations – trying, with predetermined sympathy, to see everything as Godfrey saw it – there came a renewal of self-questioning. *Had* she done everything in her power to lighten Godfrey's privation? Had she really been right in the resistance which had cost her so much pain six years ago, and again four years ago – the resistance to her husband's wish that they should adopt a child? Adoption was more remote from the ideas and habits of that time than of our own; still Nancy had her opinion on it. It was as necessary to her mind to have an opinion on all topics, not exclusively masculine, that had come under her notice, as for her to have a precisely marked place for every article of her personal property: and her opinions were always principles to be unwaveringly acted on. They were firm, not because of their basis, but because she held them with a tenacity inseparable from her mental action. On all the duties and proprieties of life, from filial behaviour to the arrangements of the evening toilet, pretty Nancy Lammeter, by the time she was three-and-twenty, had her unalterable little code, and had formed every one of her habits in strict accordance with that code. She carried these decided judgments within her in the most unobtrusive way: they rooted themselves in her mind, and grew there as quietly as grass. Years ago, we know, she insisted on dressing like Priscilla, because 'it was right for sisters to dress alike,' and because 'she would do what was right if she wore a gown dyed with cheese-colouring.' That was a trivial but typical instance of the mode in which Nancy's life was regulated.

It was one of those rigid principles, and no petty egoistic feeling, which had been the ground of Nancy's difficult resistance to her husband's wish. To adopt a child, because children of your own had been denied you, was to try and choose your lot in spite of Providence: the adopted child, she was convinced, would never turn out well, and would be a curse to those who had wilfully and rebelliously sought what it was clear that, for some high reason, they were better without. When you saw a thing was not meant to be, said Nancy, it was a bounden duty to leave off so much as wishing for it. And so far, perhaps, the wisest of men could scarcely make more than a verbal improvement in her principle. But the conditions under which she held it apparent that a thing was not meant to be, depended on a more peculiar mode of thinking. She would have given up making a purchase at a particular place if, on three successive times, rain, or some other cause of Heaven's sending, had formed an obstacle; and she would have anticipated a broken limb or other heavy misfortune to any one who persisted in spite of such indications.

'But why should you think the child would turn out ill?' said Godfrey, in his remonstrances. 'She has thriven as well as child can do with the weaver; and *he* adopted her. There isn't such a pretty little girl anywhere else in the parish, or one fitter for the station we could give her. Where can be the likelihood of her being a curse to anybody?'

'Yes, my dear Godfrey,' said Nancy, who was sitting with her hands tightly clasped together, and with yearning, regretful affection in her eyes. 'The child may not turn out ill with the weaver. But, then, he didn't go to seek her, as we should be doing. It will be wrong: I feel sure it will. Don't you remember what that lady we met at the Royston Baths[6] told us about the child her sister adopted? That was the only adopting I ever heard of: and the child was transported[7] when it was twenty-three. Dear Godfrey, don't ask me to do what I know is wrong: I should never be happy again. I know it's very hard for *you* – it's easier for me – but it's the will of Providence.'

It might seem singular that Nancy – with her religious theory pieced together out of narrow social traditions, fragments of church doctrine imperfectly understood, and girlish reasonings on her small experience – should have arrived by herself at a way of thinking so nearly akin to that of many devout people whose beliefs are held in the shape of a system quite remote from her knowledge: singular, if we did not know that human beliefs, like all other natural growths, elude the barriers of system.

Godfrey had from the first specified Eppie, then about twelve years old, as a child suitable for them to adopt. It had never occurred to him that Silas would rather part with his life than with Eppie. Surely the weaver would wish the best to the child he had taken so much trouble with, and would be glad that such good fortune should happen to her: she would always be very grateful to him, and he would be well provided for to the end of his life – provided for as the excellent part he had done by the child deserved. Was it not an appropriate thing for people in a higher station to take a charge off the hands of a man in a lower? It seemed an eminently appropriate thing to Godfrey, for reasons that were known only to himself; and by a common fallacy, he imagined the measure would be easy because he had private motives for desiring it. This was rather a coarse mode of estimating Silas's relation to Eppie; but we must remember that many of the impressions which Godfrey was likely to gather concerning the labouring people around him would favour the idea that deep affections can hardly go along with callous palms and scant means;

and he had not had the opportunity, even if he had had the power, of entering intimately into all that was exceptional in the weaver's experience. It was only the want of adequate knowledge that could have made it possible for Godfrey deliberately to entertain an unfeeling project: his natural kindness had outlived that blighting time of cruel wishes, and Nancy's praise of him as a husband was not founded entirely on a wilful illusion.

'I was right,' she said to herself, when she had recalled all their scenes of discussion – 'I feel I was right to say him nay, though it hurt me more than anything; but how good Godfrey has been about it! Many men would have been very angry with me for standing out against their wishes; and they might have thrown out that they'd had ill-luck in marrying me; but Godfrey has never been the man to say me an unkind word. It's only what he can't hide: everything seems so blank to him, I know; and the land – what a difference it 'ud make to him, when he goes to see after things, if he'd children growing up that he was doing it all for! But I won't murmur; and perhaps if he'd married a woman who'd have had children, she'd have vexed him in other ways.'

This possibility was Nancy's chief comfort; and to give it greater strength, she laboured to make it impossible that any other wife should have had more perfect tenderness. She had been *forced* to vex him by that one denial. Godfrey was not insensible to her loving effort, and did Nancy no injustice as to the motives of her obstinacy. It was impossible to have lived with her fifteen years and not be aware that an unselfish clinging to the right, and a sincerity clear as the flower-born dew, were her main characteristics; indeed, Godfrey felt this so strongly, that his own more wavering nature, too averse to facing difficulty to be unvaryingly simple and truthful, was kept in a certain awe of this gentle wife who watched his looks with a yearning to obey them. It seemed to him impossible that he should ever confess to her the truth about Eppie: she would never recover from the repulsion the story of his earlier marriage would create, told to her now, after that long concealment. And the child, too, he thought, must become an object of repulsion: the very sight of her would be painful. The shock to Nancy's mingled pride and ignorance of the world's evil might even be too much for her delicate frame. Since he had married her with that secret on his heart, he must keep it there to the last. Whatever else he did, he could not make an irreparable breach between himself and this long-loved wife.

Meanwhile, why could he not make up his mind to the absence of children from a hearth brightened by such a wife? Why did his mind fly uneasily to that void, as if it were the sole reason why life was not thoroughly joyous to him? I suppose it is the way with all men and women who reach middle age without the clear perception that life never *can* be thoroughly joyous: under the vague dulness of the grey hours, dissatisfaction seeks a definite object, and finds it in the privation of an untried good. Dissatisfaction seated musingly on a childless hearth, thinks with envy of the father whose return is greeted by young voices – seated at the meal where the little heads rise one above another like nursery plants, it sees a black care hovering behind every one of them, and thinks the impulses by which men abandon freedom, and seek for ties, are surely nothing but a brief madness. In Godfrey's case there were further reasons why his thoughts should be continually solicited by this one point in his lot: his conscience, never thoroughly easy about Eppie, now gave his childless home the aspect of a retribution; and as the time passed on, under Nancy's refusal to adopt her, any retrieval of his error became more and more difficult.

On this Sunday afternoon it was already four years since there had been any allusion to the subject between them, and Nancy supposed that it was for ever buried.

'I wonder if he'll mind it less or more as he gets older,' she thought; 'I'm afraid more. Aged people feel the miss of children: what would father do without Priscilla? And if I die, Godfrey will be very lonely – not holding together with his brothers much. But I won't be over-anxious, and trying to make things out beforehand: I must do my best for the present.'

With that last thought Nancy roused herself from her reverie, and turned her eyes again towards the forsaken page. It had been forsaken longer than she imagined, for she was presently surprised by the appearance of the servant with the tea-things. It was, in fact, a little before the usual time for tea; but Jane had her reasons.

'Is your master come into the yard, Jane?'

'No 'm, he isn't,' said Jane, with a slight emphasis, of which, however, her mistress took no notice.

'I don't know whether you've seen 'em, 'm,' continued Jane, after a pause, 'but there's folks making haste all one way, afore the front window. I doubt something's happened. There's niver a man to be seen i' the yard, else I'd send and see. I've been up into the top attic, but there's no seeing anything for trees. I hope nobody's hurt, that's all.'

'Oh, no, I daresay there's nothing much the matter,' said Nancy. 'It's perhaps Mr Snell's bull got out again, as he did before.'

'I wish he mayn't gore anybody then, that's all,' said Jane, not altogether despising a hypothesis which covered a few imaginary calamities.

'That girl is always terrifying me,' thought Nancy; 'I wish Godfrey would come in.'

She went to the front window and looked as far as she could see along the road, with an uneasiness which she felt to be childish, for there were now no such signs of excitement as Jane had spoken of, and Godfrey would not be likely to return by the village road, but by the fields. She continued to stand, however, looking at the placid churchyard with the long shadows of the gravestones across the bright green hillocks, and at the glowing autumn colours of the Rectory trees beyond. Before such calm external beauty the presence of a vague fear is more distinctly felt – like a raven flapping its slow wing across the sunny air. Nancy wished more and more that Godfrey would come in.

CHAPTER 18

Some one opened the door at the other end of the room, and Nancy felt that it was her husband. She turned from the window with gladness in her eyes, for the wife's chief dread was stilled.

'Dear, I'm so thankful you're come,' she said, going towards him. 'I began to get ...'

She paused abruptly, for Godfrey was laying down his hat with trembling hands, and turned towards her with a pale face and a strange unanswering glance, as if he saw her indeed, but saw her as part of a scene invisible to herself. She laid her hand on his arm, not daring to speak again; but he left the touch unnoticed, and threw himself into his chair.

Jane was already at the door with the hissing urn. 'Tell her to keep away, will you?' said Godfrey; and when the door was closed again he exerted himself to speak more distinctly.

'Sit down, Nancy – there,' he said, pointing to a chair opposite him. 'I came back as soon as I could, to hinder anybody's telling you but me. I've had a great shock – but I care most about the shock it'll be to you.'

'It isn't father and Priscilla?' said Nancy, with quivering lips, clasping her hands together tightly on her lap.

'No, it's nobody living,' said Godfrey, unequal to the considerate skill with which he would have wished to make his revelation. 'It's Dunstan – my brother Dunstan, that we lost sight of sixteen years ago. We've found him – found his body – his skeleton.'

The deep dread Godfrey's look had created in Nancy made her feel these words a relief. She sat in comparative calmness to hear what else he had to tell. He went on:

'The Stone-pit has gone dry suddenly – from the draining, I suppose; and there he lies – has lain for sixteen years, wedged between two great stones. There's his watch and seals, and there's my gold-handled hunting-whip, with my name on: he took it away, without my knowing, the day he went hunting on Wildfire, the last time he was seen.'

Godfrey paused: it was not so easy to say what came next. 'Do you think he drowned himself?' said Nancy, almost wondering that her husband should be so deeply shaken by what had happened all those years ago to an unloved brother, of whom worse things had been augured.

'No, he fell in,' said Godfrey, in a low but distinct voice, as if he felt some deep meaning in the fact. Presently he added: 'Dunstan was the man that robbed Silas Marner.'

The blood rushed to Nancy's face and neck at this surprise and shame, for she had been bred up to regard even a distant kinship with crime as a dishonour.

'Oh Godfrey!' she said, with compassion in her tone, for she had immediately reflected that the dishonour must be felt still more keenly by her husband.

'There was the money in the pit,' he continued – 'all the weaver's money. Everything's been gathered up, and they're taking the skeleton to the Rainbow. But I came back to tell you: there was no hindering it; you must know.'

He was silent, looking on the ground for two long minutes. Nancy would have said some words of comfort under this disgrace, but she refrained, from an instinctive sense that there was something behind – that Godfrey had something else to tell her. Presently he lifted his eyes to her face, and kept them fixed on her, as he said –

'Everything comes to light, Nancy, sooner or later. When God Almighty wills it, our secrets are found out. I've lived with a secret on my mind, but I'll keep it from you no longer. I wouldn't have you know it by somebody else, and not by me – I wouldn't have you find it out after I'm dead. I'll tell you now. It's been "I will" and "I won't" with me all my life – I'll make sure of myself now.'

Nancy's utmost dread had returned. The eyes of the husband and wife met with awe in them, as at a crisis which suspended affection.

'Nancy,' said Godfrey, slowly, 'when I married you, I hid something from you – something I ought to have told you. That woman Marner found dead in the snow – Eppie's mother – that wretched woman – was my wife: Eppie is my child.'

He paused, dreading the effect of his confession. But Nancy sat quite still, only that her eyes dropped and ceased to meet his. She was pale and quiet as a meditative statue, clasping her hands on her lap.

'You'll never think the same of me again,' said Godfrey, after a little while, with some tremor in his voice.

She was silent.

'I oughtn't to have left the child unowned: I oughtn't to have kept it from you. But I couldn't bear to give you up, Nancy. I was led away into marrying her – I suffered for it.'

Still Nancy was silent, looking down; and he almost expected that she would presently get up and say she would go to her father's. How could she have any mercy for faults that must seem so black to her, with her simple severe notions?

But at last she lifted up her eyes to his again and spoke. There was no indignation in her voice – only deep regret.

'Godfrey, if you had but told me this six years ago, we could have done some of our duty by the child. Do you think I'd have refused to take her in, if I'd known she was yours?'

At that moment Godfrey felt all the bitterness of an error that was not simply futile, but had defeated its own end. He had not measured this wife with whom he had lived so long. But she spoke again, with more agitation.

'And – Oh, Godfrey – if we'd had her from the first, if you'd taken to her as you ought, she'd have loved me for her mother – and you'd have been happier with me: I could better have bore my little baby dying, and our life might have been more like what we used to think it 'ud be.'

The tears fell, and Nancy ceased to speak.

'But you wouldn't have married me then, Nancy, if I'd told you,' said Godfrey, urged, in the bitterness of his self-reproach, to prove to himself that his conduct had not been utter folly. 'You may think you would now, but you wouldn't then. With your pride and your father's, you'd have hated having anything to do with me after the talk there'd have been.'

'I can't say what I should have done about that, Godfrey. I should never have married anybody else. But I wasn't worth doing wrong for – nothing is in this world. Nothing is so good as it seems beforehand – not even our marrying wasn't, you see.' There was a faint sad smile on Nancy's face as she said the last words.

'I'm a worse man than you thought I was, Nancy,' said Godfrey, rather tremulously. 'Can you forgive me ever?'

'The wrong to me is but little, Godfrey: you've made it up to me – you've been good to me for fifteen years. It's another you did the wrong to; and I doubt it can never be all made up for.'

'But we can take Eppie now,' said Godfrey. 'I won't mind the world knowing at last. I'll be plain and open for the rest o' my life.'

'It'll be different coming to us, now she's grown up,' said Nancy, shaking her head sadly. 'But it's your duty to acknowledge her and provide for her; and I'll do my part by her, and pray to God Almighty to make her love me.'

'Then we'll go together to Silas Marner's this very night, as soon as everything's quiet at the Stone-pits.'

CHAPTER 19

Between eight and nine o'clock that evening, Eppie and Silas were seated alone in the cottage. After the great excitement the weaver had undergone from the events of the afternoon, he had felt a longing for this quietude, and had even begged Mrs Winthrop and Aaron, who had naturally lingered behind every one else, to leave him alone with his child. The excitement had not passed away: it had only reached that stage when the keenness of the susceptibility makes external stimulus intolerable – when there is no sense of weariness, but rather an intensity of inward life, under which sleep is an impossibility. Any one who has watched such moments in other men remembers the brightness of the eyes and the strange definiteness that comes over coarse features from that transient influence. It is as if a new fineness of ear for all spiritual voices had sent wonder-working vibrations through the heavy mortal frame – as if 'beauty born of murmuring sound'' had passed into the face of the listener.

Silas's face showed that sort of transfiguration, as he sat in his arm-chair and looked at Eppie. She had drawn her own chair towards his knees, and leaned forward, holding both his hands, while she looked up at him. On the table near them, lit by a candle, lay the recovered gold – the old long-loved gold, ranged in orderly heaps, as Silas used to range it in the days when it was his only joy. He had been telling her how he used to count it every night, and how his soul was utterly desolate till she was sent to him.

'At first, I'd a sort o' feeling come across me now and then,' he was saying in a subdued tone, 'as if you might be changed into the gold again; for sometimes, turn my head which way I would, I seemed to see the gold; and I thought I should be glad if I could feel it, and find it was come back. But that didn't last long. After a bit, I should have thought it was a curse come again, if it had drove you from me, for I'd got to feel the need o' your looks and your voice and the touch o' your little fingers. You didn't know then, Eppie, when you were such a little un – you didn't know what your old father Silas felt for you.'

'But I know now, father,' said Eppie. 'If it hadn't been for you, they'd have taken me to the workhouse, and there'd have been nobody to love me.'

'Eh, my precious child, the blessing was mine. If you hadn't been sent to save me, I should ha' gone to the grave in my misery. The money was taken away from me in time; and you see it's been kept – kept till it was wanted for you. It's wonderful – our life is wonderful.'

Silas sat in silence a few minutes, looking at the money. 'It takes no hold of me now,' he said, ponderingly – 'the money doesn't. I wonder if it ever could again – I doubt it might, if I lost you, Eppie. I might come to think I was forsaken again, and lose the feeling that God was good to me.'

At that moment there was a knocking at the door; and Eppie was obliged to rise without answering Silas. Beautiful she looked, with the tenderness of gathering tears in her eyes and a slight flush on her cheeks, as she stepped to open the door. The flush deepened when she saw Mr and Mrs Godfrey Cass. She made her little rustic curtsy, and held the door wide for them to enter.

'We're disturbing you very late, my dear,' said Mrs Cass, taking Eppie's hand, and looking in her face with an expression of anxious interest and admiration. Nancy herself was pale and tremulous.

Eppie, after placing chairs for Mr and Mrs Cass, went to stand against Silas, opposite to them.

'Well, Marner,' said Godfrey, trying to speak with perfect firmness, 'it's a great comfort to me to see you with your money again, that you've been deprived of so many years. It was one of my family did you the wrong – the more grief to me – and I feel bound to make up to you for it in every way. Whatever I can do for you will be nothing but paying a debt, even if I looked no further than the robbery. But there are other things I'm beholden – shall be beholden to you for, Marner.'

Godfrey checked himself. It had been agreed between him and his wife that the subject of his fatherhood should be approached very carefully, and that, if possible, the disclosure should be reserved for the future, so that it might be made to Eppie gradually. Nancy had urged this, because she felt strongly the painful light in which Eppie must inevitably see the relation between her father and mother.

Silas, always ill at ease when he was being spoken to by 'betters,' such as Mr Cass – tall, powerful, florid men, seen chiefly on horseback – answered with some constraint –

'Sir, I've a deal to thank you for a'ready. As for the robbery, I count it no loss to me. And if I did, you couldn't help it: you aren't answerable for it.'

'You may look at it in that way, Marner, but I never can; and I hope you'll let me act according to my own feeling of what's just. I know you're easily contented: you've been a hard-working man all your life.'

'Yes, sir, yes,' said Marner, meditatively. 'I should ha' been bad off without my work: it was what I held by when everything else was gone from me.'

'Ah,' said Godfrey, applying Marner's words simply to his bodily wants, 'it was a good trade for you in this country, because there's been a great deal of linen-weaving to be done. But you're getting rather past such close work, Marner: it's time you laid by and had some rest. You look a good deal pulled down, though you're not an old man, *are* you?'

'Fifty-five, as near as I can say, sir,' said Silas.

'Oh, why, you may live thirty years longer – look at old Macey! And that money on the table, after all, is but little. It won't go far either way – whether it's put out to interest, or you were to live on it as long as it would last: it wouldn't go far if you'd nobody to keep but yourself, and you've had two to keep for a good many years now.'

'Eh, sir,' said Silas, unaffected by anything Godfrey was saying, 'I'm in no fear o' want. We shall do very well – Eppie and me 'ull do well enough. There's few working-folks have got so much laid by as that. I don't know what it is to gentlefolks, but I look upon it as a deal – almost too much. And as for us, it's little we want.'

'Only the garden, father,' said Eppie, blushing up to the ears the moment after.

'You love a garden, do you, my dear?' said Nancy, thinking that this turn in the point of view might help her husband. 'We should agree in that: I give a deal of time to the garden.'

'Ah, there's plenty of gardening at the Red House,' said Godfrey, surprised at the difficulty he found in approaching a proposition which had seemed so easy to him in the distance. 'You've done a good part by Eppie, Marner, for sixteen years. It 'ud be a great comfort to you to see her well provided for, wouldn't it? She looks blooming and healthy, but not fit for any hardships: she doesn't look like a strapping girl come of working parents. You'd like to see her taken care of by those who can leave her well off, and make a lady of her; she's more fit for it than for a rough life, such as she might come to have in a few years' time.'

A slight flush came over Marner's face, and disappeared, like a passing gleam. Eppie was simply wondering Mr Cass should talk so about things that seemed to have nothing to do with reality, but Silas was hurt and uneasy.

'I don't take your meaning, sir,' he answered, not having words at command to express the mingled feelings with which he had heard Mr Cass's words.

'Well, my meaning is this, Marner,' said Godfrey, determined to come to the point. 'Mrs Cass and I, you know, have no children – nobody to be the better for our good home and everything else we have – more than enough for ourselves. And we should like to have somebody in the place of a daughter to us – we should like to have Eppie, and treat her in every way as our own child. It 'ud be a great comfort to you in your old age, I hope, to see her fortune made in that way, after you've been at the trouble of bringing her up so well. And it's right you should have every reward for that. And Eppie, I'm sure, will always love you and be grateful to you: she'd come and see you very often, and we should all be on the look-out to do everything we could towards making you comfortable.'

A plain man like Godfrey Cass, speaking under some embarrassment, necessarily blunders on words that are coarser than his intentions, and that are likely to fall gratingly on susceptible feelings. While he had been speaking, Eppie had quietly passed her arm behind Silas's head, and let her hand rest against it caressingly: she felt him trembling violently. He was silent for some moments when Mr Cass had ended – powerless under the conflict of emotions, all alike painful. Eppie's heart was swelling at the sense that her father was in distress; and she was just going to lean down and speak to him, when one struggling dread at last gained the mastery over every other in Silas, and he said, faintly –

'Eppie, my child, speak. I won't stand in your way. Thank Mr and Mrs Cass.'

Eppie took her hand from her father's head, and came forward a step. Her cheeks were flushed, but not with shyness this time: the sense that her father was in doubt and suffering banished that sort of self-consciousness. She dropt a low curtsy, first to Mrs Cass and then to Mr Cass, and said –

'Thank you, ma'am – thank you, sir. But I can't leave my father, nor own anybody nearer than him. And I don't want to be a lady – thank you all the same' (here Eppie dropped another curtsy). 'I couldn't give up the folks I've been used to.'

Eppie's lip began to tremble a little at the last words. She retreated to her father's chair again, and held him round the neck: while Silas, with a subdued sob, put up his hand to grasp hers.

The tears were in Nancy's eyes, but her sympathy with Eppie was, naturally, divided with distress on her husband's account. She dared not speak, wondering what was going on in her husband's mind.

Godfrey felt an irritation inevitable to almost all of us when we encounter an unexpected obstacle. He had been full of his own penitence and resolution to retrieve his error as far as the time was left to him; he was possessed with all-important feelings, that were to lead to a predetermined course of action which he had fixed on as the right, and he was not prepared to enter with lively appreciation into other people's feelings counteracting his virtuous resolves. The agitation with which he spoke again was not quite unmixed with anger.

'But I've a claim on you, Eppie – the strongest of all claims. It's my duty, Marner, to own Eppie as my child, and provide for her. She's my own child: her mother was my wife. I've a natural claim on her that must stand before every other.'

Eppie had given a violent start, and turned quite pale. Silas, on the contrary, who had been relieved, by Eppie's answer, from the dread lest his mind should be in opposition to hers, felt the spirit of resistance in him set free, not without a touch of parental fierceness. 'Then, sir,' he answered, with an accent of bitterness that had been silent in him since the memorable day when his youthful hope had perished – 'then, sir, why didn't you say so sixteen year ago, and claim her before I'd come to love her, i'stead o' coming to take her from me now, when you might as well take the heart out o' my body? God gave her to me because you turned your back upon her, and He looks upon her as mine: you've no right to her! When a man turns a blessing from his door, it falls to them as take it in.'

'I know that, Marner. I was wrong. I've repented of my conduct in that matter,' said Godfrey, who could not help feeling the edge of Silas's words.

'I'm glad to hear it, sir,' said Marner, with gathering excitement; 'but repentance doesn't alter what's been going on for sixteen year. Your coming now and saying "I'm her father" doesn't alter the feelings inside us. It's me she's been calling her father ever since she could say the word.'

'But I think you might look at the thing more reasonably, Marner,' said Godfrey, unexpectedly awed by the weaver's direct truth-speaking. 'It isn't as if she was to be taken quite away from you, so that you'd never see her again. She'll be very near you, and come to see you very often. She'll feel just the same towards you.'

'Just the same?' said Marner, more bitterly than ever. 'How'll she feel just the same for me as she does now, when we eat o' the same bit, and drink o' the same cup,[2] and think o' the same things from one day's end to another? Just the same? that's idle talk. You'd cut us i' two.'

Godfrey, unqualified by experience to discern the pregnancy of Marner's simple words, felt rather angry again. It seemed to him that the weaver was very selfish (a judgment readily passed by those who have never tested their own power of sacrifice) to oppose what was undoubtedly for Eppie's welfare; and he felt himself called upon, for her sake, to assert his authority.

'I should have thought, Marner,' he said, severely – 'I should have thought your affection for Eppie would make you rejoice in what was for her good, even if it did call upon you to give up something. You ought to remember your own life's uncertain, and she's at an age now when her lot may soon be fixed in a way very different from what it would be in her father's home: she may marry some low working-man, and then, whatever I might do for her, I couldn't make her well-off. You're putting yourself in the way of her welfare; and though I'm sorry to hurt you after what you've done, and what I've left undone, I feel now it's my duty to insist on taking care of my own daughter. I want to do my duty.'

It would be difficult to say whether it were Silas or Eppie that was more deeply stirred by this last speech of Godfrey's. Thought had been very busy in Eppie as she listened to the contest between her old long-loved father and this new unfamiliar father who had suddenly come to fill the place of that black featureless shadow which had held the ring and placed it on her mother's finger. Her imagination had darted backward in conjectures, and forward in previsions, of what this revealed fatherhood implied; and there were words in Godfrey's last speech which helped to make the previsions especially definite. Not that these thoughts, either of past or future, determined her resolution – *that* was determined by the feelings which vibrated to every word Silas had uttered; but they raised, even apart from these feelings, a repulsion towards the offered lot and the newly-revealed father.

Silas, on the other hand, was again stricken in conscience, and alarmed lest Godfrey's accusation should be true – lest he should be raising his own will as an obstacle to Eppie's good. For many moments he was mute, struggling for the self-conquest necessary to the uttering of the difficult words. They came out tremulously.

'I'll say no more. Let it be as you will. Speak to the child. I'll hinder nothing.'

Even Nancy, with all the acute sensibility of her own affections, shared her husband's view, that Marner was not justifiable in his wish to retain Eppie, after her real father had avowed himself. She felt that it was a very hard trial for the poor weaver, but her code allowed no question that a father by blood must have a claim above that of any foster-father. Besides, Nancy, used all her life to plenteous circumstances and the privileges of 'respectability,' could not enter into the pleasures which early nurture and habit connect with all the little aims and efforts of the poor who are born poor: to her mind, Eppie, in being restored to her birthright, was entering on a too long withheld but unquestionable good. Hence she heard Silas's last words with relief, and thought, as Godfrey did, that their wish was achieved.

'Eppie, my dear,' said Godfrey, looking at his daughter, not without some embarrassment, under the sense that she was old enough to judge him, 'it'll always be our wish that you should show your love and gratitude to one who's been a father to you so many years, and we shall want to help you to make him comfortable in every way. But we hope you'll come to love us as well; and though I haven't been what a father should ha' been to you all these years, I wish to do the utmost in my power for you for the rest of my life, and provide for you as my only child. And you'll have the best of mothers in my wife

– that'll be a blessing you haven't known since you were old enough to know it.'

'My dear, you'll be a treasure to me,' said Nancy, in her gentle voice. 'We shall want for nothing when we have our daughter.'

Eppie did not come forward and curtsy, as she had done before. She held Silas's hand in hers, and grasped it firmly – it was a weaver's hand, with a palm and finger-tips that were sensitive to such pressure – while she spoke with colder decision than before.

'Thank you, ma'am – thank you, sir, for your offers – they're very great, and far above my wish. For I should have no delight i' life any more if I was forced to go away from my father, and knew he was sitting at home, a-thinking of me and feeling lone. We've been used to be happy together every day, and I can't think o' no happiness without him. And he says he'd nobody i' the world till I was sent to him, and he'd have nothing when I was gone. And he's took care of me and loved me from the first, and I'll cleave to him as long as he lives, and nobody shall ever come between him and me.'

'But you must make sure, Eppie,' said Silas, in a low voice – 'you must make sure as you won't ever be sorry, because you've made your choice to stay among poor folks, and with poor clothes and things, when you might ha' had everything o' the best.'

His sensitiveness on this point had increased as he listened to Eppie's words of faithful affection.

'I can never be sorry, father,' said Eppie. 'I shouldn't know what to think on or to wish for with fine things about me, as I haven't been used to. And it 'ud be poor work for me to put on things, and ride in a gig, and sit in a place at church, as 'ud make them as I'm fond of think me unfitting company for 'em. What could *I* care for then?'

Nancy looked at Godfrey with a pained questioning glance. But his eyes were fixed on the floor, where he was moving the end of his stick, as if he were pondering on something absently. She thought there was a word which might perhaps come better from her lips than from his.

'What you say is natural, my dear child – it's natural you should cling to those who've brought you up,' she said, mildly; 'but there's a duty you owe to your lawful father. There's perhaps something to be given up on more sides than one. When your father opens his home to you, I think it's right you shouldn't turn your back on it.'

'I can't feel as I've got any father but one,' said Eppie, impetuously, while the tears gathered. 'I've always thought of a little home where he'd sit i' the corner, and I should fend and do everything for him: I can't think o' no other home. I wasn't brought up to be a lady, and I can't turn my mind to it. I like the working-folks, and their victuals, and their ways. And,' she ended passionately, while the tears fell, 'I'm promised to marry a working-man, as 'll live with father, and help me to take care of him.'

Godfrey looked up at Nancy with a flushed face and smarting dilated eyes. This frustration of a purpose towards which he had set out under the exalted consciousness that he was about to compensate in some degree for the greatest demerit of his life, made him feel the air of the room stifling.

'Let us go,' he said, in an under-tone.

'We won't talk of this any longer now,' said Nancy, rising. 'We're your well-wishers, my dear — and yours too, Marner. We shall come and see you again. It's getting late now.'

In this way she covered her husband's abrupt departure, for Godfrey had gone straight to the door, unable to say more.

CHAPTER 20

Nancy and Godfrey walked home under the starlight in silence. When they entered the oaken parlour, Godfrey threw himself into his chair, while Nancy laid down her bonnet and shawl, and stood on the hearth near her husband, unwilling to leave him even for a few minutes, and yet fearing to utter any word lest it might jar on his feeling. At last Godfrey turned his head towards her, and their eyes met, dwelling in that meeting without any movement on either side. That quiet mutual gaze of a trusting husband and wife is like the first moment of rest or refuge from a great weariness or a great danger – not to be interfered with by speech or action which would distract the sensations from the fresh enjoyment of repose.

But presently he put out his hand, and as Nancy placed hers within it, he drew her towards him, and said –

'That's ended!'

She bent to kiss him, and then said, as she stood by his side, 'Yes, I'm afraid we must give up the hope of having her for a daughter. It wouldn't be right to want to force her to come to us against her will. We can't alter her bringing up and what's come of it.'

'No,' said Godfrey, with a keen decisiveness of tone, in contrast with his usually careless and unemphatic speech – 'there's debts we can't pay like money debts, by paying extra for the years that have slipped by. While I've been putting off and putting off, the trees have been growing – it's too late now. Marner was in the right in what he said about a man's turning away a blessing from his door: it falls to somebody else. I wanted to pass for childless once, Nancy – I shall pass for childless now against my wish.'

Nancy did not speak immediately, but after a little while she asked – 'You won't make it known, then, about Eppie's being your daughter?'

'No: where would be the good to anybody? – only harm. I must do what I can for her in the state of life she chooses. I must see who it is she's thinking of marrying.'

'If it won't do any good to make the thing known,' said Nancy, who thought she might now allow herself the relief of entertaining a feeling which she had tried to silence before, 'I should be very thankful for father and Priscilla never to be troubled with knowing what was done in the past, more than about Dunsey: it can't be helped, their knowing that.'

'I shall put it in my will – I think I shall put it in my will. I shouldn't like to leave anything to be found out, like this about Dunsey,' said Godfrey, meditatively. 'But I can't see anything but difficulties that 'ud come from telling it now. I must do what I can to make her happy in her own way. I've a notion,' he added, after a moment's pause, 'it's Aaron Winthrop she meant she was engaged to. I remember seeing him with her and Marner going away from church.'

'Well, he's very sober and industrious,' said Nancy, trying to view the matter as cheerfully as possible.

Godfrey fell into thoughtfulness again. Presently he looked up at Nancy sorrowfully, and said –

'She's a very pretty, nice girl, isn't she, Nancy?'

'Yes, dear; and with just your hair and eyes: I wondered it had never struck me before.'

'I think she took a dislike to me at the thought of my being her father: I could see a change in her manner after that.'

'She couldn't bear to think of not looking on Marner as her father,' said Nancy, not wishing to confirm her husband's painful impression.

'She thinks I did wrong by her mother as well as by her. She thinks me worse than I am. But she *must* think it: she can never know all. It's part of my punishment, Nancy, for my daughter to dislike me. I should never have got into that trouble if I'd been true to you – if I hadn't been a fool. I'd no right to expect anything but evil could come of that marriage – and when I shirked doing a father's part too.'

Nancy was silent: her spirit of rectitude would not let her try to soften the edge of what she felt to be a just compunction. He spoke again after a little while, but the tone was rather changed: there was tenderness mingled with the previous self-reproach.

'And I got *you*, Nancy, in spite of all; and yet I've been grumbling and uneasy because I hadn't something else – as if I deserved it.'

'You've never been wanting to me, Godfrey,' said Nancy, with quiet sincerity. 'My only trouble would be gone if you resigned yourself to the lot that's been given us.'

'Well, perhaps it isn't too late to mend a bit there. Though it *is* too late to mend some things, say what they will.'

CHAPTER 21

The next morning, when Silas and Eppie were seated at their break-fast, he said to her –

'Eppie, there's a thing I've had on my mind to do this two year, and now the money's been brought back to us, we can do it. I've been turning it over and over in the night, and I think we'll set out to-morrow, while the fine days last. We'll leave the house and everything for your godmother to take care on, and we'll make a little bundle o' things and set out.'

'Where to go, daddy?' said Eppie, in much surprise.

'To my old country – to the town where I was born – up Lantern Yard. I want to see Mr Paston, the minister: something may ha' come out to make 'em know I was innicent o' the robbery. And Mr Paston was a man with a deal o' light – I want to speak to him about the drawing o' the lots. And I should like to talk to him about the religion o' this country-side, for I partly think he doesn't know on it.'

Eppie was very joyful, for there was the prospect not only of wonder and delight at seeing a strange country, but also of coming back to tell Aaron all about it. Aaron was so much wiser than she was about most things – it would be rather pleasant to have this little advantage over him. Mrs Winthrop, though possessed with a dim fear of dangers attendant on so long a journey, and requiring many assur-ances that it would not take them out of the region of carriers' carts and slow waggons, was nevertheless well pleased that Silas should revisit his own country, and find out if he had been cleared from that false accusation.

'You'd be easier in your mind for the rest o' your life, Master Marner,' said Dolly – 'that you would. And if there's any light to be got up the yard as you talk on, we've need of it i' this world, and I'd be glad on it myself, if you could bring it back.'

So on the fourth day from that time, Silas and Eppie, in their Sunday clothes, with a small bundle tied in a blue linen handkerchief, were making their way through the streets of a great manufacturing town. Silas, bewildered by the changes thirty years had brought over his native place, had stopped several persons in succession to ask them the name of this town, that he might be sure he was not under a mistake about it.

'Ask for Lantern Yard, father – ask this gentleman with the tassels on his shoulders a-standing at the shop door; he isn't in a hurry like the rest,' said Eppie, in some distress at her father's bewilderment, and ill at ease, besides, amidst the noise, the movement, and the multitude of strange indifferent faces.

'Eh, my child, he won't know anything about it,' said Silas; 'gentle-folks didn't ever go up the Yard. But happen somebody can tell me which is the way to Prison Street, where the jail is. I know the way out o' that as if I'd seen it yesterday.'

With some difficulty, after many turnings and new inquiries, they reached Prison Street; and the grim walls of the jail, the first object that answered to any image in Silas's memory, cheered him with the certitude, which no assurance of the town's name had hitherto given him, that he was in his native place.

'Ah,' he said, drawing a long breath, 'there's the jail, Eppie; that's just the same: I aren't afraid now. It's the third turning on the left hand from the jail doors – that's the way we must go.'

'Oh, what a dark ugly place!' said Eppie. 'How it hides the sky! It's worse than the Workhouse. I'm glad you don't live in this town now, father. Is Lantern Yard like this street?'

'My precious child,' said Silas, smiling, 'it isn't a big street like this. I never was easy i' this street myself, but I was fond o' Lantern Yard. The shops here are all altered, I think – I can't make 'em out; but I shall know the turning, because it's the third.'

'Here it is,' he said, in a tone of satisfaction, as they came to a narrow alley. 'And then we must go to the left again, and then straight for'ard for a bit, up Shoe Lane: and then we shall be at the entry next to the o'erhanging window, where there's the nick in the road for the water to run. Eh, I can see it all.'

'Oh father, I'm like as if I was stifled,' said Eppie. 'I couldn't ha' thought as any folks lived i' this way, so close together. How pretty the Stone-pits 'ull look when we get back!'

'It looks comical to *me*, child, now – and smells bad. I can't think as it usened to smell so.'

Here and there a sallow, begrimed face looked out from a gloomy doorway at the strangers, and increased Eppie's uneasiness, so that it was a longed-for relief when they issued from the alleys into Shoe Lane, where there was a broader strip of sky.

'Dear heart!' said Silas, 'why, there's people coming out o' the Yard as if they'd been to chapel at this time o' day – a weekday noon!'

Suddenly he started and stood still with a look of distressed amazement, that alarmed Eppie. They were before an opening in front of a large factory, from which men and women were streaming for their mid-day meal.

'Father,' said Eppie, clasping his arm, 'what's the matter?'

But she had to speak again and again before Silas could answer her.

'It's gone, child,' he said, at last, in strong agitation – 'Lantern Yard's gone. It must ha' been here, because here's the house with the o'erhanging window – I know that – it's just the same; but they've made this new opening; and see that big factory! It's all gone – chapel and all.'

'Come into that little brush-shop and sit down, father – they'll let you sit down,' said Eppie, always on the watch lest one of her father's strange attacks should come on. 'Perhaps the people can tell you all about it.'

But neither from the brush-maker, who had come to Shoe Lane only ten years ago, when the factory was already built, nor from any other source within his reach, could Silas learn anything of the old Lantern Yard friends, or of Mr Paston the minister.

'The old place is all swep' away,' Silas said to Dolly Winthrop on the night of his return – 'the little graveyard and everything. The old home's gone; I've no home but this now. I shall never know whether they got at the truth o' the robbery, nor whether Mr Paston could ha' given me any light about the drawing o' the lots. It's dark to me, Mrs Winthrop, that is; I doubt it'll be dark to the last.'

'Well, yes, Master Marner,' said Dolly, who sat with a placid listening face, now bordered by grey hairs; 'I doubt it may. It's the will o' Them above as a many things should be dark to us; but there's some things as I've never felt i' the dark about, and they're mostly what comes i' the day's work. You were hard done by that once, Master Marner, and it seems as you'll never know the rights of it; but that doesn't hinder there *being* a rights, Master Marner, for all it's dark to you and me.'

'No,' said Silas, 'no; that doesn't hinder. Since the time the child was sent to me and I've come to love her as myself, I've had light enough to trusten by; and now she says she'll never leave me, I think I shall trusten till I die.'

CONCLUSION

There was one time of the year which was held in Raveloe to be especially suitable for a wedding. It was when the great lilacs and laburnums in the old-fashioned gardens showed their golden and purple wealth above the lichen-tinted walls, and when there were calves still young enough to want bucketfuls of fragrant milk. People were not so busy then as they must become when the full cheese-making and the mowing had set in; and besides, it was a time when a light bridal dress could be worn with comfort and seen to advantage.

Happily the sunshine fell more warmly than usual on the lilac tufts the morning that Eppie was married, for her dress was a very light one. She had often thought, though with a feeling of renunciation, that the perfection of a wedding-dress would be a white cotton, with the tiniest pink sprig at wide intervals; so that when Mrs Godfrey Cass begged to provide one, and asked Eppie to choose what it should be, previous meditation had enabled her to give a decided answer at once.

Seen at a little distance as she walked across the churchyard and down the village, she seemed to be attired in pure white, and her hair looked like the dash of gold on a lily. One hand was on her husband's arm, and with the other she clasped the hand of her father Silas.

'You won't be giving me away, father,' she had said before they went to church; 'you'll only be taking Aaron to be a son to you.'

Dolly Winthrop walked behind with her husband; and there ended the little bridal procession.

There were many eyes to look at it, and Miss Priscilla Lammeter was glad that she and her father had happened to drive up to the door of the Red House just in time to see this pretty sight. They had come to keep Nancy company to-day, because Mr Cass had had to go away to Lytherley, for special reasons. That seemed to be a pity, for otherwise he might have gone, as Mr Crackenthorp and Mr Osgood certainly would, to look on at the wedding-feast which he had ordered at the Rainbow, naturally feeling a great interest in the weaver who had been wronged by one of his own family.

'I could ha' wished Nancy had had the luck to find a child like that and bring her up,' said Priscilla to her father, as they sat in the gig; 'I should ha' had something young to think of then, besides the lambs and the calves.'

'Yes, my dear, yes,' said Mr Lammeter; 'one feels that as one gets older. Things look dim to old folks: they'd need have some young eyes about 'em, to let 'em know the world's the same as it used to be.'

Nancy came out now to welcome her father and sister; and the wedding group had passed on beyond the Red House to the humbler part of the village.

Dolly Winthrop was the first to divine that old Mr Macey, who had been set in his arm-chair outside his own door, would expect some special notice as they passed, since he was too old to be at the wedding-feast.

'Mr Macey's looking for a word from us,' said Dolly; 'he'll be hurt if we pass him and say nothing – and him so racked with rheumatiz.'

So they turned aside to shake hands with the old man. He had looked forward to the occasion, and had his premeditated speech.

'Well, Master Marner,' he said, in a voice that quavered a good deal, 'I've lived to see my words come true. I was the first to say there was no harm in you, though your looks might be again' you; and I was the first to say you'd get your money back. And it's nothing but rightful as you should. And I'd ha' said the "Amens," and willing, at the holy matrimony; but Tookey's done it a good while now, and I hope you'll have none the worse luck.'

In the open yard before the Rainbow the party of guests were already assembled, though it was still nearly an hour before the appointed feast-time. But by this means they could not only enjoy the slow advent of their pleasure; they had also ample leisure to talk of Silas Marner's strange history, and arrive by due degrees at the conclusion that he had brought a blessing on himself by acting like a father to a lone motherless child. Even the farrier did not negative this sentiment: on the contrary, he took it up as peculiarly his own, and invited any hardy person present to contradict him. But he met with no contradiction; and all differences among the company were merged in a general agreement with Mr Snell's sentiment, that when a man had deserved his good luck, it was the part of his neighbours to wish him joy.

As the bridal group approached, a hearty cheer was raised in the Rainbow yard; and Ben Winthrop, whose jokes had retained their acceptable flavour, found it agreeable to turn in there and receive congratulations; not requiring the proposed interval of quiet at the Stone-pits before joining the company.

Eppie had a larger garden than she had ever expected there now; and in other ways there had been alterations at the expense of Mr Cass, the landlord, to suit Silas's larger family. For he and Eppie had declared that they would rather stay at the Stone-pits than go to any new home. The garden was fenced with stones on two sides, but in front there was an open fence, through which the flowers shone with answering gladness, as the four united people came within sight of them.

'Oh father,' said Eppie, 'what a pretty home ours is! I think nobody could be happier than we are.'

NOTES

TITLE-PAGE

1. In the manuscript the title-page reads: 'Silas Marner:/The Weaver of Raveloe./A Story/by/George Eliot.' In a letter to John Blackwood, her publisher,
on 28 February 1861 she asked for the words 'A Story' to be removed from the
advertisement for the novel. It was omitted from all printed editions.
WORDSWORTH: 'Michael', lines 146–8 (1836 edn.). The first of many
echoes, allusions and quotations from Wordsworth in the novel. In a letter
to John Blackwood on 24 February 1861 George Eliot assumed that no one
would be interested in *Silas Marner* but herself, 'since William Wordsworth is
dead'. As in 'Michael', her novel centres on the covenantal relationship
between father and child.

PART I

CHAPTER I

1. *alien-looking men*: John Blackwood wrote to his wife on 15 June 1861 that
George Eliot had told him that *Silas Marner* 'sprang from her childish recollection of a man with a stoop and expression of face that led her to think that he
was an alien from his fellows'.
2. *winnowing-machine . . . flail*: The winnowing-machine fanned the chaff away
from the grain; the flail was used for threshing corn out of the ears by hand.
3. *rickets, or a wry mouth*: Rickets is a disease, especially of children, caused by
a softening of the bones resulting in bow legs and emaciation; wry means
contorted or twisted.
4. *tithes*: An annual tax of one tenth part of the proceeds of the land, due to
the rector of the parish.
5. *turnpike*: Road on which turnpikes or barriers were erected for the collection of tolls; hence a main road or highway.
6. *those war times*: That is, 1793–1815, when England and France were almost
continuously at war, until Napoleon was finally defeated at Waterloo. During
the war, the usual imports of foreign corn were unobtainable and so high
prices could be charged for home-grown corn.

7. *unexampled*: Without precedent or parallel.

8. *throw him on the parish*: To receive parochial relief.

9. *shell-less state*: That is, a soul without a body.

10. *tale*: Amount or number.

11. *narrow religious sect*: A Christian fundamentalist Dissenting sect with a Calvinistic emphasis on assurance of salvation, election, calling and the priesthood of all believers (see below, nn. 15 and 16).

12. *discipline*: Marked out by a spiritual experience for a special role in the Church.

13. *David and Jonathan*: Jonathan is the epitome of devoted loyalty in his relation with David, king of Israel. See I Samuel 18: 1–4.

14. *William Dane*: In the manuscript the name 'William Wake' was corrected throughout to 'William Waif', which in turn became 'William Dane' in the proof of the first edition.

15. *Assurance of salvation*: Calvin taught that membership of the elect, manifested by evidence of a good life, gave irrefutable assurance of God's eternal favour.

16. *'calling and election sure'*: II Peter 1: 10. God's act of choice in choosing an individual or group for his own special purposes.

17. *cataleptic fit*: A state of prolonged rigidity, as in a hypnotic trance.

18. *accursed thing*: After the siege of Jericho, Achan was condemned to death for concealing part of the Israelites' loot, 'the accursed thing'. See Joshua 6: 18; 7: 1–15.

19. *deacon*: In Protestant churches a lay official appointed or elected to assist the minister.

20. *three pound five*: Three pounds five shillings.

21. *not in the body, but out of the body*: See II Corinthians 12: 2–3, where St Paul describes an experience of religious ecstasy.

22. *give Satan an advantage over you*: See II Corinthians 2: 11, where St Paul stresses the need for forgiveness.

23. *drawing lots*: Following biblical precedent, the lots were cast for the detection of the guilty person. See Joshua 7: 14; Jonah 1: 7.

24. *no just God*: Like Job, Silas accuses God for his misfortunes. See, for example, Job 9: 16–24. Significant analogies are suggested in the novel between Silas and Job. (See below, Chapter 10, n. 10.)

25. *an angel who records . . . sins*: In the book of Revelation the recording angel writes down the sins of the seven churches of Asia. See Revelation 1 and 2.

CHAPTER 2

1. *Lethean*: Lethe is the river of the underworld in Greek mythology that caused forgetfulness in those who drank its waters.
2. *petition*: A prayer of supplication or entreaty.
3. *amulet*: A charm worn as protection against evil.
4. *dropsy*: An accumulation of watery fluid in the tissues.
5. *water in the head*: (Or on the brain.) Hydrocephalus, resulting in the enlargement of the head.
6. *knots in the hands*: A painful accumulation of a chalk-like substance in the joints of hands and feet, sometimes called chalkstones.
7. *familiars*: Companions.
8. *in the days of King Alfred*: The king of the West Saxons (871–99) who had a legendary reputation as the model English king.
9. *balloon journey*: The first successful balloon ascent was made by the Montgolfier brothers in France in 1782.
10. *being*: A manuscript deletion follows: ⟨The same reduction of a human life to a simple function without the consciousness of any higher end to which the function is subservient must happen to every man who has been cut off from sympathy – cut off even from that lowest egoistic interest in his fellowmen which makes their⟩ His life . . .

CHAPTER 3

1. *title of Squire*: A country gentleman, the main landowner in a rural community.
2. *game*: Wild animals and birds hunted for sport.
3. *yeomen*: Farmers on a small scale.
4. *orts*: Scraps or leftovers of food.
5. *top-knots*: A decorative bow worn on the top of the head.
6. *chines*: Joints of meat cut from the back of an animal.
7. *spun butter*: Butter worked into a fine, thread-like consistency as ornament.
8. *wainscot*: Wooden panelling on walls.
9. *King George*: George III (king 1760–1820).
10. *foxes' brushes*: Tails cut off after a hunt as trophies.
11. *distrain*: To seize someone's goods as security for a debt.
12. *a shilling to bless myself with*: That is, when coins had the image of the Cross on them.

13. *laudanum*: Any medicine of which opium was the main ingredient.

14. *to dig and to beg*: See the parable of the dishonest manager who was not strong enough to dig and too ashamed to beg (Luke 16: 3).

15. *'listing for a soldier'*: Enlisting as a private soldier rather than buying an officer's commission.

16. *the sword hanging over him*: In Classical legend, King Dionysius of Syracuse demonstrated to Damocles that being a king was not the happy state he thought it was by forcing him to sit under a sword suspended by a single hair.

17. *pulling the house over my head*: Getting me into trouble (proverbial).

18. *trumps*: The suit of cards that outranks other suits.

19. *crooked sixpence*: Carried in a left-side pocket as a lucky charm.

20. *rioting*: Unrestrained revelry.

21. *pierced by the reeds*: See Isaiah 36: 6.

22. *vicinage*: Vicinity or neighbourhood.

23. *demons . . . a ready-garnished home*: See the parable of the unclean spirit in Matthew 12: 43–5.

24. *open to her*: In the manuscript the chapter ends with ironic pedantry: 'It being the opinion of some philosophers that the absence of an alternative has a great deal to do with the faithfulness of spaniels.' The sentence was deleted in the proof of the first edition.

CHAPTER 4

1. *cover*: The woods or bushes providing shelter for wild creatures where the hunt will start.

2. *pocket-pistol*: A pocket spirit-flask.

3. *latch-string*: The cord passed through the latch-hole of old-fashioned doors by which the latch could be lifted.

4. *jacks*: A mechanical device for rotating meat on a spit.

5. *treddles*: The pedals or levers of a loom which are worked by foot.

CHAPTER 5

1. *horn lantern*: (Or lanthorn.) A lantern with windows of semi-transparent horn.

2. At this point in the manuscript, a deleted sentence – beginning: ⟨The long pipes . . .⟩ – suggests that George Eliot only introduced Chapter 6, the lengthy conversation in the Rainbow, as a second thought. 'The long pipes' reappear at the beginning of Chapter 7.

CHAPTER 6

1. *fustian*: A hard-wearing fabric of cotton mixed with flax or wool.
2. *a red Durham*: A variety of shorthorn cattle bred originally in the county of Durham.
3. *drenching*: Giving medicine to an animal.
4. *'I know what's right ... practise what I know.'*: At this time, the psalms were usually sung in rhymed verse from *The New Version of the Psalms* (1696) by Nahum Tate and Nicholas Brady. This couplet (not identified) reads like a folk version of, for instance, Psalm 119: 33: 'Instruct me in thy statutes, Lord,/thy righteous paths display;/And I from them, through all my life,/will never go astray.'
5. *'key-bugle'*: A bugle fitted with keys to increase the number of its sounds.
6. *lights*: The lungs, especially of sheep, pigs and bullocks.
7. *Charity Land*: Land bequeathed and devoted to a charitable purpose.
8. *Old Harry*: Colloquial name for Satan or the Devil.
9. *afore the Queen's heads*: At the time of the story, Queen Anne (queen 1702–14), had been the last reigning queen of England.
10. *lief*: Gladly, willingly (archaic).
11. *'bate*: Reduce, abate.
12. *plain as a pike-staff*: Originally, packstaff, the staff on which a pedlar supported his pack when resting (proverbial).

CHAPTER 7

1. *the Justice*: The Justice of the Peace, a local magistrate, usually a country gentleman of the district.
2. *strapped*: Put in a strait-jacket.
3. *mushed*: Crushed, subdued (dialect). It is worth pointing out that George Eliot was an expert on Midland dialects and their use in fiction. For example, in reply to an inquiry in 1872 from the philologist, Walter W. Skeat, she wrote:

It must be borne in mind that my inclination to be as close as I could to the rendering of dialect, both in words and spelling, was constantly checked by the artistic duty of being generally intelligible ... The district imagined as the scene of 'Silas Marner' is in N. Warwickshire. But here, and in all my other presentations of English life, except 'Adam Bede', it has been my intention to give the general physiognomy rather than a close portraiture of the provincial speech as I have heard it in the Midland or Mercian region. (*Letters*, IX. 39)

Some of the care she took to achieve this 'general physiognomy' can be seen from the revisions in the list of Textual Variants. See also, Q.D. Leavis (ed.), *Silas Marner* (Harmondsworth: Penguin, 1967), pp. 245–7.

4. *nolo episcopari*: Literally, 'I do not wish to become bishop' (Latin), signifying token resistance to high office because of one's unworthiness.

5. *'watch for the morning'*: Psalm 130: 6.

CHAPTER 8

1. *tinder-box*: Used for making a flame.
2. *the 'sizes*: The Assizes, presided over by judges of the High Court of Justice who periodically visit county towns.
3. *swinging*: (Or swingeing.) Severe, punishing.

CHAPTER 9

1. *managing-man*: Bailiff or farm-manager.
2. *to unstring*: To undo the strings of a purse.
3. *like a jack*: See above, Chapter 4, n. 4.
4. *collogue*: To intrigue or conspire.
5. *entail*: Legal restriction on the descent of an estate to a designated line of heirs.
6. *lieve*: Gladly, willingly (archaic).
7. *shilly-shally*: Indecisive or hesitant, from 'shall I, shall I'.
8. *ostler*: (Or hostler.) A stableman or groom, usually at an inn.
9. *seed . . . after its kind*: See Genesis 1: 12.

CHAPTER 10

1. *Commission of the Peace*: The authority to which Justices of the Peace belong (see above, Chapter 7, n. 1).
2. *brawn*: Meat loaf made from the head (sometimes the feet) of the pig or calf.
3. *wall-eyed*: Eye showing too much white because of a squint, hence dim-sighted.

4. *skimming-dishes*: Dishes for skimming milk or used in cheese-making.

5. *pettitoes*: Pigs' trotters.

6. *yarbs*: Dialect form of 'herbs'.

7. *took the water*: The sprinkling with holy water at baptism.

8. *the cussing of a Ash Wednesday*: The recital of prayers, including a list of God's judgements against sinners, in the office for Ash Wednesday at the beginning of Lent.

9. *trust*: Credit.

10. *comforters*: In the Old Testament, Job is offered various explanations for his misfortunes by his 'comforters'. (See above, Chapter 1, n. 24.)

11. *sacrament*: The sacrament of Holy Communion.

12. *monthly nurse*: A nurse who looks after a baby for a month after its birth.

13. *lard-cakes*: Made of dough, lard, sugar and spice.

14. *I. H. S.*: The first three letters of the name of Jesus in Greek, used as a Christian emblem. The capital Greek E resembles an H.

15. *bakehus*: The bakehouse where people who had only open fires would pay a small fee for the use of an oven.

16. *Sacramen' Day*: Those days on which Holy Communion is celebrated.

17. *'God rest you . . . Christmas-day.'*: Traditional Christmas carol, author unknown.

18. *'Hark the erol angils sing.'*: 'Hark the herald angels sing', Christmas carol by Charles Wesley, from *Hymns and Sacred Poems* (1739).

19. *toast and ale*: Toast, sometimes spiced, was often added to ale and other drinks.

20. *Athanasian Creed*: Replaces the more familiar Apostles' Creed at Morning Prayer on thirteen holy days in the Church of England; it was formerly attributed to St Athanasius.

CHAPTER II

1. *joseph*: A woman's floor-length riding coat, dull brown in colour.

2. *mob-cap*: A large cotton cap with a pouched crown and frill.

3. *puffed . . . top-knotted caps*: Padded; a top-knotted cap was a lace cap with a bow of ribbon on top.

4. *twilled silk . . . tucker*: Silk woven in such a way as to appear in diagonal lines; a tucker was a detachable yoke worn with a low-cut dress.

5. *fortin*: Fortune.

6. *hogsheads*: Large casks containing wines and spirits.

7. *a scrag or a knuckle*: The lean end of a neck of veal or mutton; and the knuckle joint of meat, used in stews.

8. *mawkin*: A slattern or untidy person (dialect).

9. *addled*: Rotten.

10. *the old king fell ill*: George III (king 1760–1820) suffered several attacks of insanity and other illnesses from 1788 onwards; in 1810 the Prince of Wales became Prince Regent.

11. *'The flaxen-headed ploughboy'*: (Or cowboy.) From the ballad-opera, *The Farmer* (1787), written by John O'Keefe, with music by William Shield.

12. *'Over the hills and far away,'*: From 'The Distracted Jockey's Lamentation', with its first line: 'Tom he was a piper's son'. Author unknown.

13. *'Sir Roger de Coverley,'*: Traditional tune accompanying English country dancing.

14. *tithe in kind*: Tithe (see above, Chapter 1, n. 4) paid in agricultural produce (kind) rather than money.

15. *springe*: Active, agile (probably dialect; this is the only recorded instance in *OED*).

16. *presto movement*: To indicate that a passage of music is to be played very fast.

17. *piert*: Lively, brisk, sprightly (dialect).

18. *slack-baked*: Insufficiently baked.

19. *offal*: Cast off, outcast.

CHAPTER 13

1. *gallanting*: To escort or attend to a lady.

CHAPTER 14

1. *the night . . . and the harvest*: Dolly's speech is full of biblical echoes; compare Genesis 8: 22.

2. *scrat and fend*: Struggle and strive to make a living (dialect).

3. *moithered*: Bothered, bewildered (dialect).

4. *ringing the pigs*: Putting a ring in the noses of pigs to prevent them rooting up the ground.

5. *'hurt nobody by word or deed,'*: From the Church of England catechism ('my duty towards my neighbour') in the Book of Common Prayer.

6. *'christened'*: The term used for baptism in the Anglican Church.

7. *Hephzibah*: In Isaiah 62: 4 the prophet proclaims Israel's approaching vindication: 'Thou shalt no more be termed Forsaken; neither shall thy land any more be termed Desolate: but thou shalt be called Hephzibah, and thy land Beulah: for the Lord delighteth in thee, and thy land shall be married.'

In the Bible, the giving of a new name confirms God's covenant with his people.

8. *haft for the handle*: Mistaking one thing for another.

9. *set up*: Arched.

10. *colly*: To blacken from soot or coal-dust (dialect).

11. *Goliath*: The Philistine giant killed by David (I Samuel 17).

12. *brownie*: An elf in folklore who does helpful work, especially household chores, at night.

13. *city of destruction*: Angels led Lot and his family away from the doomed cities of Sodom and Gomorrah (Genesis 19: 1–25). Also, at the beginning of Bunyan's *The Pilgrim's Progress* (1678), Christian sets out from the City of Destruction.

CHAPTER 15

1. *That famous ring*: Madame Leprince de Beaumont, the eighteenth-century French writer, tells the story of 'Prince Chéri' in her *Contes des Fées* (1785) in which the good fairy Candide gives the prince such a ring.

PART II

CHAPTER 16

1. *entering . . . formalities*: The manuscript version reads: 'intruding into the conversation with an absence of formalities that must shock all polite minds'. The revision for the first edition indicates that George Eliot had occasionally to rein in her irony when dealing with the people of Raveloe.

2. *weaving was going down*: A loom that could be worked by steam or water-power was invented by Edmund Cartwright in 1784 and gradually replaced the hand-looms.

3. *drawing o' lots in the Bible*: See above, Chapter 1, n. 23.

4. *mine own famil'ar friend . . . lifted up his heel again' me*: Psalm 41: 9: 'Yea, mine own familiar friend, in whom I trusted, which did eat of my bread, hath lifted up his heel against me.'

5. *dame school*: Small village school usually run by an elderly woman in her own home to teach children to read and write.

6. *Perfect love . . . human beings*: One of the many Wordsworthian echoes in the novel. Compare *The Prelude* (1850 edn.):

Nature for all conditions wants not power
To consecrate, if we have eyes to see,
The outside of her creatures, and to breathe
Grandeur upon the very humblest face
Of human life.

[XIII. 283–7]

CHAPTER 17

1. *filberts*: Hazelnuts or cobnuts.

2. *Derbyshire spar*: Various crystalline minerals mined in Derbyshire.

3. *increasing poor-rate*: The poor-rate, which was the tax levied on ratepayers for the relief of paupers, was increased to compensate labourers for lower wages when the price of corn dropped at the end of the Napoleonic Wars.

4. *Michaelmas*: The feast day (29 September) of St Michael, the archangel, and one of the four quarter-days when workers' contracts could end. The other three are Ladyday (25 March), Midsummer Day (24 June) and Christmas (25 December).

5. *Mant's Bible*: First published in three volumes in 1814 with a commentary by Richard Mant (1776–1848), the bishop of Down.

6. *Royston Baths*: A fictitious spa or fashionable holiday resort.

7. *transported*: Exiled to a penal colony.

CHAPTER 19

1. *'beauty born of murmuring sound'*: Wordsworth, 'Three years she grew in sun and shower', line 29.

2. *eat o' the same bit, and drink o' the same cup*: Compare Nathan's story to David of the poor man with his ewe lamb which 'grew up together with him, and with his children; it did eat of his own meat, and drank of his own cup, and lay in his bosom, and was unto him as a daughter' (II Samuel 12: 3).

EMENDATIONS

The following is a complete list of emendations made to the text of the Cabinet edition for the purposes of the present edition. In most cases, they represent a return to the manuscript version (MS); 1 and 2 refer respectively to the first and second edition. The inconsistent spelling of the exclamatory O/Oh has been regularized in the text in the latter form, but this is not recorded in the emendations.

	Penguin Text	Cabinet Edition
11	to [announce] their marriage	to their marriage
13	fold (MS 1)	folds
19	arranged (MS 1)	arranged,
69	most unfavourable (MS 1)	utmost unfavourable
106	for her, roused (MS 1)	for her roused
111	chair, powerless (MS)	chair powerless,
112	Baby (MS)	baby
121	Baby (MS)	baby
	it's time	its time
142	there, when (MS)	there when
	clue (MS 1)	clew
144	famil'ar (MS 1)	familiar
168	it 'ud be	it u'd be

The Penguin copy-text readings (Cabinet edition) appear first, with substantive variants from the manuscript (MS), first edition (1) and second edition (2) recorded in the second column. (See A Note on the Text for a description of the different editions of the novel.) Variations in spelling, punctuation, hyphenation, capitalization and contractions are not recorded, but the introduction or removal of dialect forms is shown.

Penguin Text (Cabinet Edition 1878)	Variants
5 polished oak	mahogany or polished oak (MS)
honest folk	honest folks (MS 1 2)
6 the ideas	the idea (1)
8 her body, for two months and more, while	her body and that for two months while (MS)
9 end. Their sense	end; and their sense (MS 1 2)
Lantern Yard	Lanthorn Yard *spelt always thus in MS; changed in proof of 1*
10 fervent men	fervid men (MS)
his inherited delight to wander through the fields	the inherited delight he had in wandering in the fields (MS 1 2)
William Dane	William Waif (MS) *spelt thus in MS (See Chapter 1, n. 14.)*
11 usual audible	usually audible (MS 1)
13 church in Lantern Yard, according to which prosecution was forbidden to Christians, even had the case held less scandal to the community. But the members	Church: [church; (MS)] prosecution was held by them to be forbidden to Christians, even if it had been a case in which there was no scandal to the community. But they (MS 1 2)
bruised. *The lots*	bruised. They rose from their knees and the lots were drawn. *The lots* (MS)

16	Power he had vainly trusted in among the streets and at the	Power in which he had vainly trusted among the streets and in the (MS 1 2)
20	functions	mere functions (MS 1 2)
21	drew forth	drew out (MS 1 2)
23	accepting gout	and accepted gout (MS 1 2)
	After ladies	When ladies (MS 1)
24	So soon as Squire	When Squire (MS 1)
	with his brother	as his brother (MS 1 2)
26	rid of you	rid of *you* (MS)
27	it is,' said	it is, Sir,' said (MS)
	get you off	get *you* off (MS)
	come herself	come over herself (MS)
29	no bodily fear	no fear of kicks and bruises (MS)
32	regard. Towards this gratification he was impelled	regard – a gratification towards which he was impelled (MS)
33	open to her.	(*See Chapter 3, n. 24.*)
35	and got his horse pierced with a hedge-stake	and 'staked' his horse (MS 1 2)
36	and to encounter	and encounter (MS 1 2)
	fact that the	fact the (MS 1)
	the stable-keeper	Jennings (MS 1)
37	gold handle	silver handle (MS)
	gold handle	silver handle (MS)
38	passing into rain	turning into rain (MS)
39	distinct in the fire-light	made distinct by the firelight (MS)
	the hook	the silver hook (MS)
42	fifteen years	twelve years (MS 1)
45	close to the Rainbow	close by the Rainbow (MS)
48	hear itself	hear itsen (MS)
49	come into these parts	came into these parts (1)
50	far north'ard	fur north'ard (MS)
	out; yet some folks	out, for – all some folks (MS) out; though some folks (1 2)
	Drumlow	Drummlow *spelt always thus in MS; changed in proof of 1*
51	we went	we got (MS 1 2)
	lasses was	lasses were (MS 1 2)
52	said the butcher	said Snell, the butcher (MS)
	queerer nor ever	queerer nor iver (MS)

54	Master Lundy	Master Snell (MS)
56	a guinea	a guinea – one guinea (MS)
57	circulations of the sap	pulsations of the sap (MS)
	Folks as had	Folks who had (MS)
	so, if anybody	so, eh, Mr Winthrop, if anybody (MS)
58	my guineas	my money (MS 1 2)
	Two hundred and seventy-two pounds	Four hundred and two pounds (MS)
	premises	primises (MS 1)
61	ascertained facts	accomplished facts (MS)
62	else, mayhap, saw	else, praps, saw (MS)
	glazier's wife	wheelwright's wife (MS)
66	Godfrey said	He said (MS)
	anger, and he	anger, but he (MS 1 2)
68	out; awaiting his father, who always took a walk	out, awaiting his father, who always went out and had a walk with (MS 1 2)
69	Fleet	Flint (MS)
	It's worse	It was worse (MS)
71	pull up, sir.'	pull up, Sir, I shall pull up.' (MS)
73	prudence. ¶ In this point . . . called old-fashioned. Favourable Chance is	prudence. And in this point . . . called specially old-fashioned. Favourable Chance, I fancy, is (MS 1 2)
78	harmless, and	harmless, like, and (MS 1)
79	Here Mr Macey . . . went on.	*This sentence added in proof of 1*
80	wife.	wife, the same exemplary woman who had described the pedlar's earrings with graphic particularity. (MS)
	funereal mourner	mourner (MS)
82	need of it	need on it (MS 1 2)
	down the cakes	down the cake (MS 1)
	which the cakes	which the cake (MS 1)
86	love and of faith in a divine love	love and divine faith (MS 1 2)
89	behind the servant	with the servant (MS 1 2)
90	since the snow	for the snow (MS)
92	for while she	for even while she (MS 1)
93	slightly proud	rather proud (MS)
94	*your* choice	your choice (MS)

98	country apothecaries	county apothecaries (1)
99	and amiably intended to smile, but the intention lost itself in small twitchings	and seemed to intend a [to *in 1 2*] smile, that [which *in 1 2*], by the correlation of forces, went off in small twitchings (MS 1 2)
100	*I* believe	I believe (MS 1)
101	front-folds – luring burly fathers	front-folds – burly fathers (MS 1)
102	irreligion – not of deeper significance than the grumbling at the rain	irreligion – not beyond the grumbling at the rain (MS 1)
103	pot o' good ale	pot of good ale (2)
105	can matter but very little.	can make but very little. (1)
106	but this very pressure of emotion that she was in danger of finding too strong for her, roused	but her supreme dread of behaving in a way that she would be unable to approve in herself in after-moments, roused (MS)
	But she was not indifferent to him *yet*.	She was not indifferent to him *yet*, though – (MS 1)
108	arms had not yet relaxed	arms did not yet relax (MS 1)
109	strange visitor	stranger-visitor (MS 1)
110	road coming towards him	road towards (MS)
112	and this roused him	and had roused him (MS)
114	there under such	under such (MS)
120	surprise	surprising (MS 1)
122	with some jealousy	rather jealously (MS)
	high hearth	open hearth (MS)
	Well, mayhap that'll do,	Well, that'll do, praps, (MS)
126	him that punishment	him punishment (MS 1 2)
127	Goliath get	Goliath, even, get (MS)
128	sorrel, and to see her moving	sorrel and moving always (MS)
129	sets 'em	sets them (1)
	hut she knew	hut for her, she knew (MS 1)
131	thing, wherewith he	thing, with which (MS 1)
132	suspicion	suspicions (MS 1 2)
	those brought up	those who are brought up (MS 1 2)
138	answering gaze	answering look (MS 1 2)
139	entering into the conversation without the trouble of formalities.	*(See Chapter 16, n. 1.)*

142	claws to one shoulder, like a design for a jug-handle, while	claws, like a design for a jug-handle, to one shoulder, while (MS)
	till Eppie	till at last Eppie (MS)
	advice was sanctioned	advice having been sanctioned (MS)
143	folks, happen,	folks, praps, (MS)
	Silas, who	Marner, who (MS)
144	a rights	a right (MS 1)
145	I've a feeling o' that now; and it makes a man feel as there's a good more nor he can see.	I feel that now – and, as you say, it makes one feel there's a good we can't see, (MS)
149	like it or no	like it or not (MS 1)
150	to the end.	to the last. (MS)
151	take tea	stay tea (MS 1 2)
	to rest	to settle (MS 1)
152	lief	lieve (MS 1)
155	'It is very different – it is . . . a woman can . . . but a man wants . . . that will . . . the fire is	'It was very different – it was . . . a woman could . . . but a man wanted . . . that would . . . the fire was (MS 1 2)
156	arrangements	arrangement (MS 1)
	sought what it was clear	sought that which it was clear (MS)
157	together, and with	together, with (MS 1)
158	her loving effort	that loving effort (MS)
168	to be the better for	to benefit by (MS 1 2)
	It u'd be	It would be (MS 1 2)
170	would make	would have made (MS 1 2)
	remember your own life's uncertain, and she's	remember that your own life is uncertain, and that she's (MS 1 2)
	more deeply	most deeply (MS 1 2)
171	shadow which	shadow that (MS)
	that was	that was (MS 1 2)
	these feelings	these feeling (1)
	but her code	but Nancy's code (MS)
	should ha' been	should have been (MS 1 2)
173	folks, and their victuals, and their ways	folks – and their houses – and their ways (MS); folks, and their houses, and their ways (1)
	dilated eyes	dilation of the eyes (MS 1 2)

174	my wish	my will (MS)
175	about Dunsey	of Dunsey (MS 1 2)
	I got *you*	I got you (MS)
178	I never was	I was never (MS)
	a sallow, begrimed face	a grimy sallow face (MS)

The complete autograph manuscript of *Silas Marner* is in the British Library (Add. MSS 34026). It was bound in leather by the publisher, John Blackwood, and returned to the author after the publication of the novel. On the first leaf is George Eliot's dedication: 'To my beloved Husband/George Henry Lewes/I give this M.S. of my fourth book/written in London, 1861.' There are revisions on most leaves of the manuscript. All those deletions that can be deciphered – apart from the accidentals of spelling and punctuation – are recorded below. Occasionally, the manuscript punctuation will differ from that of the copy-text.

In the following list, deletions are enclosed in angle brackets (⟨ ⟩). The aim of these notes is to show the different readings rather than to reproduce the exact form of the manuscript revisions and deletions; ampersands (&) are replaced throughout by 'and'.

6 counter ⟨acting⟩ balancing
   by ⟨the⟩ primitive wants ⟨of life⟩, and
   illuminated by ⟨a religious faith which would make it appear a
   heavenward pathway instead of a plain along which they plod to
   the 'parish' and the churchyard.⟩ any enthusiastic religious faith
7 phantasm of ⟨hunger⟩ appetite
   life: ⟨for it soon appeared that Marner⟩ he invited
8 to ⟨marry⟩ accept
   and ⟨unparalleled⟩ unexampled eyes
9 might ⟨help poor folks⟩ cure more folks
   It was ⟨not only⟩ partly . . . for ⟨protection⟩ protecting him
   have ⟨counterweighed⟩ counteracted
10 less truthful ⟨or less sane⟩ man
   William ⟨Wake⟩ Waif *The same revision is made whenever* William
   Wake *appears in Chapter 1. (See Chapter 1, n. 14.)*
   William, ⟨for his friend⟩ to his friend's mind
   self-complacent ⟨expression⟩ suppression

11   effort at ⟨additional signs⟩ an increased manifestation
     be ⟨justified⟩ sanctioned
     expectation, ⟨was⟩ seemed to be
     one ⟨Saturday⟩ night
13   ⟨One⟩ The other persons present, however, ⟨said⟩ began
14   have ⟨laid⟩ woven a plot
     culpable. ⟨For two days Marner sat alone, stunned by pain,
     without hope enough to create the impulse to go to Sarah; and
     on the third, the minister and a deacon came to him charged
     with the message⟩ Marner went home
15   invisible; ⟨and even⟩ nay,
     well-known ⟨faces were upturned⟩ figures
     Christianity ⟨to him, and the seed of God's kingdom⟩ and
16   bitterness. ⟨You see,⟩ The little light he ⟨had⟩ possessed . . . belief
     ⟨had made⟩ was a curtain
17   seemed ⟨dead under⟩ to have died under the bruise ⟨to⟩ that
     had ⟨four⟩ five bright guineas
     saw no ⟨object in life beyond endless weaving⟩ vista beyond
     countless days of weaving? ⟨There was no need⟩ It was needless
     hunger, ⟨lying⟩⟨standing⟩ subsisting
     the ⟨fingers⟩ palm . . . to ⟨their⟩ its full breadth
     loam ⟨of habit⟩ that was deep enough for ⟨desire to plant itself
     there⟩ the seeds of desire
     and ⟨seemed⟩ thought
     seemed to ⟨promise⟩ open a possibility
18   Silas ⟨recovered⟩ felt
     When ⟨the⟩ doctor
     must be ⟨such another⟩ a person of the same sort
     Woman ⟨knew⟩ had words
     sure ⟨and⟩ to set his face against ⟨it⟩ Marner
     their ⟨hands⟩ palms
     small ⟨range⟩ list
19   walks ⟨in order to consult⟩ for the sake of asking his aid. But the
     hope in ⟨him was at last⟩ his wisdom
     the ⟨growing⟩ growth of the sum
     or ⟨sensation⟩ sound, until the repetition has bred a ⟨desire⟩
     want
20   he ⟨placed⟩ set the iron pot

being. *(For deletion at this point, see Chapter 2, n. 10.)*

21   until the ⟨fifteenth⟩⟨twelfth⟩ fifteenth year after he came to
Raveloe. ⟨But in the Christmas tide of this year, his weaving⟩
The livelong
pieces of ⟨cloth⟩ linen
not ⟨part with⟩ change

23   unctuous ⟨water⟩ liquor

24   for ⟨she had been known to look⟩ it was well known

25   do. ⟨Everybody used to say what a fine match⟩ At one time
his ⟨station⟩ place
The ⟨light of the grey evening⟩ fading grey light

26   hundred ⟨and twenty⟩ pounds

27   I can⟨'t⟩ get ⟨any⟩ no money

28   danger[s] to be braved ⟨was one that⟩ were such as
himself ⟨beyond⟩ on the other side of confession

29   give it me, ⟨I'd nothing to do with how you got it⟩ that was all
and ⟨beat⟩ flog

32   a ⟨continual⟩ constant exasperation

34   The ⟨place⟩ spot
as ⟨he expected⟩ Dunstan was quite sure

36   could ⟨bully⟩ worry Godfrey into anything ⟨in the long run⟩.
The
the ⟨possible unpleasantness⟩ prospect

39   on such ⟨a night as this⟩ an evening
brief ⟨object⟩ purpose
were ⟨movable⟩ loose
Dunstan ⟨as if a long time had elapsed⟩ like a long while;

44   like a ⟨deserted⟩ forlorn traveller

52   queerer ⟨than ever⟩ nor iver

53   then ⟨pretend⟩ make believe

54   candour and ⟨moderation⟩ tolerance

55   Marner ⟨went⟩ was

57   was. ⟨But the most probable conclusion was that⟩ Rather

58   ⟨Three⟩ Four hundred and ⟨seventy⟩ two pounds

60   about ⟨keeping⟩ leaving his brother in suspense
direction ⟨away from⟩ opposite to the village

64   that ⟨heralded unpleasant tidings⟩ implied something
disagreeable

66 the fact. ⟨There was always the chance that his father ⟨the
Squire⟩ might take the thing differently⟩ ⟨his father might see
the thing in a light that would induce him to hush it up, rather
than turn his son out and make the family the talk of the county
for six miles round.⟩ The old *Deletion rephrased later in the
paragraph.*
men, he ⟨was heedless of⟩ allowed evils
for ⟨six⟩ ten miles

67 *Originally no chapter break here. Chapter heading added in MS later.*

69 consumed ⟨several⟩ enough bits of beef
Squire ⟨inclined to take things more good humouredly now he
had had his draught of ale⟩ after taking

70 was ⟨looking⟩ staring
guess as ⟨to the cause of this sudden inversion⟩ to what
The ⟨fact⟩ truth

71 with ⟨inventions⟩ invented motives

75 this ⟨result⟩ issue

79 to ⟨come soon⟩ lose no time

80 have ⟨argued⟩ implied
servants ⟨and who could not be spared⟩ to take the sacrament
⟨at least⟩ at one

83 or a ⟨dinner⟩ basin of gruel

85 may ⟨think⟩ judge

86 report ⟨or description⟩ of unknown objects

87 and ⟨beds and bedding was⟩ bedding

91 her ⟨cape⟩ turban

92 she ⟨made⟩ concluded this judicious ⟨observation⟩ remark

96 her ⟨movements⟩ actions

97 Nancy ⟨at that moment⟩ very markedly

100 in a ⟨low voice⟩ cold tone

103 anybody ⟨'ud⟩ could
good ⟨beer⟩ ale

104 caught ⟨in its slight whirl⟩ under the stately stamp

105 dignity and ⟨dislike⟩ repugnance
never ⟨let⟩ think
had ⟨thrown⟩ driven him

106 Godfrey ⟨seating himself on a chair opposite her⟩ with

108 down ⟨at last⟩ against

109 gurgling ⟨and chattering⟩ and making
presently the ⟨soothing⟩ warmth
were ⟨closed⟩ veiled
a ⟨beloved⟩ supremely loved

110 familiar ⟨rounded⟩ resisting outline
a ⟨tiny⟩ sleeping child

111 shabby ⟨dingy⟩ clothing
had a ⟨strong impression⟩ dreamy feeling
dying ⟨embers⟩ fire

112 was ⟨happy⟩ at once ⟨studying⟩ happily occupied with

113 had ⟨brought⟩ advanced to
left ⟨open for the sake of air⟩ free.
repeatedly ⟨and loudly⟩ declared
days, ⟨as if that was⟩ in a tone

114 for ⟨three⟩ months
snow ⟨against my house⟩ at the Stone Pits
was ⟨a wicked⟩ an evil terror
on ⟨concealment⟩ duplicity.

115 hesitating ⟨a little⟩, however,
It's ⟨been sent⟩ come to me – I've a right to keep it ⟨if I
like⟩.

116 cold and ⟨wet⟩ snow
use. ⟨And if you didn't⟩ Or else

118 on ⟨Marner's withered⟩ the weaver's queer face

119 great ⟨painter⟩ artist

121 You'll ⟨belike⟩ happen

122 docilely, ⟨putting⟩ bringing his ⟨head⟩ eyes very close
the ⟨boys⟩ lads ... the ⟨boys⟩ lads

123 teach 'em ⟨your⟩ this little un

125 blank ⟨goal⟩ limit

126 the ⟨sounds⟩ tones

127 masterful ⟨it'll be the ruin of her⟩ there'll be no holding her.
waist and ⟨defied her cleverness in tearing⟩ was long enough
from ⟨the bed⟩⟨her place⟩ her corner ... toddled ⟨back⟩ to the
bed

128 except by ⟨traversing⟩ a close search

129 morning ⟨and was going back again⟩. He turned round again
punishment ⟨except any evil consequences⟩, the burden

130 come to ⟨bind⟩ link him
137 is ⟨felt⟩ marked
     round to ⟨wait a minute⟩ look for
138 handsomely ⟨dressed⟩ clad
139 side, ⟨and entered⟩ intruding *In 1st edition* intruding *changed to*
     entering.
     done ⟨shepherding⟩ my day's work
140 with the ⟨gentle⟩ mild passive happiness
     not ⟨a scornful critic⟩ scornfully critical
     usual ⟨attention⟩ notice
141 sunning ⟨herself⟩ her white bosom
     decent ⟨cottage⟩ furniture
     village, ⟨had done⟩ did very kindly
     was ⟨old for his years⟩ none so young
142 old ⟨open⟩ brick hearth
     not ⟨before that hearth that⟩⟨there where⟩ there, when
     clue ⟨by which⟩ his
146 were ⟨thoughts⟩ questions
150 when I ⟨think on⟩ look forward to
151 spar. ⟨There is a presiding spirit of⟩ All is purity
152 yew, ⟨on their way towards Nancy's particular bed of
     chrysanthemums,⟩ Priscilla
153 hour ⟨or less⟩.
154 recalled ⟨every detail, every word and look⟩ the small details
155 everything ⟨that was⟩ in her power
     the ⟨refusal in⟩ resistance which
156 opinions ⟨had the rigidity of principles⟩ were always
157 anybody?' ¶ ⟨Godfrey had specified Eppie, then about
     ⟨twelve⟩⟨ten⟩ twelve years old, as a child suitable for them to
     adopt. It had never occurred to him that Silas would rather have
     parted with his life than with Eppie. Surely the weaver⟩ 'Yes,
     my dear *Deleted passage reintroduced two paragraphs later.*
158 now ⟨for the first time⟩ after that long concealment
     thought ⟨would be⟩ must become an object of ⟨that⟩ repulsion:
     the very sight of her would ⟨become⟩ be painful
159 not ⟨be contented⟩ make up his mind
161 ⟨The ready⟩ Jane was already
165 ⟨At eight⟩ Between eight and nine o'clock

life ⟨which would make sleep impossible⟩ under
chair ⟨forward⟩ towards
167 because ⟨linen-weaving was wanted.⟩ there's been
few ⟨poor⟩ working-folks
she ⟨isn't like the strapping girls in the village⟩ doesn't look like
168 she ⟨may⟩ might
169 was ⟨not prepared⟩ possessed
to a ⟨certain⟩ predetermined
171 the ⟨luxuries⟩ privileges
172 were ⟨capable of⟩ sensitive to
174 would ⟨interfere⟩ distract
180 love ⟨it⟩ her as myself, I've had light enough to ⟨live by⟩ trusten
by

APPENDIX: ORIGINAL PENGUIN CLASSICS INTRODUCTION BY Q. D. LEAVIS

I

It is in *Silas Marner* that we come closest to a George Eliot who is everywhere present in her letters and journal and in other people's reminiscences of her, but who has been buried by the legend of the masculine bluestocking, the editor of the Benthamite review, the admirer of Comte, the student of all the ancient and modern languages, the friend of Herbert Spencer and the consort of G. H. Lewes, that middleman of all the arts and sciences. This other George Eliot reread the *Pilgrim's Progress* while reading the newly published *Origin of Species* and having reported of the Darwin that 'it is not impressive, from want of luminous and orderly presentation', went on to note that she was 'profoundly struck with the true genius manifested in the simple, vigorous, rhythmic style' of Bunyan. This was the George Eliot who wrote to Lady Ponsonby to beg her to

Consider what the human mind *en masse* would have been if there had been no such combination of elements in it as has produced poets. All the philosophers and *savants* would not have sufficed to supply that deficiency. And how can the life of nations be understood without the inward life of poetry – that is, of emotion blending with thought?

Acquaintance with her life is still best made through the volume called *George Eliot's Life* published by her widower J. W. Cross, which he made out of selections from her journal and letters and the reminiscences he collected from her relatives and friends. The letters can now be read complete in the edition by Professor C. Haight, who has now published a biography too. Cross himself gives all the necessary details of her appearance and qualities. He tells of 'the organ-like tones of her voice', of her fine brows and musician's hands,[1] and while mentioning her 'impressive speech which claimed something like an awed attention from strangers',[2] he tries to stress her hearty laughter and humour and her pride in being a skilful housekeeper, concluding:

'She had the instinctively feminine qualities which lend a rhythm to the movement of life.' All this is borne out by Henry James's letter to his father after first meeting George Eliot: 'a delightful expression, a voice soft and rich as that of a counselling angel – a mingled sagacity and sweetness – a broad hint of a great underlying world of reserve, knowledge, pride and power – a great feminine dignity and character in these massively plain features'. Cross's account of his first meeting with his future wife satisfies one's notions of her personality but he gives a very unexpected insight into the Lewes home in 1878, when G. H. Lewes was near his end:

between bouts of pain he sang through, with great *brio*, though not much voice, the greater portion of the tenor part in the *Barber of Seville* – George Eliot playing his accompaniment, and both of them thoroughly enjoying the fun.

George Eliot was nearly sixty at this time so the anecdote should correct any false idea that she was a solemn prig.

II

It is evident that by the time George Eliot came to write *Silas Marner* her ideas about the novel had matured. She confesses that while 'there are portraits in the "Clerical Scenes"', 'that was my first bit of art, and my hand was not well in'. In *Adam Bede* she claimed there were no actual portraits from life, and rose to some theorizing about the art of fiction, offering in the text a well-known defence of Dutch pictures of 'homely existence' which is generally taken to be a defence of realism. But it is in fact a quite different argument; the intention is to plead for humble life to be treated in art on theoretic grounds of moral obligation, not aesthetic ones: 'In this world there are so many of these common coarse people, who have no picturesque sentimental wretchedness! Therefore let Art always remind us of them . . . your common labourer, who *gets his own bread*, and eats it vulgarly but *creditably* with his own pocketknife.' These are the people, she says, who have '*done the rough work of the world*'. (All my italics.) This is more Radical than even Wordsworth's grounds for choosing humble life as the subject matter for true poetry. And this Radicalism is an important constituent of *Silas Marner*.

By 1859 George Eliot could write to a friend: 'I have turned out to be an artist – with words.' And after *Adam Bede* and *The Mill on the Floss* the remarks she makes in her letters and journal about her own books and the books she reads show more sophistication and more understanding of the problems a novelist has to solve. Whereas in 1857 she was saying: 'my stories always grow out of my psychological conception of the dramatis personae', by 1866 she has completely changed her position. There are some signposts on the way: her report that 'I went to hear *Faust* at Covent Garden; I was much thrilled by the great symbolical situations – more, I think, than I had ever been before', and her numerous accounts of hearing orchestral concerts or herself playing the piano in chamber-music concerts at home, and her unexpected dictum 'The Opera is a great, great product.' In 1866 in a letter to her friend Frederic Harrison she makes an important revelation of the way in which she now (soon after finishing *Felix Holt*) recognized that she composed:

That is a tremendously difficult problem; its difficulties . . . press upon me, who have gone through again and again the severe effort of trying to make certain ideas thoroughly incarnate, as if they had revealed themselves to me first in the flesh and not in the spirit. I think aesthetic teaching is the highest of all teaching because it deals with life in its highest complexity. But if it ceases to be purely aesthetic – if it lapses anywhere from the picture to the diagram – it becomes the most offensive of all teaching . . . Well, then, consider the sort of agonizing labour to an English-fed imagination to make out a sufficiently real background for the desired picture, – to get breathing individual forms, and group them in the needful relations, so that the presentation will lay hold on the emotions as human experience – will, as you say, 'flash' conviction on the world by means of aroused sympathy.

Far from the 'portrait' being the foundation of a novel or the 'story' being dictated by her 'psychological conception of the dramatis personae', she now feels the danger of being too schematic and of failing to create convincingly and to 'group' naturally enough the lives needed to incarnate her 'ideas' *'as if they had revealed themselves to me first in the flesh'*. That is, she now starts with the ideas, and stresses what she also calls 'symbolic situations', and 'the myth' – because she is preoccupied with her *theme*. *Silas Marner* is the first novel in which she is seen to have worked like this but, as I hope to show, she did not have to do this consciously: the theme forced itself on her. *Felix Holt, the Radical* followed in theme out of *Silas Marner* and as a complement to *Adam Bede*, but the 'idea' in *Felix Holt* was a subject outside herself, it had to be read up for like *Romola* (as we see from her journal) and though this subject embodied some of her most cherished beliefs these could not be 'incarnated' so naturally in felt life as in *Silas Marner*. In 1868 she makes an observation about Greek tragedy which repeats the theory of creative composition she had explained to Frederic Harrison earlier:

The Greeks were not taking an artificial, entirely erroneous standpoint in their art – a standpoint which disappeared altogether with their religion and their art. They had the same essential elements of life presented to them as we have, and their art symbolized these in grand schematic forms.

So it was not only the concept of Nemesis that George Eliot gained from reading Greek. Her youthful enthusiasm for Scott had yielded at the *Silas Marner* period to a critical view of his inadequate ideas of composition in spite of his fertile imagination, his ability to tell a story and 'create' characters: 'But somehow experience and finished faculty rarely go together. Dearly beloved Scott had the greatest combination of experience and faculty – yet even he never made the most of his treasures, at least in his *mode* of presentation' (1861). Shakespeare, Molière ('I think the *Misanthrope* the finest, most complete production of *its kind* in the world', she wrote in 1859), Bunyan, Greek tragedy, opera, orchestral and chamber music, we see, helped her to extend the scope and richness of the novel and make a more intelligent use of her 'experience and faculty'.

III

In his reminiscences *The Middle Years*, written in his old age, Henry James when starting on his memories of George Eliot refers to her as 'the author of *Silas Marner* and *Middlemarch*', a selection from her novels intended either to represent her at her best or as covering two distinct kinds in her creative art, or both. He goes on to describe her work in general as 'a great treasure of beauty and humanity, of applied and achieved art, a testimony, historic as well as aesthetic, to the deeper interest of the intricate English aspects'. Of none of her novels is this more true than *Silas Marner*; one could only have wished that he had been specific. What deeper interest of the aspects of England, what aesthetic and historic testimony, does *Marner* represent? That it is not to be dismissed as the mere moral 'fairy tale' or '*divertissement*' of many critics we might have guessed from the quite exceptional nature of its origin, of which we luckily have an account. Our first knowledge of this book is a note in George Eliot's journal (28 November 1860): 'I am now engaged in writing a story – the idea of which came to me after our arrival in this house [a depressing furnished London house] and which has thrust itself between me and the other book [*Romola*] I was meditating. It is *Silas Marner, the Weaver of Raveloe*.' Thus at the outset Silas was identified by his trade. And we note also that this same day's entry in her journal opens:

Since I last wrote in this Journal, I have suffered much from physical weakness, accompanied with mental depression. The loss of the country has seemed very bitter to me, and my want of health and strength has prevented me from working much – still worse, has made me despair of ever working well again.

Six weeks later, in writing to tell her publisher of her new book she again stresses the involuntary nature of this new undertaking: 'a story which came *across* my other plans by a sudden inspiration'. She adds: 'It is a story of old-fashioned village life, which has unfolded itself from the merest millet-seed of thought.' On 10 March 1861 she notes: 'Finished *Silas Marner*.' Previously she had replied to Blackwood's comment, that so far as he had read he found it 'sombre', that she was not surprised and doubted if it would interest anybody 'since Wordsworth is dead', but assured him that it was not sad on the whole, 'since it sets in a strong light the remedial influences of pure, natural human relations'. Thus the Weaver's story belonged to the village life of the past and exemplified a theory congenial to Wordsworth (and Coleridge); and the impulse to write it sprang from a deep depression of health and spirits due to living in conditions which were the very negation of 'old-fashioned village life', a depression that, as we see, was morbid, since it involved irrational despair of succeeding again as a novelist, in spite of the great success of *Adam Bede* and *The Mill on the Floss*. The letter to Blackwood ends: 'It came to me first of all quite suddenly, as a sort of legendary tale, suggested by my recollections of having once, in early childhood, seen a linen weaver with a bag on his back; but as my mind dwelt on the subject, I became inclined to a more realistic treatment' – that is, she dropped the association with a fairy-tale figure. And this is borne out by her saying that she felt 'as if the story would have lent itself best to metrical rather than prose fiction', 'except that, under that treatment, there could not be an equal play of humour'. The humour is not only quite as much a characteristic of the book she finally wrote as the 'poetry', but is itself no simple matter; it contains much irony of various kinds and a great deal of pointed social criticism which no lightweight legendary tale could support, not even those art versions of the fairy tale so characteristic of nineteenth-century literature with which *Marner* might be associated if superficially read. Even the author's own account here is misleading; that something essential has been left out is proved by the truer, fuller version contained in a letter from Major Blackwood to his wife in 1861: '*Silas Marner* sprang from her childish recollection of a man with a stoop and expression of face that led her to think that he was an alien from his fellows.' Physical deformity and the stamp of alienation are the important factors; the bag then ceases to be sinister, suggestive of a figure in Grimms' Tales, and connects the man with the one in another vision that we often feel to be behind George Eliot's in *Marner*, the Man bowed under 'a great Burden upon his back' crying lamentably, '*What shall I do?*' and setting out from the City of Destruction to another country to seek salvation.[3] It is in keeping with this serious intention that the author insisted that in the title and in advertising the book the word *story* should be avoided, undoubtedly because she felt this was a misleading description, tending to make the book appear something slight and fanciful. And rightly, for in *Marner* she had found a framework within which she could present the problems that pressed on her, that life had shown her must be solved or managed, and which were more than merely personal. Though *Marner* prepares us for its successors *Middlemarch* and *Felix Holt* it is superior to these in an art of concentration that uses always the minimum – the loaded word and the uniquely representative act – an art which puts *Marner* with Shakespeare and Bunyan rather than with other Victorian novels. It is very evidently the source of Hardy's novel-writing, but he never anywhere equalled the characterization of Raveloe and the talk in the Rainbow in his efforts at the same kind of thing, nor did he ever manage to invent a plot where coincidence, as in *Marner*, is felt as part of a natural and just order of things, or a plot which, like *Marner*'s, perfectly exemplifies its theme.

Leaving aside for the moment why this book insisted on being written when its author was struggling to write a quite different novel, we ask first: why was this stooping man alien? what country did he not belong to and why?

The book begins by deliberately establishing in 'anthropological' terms the conditions of a poor nineteenth-century Christian whose burden is not Original Sin but loss of faith and of a community – in fact what the City had given him in the way of a religion and a community was not recognizable as such by the traditions of the countryside, the village life in which the English civilized themselves. To this, the original state, the man makes his way by instinct with his only skill, his loom, and all that is left of his religion, his Bible.[4] In Raveloe the Industrial Revolution has not yet been felt and it is the countryside of the timeless past of packhorse and spinning wheel, of the organic community and the unified society. To the people of Raveloe professional weaving, though necessary, is an alien way of working; it produces 'pallid undersized men, who, by the side of the brawny country-folk, looked like the remnants of a disinherited race', objects therefore of a superstitious repugnance; we are first shown the weaver through the eyes of a peasantry. The machinery *they* know is their servant; the country-bred novelist understood the real distinction between mechanical aids and a mechanized industry, and her feeling for music provided the natural human reaction: she expresses it in the countryfolk's perception of a difference in rhythm – 'the natural cheerful trotting of the winnowing-machine, or the simpler rhythm of the flail' – human or animal rhythms, contrasted with the mechanical rhythm which is *imposed* on the worker by his loom; significantly Marner is described as working *in* his look, which eventually turns him into a machine component, 'so that he produced the same sort of impression as a handle or a crooked tube, which has no meaning standing apart'. The signs of his enslavement are 'the bent, tread-mill attitude' and the short sight, produced by his work, that cuts him off from seeing his fellow men both actually and metaphorically. He is the opposite of the country craftsman like Adam Bede whose healthy livelihood made him a superior type of manhood.

Silas's solitary working round could find compensation only in an inward spiritual life and being 'incorporated in a narrow religious sect'. But the religious life available to him was not beneficial, taking as guidance a pathetically ignorant inner light ('Lantern Yard') which has proved delusive when tested. Moreover, it has deprived him of his cultural inheritance (represented, by a stroke of genius, by the medicinal herbs) without providing anything in the way of education in living instead. George Eliot presents more of the truth about dissent in *Marner* than in the earlier and very partial account of Methodism in *Adam Bede* – *Marner* is more truthful in many ways. Besides the problem of the machine toil which is dehumanizing, she has brought in another major problem of her age, the threat to the traditional heritage by the now dominant Evangelical outlook.[5] The 'little store of wisdom which [his mother] had imparted to him as a solemn bequest' (the knowledge and preparation of medicinal wild herbs) Calvinism had taught him to mistrust, 'so that his inherited delight to wander through the fields in search of foxglove and dandelion and coltsfoot, began to wear to him the character of a temptation.' This symbol is finely chosen, for it conveys that help for others, contact with nature, and a kind of education, as well as the satisfaction of knowing he is maintaining the wise lore of his ancestors, are all denied him. There is thus a multiple typicality about the case of Silas Marner. In him the dire effects of the Industrial Revolution are examined; the current form of religion, a Christian fundamentalism, has finished the effects of denaturing him by disinheriting him. How can such losses to the race be made good? – it is George Eliot who describes Marner's kind as 'a disinherited race'.

Driven by 'something not unlike the feeling of primitive men, when they fled thus, in fear and sullenness, from the face of an unpropitious deity', Silas leaves the alleys for the immemorial countryside. (It is not an accident that Raveloe lies in the 'rich central plain of what we are pleased to call Merry England', the countryside of George Eliot's infancy, which was still in essentials Shakespeare's.) To Silas, fresh from Lantern Yard, the lives of the people there seem merely unspiritual and misdirected ('women seemed to be laying up a stock of linen for the life to come' is not only humorous but has a scriptural phrasing hinting their blindness to their eternal welfare, or what seems blindness to Silas); but as we presently see, their materialism is an art of living. The clue to the basis of their lives is in a word we keep meeting: 'neighbourly'. Silas, with his refusal to mix by attending church or dropping in to gossip at the Rainbow or courting a girl, is suspect.

This is why his spontaneous attempt to help the woman, whose suffering recalls his mother's, with the herbal medicine he knows will relieve her, only projects him into the vacant office of Wise Woman, and when his honesty rejects it, consigns him to an even more undesirable one.[6] The irony is poignant, and the incident a proof that George Eliot is not sentimental about the people of Raveloe. But their superstition is more than offset by their shrewdness: they realize as soon as Silas has been robbed that this proves that far from being 'a deep un' he is only 'a poor mushed creatur'. The contrast with the stupid behaviour of the Lantern Yard brethren when they too had to find out whether Silas was telling the truth is to Raveloe's credit – the villagers' superstition does not prevent them from being wiser in the end than the town artisans who have a 'purer' form of Christianity. The Raveloe people chiefly appreciate the pagan survivals (carols, and keeping 'a jolly Christmas, Whitsun and Easter tide') but they practise the true religion of neighbourliness. The village way of life is shown to foster some virtues that the city does nothing to promote: Jem the poacher, unlike William Dane, is really an honest man barring 'the matter of a hare or so' (nobody in an English village ever believed that game was not rightly common property), the villagers don't steal money or goods if only because these couldn't be used without discovery, and cheating of any sort is despised (the dishonesty of Dunsey is covered by his birth, but to the cottagers he is 'that offal Dunsey'). Morality is also ensured because there is no privacy, and wisdom because everyone through gossip has the communal assessment of everyone's character, even the gentry's to draw on. Above all, mutual helpfulness is as necessarily practised in the village as competition in the city.

George Eliot's presentment in *Marner* of the peasant code as the justification of what she calls the 'old-fashioned village life' is so minimal an account of the civilization of the English folk that it is barely adequate even for her special purpose, so that now, when first-hand knowledge of that culture has gone for ever, and its very existence is denied by the intellectuals of our phase of civilization, the reader must educate himself into that knowledge in order to understand what *Silas Marner* is about – George Eliot could assume her readers did not need instruction of that kind. Now, something like the chapter on 'The Peasant System' in George Sturt's *Change in the Village* is essential reading for our understanding of this novel. Though the character of his village had been destroyed by the enclosure of its commons and an invasion from the town, Sturt could still at the beginning of this century recover from the older cottagers the traces of the independent life of fifty years before, and his intelligent observations really illuminate *Silas Marner* for us. Here are a few of his relevant generalizations from his data:

The 'peasant' tradition in its vigour amounted to nothing less than a form of civilization – the home-made civilization of the rural English. To the exigent problems of life it furnished solutions of its own … Best of all, those customs provided a rough guide as to conduct – an unwritten code to which, though we forget it, England owes much … The cheerfulness of the cottager rests largely upon a survival of the outlook and habits of the peasant days. It is not a negative quality … In the main the force that bears them on is a traditional outlook. In the little cottages the people, from earliest infancy, were accustomed to hear all things – persons and manners, houses and gardens, and the day's work – appraised by an ancient standard of the countryside … The people stood for something more than merely themselves.

These are confirmations and explanations of what George Eliot says in *Silas Marner* or sometimes only shows in action. But that civilization had impressive material forms too in the crafts and arts of country work and leisure, most of which have been or are being destroyed or lost, though enough evidence exists to put the case beyond dispute.[7]

George Eliot probably felt that she had already shown in *Adam Bede* the material beauty and achievement of the old order of the countryside and that she would do most by limiting her case in *Marner*. It is the moral feeling in the village, Sturt's 'ancient standard of the countryside', that she presents so appreciatively, as when Raveloe felt 'it was nothing but right a man should be looked on and helped by those who could afford it, when he had brought up an orphan child, and been father and mother to her'. And in a different way, she registers their acceptance of the hard realities, the risks which must be taken of things turning out ill, as well as the certainty of old age and failing strength, which can never be forgotten: even when admiring little Eppie, 'Elderly masters and mistresses . . . told Silas that, if she turned out well (which, however, there was no telling), it would be a fine thing for him to have a steady lass to do for him when he got helpless.' In comparison, the attention given to the gardener, the fiddler, the wheelwright and other representative figures of the community is slight indeed; even the dairy farming is done by Priscilla Lammeter offstage. We have to accept these sketches as being deliberately outlines only of the full world George Eliot registered in her childhood (G. H. Lewes said: 'She forgets nothing that has come within the curl of her eyelash') and draws on so impressively for *Adam Bede* and *Middlemarch*. The point that is kept to in this book is, how can Marner achieve reintegration into this community? Marner's private case is now merged into a general one, an illustration of how and how not to set about this. This is the purpose of that narrative in the Rainbow which is highlighted by being placed just before Silas bursts in with his tale of being robbed, the turning point of his relations with Raveloe.

The tale told in the Rainbow is recognized as Mr Macey's peculiar property and is one which Raveloe never tires of hearing and discussing. As tailor, parish clerk and brother to the foremost fiddler Mr Macey has a status and qualities that fit him for the part of Chorus; and that his narrative is important is shown by its having become a local legend to which ghosts and other folklore characteristics have accrued with time. The first part, old Mr Lammeter's story, is a contrast to Silas's experience so far. Like Silas this worthy came from 'a bit north'ard', but in contrast to Silas he was a countryman, for 'he brought a fine breed o' sheep with him' and 'it was soon seen as we'd got a new parish'ner as know'd the rights and customs o' things, and kep' a good house, and was well looked on by everybody'. So his son was able to marry into one of the best Raveloe families and 'for prosperity and everything respectable, there's no family more looked on'; in fact, their daughter Nancy is being courted by Squire Cass's heir, to everyone's satisfaction. So old Mr Lammeter's story ends happily ever after. The apparent link with the other half of the narrative is that Mr Lammeter settled at the Warrens, the estate and house left to charity by one Cliff – who is never given the respectful handle to *his* name. There is also a real link, for Cliff's story is the opposite of the other's and an awful warning of what Silas's might be: Cliff dies crazy and childless. *He* was no acquisition but 'a Lunnon tailor, some folks said, as had gone mad wi' cheating'. His madness consisted at first simply in wanting to pass as a gentleman, a kind of cheating which ended by driving him mad, for having been a tailor – that is, one who had to work sitting cross-legged – he was inevitably unfitted for the part of a gentleman, which implied, demanded, good riding.[8] Thus Mr Macey says of Cliff: 'For he couldn't ride; lor bless you! they said he'd got no more grip o' the hoss than if his legs had been cross-sticks ... But ride he would'. Cliff is the type of man who won't recognize that, however, rich, he can be nothing but what he is. Mr Macey, a tailor himself, has better sense and greater self-respect. He despises Cliff for being 'ashamed o' being called a tailor' – 'not but what I'm a tailor myself, but in respect as God made me such, I'm proud on it, for "Macey, tailor" 's been wrote up over our door since before the Queen's heads went out on the shillings'. He has his own honourable pedigree, tailors are essential, and besides he is proud of his craft.[9] So Eppie's final refusal to be raised out of the class she was reared in is shown as being consistent with this folk tradition, 'a little store of [inherited] wisdom', and not improbable or sentimental. We are given an insight into a theory of class which has nothing to do with snobbery and which rules out the passion to rise in the world socially.

Cliff's story has moreover a thematic relation to Godfrey Cass's, for Cliff, since he couldn't get accepted as a gentleman himself, determined to 'ride the tailor' out of his son against the boy's nature, bringing about his death, so that Cliff died childless. This prefigures Godfrey's fate when *his* cheating shall have produced his own nemesis as he recognizes in the end when he tells his wife: 'I wanted to pass for childless once, Nancy – I shall pass for childless now against my wish.' And Cliff's story stands also as contrast to Silas's, for the latter, by eventually assimilating himself like old Mr Lammeter, ends up by accepting 'the rights and customs o' things', being well regarded and leaving (adopted) heirs. True, Silas has to learn as a foreign language, which he never really masters and whose principles he certainly doesn't understand, what was native for Mr Lammeter; but he is saved from Cliff's fate by his humility. So this parable within a parable is the clue to the whole, and Mr Macey justly sums up in what might be an epigraph for the novel: 'there's reasons in things as nobody knows on – that's pretty much what I've made out'. There *are* laws of life, George Eliot shows, and they were 'made out' in village life although they can't be stated.[10] In Mr Macey's narrative and its affiliations with the rest of the book we have one example of the wonderfully complex organization and the unobtrusive structure of symbol and theme which make the text of *Silas Marner* so dense and rich in meanings and yet so economical in words.

The laws of life are shown in operation in what follows immediately after Silas has made known his misfortune to the village. His relations with the villagers follow the same impartial logic as before, but his impulse to turn to them for help in his trouble, and his compunction at accusing Jem of robbing him without evidence, which has stirred up memories of being falsely accused himself, have made a bridge between them. They see he is an innocent soul and in need of help. First 'contemptuous pity' replaces distrust, then the traditional neighbourly attempts to help him follow. The sympathetic ears, the good advice, the welcome presents and soothing attentions culminate in Dolly Winthrop's well-judged efforts to reach him by all the different channels she feels likely to work on him. She brings the cakes, with their religious sanction in the traditionally pricked 'good letters'; the child, as certain to touch his heart if he has one and moreover to sing a carol to move his Christmas sentiments; and a gentle remonstrance about his not going to church. All these good means fail to reach him, and we cannot but sense that something is being conveyed, in the cross-purposes and misunderstandings of their conversation, sometimes comical and sometimes full of pathos, about the difficulty of achieving any real communication between people who don't belong to the same culture. Silas doesn't even recognize the religion of church as the same Christian religion that he subscribed to in the first half of his life, for all his knowledge of the theory of salvation; here no doubt something more ironical is intended. Dolly's religion is about as far from Calvinism as possible; it is seen to be a matter of custom, traditional pieties and pagan practices, and she makes no distinction between christening and inoculation.

But George Eliot makes her point, that the ignorant village wheelwright's wife has the advantage over the city weaver who could talk knowingly about 'Assurance of salvation' in his youth. The difference between their two cultures is illustrated by the episode of the 'I.H.S.' on the lard cakes. Dolly pricks them, without knowing what the letters are, because tradition has assured her that they have a good meaning (even though she has noticed that sometimes the letters won't hold and also that the cakes don't always turn out so well); the proof that she can trust the inherited wisdom is that these same letters are on the pulpit cloth at church.[11] But Silas, who *can* read them, is yet seen to be really worse off than the illiterate Dolly, for, like her, he doesn't know what the letters stand for and unlike her he has no pious associations with them. Even if he had known what they stood for, we reflect, his chapel-formed prejudices would have prevented him from venerating them, as it had deprived him of the medicinal herbs.

Silas never does acquire the pieties inborn with the villagers. He gets along eventually by adopting all the village customs without questioning them, but never, of course, has the traditional associations which make people benefit by them. We are given an undoubtedly humorous illustration in the daily pipe-smoking which Silas takes up because it is the done thing and because he is told, against the evidence of his senses, that it is good for him. Eppie believes it does do him good and that he enjoys it, and though he would rather not smoke he does not like to set himself up against received opinion or to pain Eppie by undeceiving her. George Eliot does not press the general point here illustrated, which would have forced on us an awkward scepticism, but once again it expresses her freedom from sentimentality and her refusal to simplify, to make a 'story' by suppressing discordant facts.

All the attempts to bring Silas back to a place in the community fail because except for the case of Sally Oates they have no purchase on him and in that one case he has bad luck (as he has good luck in being sent Eppie – chance is impartial). Dolly believed the sight of her child Aaron was bound to do him good, yet this fails because Silas is too shortsighted to see Aaron's features at all. But (again the impartial law of life operate) this very short sight is just what leads him to accept another child later as his gold come back. Then all the right conditions are seen to have been met at last. The process of being restored to life,[12] which actually began with the loss of his gold, has accelerated. The aspect it seems to have of coincidence is ruled out when we consider that Eppie's appearance follows upon many attempts against Silas's isolation that occur in the natural course of events. The only fairy-tale element lies in the fact that Eppie appears on New Year's Eve, when the luck is liable to turn with the New Year, but again this is seen to be one of the essential conditions for the chance to take effect since the excitement brings on Silas's trance. What *is* unsatisfactory is the device of the catalepsy, since it is not, like Dr Manette's psychological losses of memory and reversions to another personality, a product of his misfortunes but the cause of them, posited for the plotting – after which Silas ceases to have any fits onstage. The fits were needed to make William's treachery and theft possible and to give the villagers an excuse for their superstitious horror of a man whose soul was 'loose from his body, and going out and in, like a bird out of its nest and back' (though this last is a true piece of folklore and helps to show us how primitive was the mentality of the countryman). And lastly, the catalepsy is necessary to get Eppie into the cottage without Silas knowing, so that she *seems* to him initially to be of supernatural origin. But even so the fits are worked into the pattern of an impartial operation of the laws of life: twice chance introduces a thief into Silas's home, the third time – there is a popular belief: 'The third time, lucky' – the same chance lets in Eppie, who makes good the previous losses.

Leslie Stephen's (and others') amused scepticism about an old bachelor's reception of a baby and his return to the bosom of society in consequence, seems to me superficial. George Eliot has been careful to explain that Silas, like many children of the poor, had been used to look after his baby sister and cherished that memory; he is domesticated by habit and handy by virtue of his trade, and he has Dolly's assistance. As for the Wordsworthian part of the enterprise, what follows seems to me a more plausible and particularized demonstration of Wordsworth's tenets than anything the poet ever wrote himself. The remedial influences of pure, natural human relations and a revived ability to enjoy the natural world are conveyed persuasively in exquisite detail and poetic imagery. But it is characteristic of the economical and pregnant construction of *Marner* that these Wordsworthian passages are something more than lovely episodes; besides their inherent poetical quality they are precipitations and enactments of the deeper meanings of the novel. Take only one of these and that the slightest: the influence of little Eppie in making Silas share her delight in everything outdoors or in nature 'even to the old winter-flies that came crawling forth in the early spring sunshine, and warming him into joy because *she* had joy'. We perceive that Silas is vividly imaged as being himself an old winter-fly crawling out under the reviving spring sunshine which Eppie is to him. And this passage builds up with what follows to convey Silas's gradual return to a life of feeling, ending by bringing into play again the herbs that not merely recall his mother but represent something like the traditions of the race.

Sitting on the banks in this way, Silas began to look for the once familiar herbs again; and as the leaves, with their unchanged outline and markings, lay on his palm, there was a sense of crowding remembrances from which he turned away timidly, taking refuge in Eppie's little world, that lay lightly on his enfeebled spirit.

As the child's mind was growing into knowledge, his mind was growing into memory; as her life unfolded, his soul, long stupefied in a cold narrow prison, was unfolding too, and trembling gradually into full consciousness.

We are shown also that besides reviving Silas's consciousness of the world around him and its associations with his past, Eppie makes him aware of a future happiness, so that he can deduce from the present 'in the ties and charities that bound together the families of his neighbours' 'images of that time' to come, another application of the Wordsworthian doctrine. In the spirit of Wordsworth's poetry too is the description of how Eppie forges a bond between Silas and all animate and even inanimate life: 'there was love between the child and the world – from men and women with parental looks and tones, to the red lady-birds and the round pebbles'.

Wordsworthian, we say, but the imagery drawn from nature is so apt[13] and so freshly observed that we recollect that 'George Eliot' was Mary Ann Evans, a country child, before she became a learned woman, and that on reading Wordsworth's poems for the first time on her twentieth birthday she wrote of them: 'I have never before met with so many of my feelings expressed just as I could wish them.' So Nancy's person is described as giving 'the same idea of perfect unvarying neatness as the body of a little bird', Dolly 'pasture[s] her mind' on the sadder elements of life, Godfrey sees himself becoming as 'helpless as an uprooted tree', the patched and darned baby-clothes are 'clean and neat as fresh-sprung herbs', Silas's 'sap of affection was not all gone' and the imagery that describes his shrunken life as 'a rivulet that has sunk far down from the grassy fringe of its old breadth into a little shivering thread, that cuts a groove for itself in the barren sand' recurs in various forms. But far more memorable than anything of the kind in Wordsworth is the episode of Silas's broken water-jug whose homely earthenware shape had become dear to him by association:

It had been his companion for twelve years, always standing on the same spot, always lending its handle to him in the early morning, so that its form had an expression for him of willing helpfulness, and the impress of its handle on his palm gave a satisfaction mingled with that of having the fresh clear water.

When he stumbled and broke it, he 'picked up the pieces and carried them home with grief in his heart. The brown pot could never be of use to him any more, but he stuck the bits together and propped the ruin in its old place for a memorial.' But this also has a function, to show that Silas retained even in his extreme isolation that natural piety which is a proof of being fully human[14] and without which he could not have been rescued by Eppie. It is part of the sequence of evidence proving that, though he had lost his faith, still compunction, compassion, gratitude and honourable feelings were alive in him; but it comes also from the George Eliot who wrote in a letter, during the very period when she was composing *Marner*: 'In proportion as I love every form of piety – which is venerating love – I hate hard curiosity'; who when reading the newly published *Origin of Species* the year before wrote to her friends that though 'it makes an epoch' yet 'To me the Development Theory and all other explanations of processes by which things came to be, produce a feeble impression compared with the mystery that lies under the processes.'

But it is not the Wordsworthian 'message' in any simple form that George Eliot is endorsing. 'Love had he found in huts where poor men lie; His daily teachers had been woods and rills' would not have been true in any way of Silas if he had not been shown these truths by Eppie. And Eppie's influence would have been inadequate without the village there to take them both into its neighbourly care and teach them how to live, with what Sturt calls 'the home-made civilization of the rural English'.[15] We meet one of its impressive aspects at the Red House's New Year dance where the villagers, admitted to watch by custom, discuss the characters, conduct, appearance and history of the gentry, drawing on their own experiences and showing their good sense and decent feeling while making shrewd criticisms; and earlier at the Rainbow we have seen their understanding of the 'reasons in things', of the nature of social life.

Another aspect of the character of this peasant tradition is embodied in Dolly Winthrop herself. The dual strain in the English folk tradition is represented by the marriage (happy enough) of tipsy, jovial Ben Winthrop and the grave, scrupulous Dolly, a good woman who performs Dinah Morris's function without being given a halo. We are introduced to her as one 'having her lips always slightly screwed, as if she felt herself in a sick-room with the doctor or the clergyman present' and 'inclined to shake her head and sigh, almost imperceptibly, like a funereal mourner who is not a relation'. Yet she is not to be ridiculed. What Dolly represents is the strength of the village code that makes it religious in character but as remote as possible from dogma, theology or ritual practice. How exactly she corresponds to George Sturt's account of the cottager's character familiar to him in life!

To some extent doubtless it rests on Christian teaching, although perhaps not much on the Christian teaching of the present day ... from distant generations there seems to have come down, in many a cottage family, a rather lofty religious sentiment which fosters honesty, patience, resignation, courage. Much of the gravity, much of the tranquility of soul of the more sedate villagers must be ascribed to this traditional influence, whose effects are attractive enough, in the character and outlook of many an old cottage man and woman.[16]

One of Dolly's many functions is to incite us to decide in what ways the code she lives by differs from Nancy Lammeter's, for Nancy's is seen to be as inferior to Dolly's as the Lantern Yard's is to Raveloe's. Nancy actually reminds us of Lantern Yard in the narrowness of her outlook and her arbitrary moral laws.

IV

In Chapter 3, with the introduction of the Cass family, the assumption that in this novel we are in the timeless world of 'Once upon a time' is finally destroyed. It specifies the England of the Napoleonic Wars and even the facts of economic history which were to ruin the landowning classes and their helpless labourers. Radicalism, the product of this age, comes out strongly in *Marner*, to produce later *Felix Holt, the Radical*. It is George Eliot's Radical sympathies that account for her distaste for the squirearchy and her compassion for the poor. It is no accident that makes the nemesis in *Marner* the gentleman's fate and the happy outcome of luck the cottager's, for Godfrey's history is in large and in detail an inversion of Silas's, and when their dramatic confrontation at last takes place, all the elements in the novel come into play and we are left in no doubt about the conclusions we are to draw. The nemesis that overtakes Godfrey is inextricably mixed up with his position in society and his conditioning by that; slight as his chances were of getting Eppie to live with him as his daughter, it is not until he makes clear, inadvertently, how he thinks of the working class that he alienates Eppie and Silas for ever. The Casses retire helpless and humiliated, and we feel impelled to cheer.

Mary Ann Evans was peculiarly qualified by her background and upbringing to appreciate the fine distinctions of the English class system of her day and their consequences. Her father, born and bred a carpenter like Adam Bede, 'raised himself', in his daughter's proud words, to being notable in the ways that Caleb Garth is shown to be in *Middlemarch*, but to an even better position. He had some of Adam Bede's qualities of bodily strength and character combined with Mr Garth's social submissiveness to his wife, who was 'superior' – a Dodson in family though a Mrs Poyser in nature and activities. Their daughter must therefore have been socially sensitive even without any knowledge of her father's aristocratic employers, and in due course this class of beings complicated her ideas of the social system even further, as J. W. Cross was well aware, no doubt from her own mouth. He stresses the effect of 'being constantly driven by her father' to the 'fine places' of these gentry as 'accentuating the social differences – differences which had a profound significance and which left their mark on such a sensitive character'. Coming home from her excellent education at a boarding school at Coventry a convert to the 'ultra-Evangelical tendencies' of the teachers, she was in conflict for years with her brother, whose private tutor's establishment had imbued *him* with strong High Church views. The future George Eliot was thus thoroughly equipped to feel in person all the strains and anomalies of the contemporary social and religious system, and being born in 1819 (a time of political and economic trouble) to know the distresses of the workers too.

Her escape from the blight of evangelicalism was, by her own account, and as one would expect, through literature, Scott first unsettling her orthodoxy and Shakespeare becoming the book of books for her by 1842. The evangelical fervour was, as so often, replaced by a desire to serve humanity which soon led her to a concern for social reform, and we find her rejoicing in the earlier Carlyle and even in the French Revolution of 1848; at this date we have her denunciation of England ('I feel that society is training men and women for hell') and her admiration for Louis Blanc. In 1851 she launched herself into the London of the congenial *Westminster Review* set; three years later she bravely united her life with G. H. Lewes's, and since marriage was legally impossible for him she found herself in a new position of complete detachment from the social system. (The effect was peculiar. While she shows in her novels complete emancipation from restrictive ideas of class, and while her criticisms of its causes, manifestations and effects are always penetrating, sensitive and unbiased, she is surprisingly conventional about *moral* conduct in the narrow Victorian sense.) *Silas Marner* is the only novel in which she makes class a major cause of the different treatment she gives human beings; even in *Adam Bede* both Arthur *and* Adam incure a nemesis – Adam's 'hardness' is rebuked by seeing the harshness with which Hetty's 'fall' is treated by his world (though it is true he gets a plaster by being allowed to marry Dinah). The experiment no doubt helped to equip George Eliot for the more systematic, and unprejudiced examination of society in *Felix Holt, the Radical* and for the wider-ranging impartial treatment of the whole subject in *Middlemarch*.[17] Class is dominant even in church at Raveloe (see Chapter 16) and in the last few pages we learn that Godfrey couldn't bear to stay in Raveloe on the day his daughter marries a 'low working-man' – whom *we* know to be the admirable Aaron Winthrop.

The effect of staying for the first part of the book with the peasantry and Silas is that we identify with them, so that when Squire Cass is brought before us at last he figures very large indeed, though only a very small squire. It is at once explained that these things are relative and that in his ambience he is 'quite as if he had been a lord' – this is the Lilliputian treatment which implies that a lord is only an enlarged

Squire Cass. He is then shown as typical of a class whose 'extravagent habits and bad husbandry' are preparing them for ruin when the 'glorious wartime' ends. The sarcasm at their expense is different from any irony in the previous chapters, it tends to take on a savage tone and to become caricature. The fatuous selfishness of believing wartime 'to be a peculiar favour of Providence towards the landed interest' is succeeded by this speech of the Squire's, by which we cannot but be disgusted and in which we catch the selfish indignation in the querulous rhythm:

'And that fool Kimble says the newspaper's talking about peace. Why, the country wouldn't have a leg to stand on. Prices 'ud run down like a jack, and I should never get my arrears, not if I sold all the fellows up.'

His class wants to keep the country at war for its own interest, a traditional Radical charge. His callous lack of concern for his tenants so long as he can get his rent shows he is a bad landlord too. The interior of the Red House is squalid and the sons degraded by dissipation. The villagers have already passed judgement: 'Raveloe was not a place where moral censure was severe, but it was thought a weakness in the Squire that he had kept all his sons at home in idleness', 'though some licence was to be allowed to young men whose fathers could afford it'. The villagers know that the same standard can't be expected of the gentry as of their own sons. Godfrey is 'equally disinclined to dig and to beg'. When we find that Dolly and Silas and worthy Mr Macey think of these people as their 'betters', it makes us think (along Radical lines of course).

Along with this concept of 'betters' we learn not only that the Casses are not better but that the Squire differs from the farmers of the parish only by 'that self-possession and authoritativeness of voice and carriage which belonged to a man' who has never met anyone superior to himself. As the villagers are characterized by 'neighbourly' attitudes he is distinguished by *patronizing* ones, he even feels his position obliges him 'to fulfil the hereditary duty of being noisily jovial and patronising' and he speaks 'in a ponderous coughing fashion, which was felt in Raveloe to be a sort of privilege of his rank'. This is amusing and intelligent observation, but it ceases to be amusing when we find that this has imposed itself as an acceptable image of gentility on the

villagers; Ben Winthrop even describes Godfrey with admiration as
'one as 'ud knock you down easier' than anyone – knocking you down
being the symbolic function of one's betters. All this is meant to be
subversive and expresses George Eliot's reaction to a class that must
in her childhood and youth have appeared a blot on the landscape.[18]
But active political feeling is needed to account for other manifestations
of the same situation: a very stock piece of Radical propaganda is the
picture of the Squire cutting beef off his joint for his deer-hound as he
breakfasts – 'enough bits of beef to make a poor man's holiday dinner'
– reminding us that working men could afford 'butcher's meat' at best
on only a few occasions a year.

So when we are returned to the company of the poor we feel relief.
Here is charity and fellowship and we can enter into their difficulties
and pleasures with sympathy without meeting their 'betters' again till
Eppie is at the critical stage of courtship. Then we are taken back to
the Red House (Chapter 17). True, the old Squire and the vicious
Dunsey are gone and the Lammeters' 'liberal orderliness' is in charge,
while the refinement compared with what went before suggests that
Nancy may really be a 'better'. Her attitude to adoption compared to
the villagers' is one test, and others follow. She is seen to be made up
of 'rigid principles', a conventional good woman, loving and dutiful to
her own relations but fatally limited, as is proved when she goes
with her husband to claim Eppie. 'Used all her life to plenteous
circumstances and the privileges of "respectability"', we are told, she
cannot understand that Eppie's life can have its own attractions and
compensations. This is exactly in keeping with Godfrey's conviction
that Eppie would readily fall in with his wish to adopt her, he having
formed 'the idea that deep affections can hardly go along with callous
palms and scant means'.

The ensuing drama is really instructive, no longer easily satiric.
Godfrey loses any sympathy we may have felt for him by his selfishness,
his obtuseness to the feelings of the Marners, and his dishonesty
in persuading himself that he is doing for Eppie's good what now
suits himself. This analysis of 'moral stupidity', one of George Eliot's
favourite subjects, proceeds magnificently as Godfrey finally accuses
the weaver of selfishness and reproaches him that without her real
father's (his) protection 'she may marry some low working-man'.[19]
Godfrey's brutality here is the more dreadful for not being conscious;

it is a class reaction only, not personal. We look to see Nancy's reaction to this test. But she notices no insult, and this comes as a shock to us because Nancy has been shown as superior to the rest of her world in delicacy of feeling. We are forced to realize that insulation by class destroys the power of imaginative sympathy in everyone. Nancy presses Godfrey's rights on Eppie, who answers the spirit of the insult with a passionate affirmation of class solidarity as well as of loyalty to the only father she has ever known. It is characteristic that the first thing Nancy then thinks of is relief that her family and the world now need never know about Godfrey's past and the relation with Eppie. What is uppermost in her mind is respectability; she is a variety of Dodson[20] and this is the real gulf between her and the village folk who have not yet been tainted with the religion of 'respectability' (a word which George Eliot herself puts into inverted commas here). Eppie's reaction is quite plausible if we remember what social and literary history abundantly confirm, what Sturt summarizes in this sentence: 'It seems singular to think of it now, but the very labourer might reasonably hope for some satisfaction in life, nor trouble about "raising" himself into some other class, so long as he could live on peasant lines.'

Now this constant play of ironical social criticism, and the general reflections about human nature, are what prevent the artifices (such as the elaborate parallels between Silas's and Godfrey's histories and the providential arrangements of the fits, little golden-haired girls, and so on) from being felt as artificial by the reader, for they never obtrude as such: far from being incited to work out the pattern, our attention is always being directed elsewhere. Yet without dwelling on these things we do get as we read a sense that these complexities of reference are further illustrations of those laws of life that, as the novel is concerned to demonstrate, so mysteriously exist.

They are not laws that can be stated, but as we've seen they cover parts of human experience investigated by Wordsworth and Bunyan, Cobbett and George Sturt, among others, and embody the truths of parables in the New Testament as well as the traditional wisdom expressed in folktales. The central thesis in Mr Macey's narrative at the Rainbow is the contrast between the rich man's folly and the meek man's success in living, a theme often present in folktales of course. Godfrey with his uneasy conscience and his childless hearth gets no benefit from his riches and the wife he has gained by deception, while the humble Marner household have the last word: 'I think nobody could be happier than we are.' Eppie has brought into the home, to complete it with a garden, Aaron the gardener. That his occupation is, like the tailor's deliberately chosen[21] is made quite explicit in his criticism of the maldistribution of goods – a return to the Radical vein:

there's never a garden in all the parish but what there's endless waste in it for want o' somebody as could use everything up. It's what I think to myself sometimes, as there need nobody run short o' victuals if the land was made the most on, and there was never a morsel but what could find its way to a mouth. It sets one thinking o' that – gardening does.

And we are presently told that Aaron does all the gardening for the Raveloe gentry: his kind do the world's work and have a better idea than the property owners of the right use of property, this tells us. Again we are led to ask: Who are the 'betters'?

Yet, it must be emphasized once again, the cottagers are not idealized. The coarse repartee and the illiterate arguments in the Rainbow, drink and stupid jokes and superstitions are there and coexist with great good sense and kindliness and love of children, and with the hospitality and cooperation that are obligatory in the Raveloe code. And as regards their weaknesses, the reader is always being nudged into realizing that the world in general is no better, that behaviour in polite circles can be worse.[22] Rarely is any incongruity felt when the cool voice of the anthropologizing critic modulates into the sympathetic tone which conveys all the pathos of the lives of the humble. Silas's helplessness and even the comical effects of his simplicity never prevent us from seeing that his inner life is to be respected. This is great art, and throws up scenes that remain in the memory as strangely impressive, such as that where Godfrey and his young child exchange looks without the child's giving him any recognition, turning instead to pull lovingly at the weaver's face – impressive in itself, but still more so when, having read to the end, we realize that it has forecast Eppie's eventual rejection of Godfrey in the final scene which is the result of Godfrey's refusal in this earlier scene to recognize the natural bond between them. The novel is full of dramatic ironies both of scene and speech (such as Silas's assurance to Godfrey Cass that he will keep the baby Eppie 'till anybody shows they've a right to take her away from me'). These ironies tie the book together firmly.

V

After the Radical vein has been worked out there still remains to determine the theme of Silas's past suffering in the city. Seen through Eppie's country-bred eyes the city is 'a dark ugly place' and 'worse than the Workhouse', and Silas notices for the first time that it 'smells bad'. A factory has swept away Lantern Yard (is it a relief?) and Silas can say, 'The old home's gone; I've no home but this now.' The irony latent in the name 'Lantern Yard' is brought out by Dolly's innocent encouragement to him to go back to the city to find out the truth: 'And if there's any light to be got up the yard as you talk on, we've need of it i' this world.' Actually, the Lantern Yard community could only darken counsel (there is scriptural reference of this kind implied in the constant play upon the words 'dark' and 'light' and we cannot avoid the suggestion of 'Lighten our darkness' in the offing). The social criticism in *Marner* therefore is inseparable from spiritual values. This is consonant with the early traditions of English Radicalism, which is why *Marner* had to be both a realistic novel and a symbolic spiritual history and why Bunyan, as I've shown, offered a suitable source for reference. *Silas Marner* really asks: What was it that characterized the way of life of the English village in its heyday, so that its passing has meant a heavy loss? One of the most memorable points made in the last part is that Silas's return to his birthplace is partly to enlighten the minister: 'I should like to talk to him about the religion o' this country-side, for I partly think he doesn't know on it.'

So we come back to the factors in George Eliot's personal life which forced her to undertake this book. Hating the conditions of life in London, she remembered her childhood not only for its green fields and her mother's dairy but for the whole agricultural way of life which, she saw, enhanced the aesthetic aspects of Nature as well as shaped the lives of a people whose human achievement in creating a community she deeply respected; a people whose speech, an art of expression manifested in a dialect notable for its force, rhythm, and subtlety, had a flavour quite absent from educated English. She felt her loss of these things the more for having pined for them for ten years in London among the claustrophobic streets, the choking smoke and the anonymous crowd – these facts are liberally documented in her letters and journal. An intellectual circle she had, but this was no substitute for the neighbourliness of 'old-fashioned village life'. With this sense of her own loss went her realization of what it must mean for the utterly disinherited masses, no longer a folk, deprived of a community by the forces we sum up as the Industrial Revolution, the city poor whom all the serious Victorian novelists had on their minds, inheritors as all these novelists were, whatever their formal political allegiances, of that earlier ethos of Cobbett's humane Radicalism and Carlyle's appeals to conscience.[23]

She had also the impulse at this date to give her generation the benefit of her own discovery of a point of rest – which *Marner* in its positive final serenity proves she had achieved. The authoritative account of George Eliot's spiritual history is given by herself in a letter written a year before starting *Silas Marner* (6 December 1859). She writes of her early bigoted evangelical phase, followed by her 'attitude of antagonism which belongs to the renunciation of *any* religious belief', and that she can now say that she has a sympathy with any faith that has been the expression of human sorrow and longing for righteousness: 'I have a sympathy with it that predominates over all argumentative tendencies.' Silas goes through a similar process, ending by accepting not dogmatic religion but a place in a community whose religious system has passed the pragmatic test – it visibly works as right and wise practice, and this brings personal happiness. Only Dolly appears to feel that faith must somewhere rest on, or imply, divine powers, but owing to her humility, or a sense of the remoteness of these powers, she refers to them only as 'Them above', suggesting those pagan deities ('primitive men') constantly invoked in the first two chapters. What the others describe as Providence seems to associate more naturally with their belief in Luck than with the Christian hope. The Raveloe people's attitude to church is that it provides social cohesion with some good magic attached (as in their belief in the necessity of taking the sacrament annually). Dolly's (and her creator's) conclusion that 'all as we've got to do is to trusten' is really no more than Axel Heyst's discovery in Conrad's *Victory*: 'Woe to the heart that has not learnt while young to put its trust in life.' Unlike Hardy's burden: 'Life offers – to deny',

George Eliot says that, in the long run, Life gives a fair deal, or at any rate it did in the village world.

Silas 'had ... come to appropriate the forms of custom and belief which were the mould of Raveloe life', and by blending these with 'the elements of his old faith', 'recovered a consciousness of unity between his past and present'. Personal happiness has made this possible and adequate for him, as for George Eliot herself, who had found objects to live for in Lewes and his three motherless boys, and in the creative work which Lewes had launched her on and sustained her in – and which, she wrote, 'gives value to my life'. She felt justified in sustaining a faith in the possibilities of social life, however discouraging some of the manifestations of human nature may be, and she shows in *Adam Bede* and *Silas Marner* that the old culture, of village units centring on the market town, manifested such a possibility.

There are so many meanings in *Silas Marner* that it is surprising there was room in such a short space for them all; it is a feat to have wrapped them up with such neatness, charm, poetry and wit. The remarkable stylization of *Marner*, which is really due to its being an extension of the parable form, is something quite unprecedented in George Eliot's fiction hitherto; it has no anticipation in any of the short stories that make up *Scenes of Clerical Life*; while the lax association of different centres of interest that constitutes *Adam Bede* and *The Mill on the Floss* is as different from *Marner* as is *Romola*, its successor. But we can see that in the symbolic confrontation scenes in *Felix Holt* and in the use of poetic symbolism in *Middlemarch*, the discoveries made in *Marner* have been consolidated.

1967

Notes

1. She was an accomplished pianist, performed with professional musicians in her own home, and was an ardent concert-goer and opera-addict, even accepting Wagnerian opera with sympathetic intelligence.
2. Not all: Henry James notes with some amusement mixed with his respect her 'tendency to *aborder* only the highest themes' when he attended her *salon*. But she did not find it easy to talk to a number of people, or to strangers at all.
3. There are many overtones from *Pilgrim's Progress*, e.g. Silas has to live away

from the village at the Stone-pits by the waste; a consequence of his adopting Eppie is that the waste is drained and a flower garden and fertile fields replace it; in his youth Silas has worshipped in Lantern Yard, 'a turning out of Prison Street, where the jail is'; he comes from a 'region called "North'ard"' which, while suggesting the industrial north to us, seems in the mouths of the peasants who are quoted to be in the same parts as Mr Honest's 'Town of Stupidity' where ' "we lie more off from the Sun, and so are more cold and senseless"' than even the City of Destruction itself – Bunyan consistently uses descriptions of places for allegorical purposes. It is his Giant Despair who has disabling fits, which may have suggested Silas's equally convenient 'fits'. But unlike Christian and the rest, Silas finds his reward and the end of his pilgrimage in Raveloe on earth.

4. 'The Bible as you brought wi' you from that country,' says Dolly, confirming that in spite of having lost his faith he had kept his Bible. This is precisely what George Eliot did, valuing it, says Cross, who was in a position to know, 'not only from early association, but also from the profound conviction of its importance in the development of the religious life of man'. In 1862 we find her writing of G. H. Lewes: 'He is not fond of reading the Bible himself, but "sees no harm" in my reading it.'

5. Compare an earlier novel, *Alton Locke* (1850), and we find Kingsley trying through the technique of fictional autobiography to register the deprivation suffered by the poor London boy, cut off from green fields, and – by his mother's religion – from poetry. Bewick's *Memoir* is a useful contrast to both *Alton Locke* and *Silas Marner*.

6. Again, we have in this novel as opposed to *Adam Bede* an admission of the dark side of cottage mentality. We were not shown any fear of witchcraft in the illiterate and superstitious Lisbeth Bede, only the attractive side of her supernatural beliefs, though the latter was hardly likely to exist without the former. Another aspect of this new concern for unglamorous truth lies in the poor figures chosen to represent the gentry – the rector is commonplace, the doctor tiresome, their wives are ludicrous, the squire's family all worse than unattractive, the worthy Lammeters uncharacterized yeomen farmers with daughters respectively narrow and rough; and the whole social life of the gentry is either insipid or gross. There is no figure like *Adam Bede's* Mr Irwine to embody the highest values of the scholar, the gentleman and the Christian.

7. One recent piece of rescue work that might be adduced as peculiarly relevant is *English Churchyard Memorials* by Frederick Burgess, both for its abundant illustrations, and for its scholarly understanding of how complex this culture of the countryside was and how completely its structure was destroyed by outside forces in the nineteenth century, however much against the wishes and interests of those who lived and worked there. See pp. 114–15 for why the

independent craftsmen had to leave the villages and what were the consequences to the social life of the countryside and to a typical craft that was also an art; and how 'integrity of design', the freedom of masons to work in a local idiom, and the craft tradition were all incidental 'victims of the complex changes in social conditions that are conventionally described as the Industrial Revolution'.

8. The symbolism is brilliantly chosen and is consistently used for the gentry. For example, we remember that to Silas his 'betters' were 'tall, powerful, florid men, seen chiefly on horseback', and that, to 'a young gentleman like Dunsey', to be 'reduced to so exceptional a mode of locomotion as walking' implied 'a too bewildering dreamy sense of unwontedness in his position'. So the horsewhip identifies Dunsey's skeleton very appropriately. Mr Lammeter recalls his prime by saying 'I always *would* have a good horse, you know' and Godfrey's self-reproach at letting himself be tricked into marrying a barmaid takes the form of visualizing himself as a horse sinking in the mire because he had lost 'the strong silken rope by which Nancy would have drawn him safe to the green banks'. My list is not exhaustive. I doubt whether the imagery was deliberately fixed on; it is more likely that for George Eliot the gentry in her childhood were inseparably associated by her with horse-riding powers.

9. Compare his brother Solomon who bowed to the company while he fiddled without pausing 'as much as to say that he respected the company though he respected the key-note more'. This seems to me one of those wonderful strokes in which George Eliot shows herself fully equal to Tolstoy. And Mr Macey himself, the parish clerk who led the singing in church, says complacently: 'our family's been known for musicians as far back as anybody can tell'. Here skill and talent are above money and rank, and, generally recognized as this truth is, it gives those who have them something better to pride themselves on than class superiority. Note Ben Winthrop's testimony that the Squire 'used to invite him [Mr Macey] to take a glass, only to hear him sing the "Red Rovier" ... It's a nat'ral gift.' The village is rich in natural gifts even in music alone: Ben is leader of the church choir and his gift is inherited by his boy Aaron ('he can sing a tune off straight, like a throstle'), the butcher has 'music in his soul', and two of the Rainbow gossips are known as 'the "bassoon"' and 'the "key-bugle"'.

The pride in a craft was general – hence the unforgivable sin of the London tailor. Richard Jefferies in *Amaryllis at the Fair*, based on family reminiscences, tells how old Iden the baker, who started to bake in the Waterloo era, had his favourite peel ('The peel is the long wooden rod, broad at one end, with which loaves are placed in the baker's oven') 'ornamented with silver' in his old age, 'being proud of his trade'. There is an immense amount of other evidence of the kind.

10. Compare Turgenev in *A Lear of the Steppes*: 'Everything in the world, good and bad, comes to man, not through his deserts, but in consequence of some as yet unknown but logical laws which I will not take upon myself to indicate, though I sometimes fancy I have a dim perception of them.'

11. We should be wrong, I think, to assume that George Eliot, who is inevitably amused by some aspects of this culture, does not intend a slightly Erewhonian satire on the Catholic nature of Dolly's belief.

12. In Dickens's *A Tale of Two Cities*, published in 1859, more than a year before George Eliot began to think of writing *Marner*, Dr Manette is 'buried alive' for eighteen years as Marner was for fifteen, also by an injustice. He falls back on shoemaking, and his bench and tools are for him in his isolation and misery in the Bastille what Marner's loom is to him at the Stone-pits. He relapses more thoroughly in personality than Marner, his loss of memory corresponding to Marner's trances, but is 'Returned to life' by the unexpected appearance of his unknown daughter Lucie, whose golden hair recalls his lost wife's, as Eppie's unexpected appearance and golden hair arouse Marner by recalling his lost sister. This experience and the obligation of being a father start a regenerative process in Dr Manette as in Silas which restores his powers of affection and his place in society. The parallel strikes me as too close to be accidental. While Dickens's treatment of the subject is too theatrical to be worth the close attention George Eliot's demands, I am bound to say that the case history of Dr Manette is much more interesting than what we are shown of Marner in his despair and after. But Silas is meant to be representative, so George Eliot could not afford to do through him the kind of analysis that Dickens did, even if she had been tempted to do a piece of pioneering investigation into the psychological effects of isolation and despair – nor was she, like Dickens, attracted by abnormality. Silas's state is too predictable. 'Silas was both sane and honest', we are told, and he remains so all through his sufferings. And he is too simple to make new values for himself in contempt of his treatment by his society, as Hester Prynne, the *esprit fort* of *The Scarlet Letter*, had done in her isolation. The robbery occurs such a short time before Eppie reaches Silas that we don't have to ask whether this final loss would have pushed him over the edge, although in fact it is shown to start the process of reintegration for him. Nor is the account of why he became a miser interesting – and it belongs too much to the mere symbolism of the gold.

13. Even the author's generalizations tend to be cast in the same appropriate kind of metaphor, e.g. 'language is a stream that is almost sure to smack of a mingled soil', and 'that habit of looking towards the money and grasping it with a sense of fulfilled effort made a loam that was deep enough for the seeds of desire' and 'before such calm external beauty the presence of a vague fear is more distinctly felt – like a raven flapping its slow wing across the sunny

air'. These and many of the other images in *Marner* are Shakespearian rather than Wordsworthian.

14. Another instance of this is Eppie's insistence when she is planning her garden on taking in the furze bush, under which her mother was found dead in the snow. '"Ah child," said Silas . . . "it wouldn't do to leave out the furze bush"'. The feeling here, left so delicately for us to grasp without help from the author, gets some emphasis by Eppie's adding: '"and just against it I'll put snowdrops and crocuses, 'cause Aaron says they won't die out, but'll always get more and more."' Of course to people like the English poor who religiously planted flowers on family graves and tended them every Sunday, the associations make the feeling clear without any more needing to be said; and Shakespearian as Eppie's poetic statement is, it is still quite plausible in the circumstances as natural speech.

15. George Eliot's understanding of the relation of the peasant to his environment is better, because more intimate, than Wordsworth's, and this she conveys admirably in *Silas Marner* and *Adam Bede*. Compare Sturt:

He did not merely 'reside' in it; he was part of it, and it was part of him . . . Out of all these circumstances – the pride of skill in handicrafts, the detailed understanding of the soil and its materials, the general effect of the well-known landscape, and the faint sense of something venerable in its associations – there proceeded an influence which acted upon the village people as an unperceived guide to their conduct, so that they observed the seasons proper for their varied pursuits almost as if they were going through some ritual – and to neglect the well-known signs which hinted at what should be done, was more than bad economy; it was dereliction of peasant duty . . . and all the customs which their situation required them to follow sustained their belief in the ancestral notions of good and evil. In other words, they had a civilization to support them. (*Change in the Village*: 'The Peasant System')

16. George Sturt, *Change in the Village*, p. 110.

17. *Marner* is the first of her novels to take an anti-Cinderella shape, but thereafter the pattern becomes compulsive. Eppie who renounces her birthright as the Squire's heiress to marry a working man is followed by Esther (in *Felix Holt*) who rejects a rich suitor and forfeits her inheritance to marry a poor, class-conscious Radical artisan, while the same idea dictated Dorothea's sacrifice of fortune and status to marry a Radical politician, who is further to be deplored as an artist. This addition is then developed in the subplot of *Deronda*, where the heiress Catherine Arrowpoint refuses a future peer and breaks with her county family to marry a foreign composer with subversive political views. The Cinderella story was the basis of much popular fiction but no temptation to George Eliot, who savoured a rare kind of success. She may have well felt,

also, that happiness has to be paid for by some painful sacrifice, as she had found herself when having to choose between 'respectability' and union with Lewes (which cut her off from her family and put her at a disadvantage socially).

18. Compare Squire Donnithorne and his daughter in *Adam Bede*, and the exploration of the unattractive attitudes both of Arthur Donnithorne himself and of the rector's mother. *Silas Marner* differs only in being more forthright and quite disenchanted in its presentation of the gentry.

19. So striking is this that it leads one to infer that 'Cass' was chosen for its suggestion of 'crass', as Dunstan ('Dunsey') obviously was for its association with 'dunce'.

20. Nevertheless, like the Dodsons in *The Mill on the Floss*, she gets very fair treatment, and the virtues of her kind are scrupulously credited to her. And at the earlier crisis she has given us as well as Godfrey a surprise, in her admirable reaction to the history her husband has so long concealed because he thought it would alienate her: '"Do you think I'd have refused to take her in, if I'd known she was yours?"' – she puts the duties of kinship before all else. Compare Flora Thompson's record of her knowing a 'rough' countryman 'who, when told for the first time, ten years after marriage, that his wife had an illegitimate daughter of sixteen, and stricken with tuberculosis, said: "You go and fetch her home at once and look after her. Your child's my child and your home's her home"' (*Lark Rise to Candleford*, p. 400).

21. As is his name, not merely biblical but actually that of the high priest himself.

22. Horse dealing is said to be the manner in which 'many human transactions [are] carried on'.

23. It is irrelevant to object that city craftsmen were, at times, better off, or had access to the enlightened culture of the educated class in some northern towns. Carlyle's comment on London in 1831 is significant: 'Miserable is the scandal-mongery and evil-speaking of the country population: more frightful still the total ignorance and mutual heedlessness of these poor souls in populous city pent.'